M.R. Mackenzie is the author of character-driven crime fiction novels set in Glasgow, including an ongoing series of mysteries featuring criminology lecturer Anna Scavolini.

The first book in the series, *In the Silence*, was shortlisted for the Bloody Scotland Scottish Crime Debut of the Year and longlisted for the McIlvanney Prize for Scottish Crime Book of the Year 2019.

Praise for M.R. Mackenzie

'One of the most consistently accomplished writers on the current scene.' FINANCIAL TIMES

'Mackenzie has come up with something that defies easy definition and is truly original.'
NB MAGAZINE

'Brings a fresh new voice to the field of Tartan Noir.'
JAMES OSWALD

'Writes with precision and passion.' CARO RAMSAY

'An immersive slow burn of a tale, peppered with disquieting fire-crackers of revelation.'
MORGAN CRY

'Up there with the best contemporary authors working today.' DAVID B. LYONS

ALSO BY M.R. MACKENZIE

Anna Scavolini Mysteries
In the Silence
Cruel Summer
The Shadow Men
Women Who Kill
The Reckoning
The Secrets We Keep

Standalone Novels
The Library Murders
Bury Your Secrets

Box Sets
The Anna Scavolini Mysteries – Volume One

M.R. MACKENZIE

THE SECRETS WE KEEP

AN **ANNA SCAVOLINI** MYSTERY

MAD HOUSE

Copyright © 2025 M.R. Mackenzie

All rights reserved. No part of this book may be reproduced in any form or by any electronic or mechanical means, including information storage and retrieval systems, without written permission from the author, except in the case of a reviewer, who may quote brief passages embodied in critical articles or in a review.

This book is a work of fiction. Names, characters, places and incidents are either the product of the author's imagination or are used fictionally. Any resemblance to actual persons, living or dead, or to actual events or locales, is entirely coincidental.

Cover design by
Tim Barber / Dissect Designs

Typeset in 10.5 pt Baskerville

First published in 2025 by Mad House

ISBN: 978-1-9160948-8-8

Text version 1.0

mrmackenzieauthor.com
facebook.com/MRMackenzieAuthor
author.to/mrmackenzie

CAST OF CHARACTERS

Professor **Anna Scavolini** – Professor of Criminology; former Course Director, Criminology MA, Kelvingrove University

Zoe Callahan – Anna's best friend

Jack Scavolini – Anna's son

Paul Vasilico – Detective Chief Inspector, Specialist Crime Unit

Jen Brinkley – Anna's friend; freelance IT security specialist

Dr **Fraser Taggart** – Head of School of Social and Political Sciences; Senior Lecturer in Political Theory, Kelvingrove University

Dr **Farah Hadid** – Teaching Associate in Criminology, Kelvingrove University

Professor **Hugh MacLeish** – Professor of Sociology; former Head of Department of Law and Social Sciences, Kelvingrove University

Sal Brinkley – Jen's sister; Zoe's girlfriend

Ewan and **Maisie Brinkley** – Jen's twin son and daughter

Grace Dunphy – Anna's former student

Maybe we are nothing more than the confidences we keep, plastered over with a distraction of skin and bone and shadow.

Jodi Picoult, *Mad Honey*

PROLOGUE

Glasgow
Saturday 28 December 2019

If she'd just made time to listen, things could have turned out so very differently.

The setting was the house on Clarence Drive; the occasion Anna Scavolini's non-denominational midwinter gathering cum farewell party. The tall, narrow townhouse was packed to the rafters – a motley assortment of friends, friends of friends and other assorted hangers-on, many of them gathered under the same roof for the first time.

Zoe and Sal had come, of course, along with Sal's big sister Jen, and Jen's twin three-year-olds, Ewan and Maisie. The twins had quickly formed a triumvirate with Jack, which subsequently became a quadrumvirate with the arrival of Mandy and her nine-year-old daughter, Ruby. As the oldest of the group, Ruby wasted no time in taking charge, marshalling her more diminutive underlings up the stairs for a rowdy game of tig, the rules and conditions of victory to be devised and enforced solely at her discretion.

Pamela Macklin was there too, having made it through

from Edinburgh on time – an obvious point of pride for her – as well as Farah Hadid and her boyfriend, Émile. Marion Angus had turned up as well, accompanied by her long-term partner, Ben, who compensated for Marion's verbal diarrhoea by barely speaking at all. The next-door neighbours, Jim and Arianne, a pair of well-to-do retirees with a fondness for involving themselves in other people's affairs, had also put in an appearance. They and Anna weren't exactly *friends* in the strictest sense, but given that they shared an adjoining wall, she could hardly conceal the fact that she was throwing a jamboree from them. Besides, they'd promised to keep an eye on the house, and its new tenants, while she was away, so she figured the least she could do was involve them in the proceedings.

And then there was Paul Vasilico, who she could probably have got away without inviting but had nonetheless felt compelled to – both for old times' sake and because she'd been serious when she'd promised not to lose touch with him again, and wanted to demonstrate the depths of her seriousness. She'd been anticipating a degree of awkwardness between them, but the reality was that she'd been so busy playing the attentive host – making sure everyone had a drink in their hand at all times; constantly nipping back and forth to the kitchen to check that the mini quiches weren't burning in the oven – that he'd barely had an opportunity to do more than nod to her in passing, and she back at him. At that particular moment, Jim, having clearly identified him as a man with similar priorities to his own, had collared him and was subjecting him to an extended soliloquy on the persisting issue, in spite of several sternly worded letters to the council, of non-residents hogging all the parking spaces on the street. Judging by Vasilico's expression, he was already regretting not having had somewhere else to be.

All told, the house was fuller that night than it had ever been in all the time Anna had lived there, and possibly even since it had been built. In fact, there were so many people clustered into the living room, it was nigh on impossible to get from one end to the other without sucking in her chest and shimmying sideways. Half of her was regretting having invited so many people to a single gathering, while the other half took genuine pleasure from the realisation that she actually had more friends than she'd thought. Now that it came down to it, she was going to miss having them all a mere walk or train ride away.

Still, with change came new opportunities. New opportunities, a new university, and a chance to put the events of the last year firmly in the rearview mirror.

'It's a one-year part-time lecturing contract,' she explained to Arianne, who'd managed to catch her in between trips to the kitchen. 'They're trialling a dedicated criminology undergraduate programme and they want someone with experience of running one to help them get it off the ground.'

'And what brought this on?' said Arianne, swirling her glass of cognac. 'Is the pay better in Perugia, or did you just fancy the change?'

Actually, Anna felt like saying to her, *it's because my boss at Kelvingrove stabbed me in the back and hung me out to dry after the entire university received sexually explicit images of me in their inboxes.*

But, of course, she didn't. Arianne Faulkner might well be the only person here tonight who *didn't* know she'd been the victim of a revenge porn operation perpetrated by a group of militant male supremacists, and she wasn't about to enlighten her now.

'Well,' she said, adopting a light-hearted tone, 'they don't have Scottish winters there, for a start.'

'*Tell* me about it,' said Arianne, who never missed an opportunity to shift a conversation to herself – for which, in this instance, Anna was profoundly grateful. 'At my grand old age, I feel the cold in my bones more with each passing year …'

But Anna was no longer properly listening. Her mind was

wandering back to the events that had followed her tendering her resignation at the start of the month. Her walking out of Fraser Taggart's office, leaving him in a state of stunned inertia. The frantic calls from colleagues, pleading with her to tell them that the rumours weren't true. The eventual intervention from the Principal himself, impressing on her how valued a colleague she was, imploring her to reconsider. Eventually, in a last-ditch effort to persuade her, he'd offered her a period of unpaid leave, during which she would be free to pursue other ventures, including taking on paid work elsewhere.

'Give it a year,' he'd said, 'and we'll see how you feel then.'

And so, with no small amount of scepticism, she'd agreed to give it a year, and had duly withdrawn her resignation and immediately set about burning through the backlog of annual leave she'd accrued in order to avoid the resulting awkwardness of having to face her colleagues before her period of leave took effect at the start of the new year. It was hard not to feel like she'd basically been browbeaten into submission, and that any decision about her future at Kelvingrove had merely been deferred. Mind you, there was something undeniably gratifying about knowing that her presence there was so valued that the Principal would consider staging such an extraordinary intervention to secure her continued affiliation.

She'd had no communication whatsoever with Fraser throughout any of this. Anna strongly suspected he'd been ordered by the Principal to keep a low profile – no doubt after being given a summary bollocking for allowing this situation to ever arise.

'… and what do you make of this virus that's doing the rounds in China?' said Arianne, interrupting Anna's thoughts. 'They were talking about it on the radio this morning, so they were. They're saying it's this super-charged new type of flu.'

'Nothing for us to fret about, I'm sure,' said Jim, breaking away from Vasilico to insert himself into the conversation.

'There's nothing to be gained from concerning ourselves with goings-on nearly five thousand miles away.'

'But—'

'Mark my words: in a few weeks, it'll all've blown over and we'll be left wondering what all the fuss was ever about.'

Anna caught Vasilico's eye. He gave a rueful grimace, which she returned, then swiftly averted her eyes and scurried back to the kitchen with her tray of empty glasses.

She was bending down to check the mini quiches for the umpteenth time when she heard movement behind her. She stood up and turned to see Vasilico shutting the door behind him. The chatter from the living room, so overbearing until now, was muted to a distant murmur.

'Paul,' she said, a trifle flustered. 'What's up? D'you need something in your glass?'

'What?' Vasilico appeared momentarily confused. 'No, my glass is fine, thanks. My cup runneth over. I just wanted to get you to myself for a bit.'

'Jim's been talking your ear off, I see,' said Anna, steadfastly ignoring the implications of what he'd just said. 'I swear, there's not a topic on this earth he doesn't consider himself an expert in.'

'Yes, he's quite something. He's just been explaining to me how he'd solve Brexit, the Northern Ireland border and world hunger in ten minutes flat if the politicians would just give way to him.'

'Goodness. They don't realise what they're missing.'

She could hear the way her voice sounded: high and artificially chirpy. She knew she was babbling, filling the space between them to avoid having to acknowledge the outsized pachyderm in the room.

Vasilico stepped towards her. 'Anna …'

'Are you sure I can't get you something to drink?'

But before Vasilico could respond, they were interrupted by the creak of the door. They turned to see Ben tentatively poking his head in. He blinked uncertainly from behind his thick, full-rim glasses as he regarded the pair of them, barely ten centimetres apart at the hob.

'Not interrupting anything, am I?'

'Absolutely not,' said Anna, both too quickly and too emphatically. 'We were just ... *I* was just checking on the oven.'

'Oh, good,' said Ben, with palpable relief. He stepped into the kitchen, tucking a loose strand of long, lank hair behind his ear. 'Actually, about that.' He glanced at the oven. 'I, uh, just wanted to make sure ... you're remembering Marion's gluten-free?'

'She's what now?' said Anna, a rictus grin stretched taut across her features.

'Aaaaand that's my cue to leave,' said Vasilico.

And before Anna could plead with him not to abandon her to her fate, he slipped past Ben and ducked out.

'You *did* remember, didn't you?' said Ben. 'She'd never say anything herself – you know how she is – so I thought I ought to check.'

Anna continued to gaze back at him. Her cheeks were aching from keeping the smile fixed on her face. She knew she should stop grinning, but she'd held it for so long now that she couldn't think of a way of changing her expression without it looking even *more* unnatural. Ben continued to gaze at her expectantly.

'Of ... *course* I remembered.' She forced a laugh, which only succeeded in making her sound faintly unhinged. 'What sort of a host d'you take me for?'

Ben relaxed instantly. 'Oh, thank God. Cos, you know, gluten makes her bloat like nothing on earth and then she gets diarrhoea for days and ... well, you get the picture.' He turned to go. 'Thanks for putting my mind at ease. I'll let you get back to it.'

And with that, he slipped out, leaving Anna to contemplate this new and unanticipated dilemma.

She racked her brains, trying to think which of the various foodstuffs she'd procured for the evening meal qualified as gluten free. The mini quiches were out, for a start ... as, presumably, was the chocolate torte she'd bought for dessert. The vegetable dip would be OK, surely – if not the dip itself then certainly the vegetables. Was she seriously contemplating leaving Marion to gnaw on cucumber and carrot sticks while the rest of them tucked into a lavish buffet spread?

She was just weighing up how straightforward it would be to slip out of the house undetected and hot foot it to Sainsbury's when the door opened once again. This time, it was Zoe.

'*What?*' Anna almost snapped.

Zoe took a step back. 'Jeez-*o*, doll. Don't be getting yer underthings in a twist. Jist thought ye'd be wanting tae know yer old CO's showed up.'

'My what?' Anna was in no fit state to deal with euphemisms.

'Y'know – auld guy with the big belly and the dandruff. Used tae be yer boss till they kicked him tae the kerb.'

'You mean *Hugh?*' Anna found herself torn between relief and exasperation.

'Aye, that's the geezer. Also, just so's ye know – reckon he's been on the sauce.'

She mimed necking from an open bottle, pulled a grimace and slipped out, the sounds of the party swallowing her up as she disappeared from view.

Anna leant both sets of knuckles on the work surface, inhaled a deep breath and counted to five. She'd invited Hugh, of course, and had been somewhat surprised when, despite promising he'd be there, he hadn't arrived with the other guests. But then, she'd been so busy dealing with a full house and keeping a dozen plates spinning that his absence had soon slipped her mind. And now, apparently, here he was, better late than never – and *drunk*, if Zoe was to be believed. What else was this night going to throw at her?

Steeling herself, she rearranged her face into what she hoped was a passable facsimile of orderly serenity and strode out into the hallway. There, just as Zoe had said, was Hugh. He did indeed appear to be somewhat the worse for wear, leaning against the wall for balance and breathing heavily through his open mouth. Farah was with him, speaking to him urgently in a low voice, though she clammed up at the sound of Anna's approach and took a step back, arms folded about herself, almost as if she'd been caught doing something illicit.

'I'll leave you to it,' she said in a low voice.

And then, with one last, foreboding look at Anna, she hurried off, heading back into the living room to join the others.

For a moment, Anna was tempted to go after her. *Please*, she wanted to say, *don't leave me to deal with this on my own*. But the moment had passed, and she knew, judging by the state Hugh was in, that leaving him on his own, even for a few seconds, would be the height of irresponsibility. So instead, she once more gritted her teeth and turned to face the music.

'Hugh,' she said, trying to maintain her smile. 'You made it.'

Hugh didn't so much turn as roll round to face her, his features broadening into an expression of unapologetic joy.

'Anna,' he slurred. 'Oh, Anna, Anna, Anna. You were always the best out of all of us. Did I ever tell you that? If I didn't, I should've, and I'm sorry. Sorry, sorry, sorry. Sorry about how things turned out. Sorry about all of it.'

'It's fine, Hugh,' said Anna wearily. 'You know I don't hold you responsible for any of it. The people to blame … well, they're not under this roof tonight.'

'It's a waste. A bloody waste is what it is.'

Hugh poked an index finger in Anna's direction for emphasis, but overshot and jabbed her right in the clavicle. Seeming to realise his mistake, he withdrew his hand into a clenched fist and had the good grace to look suitably ashamed by his faux pas.

Doing her best not to take this apparently unintentional act of assault personally, Anna gripped Hugh's arm and led him over to the stairs. With her help, he managed to lower himself onto the bottom step and sat there, head tilted backwards, mouth hanging slack, while she stood, gazing down at him. Right now, her overriding feeling towards him was one of pity, but pity tempered by something else: a degree of repellence which bordered on disgust, as much as she didn't want to admit it. She'd never seen him like this before; had no idea he was even *capable* of getting himself into this sort of state, and she wished now that she'd remained none the wiser.

'What's going on, Hugh?' she implored him. 'D'you want me to call Miriam?'

'No!' said Hugh immediately, growing seemingly alarmed at the invocation of his adult daughter's name. 'I ...' he began, then seemed to think better of what he'd been about to say and shook his head vehemently. 'No,' he said again. 'Don't want to trouble her.'

'Well, is there someone else I can get for you? Someone who can—'

'No. You. Only you. Need to talk to you. Need to tell you things.'

'Well,' said Anna, once again with forced levity, 'no time like the present. Let's hear it.'

But at that moment, there came an anguished shriek from overhead, followed by a series of short, sharp wails.

The children, Anna immediately thought. Something must have happened to one of the children. Now that it occurred to her, they *had* been suspiciously quiet for a good long while.

Without another word, she left Hugh where he sat and hurried up the stairs, wondering just what the hell was going on up there.

She soon found out. Ewan was on his hands and knees at the edge of the second-floor landing, his head wedged between two of the wooden balusters that formed the guardrail. He continued to wail while the other three children stood in a semi-circle around him, all trying their hardest not to look shifty. Well, Jack and Maisie were trying. To Anna's eyes, Ruby looked altogether too pleased with herself.

Anna stared at the sight before her in disbelief. 'What the actual *fuck*?'

The inadvertent chortle that escaped from Ruby did little to lessen the impression of her guilt.

It took several minutes and the combined interrogation skills of several of the adults to finally get to the bottom of what had happened. Apparently, Ruby had declared that Ewan had a fat head, and, in the face of his vociferous denials, had encouraged him to prove her wrong by pushing it between the balusters. He had duly done so and was now wedged tight – a situation which, in Ruby's eyes, ably proved her point. Now, at least half the guests were clustered round him, each – in the apparent belief that they were being helpful – offering their own solutions to the problem, from rubbing butter on Ewan's cheeks to calling out the fire brigade. Mandy, meanwhile, declared that they were 'bloody eejits, the lottaya,' while Sal did her best not to collapse in a fit of giggles, even as Jen, down on her knees and rubbing Ewan's back soothingly, shot her sister an angry glare and told her it wasn't bloody funny.

'I mean,' said Sal, wiping her eyes, 'I know it's not, but it also sort of *is*, y'know?'

Ewan, meanwhile, having apparently worn himself out, had ceased wailing and settled instead for letting out periodic self-pitying moans, which presumably required less energy and effort.

In the end, it required nothing so drastic as summoning the

fire brigade. Nor was Anna required to fetch the Lurpak. It was Mandy who eventually pointed out that, since Ewan's head was indeed the largest part of his anatomy, it would make more sense if he simply followed through on what he'd already started and pushed the rest of himself through the gap between the balusters. He took a great deal of convincing, but eventually he complied, and succeeded in squeezing his entire body through without too much effort, while Émile balanced precariously at the top of a stepladder on the half-landing below, ready to receive him.

By the time Ewan had been consoled, by multiple cuddles from Jen and an extra-large slice of chocolate torte, there wasn't much left of the evening, and the guests began to drift away. Marion and Ben were among the first to leave, the issue of the lack of gluten-free food thereby resolving itself naturally. Jen and her brood followed shortly afterwards, an exhausted Ewan fast asleep on Jen's shoulder; then, once the coast was clear, Mandy left too, dragging a recalcitrant Ruby by the arm and being heard to mutter darkly at her that she 'couldnae take ye *anywhere*.' The remaining guests nibbled at the buffet (minus the mini quiches, which had burned to a crisp while the drama was unfolding upstairs), but the spark seemed to have gone out of the event, and, before long, they too were making their excuses and preparing to vacate the premises.

Vasilico was the last to leave. Anna saw him out to the front step, where they stood facing one another, neither seemingly wanting to bring things to a close, but both afflicted by the same awkwardness that had characterised all their interactions of late.

'Well,' he said, breaking the silence, 'I guess this is it.'

'It's only for a year,' said Anna. 'That's no time at all. I'll be back before you know it.'

A strained silence unfolded. Eventually, Vasilico cleared his throat.

'So, ah, when's the big moving day?'

'Soon,' said Anna. 'We need to be out of the house by the sixth for the new tenants moving in. My contract with Perugia doesn't start till the first of February, but I'd like to be there early so I can get Jack settled in before I begin teaching.'

'Well, maybe I'll come and visit you.'

'There's an idea.'

Again, Vasilico hesitated. For a moment, she wondered if he was going to attempt to kiss her – if not on the lips, then at least on the cheek. She wasn't sure how she'd respond if he did.

But, in the event, the moment passed without incident. A few seconds later, he stirred, then gave her an unusually formal nod.

'Well ... safe travels.'

And, with that, he turned and headed off into the night.

Long after he'd disappeared from sight, Anna remained on the top step, barely noticing the chill of the concrete on her bare feet. There was a lot still to be done before the sixth. She had to finish packing, and the things she and Jack weren't planning to take with them to Perugia would have to be put into storage. The small apartment she had lined up there – in the city centre, a stone's throw from the Piazza IV Novembre and within walking distance of the university – couldn't possibly accommodate all the clutter they'd accumulated over the years; nor would it be practical to ship everything over there from Glasgow. She still needed to pin Jack down on which Lego sets he wanted to take with him – not a conversation she was looking forward to.

At least she wouldn't have to chase Zoe about packing up her stuff. She'd already vacated the premises a week ago; her and Sal were staying with Jen and the twins till they got their own place sorted out. No doubt about it, it was going to be tough, having fifteen hundred miles separating them after having lived under the same roof for the last four years. But at least they'd both have plenty to keep them occupied – Anna with her new post in Perugia, Zoe with the Childhood Practice course she'd enrolled in, and which was due to start in just over a week's time.

Anyway, she told herself, it wasn't for ever. Just for twelve months.

She sucked in a deep breath through her nostrils, held it for a moment, then let it out. She wasn't looking forward to saying goodbye to all of this: the city she'd been born in, the house she'd occupied for the last nine years, the friendships she'd forged. But, all the same, she was glad to be drawing a definitive line in the sand. 2019 had, all told, been a bloody awful year, what with the Sandra Morton affair, followed hot on its heels by her ordeal at the hands of The Reckoning. She'd be glad when it was over.

2020 couldn't possibly be any worse.

It was only after she was back inside, the door securely locked behind her, that she realised there was no sign of Hugh. He must have left while the crisis with Ewan had been unfolding upstairs. What had he wanted to talk to her about, she wondered, and what had prompted him to get himself into such a pitiable state? Her eyes strayed to the phone on the hallway table. She really ought to call him – to make sure he'd got home safely, if nothing else.

She shook her head, banishing the idea from her mind. Whatever was going on was his business, unless he chose to share it with her. And he had, it seemed, changed his mind about doing so – or else, surely, he wouldn't have snuck off without so much as a by-your-leave. Besides, she had enough on her plate without involving herself in someone else's affairs. She'd done more than enough of that lately, and it never ended well.

Whatever problems Hugh was facing, he was going to have to solve them himself.

TIMELINE

31 January 2020. First confirmed case of COVID-19 in Italy. All flights to and from the People's Republic of China suspended.

22 February. First deaths from COVID-19 in Italy.

4 March. The Italian government orders the closure of all schools and universities.

9 March. As the virus spreads to all regions of the country, a nationwide lockdown is enacted.

20 March. Restrictions are further tightened. Sporting activities are banned, parks and playgrounds are closed, and movement across the country is tightly controlled.

21 March. All non-essential business and industry closed.

May. Restrictions slowly begin to ease.

3 June. Freedom of movement restored.

September. Schools and universities reopen.

DEATH NOTICES SECTION, GLASGOW TRIBUNE, 18 MAY 2020

It is with great sadness that we announce the peaceful passing, following a brief period of illness, of **Edward Hugh MacLeish**, aged 66, on Friday 15 May. Beloved father of Miriam, husband of the late Geraldine, formerly Professor of Sociology at Kelvingrove University.

A funeral service will be held on 19 May, 2 p.m., at Clydebank Crematorium. Due to current restrictions, mourners are limited to immediate family members, but a livestream will be accessible at https://tinyurl.com/fj8xextx.

Family flowers only, please. Donations, if desired, to the Scottish Cancer Foundation.

PART I

THE LONG ROAD HOME

1

Perugia
Wednesday 11 August 2021

Anna stood at the head of the high-ceilinged drawing room on the second floor of the Palazzo Florenzi. Historic paintings adorned the walls and a chandelier hung overhead, but the sense of historicity was blunted somewhat by the laminated signs commanding all and sundry to adhere to the government-mandated regulations regarding mask-wearing, social distancing and regular lateral flow testing. Five rows of seats faced the front, each a metre apart, the space between them marked by two strips of tape on the floor forming a stark white 'X'. The blinking red LED of the camera mounted on a tripod facing her served as a constant reminder that the lecture was being beamed live into the bedrooms of those students who either chose not to attend in person or hadn't been sufficiently quick off the mark to secure one of the limited spaces available. Beyond the camera, the eyes of around twenty-five students gazed back at her, their faces covered by masks of a variety of styles and colours. Their facial expressions might have been hidden from view, but their eyes shone with an attentive fervour.

'*Oggi finiamo qui,*' she said. '*Grazie a tutti, e buona fortuna.*'

As she dipped her head and took a step back, the students broke into a round of what appeared to be spontaneous applause. It started with just a couple of them in the front row, then quickly spread until it engulfed the entire room. As the applause continued, Anna, a little overwhelmed, felt her lips extending into an embarrassed smile, and was grateful that her own snuggly fitting mask concealed her blushing cheeks.

The applause petered out. The students gathered their things and began to leave, forming an orderly, one-metre-apart queue for the door on the right, designated as the exit. As Anna packed away her laptop, one of the students, a girl of about twenty with an incongruous (and slightly manic-looking) cartoon smile design on her mask, broke off and approached her.

'*Professoressa*, I just wanted to tell you how much I've enjoyed this class.'

'Oh,' said Anna, slightly wrong-footed by this unexpected approach. 'Well, I'm glad you got something out of it.'

'To tell the truth,' the girl – Gabriela, *that* was her name – went on, 'I only took it because I needed the grade points. My major is in comparative literature. But I've realised now that's not really where my heart lies. I want to be a criminologist.'

'That's ... that's wonderful,' said Anna, genuinely touched and not sure how else to respond.

'Actually, I was wondering if you could give me any advice about applying to different universities.'

Anna felt her eyes straying inadvertently towards the wall clock. She managed to stop herself, but not quickly enough.

'I don't mean right now,' said Gabriela hastily. 'But if I could contact you at a more convenient time ...'

'Well,' said Anna, silently cursing herself for being so transparent in her desire to beat a hasty exit, 'I'm not sure how much longer my university email will be active, but …'

She took a notebook from her bag, tore a scrap of paper from a blank page and scribbled on it, before handing it to Gabriela.

'There. That's my personal email. Send me a message and I promise I'll get back to you.'

Gabriela took the paper, practically gushing with gratitude. 'Oh, thank you, *Professoressa*. I will. And enjoy your summer vacation.'

Anna smiled. 'You too.'

Gabriela thanked her once again, then practically curtsied and hurried off to join her friends.

Shaking her head in amusement, Anna resumed her packing.

Ten minutes later, she exited the small corner office she'd occupied since the university reopened its doors the previous September, the handful of personal effects she'd accumulated there crammed into her shoulder bag. The multi-storey Palazzo Florenzi had been built in the eighteenth century, passing through the hands of various members of the aristocracy before finally coming into the possession of the university and serving as the headquarters of the Department of Philosophy, Social Sciences and Education, and it still had more than a whiff of a stately home about it.

She set off down the stairs and was making her way along the ground-floor corridor towards the exit when she heard someone calling her name behind her. She turned as Silvia Arrighi, the department's elegant sixty-year-old director, came clomping after her in her heeled brogues. Anna stopped to wait for her.

'I was hoping to catch you before you left,' she said. 'I just wanted to thank you for everything you've done for us during the last eighteen months – particularly under such ... trying circumstances.'

'It's been a challenging time for everyone,' Anna said.

That might well have been the understatement of the new millennium. Those eighteen months had been nothing short of surreal, from the daily reports about the spread of the virus to the announcement, when she'd barely got her feet under the table, of the university's closure, followed by the nationwide lockdown that confined her and Jack to their little apartment on Via Gianna Brezzi for weeks on end. Then there was the resumption of classes in the form of remote learning, with all the trials and tribulations associated with unfamiliar and cumbersome technology (she swore, if she never attended another Zoom meeting, it would be too soon) – followed, after a few months, by a move to hybrid teaching once the university reopened its doors, punctuated by a succession of mini-lockdowns to tackle local flare-ups, each resulting in temporary, often last-minute, closures. All told, it had been an uncertain, frustrating and at times genuinely frightening period in her life, and being in a new job, in a new city, where she didn't know anyone, hadn't helped. And yet she knew, if she had the option to wind back the clock, she'd still have made the same choice to abandon everything and relocate to Perugia.

'Well, you more than rose to the occasion,' said Silvia. 'I've heard nothing but praise from the students.'

'I'm glad,' said Anna. Then, mindful of the time, 'Do you mind ... ? I've arranged to meet someone.'

'*Certo, certo.* I wouldn't dream of delaying you further. But I wanted to emphasise how much we've appreciated having you with us, and ... well, I wanted to see how you'd feel about potentially making it more permanent.'

'Pardon?'

'I've been given authorisation by the Deputy Rector to offer you a permanent contract as a full faculty member. It's a full-time position with a *very* competitive salary, not to mention a guaranteed research budget and a variety of other perks which are detailed in the written offer of employment. I know your intention was always to return to Scotland once your contract here ended,' she continued, before Anna could speak, 'but you've extended your stay with us once already, and – well, I think the last year and a half has caused several of us to reevaluate our lives.'

'It's … I'm not sure what to say,' was Anna's eventual response. Her eyes involuntarily glanced towards the door, aware of the passing time.

'Of course,' said Silvia hastily, 'I don't expect a decision immediately.' She waved her hands theatrically, as if shooing Anna away. 'Go. Enjoy your vacation. Take a week to think about it. But if you *do* decide to accept, know that the entire department would be honoured to have you as a colleague.'

Her mind abuzz, Anna traversed through the narrow, winding streets, up the steps of the Via Appia, to the Piazza IV Novembre. The historic public square teemed with a mixture of tourists, students and the handful of locals who'd come out to enjoy the late afternoon sun, now that the worst of the day's heat had passed. Anna made her way through the crowd and took a seat on the steps of the Cattedrale San Lorenzo, facing the fountain in the middle of the square. The sun might have passed its peak, but, as she removed her cardigan and stowed it in her bag, she was grateful for the thin sleeveless summer dress she'd picked out that morning. There was a reason why Italians – those who have the luxury of doing so, at any rate – fled the cities en masse for the countryside and the coast in August. She'd be joining them herself before long, now that teaching was over at last – and would have done so considerably earlier, if the constant lockdowns and related upheavals hadn't prolonged the academic year well into the summer months.

She heard a shout and looked up, a smile spreading across

her face as she saw Jack running across the piazza towards her. He barrelled into her and threw his arms round her, practically knocking her over in the process: now five and a half years old and pushing fifteen kilos, he nonetheless remained blissfully unaware of his own strength.

'Hey, Trouble,' she said, returning the hug, then prying him off her gently but firmly. 'What have you been up to?'

Jack grinned. *'Abbiamo preso un gelato,'* he chirped.

'Oh, che bello. Quali gusti?'

But Jack was now bored of speaking Italian. 'I had chocolate,' he responded in English, 'but Francesca wouldn't let me taste her pistachio.' He sounded genuinely aggrieved.

'Is that right? Well, if you wanted pistachio, perhaps you should have asked for that instead of chocolate, then?'

Jack considered this for a moment, then shook his head. 'No,' he said, his tone final.

'No? So you reckon you should be able to have your cake and eat it, then?'

Jack frowned. 'We didn't have cake.'

'Neither you did,' Anna agreed. She got to her feet. 'Speaking of which, where are …'

But even as she shielded her eyes against the sun, she spotted them, making their way across the piazza towards them: nine-year-old Francesca, all gangly limbs and long, uncombed hair, and her father, Matteo, tall and sinewy in a clay-stained T-shirt and old jeans. Spotting them, he grinned and raised a hand in greeting.

'Caio, Anna!'

Returning the wave, Anna took Jack's hand and headed down the steps to join them.

'Hey, you two. Been having a grand old time without me, by all accounts.'

'Nonsense,' said Matteo amiably. 'It's been deeply trying for us all.' He took Anna's bag from her. 'So, no difficulty in getting away, then?'

'It's all good.'

'And you're completely finished with work? No possibility of some last-minute catastrophe luring you back into the office?'

Anna smiled firmly. 'I give you my word, nothing will prevent the four of us from being at Lago Trasimeno by lunchtime tomorrow.'

They headed south across the piazza, Anna and Matteo strolling side by side while Jack and Francesca ran on ahead. *Where do they find the energy in this heat?* Anna wondered.

'Jack didn't cause any trouble, did he?' she said.

They tended to shift between English and Italian freely, but she was making a conscious decision to speak the latter now. Jack was far enough ahead that the odds of him hearing her were low, but she still preferred to add an extra layer of 'protection'.

'Well,' said Matteo airily, 'he did threaten to strangle Francesca with her own intestines.' He saw Anna's aghast look and smiled. 'I'm joking. He's been a model citizen from start to finish.'

Anna felt the tension leaving her. During their time in Perugia, Jack had been on a much more even keel. Indeed, it might even be fair to say he'd blossomed here – in spite of the strictures of lockdown, and helped in no small part, no doubt, by her greatly reduced working hours having allowed her to devote vastly more time to him than in the past. Nonetheless, she remained mindful of the various incidents that had occurred in their last few months in Glasgow – the tantrums and the biting – and remained alert for any signs of a return to 'old ways'.

'And you know we always enjoy looking after him,' Matteo continued. '*Both* of us. Especially Francesca. She's never had someone to boss around before.'

They watched the two children, hiding in adjacent archways up ahead, periodically peeking out at one another and cackling uproariously, as if it was the funniest thing in the world.

Anna smiled to herself. She couldn't deny that it had been a stroke of extremely good fortune to have found herself living in the same apartment block as a fellow single parent. It had been Matteo who'd proposed they form a bubble, pooling their resources, as it were, and for all intents and purposes becoming a de facto family unit. Especially during the first few weeks of lockdown, when everyone was cooped up indoors and venturing outside was limited to essential business only, it had been a godsend to have another child around for Jack to interact with at such a crucial stage in his development. She shuddered to think what the impact would have been on him if he'd had no contact with anyone besides herself. Once the restrictions had eased and some semblance of normality slowly began to creep back into their lives, they'd continued their arrangement, looking after each other's offspring whenever the other had to go out. Matteo, a sculptor by trade, had his studio in the spare room of his apartment, while Anna's contract only called for her to be at the university three days a week, meaning it was rare indeed for a situation to arise whereby one of them wasn't around to play childminder.

And there were other advantages, too, to having an available bachelor just across the hallway, as Anna had soon discovered …

They enjoyed a lazy evening meal in the open-air courtyard of the apartment block, Anna and Matteo emptying the better part of a bottle of Sangiovese between them. Jack and Francesca soon tired of watching their parents drink wine and listening to them talk about boring grown-up things, and, to give him and Anna some peace, Matteo fetched the portable sprinkler and set it up at a precautionary distance from the table. Word soon got around and they were joined by a handful of other children from the adjacent buildings, who eagerly abandoned their clothes in an untidy heap on the patio and hurried to enter the fray. As they ran naked through the revolving spray of water, their squeals and whoops carrying in the still evening air, Anna filled Matteo in on her conversation with Silvia.

'And what are you currently thinking?' said Matteo, asking the one question Anna had been hoping he wasn't going to ask while knowing full well that there was no way he *wouldn't*. 'What's your gut feeling?'

Anna inhaled a deep breath. 'My gut feeling … is that it's an extremely generous offer, and anyone in my position would be chomping at the bit to accept it.'

'But …' prompted Matteo, who knew her mind better than she cared to admit.

'But I honestly don't know.' She tried to explain: 'I took it for granted that I'd be going back to Glasgow once my contract here came to an end. OK, so they extended it from twelve to eighteen months after the whole world went topsy-turvy, and my employers in Glasgow were magnanimous enough to extend my leave of absence, but I always assumed this was a temporary thing. But lately …'

She watched Jack at the other end of the courtyard, hands on his hips, gabbling away in an idiosyncratic mixture of English and Italian while waggling his crooked little penis at the other children with the lack of inhibition only a child could possess.

'Look at him. He's so …' She waved her hand, giving up on trying to find the appropriate word. 'Honestly, I think bringing him out here was the best thing I could have ever done for him. You'd think he'd lived here all his life.

'And it's not just him,' she continued, as if she needed further justification. '*I* feel it too. Back in Glasgow, I was like this rubber band just waiting to snap. But here … well, I feel like I can actually *breathe*, for the first time in I don't know how long.'

There were other things too, which she didn't elaborate on. Things like the fact she no longer carried constant tension in her shoulders or suffered from headaches that lasted for days on end – things that, over the years, she'd resigned herself to accepting as simply being part and parcel of her life. She'd even been able to dispense with the hated dental splint (something she used to wear every night) since she was no longer grinding her teeth in her sleep – a habit she'd had since she was a teenager.

'And I know some of that'll change if I accept this position,' she went on. 'I'd be going back up to working full-time, taking on administrative duties again, but …' She shrugged helplessly. 'At the end of the day, it's not about the workload or the pay or the guaranteed research budget. It's about where I belong. And I'm just not sure where that is.'

She fell silent and leant back in her chair, feeling unexpectedly spent after this tortuous speech.

'It sounds to me,' said Matteo slowly, 'like you're talking yourself round to a decision you've already made.'

'And I don't suppose I can prevail on you to play devil's advocate.'

'I'm not sure it'd be in my interest.'

Anna glanced at him sidelong. Their eyes met, and they both shared a soft, knowing smile.

There was silence for a moment as they continued to watch the children. Matteo stroked the bristles on his chin with a calloused thumb as he pondered the matter.

'We've got the villa at Lago Trasimeno for two weeks,' he said eventually. 'That's two weeks for you to weigh up the pros and cons on either side. They can wait that long for their answer.'

Anna considered this, then nodded her assent.

'Deal.'
They clinked glasses together, sealing the agreement.

2

Anna collapsed onto her back, gulping down air. Matteo flopped down next to her on the bed, his own breathing no less laboured. He nuzzled her shoulder.

'*È stato bello?*'

'*Lo è stato,*' she confirmed.

She lay there in the darkness, gazing up at the ceiling. The thin curtains fluttered as a gentle breeze wafted through the open balcony shutters. Her breathing gradually slowed, the sweat cooling on her body. She sensed the even in and out of Matteo's breath next to her, their bodies almost but not quite touching.

'It would be nice if we could lie like this all night,' said Matteo, breaking the silence.

'You know we can't,' she said, almost automatically.

She felt him recoil ever so slightly, as if a part of him had been hoping for a different response, even though this was a conversation they'd already relitigated countless times.

'I know, but … it would be nice.'

'We agreed it was best for both of them.'

'I know. I just think perhaps it's time for us to re-evaluate that decision. I think they're ready for the truth.'

Anna said nothing. Matteo's words hung there like a leaden weight in the air. They continued to lie there, their shallow, even breathing the only audible sound in the otherwise still room.

These conjugal visits had started roughly six weeks after the first lockdown was called. At the time, it had felt like a natural extension of their existing partnership, such as it was. It even had a whiff of the forbidden thrill about it, creeping on tiptoe across the hallway to the other's bedroom once both children were asleep, then sneaking back again while it was still dark.

They'd been sleeping together in secret for nearly a month before they finally had a frank and honest conversation about what they were doing. By mutual consensus, they'd agreed not to tell either of their children. At the time, it had been less than a year since Francesca's mother had abandoned her and Matteo for a man who'd made it clear he had no interest in acquiring a stepdaughter. It was all still too raw, Matteo had said, for her to cope with the idea of her father being in a new relationship. Anna, for reasons of her own, had been only too keen to agree.

Of late, though, Matteo had been dropping increasingly unsubtle hints about a desire to come clean to Francesca – meaning that Jack, too, would inevitably have to be brought into the picture. Over the last couple of months, the balance had shifted, from Matteo having been the instigator of the clandestine nature of their arrangement to Anna being the one insisting they retain the status quo in the face of Matteo's clear desire for change. And she wasn't completely lacking in self-awareness. She could see that, from the outside, their secrecy looked increasingly absurd with each passing day.

And yet, still, she resisted.

Levering himself up on his elbow, Matteo fixed her with a probing look. Finding herself unable to meet his dark eyes, she quickly looked away.

'Jack isn't stupid, you know,' he said, his tone gentle but pointed. 'Neither is Francesca. They'll work it out eventually.'

Anna continued to avoid his gaze.

He sighed. 'But you're right. This was what we both agreed, and so this is how it will stay – until *both* of us are ready.' He reached across and tucked a stray strand of hair behind her ear. 'Anyway,' he added, a touch unconvincingly, 'we're fine just the way we are.'

Anna gazed up at him, feelings of gratitude and relief vying for dominance with the lingering pang of guilt that gnawed at her gut.

'You're sure you're OK with this?'

Matteo smiled. *'Sto bene.'*

She returned the smile, a trifle more uncertainly, then watched as he slid out of bed and crossed over to the chair where he'd left his clothes. He pulled on his jeans and zipped them up. Then, tucking his T-shirt and trainers under one arm, he made his way back over to the bed, leaned over her and kissed her lightly on the cheek. She felt the trace of another smile, this one unforced, flicker on her lips. Then he straightened up and slipped out of the room, shutting the door behind him. She listened to the sound of his bare feet padding away down the stone corridor, then the apartment door opening and shutting.

As she lay there in the dark, her phone, lying on the nightstand, began to ring, its screen lighting up the entire room. Scrambling across the bed, she snatched it up and answered it before the second ring was over, not bothering to check the caller ID in her rush to silence it before it woke Jack, slumbering in the room next door.

'Pronto?'

'Hello – Anna?'

A man's voice. Scottish accent.

'Who's this?' she said, switching to English.

'It's, ah, it's Fraser. Fraser Taggart.'

'Fraser,' she said stiffly, recognising his voice before he'd finished saying his name.

She tugged the bedsheet around her body, even though she recognised the pointlessness of such a move. She hadn't forgotten the pictures of herself that had been leaked to the entire university less than two years earlier, nor that he was among the people who she knew for a fact saw them before the email containing them was recalled.

'How are you?' she said, aware of – but unconcerned by – the harsh note in her voice that belied the seemingly civil question.

'I'm well,' said Fraser, sounding almost surprised to be asked. He gave a slight chuckle. 'As well as anyone can be in this crazy new world we seem to have found ourselves in. How's Perugia?'

'You know what, Fraser?' she said pointedly. 'It's actually really great – thanks for asking. I'm surrounded by culture and history, I get an average of 2,000 hours of sunshine a year, and I get to work with some really, *really* solid people.'

She'd thought, perhaps, that not having had any contact with him in the last eighteen months plus might have caused her feelings towards him to have mellowed a little. Now that she was faced with him at the other end of the phone, though, she realised she was as livid with him as ever and in no mood for shooting the breeze like they were old friends. Especially not at – she checked the display on her phone – *quarter past midnight!*

'Were you calling about something in particular, or did you just want to check whether I was still awake at twelve fifteen?'

'Twelve fif …' Fraser began, before groaning as realisation dawned on him. 'Of course. I was forgetting you were an hour ahead.'

Of course you were, Fraser.

'Um … I can call back in the morning if …'

She considered telling him to do just that, then blocking his number. But she couldn't. Whether she liked it or not, she still had unfinished business with her old boss. Whatever decision she ended up making about her future, she was going to have to deal with him again at some point in the not-so-distant future. Scorched earth was not a viable policy. She massaged the skin between her eyebrows with her free hand and suppressed a weary sigh.

'No,' she said, with as much forbearance as she could muster, 'you might as well say your piece now.'

'I'm grateful. And, I hasten to add, this won't take long, but the fact of the matter is I have ... well, something of a proposition to put to you.'

'Go on,' she said, already growing impatient.

'Actually, it concerns a certain former mutual friend of ours. Hugh MacLeish, to be precise. You're, ah, aware he passed away last spring?'

'It hadn't escaped my notice, no.'

It had been Farah Hadid who'd alerted her to the news, calling her the day after it had happened in a state of numb shock. She'd have flown back for the funeral had the travel restrictions at the time not made it impossible. Instead, she'd settled for watching the livestream on her laptop. Never the most emotionally expressive of people, she'd nonetheless blubbed through the better part of the service and had been glad she'd arranged beforehand for Matteo to take Jack out with him and Francesca, giving her the apartment to herself.

'Of course, yes.' Fraser at least had the good grace to sound chastened. 'Well, anyway, it relates to something Hugh was involved with towards the end of his life. Something I was wondering if I might persuade you to take a look at.'

'Is this about that research he was doing into the effects of austerity?' said Anna, wondering what could have possessed Fraser to ring her up at such an ungodly hour to discuss this. 'I told him at the time, I thought that was more his bag than mine.'

The project in question, for which Hugh had received funding in the year prior to Anna's departure, had aimed to investigate the relationship between austerity as a political strategy and crime – more specifically the ways in which it disproportionately affected women, minorities and the poor, pushing them into criminal activity. From what Anna could gather, the project had languished for some time, and, on various occasions during the second half of 2019, Hugh had attempted to persuade her to take it over, on the grounds that there was significant overlap between their respective disciplines. Anna, who'd had more than enough on her plate, had resisted these overtures, and hadn't been banking on Fraser picking up where Hugh had left off.

'It honestly might be easier if we could discuss this face to face,' said Fraser. 'Are you planning to be in Glasgow at any point in the next couple of weeks?'

'It's not something I had on my list of things to do, no.'

In truth, she *had* been planning to pay a visit to Glasgow at some point before too long – especially now that the requirement to quarantine had been lifted for fully vaccinated travellers arriving from Europe. There were a handful of jobs she needed to take care of there, including a complaint from the couple she was letting the house to about water damage in the living room; things that ideally required her to be there in person and which she'd been putting off for some time. But she wasn't about to be railroaded into coming by Fraser – especially over something she'd already indicated didn't interest her.

'Pity,' said Fraser. 'Quite apart from the business with Hugh, there's the small matter of your impending return to work. The next teaching year begins in just over six weeks, and – well, we could do with knowing where things stand *vis-à-vis* your employment status here.'

Did he REALLY just say 'vis-à-vis'*?*

'Look,' Fraser went on, 'I wouldn't normally suggest this,

but if I covered your travel expenses, would you consider making the trip – perhaps, say, within the next week or so? I really *would* like to catch up with you. For old times' sake, if nothing else.'

For a moment, Anna couldn't think how to respond. Why the hell couldn't he just say whatever he had to say to her over the phone? Hadn't they all spent the last year and more learning, by virtue of necessity, that it was perfectly possible to hold the vast, *vast* majority of meetings remotely instead of insisting on having them face-to-face?

But then, she thought, perhaps it *would* be good to go back. She recalled Matteo's words earlier, about her talking herself round to a decision she'd already made. It wasn't quite as simple as that. An element of doubt remained, but it was a small one, and she now wondered whether a final visit to her old haunts might be what was required to force her to make the decision she knew, in her heart, she wanted to. A farewell tour of sorts, laying the ghosts of the past to rest. And, in spite of how abysmally Fraser had treated her during the Reckoning business, if she *was* going to sever her ties with Kelvingrove, she somehow felt she owed it to him to tell him to his face.

With a heavy heart, she made her decision.

'All right. If you can find me a flight out of Perugia late tomorrow morning or early afternoon, I'll come. Tomorrow, mark you,' she added, before Fraser could respond. 'Any later and you can forget it. I'm supposed to be going away on holiday.'

'Of course,' said Fraser.

He sounded slightly surprised, though whether by the specificity of her request or because he hadn't expected her to agree under *any* circumstances, she didn't know. For a moment, she wondered if she'd given in to him too easily.

'I'll look into flights,' he went on, 'and call you back shortly.'

'Don't bother. Just forward me the details and I'll make the booking. You can reimburse me later.'

'I'll do that. Oh, and Anna? Thank y—'

She hung up before he could finish. Already, her mind was turning to the practicalities. She was fully vaccinated and, as required by all university employees, had been testing regularly, with all the evidence readily at hand, meaning there were no barriers she could think of to her travelling. So, tomorrow morning, Matteo could drive up to Lago Trasimeno as planned with Jack and Francesca, while she flew to Glasgow, met Fraser, they both said whatever they had to say to one another, she took care of the few bits of business she had there, then flew back to Italy and headed up to Lago Trasimeno on her own steam to join the others – at most, a couple of days later than she intended. Couldn't be simpler.

Now she just needed to tell Matteo the lay of the land.

3

Thursday 12 August

It was fair to say Matteo wasn't overly enamoured by the plan when Anna put it to him, though he did reluctantly agree that, if Anna's presence *was* required in Glasgow, then it made more sense for her to miss the first couple of days of their holiday than to interrupt it further down the line. He warmed further to the proposal when Anna told him or her intention for it to serve as a final tying up of loose ends before definitively drawing a line under that period in her life.

Shortly after 8:30 that morning, Matteo, Jack and Francesca all bundled into Matteo's ageing Fiat, along with toys, swimwear and enough clothes and other provisions to see them through the next fortnight. Anna kissed Jack goodbye, promising to see him soon, but he was already buckled into the backseat, too engrossed in the cartoon playing on his tablet to do more than grunt in her general direction.

'I should be with you by Friday night,' she said to Matteo, as he got behind the wheel. 'Saturday at the absolute latest. I'll let you know what's happening once I know for sure.'

She gave his shoulder a brief, affectionate squeeze through

the open window, unnoticed by the two children. And then they were off. She stood at the kerbside, waving them off as the Fiat rumbled up the narrow street.

She couldn't ignore the twinge of anxiety – and no small amount of self-reproach – she felt over palming Jack off on Matteo, even if it *was* only for a couple of days. But then, she told herself, this was always on the cards. If she planned to stay in Perugia, she'd have had to go back to Glasgow to settle up at some point, and it made sense for her to go by herself rather than take Jack with her. She could get done what she needed to do a whole lot quicker without having to drag him around everywhere with her – and besides, she thought, it avoided the possibility of him deciding he preferred Glasgow to Perugia. As far as she could tell, he'd largely forgotten about his old life, but every now and then he'd still say things out of the blue like 'When are we seeing Ewan and Maisie?' or 'When do I go back to playgroup?' She strongly suspected he had no real conception of just how much distance now lay between him and the places and people he'd come to know so well during the first four years of his life. Whenever he mentioned them, the way he spoke about them led her to believe that, as far as he was concerned, they were just a short car ride away, and all that prevented him from visiting the Lego shop in Buchanan Galleries or tearing around Dowanhill Park with Ewan and Maisie was the restrictions on travel and social mixing imposed by the pandemic – something that, in contrast, he seemed to have no difficulty at all in understanding, and accepting. Now that she thought about it, there was something profoundly depressing about that fact.

She reminded herself she really *was* just going away for a couple of days – an incentive, if there ever was one, to get everything she needed to do done in double-quick time. Besides, Jack needed to get used to her not being constantly on hand before he started school in the autumn. That, too, she realised, reinforced her need to make a decision soon about where her future lay. Wherever they ended up living, she was going to have to get him enrolled at a local school. That or home-school him – something she'd always sworn she'd never do. In fact, she thought, there was a strong chance she was already too late to arrange anything for him in Glasgow. The schools in Scotland always went back early – possibly even as soon as the following week.

She stirred and realised she'd completely lost track of how long she'd been standing there at the kerb. Muttering a hasty apology to the elderly woman who'd been patiently waiting for her to stop blocking the pavement and let her pass, she hurried back inside to finish her own packing.

She dug out her old wheelie case, battered and worn from constant use and covered with the remnants of umpteen different luggage stickers. In addition to underwear and toiletries, and a raincoat to combat the inevitable Scottish summer weather, she packed three changes of clothes: one for today, since she'd no doubt be as sweaty as a builder's cleft by the time she touched down, one for tomorrow, and an extra one for the day after just to be on the safe side, though she told herself she wouldn't need it.

Just a flying visit.

The flight Fraser had identified for her, and which she'd booked at 2 a.m. that morning, departed San Francesco d'Assisi Airport at 11:05, with a connecting flight at London Stansted, touching down in Glasgow at 15:10 local time. She'd be gaining an hour – not great off the back of a decidedly interrupted night, but she could hardly expect the entire country to wind its clocks forward to accommodate her.

She took a taxi to the airport, arriving in plenty of time for check-in and the enhanced security process, which included taking her temperature and running through a seemingly endless series of questions about her own health and whether she could have been exposed to anyone with COVID in the past week. By far the biggest source of delay, however, was her personal alarm, a device which resembled a standard wristwatch but was designed to emit an ear-splitting 125-decibel siren when activated. She'd procured it in the aftermath of the Reckoning affair and now never left the apartment without it, but she hadn't anticipated the security staff treating it like an unexploded IED. Eventually, however, she managed to persuade the stone-faced head of security that she *hadn't* jerry-rigged it in her garage and it *wasn't* going to explode once they were 35,000 feet in the air, and was waved through with the forced, condescending smile of a man who clearly thought women's safety concerns amounted to a whole lot of fuss about nothing.

The flight wasn't full, but still too busy for her liking. In days gone by, she'd have thought nothing of being crammed like a sardine into an enclosed box filled with nothing but recycled air. Now, though, she was hyper-aware of just what a tinderbox the cabin really was, and found herself tensing at every stray cough and throat clearance. What if she caught the virus on the flight? She'd be unable to travel back to Italy until she was negative. She might not see Jack for over a week. He'd think she'd abandoned him.

Get a grip, Scavolini, she told herself. *You're acting like it's a done deal. You're masked, you're vaccinated up the wazoo, you're taking all the precautions you possibly can. Just sit back and go with the flow.*

They landed in Glasgow a few minutes ahead of the scheduled time of arrival. Getting through security took longer than expected thanks to the additional, post-Brexit layers of bureaucracy now being placed on travellers arriving from the EU. She was travelling on her Italian passport – which she'd qualified for during her ten-year sojourn at the Sapienza in her twenties and had continued to renew – almost as a point of principle, and had never felt more glad that she had it than on the morning of 24 June 2016 when she woke to discover that the island she then called home – the southern half of it, at any rate – had narrowly voted to commit collective hara-kiri. In retrospect, she'd often wondered if the seeds for her eventual relocation to what her mother (her own status as a resident of France now the subject of protracted wrangling with the relevant authorities) would have quaintly referred to as 'the Continent' had been planted on that very day.

After texting Matteo to let him know she'd landed safely, she headed through the terminus, tugging her case behind her as she weaved through the crowds of business travellers and holidaymakers, giving everyone as wide a berth as possible.

Exiting through the sliding doors and out into the open air was like stepping into a walk-in freezer. They'd been informed by the captain when they landed that it was a balmy eighteen degrees in Glasgow, but after becoming so heavily acclimatised to the heat of the Perugian summer, she'd have believed him if he'd told them it was in single digits. She hugged her arms through the fabric of her long-sleeved corduroy shirt and wished she'd had the forethought to bring something heavier-duty than a flimsy polyester raincoat. She gazed up at the sky, a thick blanket of grey cloud between her and any hint of sunlight. Somehow, it managed to feel more oppressive than Perugia at the height of the summer season, when the mercury regularly passed thirty – like being smothered by a thick, grey duvet.

As the shuttle bus trundled along the M8 towards Glasgow, her sense of trepidation steadily grew. To say her recent memories of the city weren't exactly rosy would be understating the matter something rotten. But it wasn't just that. Being forced, by the small matter of a global pandemic, to remain away for so long had made it possible for her to avoid confronting what it would mean to definitively cut her ties with the place. Until now, she'd been cocooned from the wider ramifications, allowing herself to behave as if her decision would impact only her – and Jack, of course. And Matteo, she supposed. But the prospect of coming face to face with her friends and co-workers – people she cared about, and who cared about her – was one she dreaded. Despite constantly reiterating to herself the need to put herself first, it was hard to shake the feeling that she was somehow letting them down – especially her colleagues, whom she'd essentially strung along for the last eighteen months, allowing them to believe her return to the fold was imminent. She resolved to keep as low a profile as possible during her visit: get in, get out, and avoid seeing anyone she didn't absolutely have to. She thanked her lucky stars unnecessary socialising remained something of a convenient taboo.

Conversely, the one person she genuinely *did* want to see, and deeply regretted not being able to, was Zoe, currently off hiking in the Brecon Beacons with Sal. Throughout the pandemic, they'd stayed in touch with weekly FaceTime calls – an absolute godsend as far as Anna was concerned. It had been somewhat surreal following Zoe's life from a distance, participating in the virtual housewarming party she and Sal threw once they'd moved into their new flat, as well as seeing her successfully completing her HNC and starting her job as an early years practitioner at the nursery in Broomhill. She told herself there'd be plenty of other opportunities for them to see one another, especially as the world increasingly got back to normal. And yet, there was something about coming back to a Zoe-less Glasgow that just felt all sorts of wrong – as if it wasn't truly Glasgow without her there.

She watched through the grimy window as the bus crawled through the city centre, seeing the familiar streets as if through fresh eyes. A lot, it was clear, had changed since she was last there. The pavements were virtually empty, and the number of boarded-up shopfronts and FOR SALE and TO LET signs seemed to almost match in number those that were open for business. The city centre had already been in a state of decline when she left, thanks to the machinations of racketeering landlords and a series of municipal planning failures, but the pandemic appeared to have accelerated the process tenfold. Now, it was just a hop, skip and a jump away from being a veritable ghost town.

She got off the bus at Hope Street. Having failed to summon a taxi from any of the local companies whose numbers she had on her phone ('We've a shortage of drivers on at the moment,' the dispatcher of one firm apologetically informed her) and reluctant to pay the exorbitant fees associated with the black cabs that lined the rank outside Central Station, she lugged her case up to Buchanan Street and took the subway to the West End. She was due to meet Fraser in Kelvingrove Park at 4:30, and, by the time she finally emerged from the station at Kelvinbridge, she found herself with just under half an hour to kill. She stopped at a café on Otago Street – a regular haunt of hers in days gone past – for a cappuccino, more to pass the time than because she was actually in need of sustenance. Then, after successfully persuading the owner to let her leave her case behind the counter for an hour or so, she headed on down to the Kelvin Way, arriving at the northwest entrance to Kelvingrove Park with a few minutes to spare.

In the end, Fraser was almost a quarter of an hour late, trotting along the path towards her with his jacket tucked under his arm – looking, to Anna's mind, more than a tad absurd in his ultra-tight shirt and chinos. He came to a halt an arm's length from her, and they did that awkward little half-dance that had become so common in the world they now inhabited, attempting to mark the occasion in some way that didn't involve physical contact. Not that she would ever have considered hugging Fraser – or even, after the way he'd handled the business with the photos, shaking his hand.

'Travel work out OK?' he asked, once they'd dispensed with the formalities, or lack thereof.

'Apart from not being able to summon a taxi for love nor money.'

Fraser gave a rueful grimace. 'Yes, I've noticed that. A lot of the drivers found alternative work during lockdown, I gather. Still, you made it here in one piece.'

'So it seems.'

'Well, I'm grateful to you for making the trip, especially at such short notice. I appreciate Glasgow's a little out of your way these days.' He gave a small, awkward laugh, before his expression became serious. 'And I'm sorry we're meeting under such unhappy circumstances. It goes without saying that Hugh was a much-loved and valued colleague.'

For Anna, who'd witnessed firsthand how the university, and Fraser in particular, had treated Hugh following the restructuring that had led to his old position of head of department being eliminated, these words rang decidedly hollow, but she'd promised herself she wasn't going to get into a slanging match with him. At least, not yet.

'He was, yes,' she agreed blandly.

'I don't know about you, but I still can't quite grasp that he's gone. I keep expecting to come across him shambling down the corridor towards me, battered old briefcase in hand, wearing one of those garish woollen neckties he was so fond of.'

Anna smiled dutifully, finding the comment more condescending than genuinely affectionate.

Fraser nodded, smiling fondly. 'Yes, he was quite a character, our Hugh. Memory like a sieve, bless him – always turning up late for meetings, full of apologies and telling us all how unlike him it was to forget. D'you remember that time he stood waiting for three quarters of an hour in the Mitchison Room, wondering why no students had shown up, only for it to turn out it was because they were all waiting for him over in the Rutherford Building?'

Now this just felt like cruelty – not *conscious* cruelty, perhaps, but the lack of thought only made it all the more objectionable.

'He made a lot of difference to a lot of people's lives,' Anna said pointedly.

'Yes,' Fraser agreed, cheerfully failing to pick up on her rebuke, 'and I'm determined to honour the contribution he made to the field in some way – to ensure that *something* positive comes from it all. That's why I've been labouring so hard behind the scenes to make sure this scholarship comes to fruition.'

'Scholarship?'

'Of course, you won't be abreast of any of this, what with you having departed for sunnier climes. Earlier in the year, we received an approach from a wealthy benefactor. I'm guessing you're familiar with Dame Jackie Gordon.'

'The great philanthropist,' Anna nodded. 'Yes, I've heard of her.'

'Well, she's offered to fund a grant in Hugh's name, to be made available exclusively to students from marginalised backgrounds. Levelling the playing field, as it were – making a postgraduate career in the social sciences a more attainable reality.'

Why did she get the feeling she was being buttered up for something? And yet, it seemed churlish to think of what Fraser had just described in anything less than wholly positive terms – a genuinely lovely way to honour the man's legacy. So she simply nodded thoughtfully and said, 'He'd have liked that.'

'Yes, I think so too,' said Fraser. 'Of course, it's still early days. Nothing official's been announced yet – so, needless to say, keep this under your hat for now.' He gestured to her. 'Shall we?'

They set off along the footpath at a leisurely pace, Fraser

with his jacket slung over his shoulder, his free hand in his pocket. Stealing a glance at him, Anna thought he looked older – more drawn about the face, his hairline having receded a good couple of centimetres compared to what she remembered. Or maybe it was just that she'd successfully managed to scrub her memories of him from her mind.

'Tell me,' he said, as they tramped along, side by side, 'how much do you know about the circumstances surrounding Hugh's death?'

'Just what was in the death notice in the *Tribune* and what Farah told me,' Anna replied, still wondering what all this was leading up to, 'which amounted to the same thing. He passed away last May after a short illness.'

Fraser glanced briefly at her, his expression inscrutable. 'And you've not had any contact with his daughter?'

'With Miriam? No. I *had* thought to get in touch, but …' She hesitated. 'But I decided there was nothing I could say to her that she hadn't heard a hundred times already.'

Plus, there were the pathological insecurities she experienced about situations that made her feel emotionally vulnerable – the same insecurities that had caused her to miss her own father's funeral fifteen years earlier. She'd procrastinated for so long about reaching out to Miriam that, eventually, so much time had passed that any belated message of condolence would only have succeeded in drawing attention to her failure to get in touch on a more respectable timescale.

'Yes, she's not had her sorrows to seek, that one,' Fraser agreed. 'Little brother dead when she was barely more than a mite herself, then losing her mother to cancer just a few years ago. And now old Hugh.'

Anna, still lost in her own thoughts, didn't respond. She wasn't clear about the precise details of what had happened to Alfie, the younger of Hugh's two children – only that he was killed in some sort of domestic accident when he was just a toddler. And she only knew that much from whispered gossip among the university staff. Hugh had never spoken to her about it, and it wasn't the sort of thing you asked about. Of his wife, Geraldine, she knew only a little more. It was fairly common knowledge that Geraldine had survived a bout of cancer in her early forties. As to what type, no one had been able to shed any light – only that it had returned in 2015, and from there it had been a short and painful downhill battle. Never one to share much about his private life, Hugh had kept from his colleagues what the family was going through until very near the end. Anna, who'd never met Geraldine while she was alive, had attended the funeral to show her support to Hugh. It was there that she'd met Miriam for the first time – an odd, rather flighty young woman roughly eight years her junior, who, from her spaced-out appearance and vacant stare, was either heavily self-medicating or disassociating with a vengeance.

'Truly, my heart goes out to her,' Fraser went on, shaking his head sadly. 'You can hardly blame her for lashing out.'

'Lashing out?' repeated Anna, shaken out of her reverie by this apparent non-sequitur.

Fraser halted and turned to face Anna, a pained grimace on his face. 'There was an, um ... something of a *confrontation* at the funeral. You'll be aware that the rules at the time meant no more than six people were allowed to attend the service.'

Anna nodded, still wondering where this was going.

'But a whole gaggle of us gathered outside the crematorium to pay our respects. There must have been upwards of sixty there, all told – staff and students alike, spread all throughout the grounds to adhere to the two-metre rule.' He smiled briefly, as if to acknowledge the faint absurdity conjured up by the image. 'Anyway, at the end of the service, the mourners all trouped out, Beryl – Hugh's sister – and her husband and kids leading the pack. And while Beryl was thanking us all, saying it meant the world to her that we'd all shown up to see her brother off, out came Miriam. And straight away, she homed in on me and started screaming at me, saying all this was my fault and how dare I show my face. I'm convinced she'd have gone for me if a bunch of people hadn't stepped in to hold her back.'

Anna shook her head, trying to make sense of all of this. 'I don't understand. Why would it be *your* fault Hugh was ill?'

Fraser sighed. 'That's just it. Hugh wasn't sick. That's merely a story the family put out because they figured it was more palatable than the truth.'

'Which was … ?'

Fraser hesitated, briefly looking left and right to make sure no one was within earshot, then took a couple of steps closer to Anna, in flagrant violation of the same two-metre ruled which he'd invoked just moments earlier. Under normal circumstances, she'd have taken a step back, but she was now so desperate to know the truth that she remained stock still even as she felt his warm breath on her face.

'The truth,' he said, lowering his voice, 'is that Hugh died by suicide.'

4

'He *what?*'

Anna gaped at Fraser, the ground seeming to shift beneath her feet as she struggled to process what she'd just heard.

'I gather that's the approved terminology these days,' said Fraser, seemingly oblivious to her bewilderment. 'Apparently, he left a note, laying it all at my door – accusing me of usurping him and pushing him to the sidelines. Which is flagrant nonsense, incidentally,' he added hotly, 'for a whole host of reasons. But still, that's presumably where Miriam got the idea from. She even wrote to the Senior Management Group, demanding my removal as Head of School. I'm happy to say cooler heads prevailed on *that* front.

'The point is,' he went on, as Anna continued to reel, her thoughts bouncing all over the place as they tried desperately to identify some solid ground on which to find purchase, 'I don't believe it. I don't mean about it being a suicide. That much appears to be true, or else why lay into me in front of everyone like that?' He shook his head. 'No, it's his reasons for having killed himself that I believe are contestable.'

Anna stared at him expectantly, waiting for him to elaborate. But, to her immense frustration, he instead turned from her and walked on up the path.

She set off in hot pursuit. They were making their way along the Kelvin Walkway, the river bubbling and gurgling alongside them. Birdsong mingled with the sound of the water, giving the whole scene an air of gentle tranquillity which seemed utterly inappropriate given the subject under discussion.

After a minute or so, Fraser began to speak again.

'Shortly before he died, Hugh conveyed to me that he was in some sort of difficulty. He told me he'd made mistakes and that they were catching up with him. "My chickens have come home to roost," were the words he used. He said he had secrets which had the power to ruin him completely, and that someone was threatening him with exposure.'

'He was being blackmailed?' said Anna, still not quite prepared to believe what she was being told.

'He didn't use that word,' said Fraser carefully. 'But … that was what I took him to mean, yes. I tried to get him to elaborate, but he wouldn't tell me anything more. He said he wanted to "make things right" – again, those were his words – and that if I just gave him some time, he'd explain everything.

'But we never did get to have that conversation. I didn't see him again after that brief exchange, and, not long afterwards, I heard the news that he was dead.'

An unhappy silence settled between them. The birds continued to chirp. The river continued to gurgle and flow. There was something almost companionable about their silence – something Anna would have previously considered unthinkable. Whatever bitterness she felt towards Fraser had been superseded by a shared concern for Hugh and whatever trouble he'd found himself in prior to his death.

At length, she was aware of herself speaking, half to herself.

'He was trying to tell me something that night.'

She realised Fraser was looking at her quizzically.

'At my farewell party,' she explained. 'He showed up late and under the influence. There was something he wanted to tell me, but I ... was distracted. He left before I had a chance to come and find him.'

Fraser said nothing, but he nodded softly, as if he understood this all too well. 'I've kept this to myself for the better part of fifteen months,' he said, his words appearing to bear no relation to what she'd just said. 'You're the first person I've told. I didn't want to besmirch Hugh's memory – to give anyone cause to think there was any possibility that he was anything less than squeaky clean. In a way, I almost *welcomed* Miriam's accusations. At least, that way, the focus was firmly on me and my apparent shortcomings rather than his.

'But I can't let this go. I need to know what was going on: what Hugh had got himself involved in and who was making his life such a misery that he saw no way out other than to end it.'

They came to the southern edge of the park, where the river curved away to the right under the Kelvin Way Bridge and the footpath continued on towards the Kelvingrove Art Gallery. Anna halted and turned to face Fraser.

'There's one thing I don't understand in all of this. Why are you telling all this to me? And why fly me nearly fifteen hundred miles just to hear it?'

'Surely that should be obvious.'

'Well, it's not.'

Fraser gave a silent, exasperated laugh, as if he regarded Anna as being deliberately obtuse.

'Come on, Anna. You can't kid on you don't have a certain ... reputation when it comes to these things.'

Anna couldn't help rolling her eyes, though she knew better than to try to deny it. She'd heard this pitch before, and, whether she liked it or not, knew there was some truth in it.

'I want to ask if you'd be prepared to find out who was

putting pressure on Hugh,' said Fraser, 'and what they were using to blackmail him.'

'Why not take your concerns to the police?'

'For the same reason I know you'd do the same if you were in my position: because I'm worried about what they might find out.'

Anna folded her arms and looked at him expectantly. She knew what he was driving at, but was determined to make him spell it out.

'Look,' said Fraser, adopting a tone that was clearly intended to make him appear the very picture of a reasonable man, 'neither of us wants to think less of Hugh. We can agree on that much. But if it *does* transpire that he was involved in something shady … wouldn't you rather have some control over the spread of that information?'

Anna said nothing. It sounded squalid and underhanded … but she couldn't deny he had a point.

'There's another reason why it should be you,' Fraser added.

'Oh yes? What's that?'

'His daughter will actually *talk* to you.' He gave a rather wincing smile. '*I* may be persona non grata as far as she's concerned, but you – you were always Hugh's golden girl, if you'll permit me to make so bold an observation. I doubt the regard in which he held you will have been lost on Miriam. That's got to count for something, surely. At any rate, she's unlikely to attempt to physically assault you if you turn up at her door without an armed escort.' He smiled encouragingly, as if inviting Anna to acknowledge his joke.

Anna sighed. 'Fraser …'

'Yes?' he said immediately, unable to hide his anticipation.

'I've put this sort of thing behind me.'

His face fell.

'Any time I get involved in something like this, all that

happens is I end up endangering both myself and the people I care about.'

And a bunch of the people I ought to be able to rely on invariably let me down, she wanted to add but didn't.

Fraser pulled a strained expression. 'That's a bit of an exaggeration, surely.'

She laughed incredulously. 'I'm not sure if it escaped your notice, but just under two years ago I had my life turned inside out because I pissed off the wrong set of people. What makes you think I'd voluntarily sign up for that again?'

'This is different. You wouldn't be going up against a bunch of sad little womanhaters who've sworn vengeance against the entire female population.'

'I don't know *what* I'd be going up against,' she exclaimed in exasperation. 'That's the entire point!'

The volume of her outburst only made the silence that followed all the more pronounced. Plainly suffering from second-hand embarrassment, Fraser glanced around uncomfortably, but there was no one else within earshot.

'Look,' he said, a note of frustration now entering his voice as he turned to face her again, 'I'd do it myself if I thought I'd get anywhere, but I've well and truly blotted my copy book with the very people I'd need to persuade to talk to me. Besides, you've something of a track record when it comes to finding out things that no one else can. You can't pretend otherwise.'

She said nothing.

'Pretend it's not me asking you, if that would help. Pretend it's Hugh's family – or better yet, Hugh himself.'

She continued to say nothing, but she felt the muscles in her jaw tightening.

'You said he was trying to tell you something the last time you saw him,' Fraser continued. 'That can only mean he wanted you to help him.'

'Stop.'

'Stop what?'

'Trying to use emotional blackmail on me. It's cheap and grubby.' She paused. 'Not that you need much help in that department.'

'I probably deserved that.'

The almost cheerful manner with which he accepted the insult only served to bolster her ire. But even as she prepared to deliver a fresh riposte, she knew, with a sinking feeling, that the die was already cast; that his efforts to prick her conscience had worked and that she was going to accept this undertaking. Moreover, that she was *always* going to accept, whatever she might claim to him – or to herself.

She gave Fraser a long, hard look. He continued to meet her gaze, the expectant, vaguely desperate look in his eyes reminding her of a dog waiting to be given a belly rub.

'You're an arsehole, Fraser,' she said.

Naturally, she recognised the inherent folly in speaking like this to the man who was, until such time as she formally tendered her resignation, still her line manager. And yet, the expression on his face was not one of anger but unbridled joy. For that reason alone, she wished she could take back her words.

'Anna, you're an absolute diamond,' he purred. 'I know we've had our ups and downs, but I'm glad you're able to look past our differences to—'

'Don't kid yourself,' she snapped. 'We're not friends, Fraser, OK? This isn't about looking past our differences or letting bygones be bygones. If I do this, the only person I'll be doing it for is Hugh.'

'Hey,' said Fraser, continuing to be infuriatingly amiable in the face of her opprobrium, 'I'll take it. And, if it helps galvanise you at all, feel free to channel all that ill-feeling towards me into getting to the bottom of whatever was going on in Hugh's life. All I ask is that, whatever you uncover, you share it with me so the two of us can make a joint decision about what to do with it.' He hesitated. 'Does that ... does that sound reasonable?'

Anna considered his request for a moment, then gave a curt nod.

'Fine.'

She glanced off to the side as she spoke, not quite able to bring herself to look at him directly.

'Thank you,' said Fraser, mercifully avoiding a repeat of his earlier exuberance. 'For what it's worth, I'm glad it's you who's looking into this. If anyone can ferret out the truth, it's you. I know you'll find this hard to believe, but I cared a lot about Hugh. It's caused me no end of distress, this last year or so, to think—'

'I have a few provisos, of course,' she cut in, halting his self-indulgent homily in its tracks.

'Naturally.' Once again, he sounded decidedly chastened.

'You're to let me do this without interference. You don't pester me with endless phone calls and demands for updates. You wait for *me* to get in touch with *you*.'

'Of course.'

'And another thing. I plan to be in town for a couple of days while I take care of some unfinished business. Three at the absolute *most*. If, during that time, I succeed in getting to the bottom of this Hugh business, then so be it. But either way, I'll be leaving before the end of the weekend, come hell or high water.'

Fraser opened his mouth to say something, then stopped, seemingly changing his mind.

'Duly noted.'

She wondered if he'd been about to launch into an impassioned attempt to get her to reconsider her self-imposed deadline, or to merely voice his disbelief that she'd ever willingly walk away from a job unfinished, let alone one of this nature ...

But then, perhaps she was merely projecting her own incredulity onto him.

They headed back up the Kelvin Way. Once again, Anna was struck by how quiet it was. Of course, it was still the summer holidays, which accounted for the lack of students – but even so, she couldn't get over the near-total absence of noise – of voices, of traffic. Even the birds sounded unusually quiet for the time of year. She said as much to Fraser, more to fill the silence than anything else.

'It's a rare old wheeze, this "work from home" lark,' he agreed. 'Quite remarkable that it took a worldwide pandemic for our overlords to realise how inefficient it was to force everyone into the office every day, whether or not they had any actual need to *be* there.'

Anna nodded but didn't respond. Her mind was once more on Hugh, and on the task that lay ahead of her.

'Tell me something,' she said.

'I'll try.'

'You saw far more of Hugh in the last year of his life than I did. Do you have any theories as to what sort of trouble he was in?'

Fraser gave a pained grimace. 'I wish I did. I've racked my brains over and over again. Gone back through all our old conversations, trying to figure out whether there was some clue I might have missed.' He shrugged helplessly. 'I've got nothing.'

She'd figured as much. Leave it to Fraser Taggart to be utterly unobservant about the mental state of the people around him.

'Any feel for where you're going to begin your enquiries?' he asked tentatively.

'I think I might do as you suggested and pay Miriam a visit. She's still at the family home on Hendon Drive, I take it?'

She'd always found it something of a head-scratcher that Hugh's daughter had continued to live with him into her thirties. When *she'd* been a teenager, she couldn't wait to get out from under her parents' thumb – but then, she supposed, perhaps she was just projecting her own experiences onto Miriam.

Fraser nodded. 'So I gather. Not that I've had any communication with her since … well, you know. But I haven't heard anything to suggest she's moved out.' He paused, then added hesitantly, 'You'll, ah, be heading over there straight away?'

'No time like the present.'

Fraser nodded, seemingly approving of this decision. She felt like pointing out that she wasn't on the company clock here – that she was entitled to carry out her enquiries at her own pace. But then, that would be needlessly petty. After all, *she* was the one who'd set a hard limit on her time here.

'There's something I need to say,' she said.

'Go on.'

'There's no guarantee I'll find out anything. And if I *do*,' she added, before Fraser could respond, 'it's entirely possible it'll mean learning things about Hugh that we'll both end up wishing we hadn't. That's invariably what happens when you start digging into someone's life – whether they're being threatened with exposure or *not*.'

'I'm aware of that,' said Fraser quietly. 'It seems to me, though, that, if my interpretation of his last words to me is correct, someone drove him to this. That means someone has blood on their hands – figuratively speaking. I'd want to see them held to account, wouldn't you?'

Anna didn't trust herself to respond. But yes, she thought, she'd want that very much. Retribution might not be the noblest of goals, but it *was* a powerful motivator.

'And is there anything else you can think of that I should know?' she asked instead. 'Anything about your last conversation with Hugh that you haven't told me?'

Fraser considered this for a moment, then shook his head.

'I don't think so, no. It was a frustratingly brief exchange, and even more frustratingly cryptic. Perhaps, if I'd pressed him harder …' He made a vague gesture with one hand. 'But at the time, I had no idea it would be the last conversation we'd ever have.'

Anna nodded soberly and tried not to think about her *own* final conversation with Hugh, perched drunk and disorderly on the stairs of the house on Clarence Drive.

They walked on in silence for a while, eventually coming to a halt at the foot of University Avenue.

'Hmm,' said Fraser, as if mildly amused. 'Back where we started, more or less. I suppose this is where we part ways. Um … if you don't mind my asking, have you organised anything in terms of accommodation while you're here? You're more than welcome to our spare room,' he added quickly. 'It's not being used for anything apart from some old boxes, and both myself and Catriona would be delighted to have you.'

'Oh, I've already booked into a hotel,' said Anna, the lie leaving her lips as easily as if it were the truth. She wasn't keen on the idea of feeling in any way indebted to Fraser, or of sharing a roof with him and his equally vapid wife, in whose company she'd once spent an excruciatingly tedious half-hour at a function for university staff and their significant others.

'Pity,' said Fraser. 'I should have thought to say something sooner. Still, if you're happy with your present arrangements …'

'I am.'

They stood facing one another, neither seemingly knowing how to break this off. Eventually, Anna took the initiative.

'Well, I'd better get to it.'

She turned to go.

'Oh,' said Fraser, 'I just remembered.'

She stopped. Turned to face him.

'Last year, while we were cleaning out Hugh's old office, I found something that might be of interest: his diary from the previous year. That is, 2019. The last full year of his life. I've spent umpteen hours poring over it, trying to figure out if it contained some clue as to what had been going on with him. Perhaps you'll have more luck than me.'

'Have you got it?'

'Not with me, no.' He winced sheepishly. 'I meant to bring it today, but it slipped my mind. Here's a thought, though. I'm away at a conference all day tomorrow, but what's say I swing by your hotel and drop it off en route?'

'That would be ... ideal,' said Anna, realising she was at imminent risk of her lie being exposed.

'Where did you say you were staying?'

'I didn't.' She thought quickly. 'Um, it's the Great Western Inn.'

It was the first place that came into her head: a large chain hotel on Great Western Road, across the road from the old Willow Bank Academy playing fields. It was far from the cheapest option on the table; she'd originally planned to check into a budget Travelodge in the city centre. But now that she thought about it, she realised having a base of operations close to the beating heart of the West End might not be the worst idea.

'Excellent,' said Fraser. 'I'll be there with it shortly after eight. I'll, uh, leave it at reception in case you're having a lie-in.'

And, on that rather awkward note, they went their separate ways, Fraser heading back up the hill towards the university while Anna made for Otago Street.

It was only after she'd rounded the corner that it occurred to her that the subject of her future at Kelvingrove – or lack thereof – had never once come up in their conversation.

5

Anna picked up her case at the café, then walked the roughly three kilometres to the Great Western Inn. She was in luck: there were currently several vacancies, and, though the receptionist did his best to put a positive spin on things, it was clear from reading between the lines that, as with so many other professions, the pandemic had hit their trade hard.

She headed upstairs to her room on the second floor to drop off her luggage, and to have a quick wash and change of clothes. The room was decently sized but sparsely furnished – which suited her just fine, as she only intended to use it for the three S's: showering, sleeping and shitting. It was also extremely warm, the radiator under the window running full tilt despite it being the middle of August, with no apparent means of controlling it. It was the first time she'd felt hot since she'd arrived in Glasgow – oppressively so, in fact, even though she knew that, objectively, the temperature in the room was lower than it would be in Perugia at this time of day, even in the shade.

A couple of hours back in Glasgow and she'd already gone native.

Once she'd got her things unpacked, she FaceTimed

Matteo and, after exchanging some brief words with him, asked him to pass the phone to Jack, who chattered away contentedly as he treated her to a guided tour of the villa and its garden.

'It looks lovely,' she told him. 'I can't wait to join you there in another day or two.'

It was close to 7 p.m. when she finally set off, walking south along the perimeter of Gartnavel Hospital towards the railway station at Hyndland. The MacLeish family home was in Westerton, a leafy suburb just beyond the city's northwestern marches, barely more than a five-minute journey by rail. She boarded the first westbound train that pulled into the platform, choosing what looked to be the carriage with the fewest occupants. At one end, a gaggle of teenagers on e-scooters were clustered by the doors, their loud, overly excited voices seeming to fill the entire carriage. They were wearing those flimsy, disposable blue masks you saw everywhere these days, more often than not lying trampled on the ground ... though, in their case, 'wearing' might have been a bit of an overstatement. A couple of them had their masks covering their mouths, if not their noses; the rest had them pulled down below their chins, which Anna doubted was doing very much to halt the spread of the virus.

But that was nothing compared to the corpulent, briefcase-toting man in the ill-fitting suit who'd boarded the train behind her and had opted for the seat just across the aisle from her. Bare-faced and breathing heavily, she might have given him the benefit of the doubt and assumed he had some sort of condition that exempted him from masking, were it not for the fact that he'd been wearing one when he'd boarded the train, only to remove it the moment the doors closed. She briefly toyed with either confronting him herself or raising the matter with the conductor, currently making his way down the gangway towards them, then caught herself.

What have I become? she thought. *I've turned into a total clype. This virus has made hall monitors of us all ...*

The MacLeish family home was located in the heart of Westerton's garden suburb, a conservation area characterised by its abundant foliage and quaint, Arts and Crafts-style houses, with long, sloping roofs and gable windows. The trees overhanging the road up from the station were in summer's full bloom – a vast sea of verdant hues that was almost overpowering on the eyes until you acclimatised to it. You didn't see green quite like this in Perugia, that was for sure. Back in 2011, when Anna had first moved back to Scotland after a decade in Rome, she'd briefly toyed with the idea of settling here herself, before concluding she'd go stir crazy this far from the city centre, even with the perk of a regular train service to connect her to the 'real world'. It represented a form of living that was just too quiet and sedate for her, though she could see why it appealed to some people. For her, the West End had offered an acceptable compromise: picturesque but with a pace of life that wasn't verging on glacial.

The MacLeish house – a detached two-storey villa of blonde sandstone – lay in the shadow of the Cairnhill Woods, about a ten-minute walk uphill from the station. Hugh had once told her he and Geraldine had acquired it as a fixer-upper in the early eighties, back in the days when it was still possible for young newlyweds to get a foot on the property ladder without a sizeable cash injection from their parents. As Anna stepped through the front gates and followed the gravel driveway as it arced round a tall, solitary fir tree, the house hove into view, looking decidedly the worse for wear. The ivy growing up the front of the building was overgrown and hanging off the wall in places, the mullions of the large bay windows showed signs of cracking, and the lawn was in serious need of mowing. If Anna hadn't known better, she'd have assumed the place had been left abandoned and unoccupied since Hugh's death.

She approached the front door and rang the bell. A long wait ensued, during which she had a chance to eye up her surroundings and notice further evidence of neglect: the weeds poking out of the gravel, the cloudiness of the window next to the door, the smashed remnants of a fallen roof tile lying on the ground a few metres away. As she inspected her own fingernails while she continued to wait, she heard a vehicle coming to a halt in the street beyond the driveway, followed by a door slamming, then footsteps crunching up the gravel. She turned as a man in a DHL uniform and the ubiquitous face covering shambled into view, lugging a large and obviously heavy box with 'The Wine Society' emblazoned on it. He came to a halt next to Anna, deposited the box on the ground and nodded to her in a knowing fashion, as if he recognised a fellow traveller facing the same predicament as himself. She nodded back. Then, as the silence between them stretched out to the point of awkwardness, she rang the bell again.

'That doesn't work,' he said. 'You have to do it like this.'

He stepped past her and hammered on the door with his fist. A moment later, a voice called out from somewhere inside.

'All right, calm your tits! I'm coming.'

They waited a few seconds longer. Then, the shimmering outline of a figure appeared behind the frosted glass. The door swung open and a woman gazed out at them balefully.

Miriam MacLeish was thirty-two years of age but could be mistaken for someone much younger, with her delicate, almost cherubic features, large brown eyes and pale, borderline translucent skin. She had dark hair in a messy blunt cut which looked suspiciously like she'd hacked at it herself with the garden shears, and was wearing an oversized denim shirt that reached to just above her bare knees. The shirt was splattered with a variety of hues of paint, and, from its dishevelled appearance and misaligned buttons, looked like it had been hastily thrown on moments before she arrived at the door. She rubbed sleep from one eye with a balled fist and glowered at the deliveryman.

'You again?' she said. 'What do you want?'

'Got another load of vino for you,' he said cheerfully.

She sighed irritably. 'What, *again*? I told you to stop bringing it. The man who ordered it doesn't live here anymore.'

'Hey, I'm just the delivery boy. You need to take it up with the supplier.'

For a moment, she merely scowled in his direction. Then she sighed again.

'All right. You might as well dump it with the rest.'

He hoisted up the box with a grunt and followed Miriam into the house. Anna – seemingly unnoticed by Miriam for the time being – saw that the hall corridor was filled with similar boxes, piled high on top of one another, all bearing the same logo. The man deposited his load and emerged from the house, cracking his knuckles and looking altogether too pleased with himself. Miriam was hot on his heels.

'I don't want you bringing any more of these,' she informed him, her voice high and haughty in an attempt to sound authoritative, which only made her sound even younger than she looked. 'You can see for yourself no one's drinking them.'

'So put them on eBay, then,' he shrugged. 'You'd probably make a killing.'

Anna got the impression being hectored like this by Miriam was not a new experience for him.

He strolled past Anna, shooting her a wry eyebrow-raise as he went, and headed off, whistling a jaunty tune as his footsteps crunched down the driveway.

Miriam watched till he'd disappeared round the bend, then

shook her head in disapproval. 'Seriously! The complete *nerve* of some people.' She turned to Anna, giving the unmistakable impression that she wasn't so much noticing her for the first time as only now deeming her worthy of her attention. 'And what can I do for *you*? I hope you're not with the Liberal Democrats. I told the last one of their lot who showed up at my door I wouldn't consider voting for them – not for all the gold in China.'

'It's Anna,' said Anna, surprised and, she had to admit, a little put out that Miriam hadn't recognised her. 'Anna Scavolini. I worked with your dad.'

'Anna?' She frowned, rolling the word around in her mouth as if trying to decide whether she liked the taste of it. Then her expression brightened. 'Anna! Anna Scavolini! Of course! How nice! What are you doing here? They said you'd gone away.'

She looked and sounded genuinely overjoyed, as if Anna was a long-lost friend who'd come back to her against all the odds. It was all a bit overwhelming, and Anna had to stop herself from taking a protective step back.

'Oh, but never *mind* all that.' Miriam batted her own question away with a wave of her hand. 'You're here, and it's wonderful to see you, whatever the occasion. Come in, come in.'

Anna hesitated. 'Um … do you want me to put on my mask?'

Miriam snorted. 'Oh, pish posh. I've had all my shots. Get *in* here!'

Fearful that, if she delayed for a moment longer, Miriam would physically *yank* her inside, Anna hastily did as she was told. As she stepped into the hallway, she realised that the state of disrepair that was evident outside extended to the house's interior as well. In addition to the multiple boxes of wine that lined the long, wood-panelled corridor, a dead plant lay wilting in a cracked jardinière, and the carpet looked like it hadn't felt the caress of a vacuum cleaner in years.

'Daddy had a standing order with The Wine Society,' said Miriam, seeing Anna's eyes skirting over the boxes. 'I've tried to get them to cancel it, but they want his account number and all manner of other obscure information. I said what did they expect me to do – hack into his email account for them? But they wouldn't budge, and so here we are.' She shrugged, letting her arms fall to her sides with a slap, and gave a rather sheepish smile.

Anna's eyes drifted sideways to the console table by the door, where a hefty stack of letters lay unopened, the words 'FINAL NOTICE' stamped on the top one in ominous red. Miriam caught her looking and hastily slid them behind the nearby key bowl – a move so plainly intended to be surreptitious, it only succeeded in drawing even more attention to itself.

'Can I get you something to drink?' she said, transparently insistent in her desire to change the subject. 'I think there's some orange squash in the fridge, or we could crack open a cheeky bottle of vino if you've a hankering for something stronger. I mean,' she gestured to the boxes that lined the corridor, 'it's not like we're in short supply.'

'Just some water would be grand, thanks.'

'If you're sure.' She sounded a bit disappointed. 'Well, head on through to the sitting room and make yourself at home. Be with you in two shakes of a lamb's tail.'

She disappeared through to the kitchen, leaving Anna to find her own way to the sitting room, which, by process of elimination, she determined was at the end of the corridor. The room was high-ceilinged, with large bay windows overlooking the back garden, much of its space taken up by a bulky, floral-patterned sofa set. An assortment of china ornaments lined the mantelpiece and various side tables. All told, it conveyed the taste of a woman of a certain age. Anna suspected Geraldine had been chiefly responsible for the décor and that it hadn't changed significantly since her passing six years ago.

Her gaze settled on a pair of matching stone urns occupying pride of place at the centre of the mantelpiece. They were smaller than she'd expected. Incredible – and a little unnerving – to think that fire could reduce a human being to a pile of ashes capable of being housed in a container less than thirty centimetres tall. Her own father had been buried, of course, in keeping with the traditions of his faith. She wasn't sure which she regarded as the starker reminder of the impermanence of this existence: incinerated in an oven or left to decompose below the earth until all that was left was a pile of old bones.

She stirred at the sound of footsteps, and turned as Miriam came into the room, a glass of water in each hand. Seeing Anna standing beside the urns, she halted abruptly, a stricken expression briefly crossing her face.

'Here,' she said, swiftly regaining her composure. 'I wasn't sure if you wanted fizzy or still, so I brought both.'

She stepped forward, holding both glasses out towards Anna. More out of politeness than because she actually felt thirsty, Anna took one at random. They stood, facing one another awkwardly, neither seemingly knowing how to break the impasse.

'Sorry,' said Anna eventually, half-gesturing to the urns. 'I was just …'

'That's ok,' said Miriam. 'I'd hardly've have put them on display if I'd a problem with people gawping at 'em. Not that I've exactly had a surplus of visitors in the last year and a half. Actually, I think you might be the first. Did you watch the livestream?'

'Livestream?' Anna repeated, momentarily confused as to what Miriam was talking about. 'Oh, I mean, I did, yes.'

'What did you think? I thought it turned out quite well, all in all. I'd never organised something like that myself before –

and Auntie Beryl, *she* was about as much use as a rubber cheese-grater.' Miriam's eyes flared with sudden indignation. 'Wanted a share of the ashes, so she did. But I put my foot down. I said to her, "You swan off to the Southern Hemisphere and don't even bother sending a Christmas card for the better part of twenty years. I'll be arse-badgered if I let you make off with his remains." She didn't like that much – but still, I won in the end.' Her tirade ended as suddenly as it had begun, a sweet but unmistakably triumphant smile serving as the coup de grâce.

Anna managed a strained smile in response, though she wasn't sure what to make of any of this. The cheerful, almost flighty demeanour interspersed with abrupt bursts of petty vindictiveness; the vaguely manic speech patterns and mannerisms – she was far from convinced Miriam was all there.

'How have you been coping?' she ventured. She knew it was a vapid question, but she wasn't sure what else there was to say.

'Oh, I get by about as well as anyone, I expect,' said Miriam airily. 'I suppose I'm used to death by now. First Alfie, then Mum, and now Daddy. All shuffled off the mortal coil.' She sighed heavily. 'For they are all there but one: I, Miriam, last of the MacLeishes.'

They stood there in silence for a moment, Anna hoping her expression appeared suitably reflective. She was wondering if she should clasp her hands and bow her head – that, or raise her glass in toast – when Miriam snorted and rolled her eyes.

'It was a joke. *Jesus!* Lighten up, why don't you?'

She slouched over to the nearest sofa and sat, setting the spare glass of water on the coffee table and folding one long, pale leg under her. Anna settled on the facing sofa, glass in hand, still untouched.

'Seriously,' Miriam continued, 'I'm fine. It's been over a year now. I've ... adjusted. Become acclimatised to the new normal. And there's certain advantages to having the place to myself. I can stay in bed till noon if I feel like it, without anyone moaning at me to get up. And I get to paint in peace without any distractions.'

Anna gave what she hoped was an empathetic nod and took a sip of water. She knew Miriam had gone to art school; that, since graduating, she'd devoted herself entirely to the craft; that she'd never had what might be described as a 'real' job. If she was being honest with herself, she'd always taken something of a dim view of what she perceived as Miriam's parents indulging her, essentially providing for her – and putting a roof over her head – long into adulthood while she indulged a pastime that couldn't possibly make her a decent living. But then, Anna supposed, that possibly revealed a lack of imagination on her part – an unconscious belief that it wasn't real work if it didn't involve going to an office every day and doing something soul-destroying. Wasn't she, herself, in a sort-of-relationship with a sculptor? And hadn't her own parents taken the exact same view towards her determination to pursue a degree in criminology instead of a more 'high-value' qualification? Besides, unless she'd somehow inherited enough money from her parents to live on – which Anna, who had a good feel for how much money Hugh had made, seriously doubted – the days of indulging her artistic whims at their expense were well and truly over now.

'So come on,' Miriam leant forward eagerly, hands squeezed between her thighs, 'tell me, what brings you here?'

'Oh, various things,' said Anna, immediately launching into the same spiel she suspected she'd be using on everyone with whom she came into contact over the course of her stay here. 'Tying up some loose ends, mostly. It's my first time back here since the pandemic, and I—'

Miriam interrupted with a childish, high-pitched squeal of amusement, as if Anna was being hopelessly dense. 'Oh, I didn't mean *that*! I mean *here* – as in, sitting here in this room, having a conversation with me. Don't tell me you just happened to be in the neighbourhood and thought you'd drop in and see me.'

'Well, I mean, actually …' Anna began, now finding herself very much put on the spot. 'To pay my respects, I suppose. And to apologise.'

Miriam blinked in surprise. 'Apologise? What for?'

'For not coming sooner. For not reaching out when your dad passed away.' She exhaled a heavy breath. 'And for not keeping in touch with him after I went away. He was … he was a good friend to me while I was at Kelvingrove, and I can't help feeling I may have taken that for granted.'

In a trice, Miriam was leaning across the sofa towards her, eyes wide with concern. 'Oh, Anna, he didn't think that. Not at *all*. He talked about you all the time, about how proud of you he was. Not in a sanctimonious, patriarchal sort of way, of course,' she quickly clarified. 'He was always super-respectful. He talked about how you'd built the criminology programme up from nothing in just a few years; about how honoured he was to count you as a colleague and a friend.' She gazed into Anna's eyes with such an intensity that it was almost physically painful. 'He knew you cared,' she said, her tone so earnest it bordered on pastiche.

Anna managed a small, tight smile of gratitude, even as her guilt over having somehow managed to turn this conversation into an exercise in assuaging her own conscience twisted like a knife in her gut.

Belatedly, Miriam seemed to become aware of the awkwardly intimate turn their conversation had taken. Straightening up, she blew out an exaggerated breath. 'So, this pandemic, huh? Crazy couple of years we've been having.'

'That's putting it mildly,' agreed Anna, glad to have something concrete and uncontentious to respond to. There was something to be said for a global pandemic when it came to giving everyone a shared experience to grouse about – a ready-made icebreaker for every possible social situation. 'I suppose it won't have affected you much.' She gave an awkward laugh. 'I mean, in your line of work, you must've spent a fair amount of time holed up in the house to begin with.'

Miriam frowned as she considered this. 'You know, it's strange. Right about the time it all kicked off, my commissions went off a cliff. Suddenly no one wanted to buy fine art paintings. Funny how that works. Plus, it's hard to feel inspired while you're staring at the same four walls all day.' Her expression brightened. 'So what about you? Sounds like this move to Italy's a permanent thing, then?'

Anna nodded uncertainly. 'It's looking that way.'

Miriam gave a dark look. 'Well, if you ask me, you're well out of that place. Snakes and vipers, the lot of 'em – and that walloping thundercunt Fraser Taggart the worst of all of them.' Her eyes flared again in fresh anger. 'You know he made Daddy's life a misery? Made him feel totally inadequate, having him jump through hoops to prove himself.' She snorted. 'As if *he* had anything to prove to *them*, all the years of his life he gave that place – and for what?'

'He made a lot of difference to a lot of people's lives,' said Anna gently. 'And he left behind a legacy the Fraser Taggarts of this world can't touch.'

'What's the point of a legacy when you're bloody dead?' Miriam snapped. 'I tell you, that last year of his life was pure *hell.*'

'In what way?' asked Anna. 'What was he like, those final months, after I went away? I mean, if it's not too insensitive a question.'

She was glad that Miriam, of her own volition, had brought the conversation to the very line of enquiry she'd come here to pursue. All the same, she sensed the need to tread carefully, to avoid giving her any reason to suspect that this was a fishing expedition.

'It's not too insensitive, no,' said Miriam, though with a brittleness to her tone that suggested otherwise. 'What was he like?' She frowned, pondering the question. 'To be honest, it's kind of hard to say. It's not as if I saw a whole lot of him. He was out at work during the day … and a bunch of evenings too, as I recall. He seemed to be working harder than ever, *despite* the demotion.' Her face darkened again. 'That shithole Taggart, riding him like a fucking bronco.

'You know I wrote to them?' she added, an almost accusatory note entering her voice, as if Anna was somehow guilty by association. 'Told them exactly what he'd done. But nothing came of it, of course. Closed ranks to protect their own. *So* bloody predictable.'

Anna would never have dreamed of saying as much, but, privately, she wondered what Fraser could possibly have been doing to exert the level of pressure on Hugh that Miriam was describing. His workload had unquestionably been considerably lighter after he lost his position as head of department in early 2019, and even the most disorganised of individuals – which, admittedly, Hugh *had* been – would surely have found the time to do the additional paperwork they'd all been landed with after the restructuring, and with which she'd grappled in the months leading up to her departure.

'What about once lockdown started?' she asked. 'The two of you must have seen more of each other then – cooped up in the house together all day.'

'Not really,' retorted Miriam, bristling at what she seemed to regard as an unreasonable question. 'It's a big house, and we were both still working. He was sequestered in his office all day and I had my painting to do. I'd a big project on. I was doing some portraits for a client who was paying above the odds for them, so I was hardly going to half-arse it. Plus, it's not like I've ever kept what you'd call regular hours. A lot of times, I'd only be coming to when he was already winding down for the day. Going into lockdown only fucked up my circadian rhythm even more.'

'I'm sorry,' said Anna, as tactfully as possible, 'but I'm just trying to make sense of it all. If you really saw so little of him, what was it that made you so convinced his life was hell?'

'He killed himself, didn't he?' Miriam snapped, and, for a moment, her porcelain features contorted into something bitter and ugly. 'What more proof do you need? He laid it all out in a suicide note – addressed to *me*, thank you very much. Written in his usual rambling, circumlocutory style, though it set out how he felt plainly enough. There was a lot of talk about feeling worthless and surplus to requirements, with a side order of being shat on from a great height by a certain you-know-who.'

'Did he actually mention Fraser Taggart by *name*?'

Miriam snorted. 'Of course he didn't *name* him. Since when was that ever his style? But anyone with half a brain could join the dots and work out who all those references to "management" and "the university" *really* referred to.

'You want to read it?' She suddenly lurched forward, leaning her entire body across the sofa's armrest towards Anna. 'Is that what you're after? Would that put your doubts to rest? Well, I'm sorry, but you can't. The police took it away with them, so you'll just have to get your ghoulish kicks from elsewhere.'

Anna knew better than to say anything. She realised she'd pushed things too far; that she'd ignored the warning signs that Miriam was on the verge of snapping – and yet she'd ploughed ahead, eyes so firmly fixed on the ultimate prize that she'd failed to spot the tripwire she was about to walk right into.

At length, Miriam relented. Her expression became contrite, and she withdraw from the arm of the sofa, scuttling backwards like a pallid, long-limbed beetle. 'I'm sorry,' she muttered, lowering her eyes to avoid meeting Anna's. 'It was wrong of me to accuse you like that. It's just …' She sighed. 'People can be such *ghouls*. They swarm around a bereavement like flies on shit, leeching off your grief, salivating for all the gory details – always under the pretext of *concern*, of course. It's as if they want me to perform – to rend my clothes and weep buckets. Well, I *have* wept, behind closed doors. Whatever happened to grief being a private matter? What happened to not making a scene?'

Once again, Anna found herself at a loss for what to say. A simple 'you're right' would hardly have sufficed, and yet she struggled to think of a single word in Miriam's soliloquy with which she disagreed.

'I was the one who found him, you know.'

Miriam's sudden, unprompted admission shook Anna from her train of thought. She had, now that she stopped to consider it, always assumed as much – it stood to reason, given that the two of them had lived together – but she'd never actively considered the precise circumstances under which it must have happened, or the impact on Miriam. Now that she thought about it, she didn't even know the cause of death, other than that it was self-inflicted.

'I'm sorry,' she said eventually. 'Did he … did he suffer?'

'According to some, it's practically the most painless way to go there is.'

Anna merely looked at her quizzically.

'Daddy gassed himself with the car exhaust,' Miriam explained, her tone disturbingly matter-of-fact. 'I got home from my daily constitutional, and there he was – note lying propped open on the dashboard, ready for me to find. Spared me a grisly treasure hunt, at any rate.'

'I'm sorry,' said Anna again, not knowing what else *to* say.

'You're wondering if I regret not making more time for him while he was still alive. Don't try to deny it. I would be too if I was in your shoes. And yes, of course I do. They always say you don't truly understand how much someone means to you till they're gone. Well, it's true. He was a feckless, scatter-brained old so-and-so who always left the toilet seat up and would've lost his own head if it wasn't firmly attached to him

… but he was still my daddy, and I miss him more than words can hope to describe.'

She fell silent, head lowered, picking unhappily at her fingernails. A heavy pall seemed to settle on the room. Anna, for want of something she could actually *do*, sipped slowly from her water glass, trying to make it last.

After a minute or so, Miriam stirred. 'But listen,' she said, leaning towards Anna again, her demeanour once more that of someone thrilled to have unexpectedly reconnected with an old friend, 'let's not talk about all *that* anymore. Tell me about yourself. I'm gagging to know what you've been up to since we last saw each other.'

So Anna told her all about Perugia: the weather, the architecture, all the improvements to her general quality of life. Miriam made various noises of approval and longing, some of which verged on orgasmic. 'It sounds absolutely *divine*,' she purred at one point, and Anna couldn't help but agree. Articulating her feelings about the place out loud to someone with no personal skin in the game only served to clarify in her own mind that the decision she pretended she still had to make was a foregone one.

'And is there someone waiting for you back there?' Miriam asked, clasping her hands with girlish glee.

'Well, there's my son, obviously,' said Anna, deliberately missing the point.

'Anna.' Miriam shook her head reproachfully. 'There's no need to be coy. It's just us girlies here. Have you got a special someone you're not telling me about?'

'Perhaps,' Anna equivocated, not quite managing to stop the flicker of a reflexive smile.

Miriam smiled knowingly. 'I see. So *that's* how it is.'

'What?' Anna felt her shoulders tensing defensively.

'Oh, nothing,' Miriam continued to smirk. 'Your secret's safe with me.'

They continued to talk for a while, trading various small items of gossip and lamenting all the ways, great and small, in which the pandemic had impacted their lives. Eventually, Anna declared that she really had to be going. Miriam, evidently disappointed, tried to press her into staying, but Anna insisted, stating – not untruthfully – that she was worn out from the day's travels and intended to have an early night.

Miriam relented and saw her to the door, late evening birdsong greeting them as they stepped out into the driveway.

'Will I see you again before you go?' asked Miriam, bare feet perching gingerly on the gravel.

'I don't expect so,' said Anna. 'This really is the very definition of a flying visit.'

'In that case, you absolutely must come for supper some night.'

It sounded more like a command than an invitation. Anna opened her mouth to respond, then stopped, not sure what to say.

'Well,' she began weakly, 'I mean … I wouldn't like to impose.'

'It's no imposition. It's the least I can do. I still haven't thanked you properly.'

'Thanked me? For what?'

Miriam shrugged limply. 'For everything, I suppose. But most of all, for being there for Daddy. It's comforting, somehow, to think he had at least one friend in that nest of vipers.'

More than anything else, Anna found herself consumed by a horrendous, gut-wrenching sense of guilt over being the recipient of gratitude she was convinced she didn't deserve – not after her failure to properly listen to Hugh the last time he'd tried to talk to her.

'So will you come?' Miriam's eyes oozed eager expectation.

'We'll see,' said Anna eventually, reluctant to refuse

outright. 'I've got a fair amount to fit into the next couple of days.'

Not least trying to find out what caused your father to take his own life, she thought.

Again, they did that familiar thing of standing there awkwardly, unable to shake hands or hug or do anything that would draw a definitive line under this encounter. Not that Anna had ever been a hugger at the best of times, or felt she knew Miriam well enough to have initiated one, even in a pre-COVID world. But still, there was something undeniably inelegant about how the virus had turned social interactions into such strangely stiff, formal affairs.

'Well,' said Miriam eventually, 'see ya. Or not, as the case may be.'

Then she turned and headed back into the house, pausing briefly to glance over her shoulder at Anna one last time before shutting the door. Anna watched until her shimmering shape disappeared behind the frosted glass, then headed off down the driveway.

6

It was 9:30 p.m. by the time Anna got back to the Great Western Inn, at which point she suddenly realised just how incredibly hungry she was. She hadn't had anything to eat since the sandwich she'd wolfed down at the airport at Stansted, and the fact her day had gained an hour thanks to the time zone jump meant that, if she was still back in Perugia, it would, in fact, have been half-ten by now – seriously late for sitting down to an evening meal, even by the more relaxed Mediterranean standards to which she'd become accustomed. She headed through to the restaurant (deserted apart from the bored-looking young man on duty at the bar, who kept yawning behind his mask), chose a table near the back and turned her attention to the menu.

Over food and a glass of Merlot, she took stock of the day's events. She remained convinced that Fraser had sent her on a fool's errand; that the odds of her discovering anything about the circumstances leading up to Hugh's death, especially in so short a space of time, were staggeringly remote. She felt desperately sorry for Miriam, and was convinced that behind all the flippancy and false bravado was a deeply unhappy young woman who'd had tragedy after tragedy heaped on her from a young age and had now been left to fend for herself as the last surviving member of her family. From the general state of the house, the unwanted wine deliveries and the stack of unpaid bills she'd glimpsed, there could be little doubt that at least a part of Miriam continued to live in denial about her newfound situation.

She thought back to the parts of their conversation that had stuck in her head. She was left with the impression that Miriam's blaming of the university in general, and Fraser more specifically, for Hugh's death was based more on her own general (albeit probably not ill-founded) preconceptions – and, of course, the suicide note.

The note.

It seemed a remarkably un-Hugh-like thing to do – sticking the proverbial knife into the people who'd wronged him, however obliquely. And yet, the act of suicide was un-Hugh-like in and of itself – at least based on her own, admittedly less than wholly objective, perception of the man. It went without saying that, to take his own life, he must have been truly desperate. As such, attempting to reconcile any of this with his normal patterns of behaviour was arguably a fool's endeavour.

And then there was what Fraser had told her about Hugh's references to being threatened with exposure. She'd pushed things as far as she felt she safely could with Miriam, but had drawn the line at asking her if she knew anything about him being blackmailed. And, on the surface of it, Miriam seemed unwavering in her conviction that Hugh's death was entirely down to the pressure heaped on him by his employers. If she knew anything about the blackmail, she was keeping her cards decidedly close to her chest.

What *had* Hugh been trying to tell her at the party? For at least the dozenth time that day, she cursed herself for not having made more of an effort to talk to him when he'd made his overture to her. An overture which she'd either failed to correctly comprehend, or perhaps, she was now forced to admit, deliberately misunderstood because the prospect of Hugh telling her something potentially sensitive made her uncomfortable. She remembered how, that night, she'd responded to his need to 'tell her things' with forced levity; how, deep down, she'd been almost glad when the crisis with the children had unceremoniously interrupted them, and doubly so when she'd realised he'd left without seeking her out again.

There'd been other occasions too – various moments during her last few weeks at Kelvingrove when he'd dropped by her office for a seemingly impromptu chat or invited her to join him for lunch at the university canteen. She'd turned him down each time, either too busy with work or preoccupied by her investigation into The Reckoning, always insisting they'd get together some other time, but failing to make good on any of her multiple promises. How many of these would-be *tête-à-têtes* would have afforded him the chance to open up to her about his problems if she hadn't killed each of them at conception?

We're not friends, Fraser, OK? If I do this, the only person I'll be doing it for is Hugh.

At the time, she'd meant it as a somewhat flippant retort – a way of putting Fraser firmly in his place. But now, as she sat there, gazing into the dregs of her Merlot and wondering whether she should have another and risk it wreaking havoc on her sleep cycle, she realised the statement had held far more meaning than she'd recognised at the time. On some level, she *did* feel she owed it to Hugh – to pay him the attention in death that she'd failed to in life.

In the end, she didn't have the extra glass of Merlot. She headed upstairs to her room and prepared to turn in, even though it was barely quarter past ten and still partially light outside. The room was still far too hot, so she rolled the duvet over to the opposite side of the bed, then stripped down to her underpants and slid under the freshly pressed white sheets. She was expecting to toss and turn for a while before she nodded off. First nights in a strange bed were always like that for her. But, as it turned out, she was asleep within minutes of turning out the light.

PART II

ASKING FOR A FRIEND

7

Friday 13 August

She was awake shortly before 6:30 the following morning, feeling considerably better rested than she'd anticipated. Light was poking through a crack in the curtains, and, when she got up and thrust them open, bright sunshine streamed in through the east-facing windows.

Knowing better than to assume it would last indefinitely – this being the West of Scotland in August, after all – she put on the leggings and tank top she'd brought with her, filled her water bottle from the sink and headed straight out for her morning run.

She'd got back into running – a habit she'd maintained till she was pregnant with Jack and never got round to picking up again after his birth – once the initial, ultra-stringent round of restrictions had been eased the previous year and leaving the house for daily exercise was once again permitted. Initially, it had simply been a means to combat the cabin fever, but once she'd powered through the initial weeks of aching lungs and legs, she'd started to genuinely enjoy the act of pounding through the deserted streets of the city first thing in the morning and found herself wondering why she'd taken so long to get back on the wagon. She'd lost weight as a result, finally shedding the last few kilos of baby fat that, until now, had stubbornly refused to budge. She might not be in any danger of turning into one of those stick-thin yoga mums anytime soon, but she now felt far more comfortable in her own skin than she had in a long time.

She wasn't following any particular route plan, but she knew she wanted to get away from the fumes and fracas of Great Western Road as soon as possible, so she set off in an easterly direction, heading down Hyndland Road and along University Avenue, before turning into Kelvingrove Park and striking the Kelvin Walkway as it wound its way north and then west, following the river's trajectory through the leafy parkland on the southern outskirts of Kelvinside. She crossed the Ha'penny Bridge, then headed down through the residential streets west of Botanic Gardens and back onto Great Western Road, bringing her back more or less to where she'd started. She checked her phone. Just over six kilometres in under forty-five minutes. Not bad at all.

She was doing a gentle loop of the pond at the back of the hotel as part of her post-run cooldown when her phone began to ring, alerting her to an incoming FaceTime call. Slowing to a walk and gulping down air, she retrieved it from her armband and examined the screen. Her eyes lit up in unexpected delight when she saw the name on the caller ID. She hit the 'Accept' button.

'Zoe!' she exclaimed, as her friend's features filled the screen. '*This* is a surprise! What's the occasion?'

She could see from the view behind Zoe that she too was outdoors – tramping along a gravel path, judging by the crunching sounds on the call. Stonewashed bungalows passed her by on one side; on the other, an overgrown hedgerow. Her complexion was unusually ruddy, the bridge of her nose red with sunburn, her freckles more prominent than ever.

'Eh,' Zoe shrugged, 'woke up at the crack o' dawn and didnae fancy laying in bed so I figured I'd go for a daunder. Decided tae gie ye a bell, seeing as ye're an early burd yersel.'

'Well, it's nice to hear from you, whatever the occasion. So how's Wales?'

'Aye, doll, 's been smashing. Dead picturesque. Quiet, but. Seen mair sheep than people, last week or so.'

Anna grinned. She knew Zoe hadn't coped well during lockdown – unsurprisingly, given her normal disposition. This, her first actual getaway in at least six years, was as much a mental health holiday as a sightseeing one.

'Got anything special planned for the day?'

Zoe wrinkled her nose. 'Well, once Sal surfaces, we'll get some brekkie, then we're heading off tae climb Lord Hereford's Knob. I mean, ye cannae come all the way tae Wales and not climb Lord Hereford's Knob, can ye?'

Anna agreed that you couldn't.

'What about Snowdon?' she said, referring to the highest mountain in Wales. 'Any ambitions to fit *that* into your itinerary?'

Zoe pulled a dubious face. 'Eh. Might be a bit of a tall order – seeing as I'm not in proper training.'

'Yeah, that's probably wise.'

'I mean, I totally *could* if I felt like it. Just …'

'Hey, I believe you. Thousands wouldn't.'

They both laughed, enjoying the easy banter despite the miles that lay between them. Then, as Anna rounded the corner of the pond, Great Western Road coming into view over her shoulder, Zoe frowned.

'Haud on – are you in *Glesga*?'

Anna faltered. For a second, she considered switching off the camera in a belated attempt to cover her tracks, before realising how utterly pointless that would be.

'Uh, I am, yeah,' she admitted, rather shamefacedly.

'What the frick, Anna?' Zoe looked and sounded genuinely affronted. 'How'd ye no tell me?'

'Well,' said Anna, feeling a bit like a child caught by one of her parents at home when she was supposed to be at school, 'I mean, it was all seriously last-minute, and really, I've just stopped by to deal with some super-boring admin-y type things. Plus, you're all the way down in South Wales—'

'Aye,' said Zoe, palpably frustrated, 'but ye should've *told* me!'

She was silent for a moment. Anna stood on the edge of the hotel car park, waiting for the admonishments to continue.

'Well, no matter,' she said eventually. 'I'll see ye when I get back on Tuesday.'

Anna didn't respond.

Zoe's eyes narrowed. 'What is it?'

'Zoe,' said Anna, with a heavy sigh, 'I honestly don't think I'll still be here by then. Like I said, I'm just here to deal with some loose ends and—'

'Oh. Right.'

There was a definite whiff of 'so *that's* how it is' in Zoe's tone.

'There'll be other opportunities,' Anna insisted, not sure she really believed it. 'And I'm not saying I'll *definitely* be gone by Tuesday,' she added, a touch desperately. 'There's still an outside chance. But I really haven't factored in an extended stay, and Jack's waiting for me back in Italy …'

'Right, well,' Zoe's tone was now briskly businesslike, 'in that case, I'll come up the road early.'

'What?'

'Aye. 'S nae biggie. If we set off the now, we'll be home by late afternoon. I'll explain tae Sal. She'll be cool wi it.'

Anna pinched the bridge of her nose. 'No, Zoe. Don't do that. Please. Don't cut your holiday short on my account. Your accommodation's probably booked till Tues—'

'I don't gie a *monkey's* about that!' Zoe almost shouted in frustration. She stopped, realising how disproportionate her response had been to the perceived offence. When she continued, it was at a more reasonable level, though the note of plaintiveness in her voice was palpable. 'I havnae seen ye in nearly two *years*.'

'I know, but …' Anna massaged her forehead with her free hand. 'Look, you need time to decompress – 'specially now you're a working woman. If you ask Sal, that's what she'll tell you. Plus,' she added, perhaps a touch inadvisably, 'I've got a seriously packed couple of days ahead of me. I'm probably not going to have a whole lot of free time.' She belatedly realised how this sounded. 'I mean—'

But Zoe had got the message loud and clear. 'Naw,' she said, with a note of weary forbearance, 'it's fine. You do what ye need tae do, then get yersel back tae Jacko toot suite.'

'Zoe …'

'Seriously, it's all good. Like ye said, there'll be other opportunities.'

Feeling like a second-rate heel, Anna managed a meek smile. 'Cheers, pal. Thanks for understanding.'

'Give Jacko a big slobbery kiss fae me.'

'You can give him one yourself next time you see him.' She paused. 'Take care, Zo. Have fun with Lord Hereford's Knob.'

'Be a pretty sorry excuse for a knob if I didnae.' Zoe cackled gleefully, some of the awkwardness dissipating. 'Later, 'gator.'

The phone gave its little two-note 'woop-woop' sound as the call ended, Zoe's face replaced for a few seconds by the photo of Jack that served as the lock screen, before it too disappeared.

Anna remained standing there, gazing at the blank screen, imagining all the ways in which the conversation could have gone differently. Gone *better*. Then, she returned the phone to its holder, exhaled a heavy breath and continued across the car park.

8

Anna returned to the hotel to discover that Fraser had been and gone while she was out, and had left Hugh's 2019 diary for her with the receptionist on duty. She took it upstairs to her room, where she showered and got dressed, selecting the short-sleeved summer dress which she'd – perhaps rather overoptimistically – brought with her. Knowing how a typical Scottish summer played out, there was a strong chance this would be the only day she'd be able to get away with wearing it.

She headed down to breakfast, taking the diary with her. The restaurant was empty apart from a couple in their sixties, dressed in golfing attire, seated at a table by the window and muttering to one another over the remains of their meal. Partly because she suspected it would mean her being served quicker and partly out of sheer, unabashed nosiness, Anna chose one of the adjacent tables and tuned into their conversation while pretending to check her phone. It transpired that they'd come up from Sevenoaks the previous day and had both had a thoroughly rotten night on account of the central heating. As a result, they were cutting their stay in Glasgow short and starting the next leg of their holiday prematurely. As Anna had surmised, they were both keen putters and were heading up to

St Andrews for the golfing. She wondered if this would leave her as the hotel's sole occupant. Given that she'd yet to encounter any other guests, it didn't seem beyond the realms of possibility.

While she ate, she made her way through Hugh's diary – an initial quick skim, then a slower, more methodical pass from cover to cover, reading each entry carefully. It took some time for her to decipher his handwriting and the chaotic manner in which he'd set down his thoughts, and in places she was forced to give up trying to make sense of his rapid, careless scrawl. He seemed to have used his diary primarily to record his appointments – both his lectures, meetings and student supervision sessions, and those of a more personal nature:

TUESDAY 15 MARCH

1 p.m. 4th yr Soc. Just. lect Rutherford Bldg

SATURDAY 25 MAY

6 p.m. dinner w/ Willie & Mgt, Tickled Trout

MONDAY 24 JUNE

11 a.m. sup mtg Bella Rogers (ch 3 draft feedbk)

FRIDAY 11 SEPTEMBER

10:45 a.m. optician's

The university appointments – which were initially quite numerous, to the extent that it was unusual for any weekday to have fewer than three entries – grew increasingly sparse from the first week of March onwards, when the Great Restructuring took place and his position as head of department was eliminated. On paper – on *this* particular paper, at any rate – there was precious little evidence of Fraser having hounded Hugh, making him jump through hoops in the way Miriam had claimed. True, there was the occasional reference to a 'catch-up mtg' with him, but they were considerably fewer in number than the constant one-to-ones with which Anna had had to contend in her role as course director of the criminology MA. Indeed, the overriding picture the diary painted was of a man with a considerable amount of spare time on his hands. If he *was* involved in any shady practices, he certainly didn't appear to have been foolhardy enough to record them here.

It wasn't until she'd begun to go through the diary for a third time, perched cross-legged on the bed back upstairs in her room, that she finally noticed something. At first, she assumed it was nothing of any great significance: either a printing error or simply part of the ornate, swirling border artwork that ran along the three outer sides of each page. It took the form of a black dot, less than a millimetre in size, on the page corresponding to Friday 8 March. The indentation, carrying through to the page underneath, confirmed that it was made by a pen and not part of the original printing.

As she continued to work her way through the diary, she discovered that similar dots appeared in the margin on multiple days, starting in the second week of March and continuing through to the end of 2019. They were sporadic at first, but grew in frequency from around mid-April until June, during which it was unusual for more than a couple of days to pass without one appearing. From the end of June, they became sporadic once again, tailing off as the year waned, with a mere two in the month of December: one on the second of the month and another on the nineteenth.

She sat upright, stretching her neck as she pondered the meaning of her discovery. It seemed not unreasonable to conclude that the dots were some sort of code – something whose meaning Hugh hadn't wanted to be apparent to anyone who happened to get their hands on the diary. She spent a further half-hour carefully recording the dates on which the dots appeared, trying to identify some sort of pattern, but if there *was* one, it wasn't one she could detect. She wondered whether Fraser had noticed them. It seemed unlikely, or he'd presumably have mentioned it to her yesterday. Still, she made a mental note to ask him once he was back from his conference.

She wondered, too, whether he had Hugh's diary for 2020, which would cover the months immediately prior to his death. That, in her mind, would constitute the *real* prize. Again, it seemed doubtful, otherwise he'd surely have offered it to her as well. Doubtful, but not impossible: Fraser, in her experience, was more than capable of failing to consider the head-slappingly obvious.

She folded her arms behind her head, resting the back of her skull against the wall behind the bed.

'What were you up to, Hugh?' she mused.

9

Partly to give herself an opportunity to think and partly because she figured she might as well make a start on tackling the business that had brought her back to Glasgow in the first place, Anna left the hotel and set out on the twenty-minute walk down to her old house on Clarence Drive. She'd emailed the married couple she was letting it to the previous morning, letting them know she was going to be in town for the next couple of days and would swing by at some point to take a look at the leak they'd drawn her attention to, though she hadn't had a response from them yet. It occurred to her, as she climbed the steps to the front door, that there was no guarantee anyone would be in at ten o'clock on a Friday morning. They both worked in finance, and one of the few things she knew about the profession was that long hours came with the territory.

As it turned out, she'd only been standing on the doorstep for a few seconds and had just finished putting on her mask when the door swung open and Colin, one of the two tenants, was beaming out at her, as if she was the most welcome guest he'd received all year.

'Anna! We wondered if you might appear at some point today.'

He was in his early thirties, trim and athletic, dressed in a silk shirt and tight chinos – the sort of look Fraser so often shot for, but lacked the youthful comportment to pull off.

'Hi, Colin,' she said. 'Um ... this isn't a bad time, is it?'

'Of course not! Come in, come in!'

She stepped over the threshold, briefly registering just what an odd experience it was to be invited into what was technically still her home.

'How was your flight?' Colin asked. Then, not waiting for a response, 'It's an absolute faff, isn't it? All these lateral flow tests and temperature checks and forms to fill out. Justin and I found out the hard way when we flew to Zermatt in June for the skiing. Almost more trouble than it's worth, if you ask me ...'

As he spoke, Anna's eyes skimmed over the hallway, silently noting all the things that had changed. There was the framed *Some Like It Hot* poster hanging on the wall, the console table had been moved to the opposite wall, and next to the doormat was a shoe drop housing multiple pairs of polished leather brogues.

She realised he'd finished speaking and that she had no idea what he'd just said.

'I'm sorry, you were saying ... ?'

Colin looked momentarily thrown. Evidently, people not listening to him was a novel experience for him. 'I was just saying, you've certainly chosen the right time to visit. This is as close to an actual summer's day as we've had all year. But then,' he added, 'I imagine this is like the depths of winter compared to what you're used to these days.'

Anna gave a slight smile. 'Almost.'

At that moment, there was a sound of footsteps and the other half of the power couple came jogging down the stairs, beaming with abandon. In virtually every respect, Justin was Colin's double: same dress sense, same sleek pompadour haircut, even the same hundred-kilowatt teeth. Not for the first time, Anna felt there was something vaguely incestuous about the pair of them.

'*There* she is! For the love of all that's holy, take that awful thing off,' he implored her, referring to her mask. 'If they let you into the country, it's safe to say you're not contagious.'

Anna did as she was asked, a little reluctantly. *She* might not be contagious, but she'd be lying if she said she was entirely confident the same applied to *them*.

'That's better,' Justin nodded approvingly. 'So much nicer when you can actually see a person's *whole* face, don't you think?'

If Anna had paid for a set of gnashers like theirs, she might have been tempted to agree.

'Shall we take a look at the damage?' she suggested. 'I don't want to take up too much of your time.'

Together, they trooped through to the living room. Upon entering, Anna immediately noticed the sickly-sweet smell of burning incense – something she'd never had in the house when it was … well, *her* house.

'It's just here,' Colin gestured.

The damage, mostly contained to the left-hand corner of the wall facing the street, was considerably worse than she'd been expecting. The patch of mould, running from the ceiling to approximately halfway down the wall, had expanded significantly compared to the photos Justin had emailed to her just a couple of months ago.

'Wow,' she said. 'You really weren't kidding.'

'Right?' said Justin. 'We don't like to make a fuss, but …'

'… well, we're not sure how hygienic it is,' Colin finished on his behalf. 'You hear about people getting brain rot from mould exposure.'

'Didn't that happen to JK Rowling?'

'No, I think that was a different children's author. And we

thought – didn't we, sugar-bun?' – this aside directed at Colin rather than Anna – 'we thought Anna here would probably want to look into it PDQ in case it's a sign of something more severe.'

'Yes, we wondered about a burst pipe, or perhaps some external structural damage.'

Anna couldn't help noticing that it was always 'we' with them and never 'I' – as if they were a hive mind, incapable of independent thought or action. Perhaps that's just how it is for married couples, she thought.

'There's some upstairs as well, if you want to take a look?' said Colin, gesturing hopefully towards the hallway.

'Some' turned out to be a wild understatement. The corresponding wall of Anna's old bedroom – now a home gym, complete with the ubiquitous CrossFit bike – was black from floor to ceiling, with an ominous-looking spider's web of the stuff expanding outwards across the latter. Anna quickly determined that this was above her pay grade and that her only option would be to call on the services of a professional – to the evident disappointment of Colin and Justin, who, it seemed, had been half-hoping she'd roll up her sleeves and tackle the problem herself right there and then. Promising to update them as soon as she'd managed to track down a tradesman, she departed as quickly as she felt was polite. She already felt like something of an intruder in her own home, and sensed – despite their bonhomie and evident relief that she was finally taking steps to address the problem – that they wanted her out of their hair so they could get on with their day.

She stood at the top of Clarence Drive, gazing past the rows of shops and flats as Hyndland Road curved south into the heart of the West End. The university was less than a mile's walk from where she now stood. As wide a berth as she'd given it yesterday, she couldn't deny that she had something of a hankering to see the place – partly to remind herself of what it looked like, and to see whether it had changed at all since she'd last been there. But it was also about settling old scores and laying the ghosts of the past to rest; about having one last tramp through those stately grounds before she said goodbye to it once and for all.

Besides, there was one other very good reason for visiting it, which was that there was only so much a diary could tell you. Far more insightful would be the recollections of the people who'd worked closest with Hugh and had known him best. The people who'd observed his demeanour firsthand in the final months of his life – at least until lockdown had scattered them all to the four winds. She could, of course, simply pick up the phone – ring up some of his old colleagues from Sociology and see if any of them was willing to speak to her. But where was the fun in that? She wanted to see the old place, didn't she? Might as well kill two birds with one stone.

She glanced back down Clarence Drive, taking a last look at her old house; at the sandstone exterior and high bay windows that had seduced her so readily a decade ago when she'd put down the deposit. A pang of something that might almost have been longing briefly coursed through her. Then she turned about face and set off towards her soon-to-be-former place of employment.

10

As she made her way up the pavement, she was once again struck by just how quiet everything was. Normally, the air would be full of the chatter of students heading between lectures or loitering outside the various buildings on and around the hill to which the university laid claim. Now, though, you could practically hear a pin drop. She reminded herself it was still the summer vacation; that it stood to reason there would be fewer students around than during term time. But even so, she couldn't remember it ever being this ... dead.

That feeling continued when she entered the Hutcheson Building, the tall granite eyesore that had been home to the School of Social and Political Sciences since the restructuring. Her footsteps sounded positively thunderous on the linoleum floor, and she didn't encounter another soul until she reached the third floor and crossed paths with a young man in rolled-up shirtsleeves, wearing a facemask with a cartoon chicken on it.

'Excuse me,' she said, stepping in front of him.

He stopped, looking at her with wide, slightly apprehensive eyes.

'Can I help you?'

It occurred to her that she didn't know him – or, at least,

she didn't *think* she did. It was hard to tell behind the mask. In any event, he didn't seem to recognise her either, though he might well have been experiencing the same difficulty as her, and for the same reason.

'Sorry,' she said, a bit flustered now that she realised she hadn't properly thought this through. 'I'm looking for someone, but I'm not entirely sure where to start.'

'Oh. Who is it you're after?'

'Well, someone from Sociology, ideally. Nicola Giersch, or perhaps Stuart Colgan or Kez Dixon?' she suggested, name-checking the handful of personnel whose names she remembered.

'I'm not sure …' The young man's furrowed brows betrayed his increasing discomfort. 'I only started here in April. Plus, I'm in Central and Eastern European Studies myself. Not a ton of crossover with Sociology. Anyway,' he went on, glancing up and down the corridor as if to illustrate his point, 'to be honest, I don't think there's many folk in today. It's Friday and, you know …'

'… and you drew the short straw.'

'Something like that.'

From the crinkling of his eyes, she sensed he was smiling ruefully.

'Well, thanks for your time.' She stepped out of the way to let him pass.

'Don't mention it.'

He turned to go, then stopped, glancing back at her over his shoulder.

'Um … I hope you find who you're looking for.'

'Me too.'

But she said it to herself under her breath, her mask muffling the words to the point of being inaudible.

As he disappeared round the bend at the end of the corridor, she remained where she was, pondering her options. Any fears she might have had about the prospect of running into her old colleagues appeared to have been seriously misplaced. Perhaps this had been a waste of time after all?

She was on the verge of throwing in the towel when a sudden thought occurred to her.

Lorraine.

She made her way up the hill to the main building, then upstairs to the second level, through the cloisters and the passageway beneath the belltower until she came to the registry office. Feeling decidedly like an intruder, she cautiously pushed open the door to the tiny, airless room, into which multiple desks and filing cabinets had been crammed. Half a dozen people – predominantly older women – were hard at work, their snatches of murmured conversation barely audible below the hum of their computers, a pair of rattly fans stationed strategically at opposite ends of the room, and the near-continuous clacking of their keyboards. A couple of them glanced up briefly at Anna, who made a beeline for the desk at the back of the room, behind which a woman in her mid-sixties with closely cropped grey hair, tortoiseshell glasses and the sort of stiff, upright posture Anna normally associated with people in costume dramas was seated. As Anna reached the desk, the woman, who hadn't once looked up, raised a finger, silently ordering her to wait, while she continued to type one-handed. Anna obediently stood in silence for a few more seconds until the woman finally finished tapping, then folded her hands in front of her and lifted her head.

'Well, well,' she said, in a tone that suggested she'd always known this day would come, 'the bold Professor Scavolini returns.'

'Hello, Lorraine,' said Anna. 'Long time, no see.'

'And to what do I owe this unexpected delight?' Lorraine enquired, peering at Anna over the top of her glasses.

It was at times like this that Anna wished she was better at reading sarcasm. With Lorraine, the line between obsequious fawning and withering contempt was an exceedingly fine one.

Concluding that the most diplomatic response was to take Lorraine's words at face value, Anna pasted on a smile. 'I'm spending a couple of days in Glasgow,' she said. 'I was in the area and thought I'd drop by – you know, for old times' sake.'

Lorraine maintained her familiar, poker-faced expression.

'I mean, it just feels like I've never properly thanked you for everything you did for me over the years. I'm not sure I ever fully appreciated just how indispensable you really were to the smooth running of the department. I feel ...' She affected a sheepish shrug. 'Well, I thought maybe I could take you out to lunch as a way of saying thank you.'

Lorraine, who'd listened to this proposal without giving any impression of being moved by it one way or the other, pursed her lips in contemplation. 'I shall have to consult my diary. Which day did you have in mind?'

'Actually, I was thinking right *now*.'

Lorraine made a show of examining her watch. 'It's a *little* early for lunch,' she said, with more than a whiff of disapproval.

'I know,' said Anna, 'but I'm afraid I can't stay for long, and I've got a pretty packed schedule for the next couple of days ...'

None of this was, strictly speaking, untrue, but she could nonetheless feel herself becoming increasingly flustered as she struggled to justify what she had to admit was a rather odd proposition. She'd probably have baulked *herself* if someone had invited her to lunch at 11:30 in the morning.

An idea struck her.

'We could go to Clarissa's,' she said, naming a local tearoom to which she remembered Lorraine being particularly partial. 'It's not far, and ... I mean, it's never too early for an Earl Grey and a slice of carrot cake, right?' She smiled awkwardly, awaiting Lorraine's judgement.

For several seconds, Lorraine neither responded nor gave any indication as to what she was thinking. Then, eventually, she gave a slight, almost imperceptible nod, Anna's proposal having evidently passed muster.

'I'll fetch my coat,' she said.

11

At the time of Anna's departure, Lorraine Hammond had been one of three secretaries attached to the School of Social and Political Sciences, and, before that, the now defunct Department of Law and Social Sciences, where she'd worked closely with Hugh in his old role as department head. She'd transferred to the central registry office the previous September; Anna remembered the mass email from Fraser, thanking her, with cloying insincerity, for her 'decades of tireless service'. She'd also remembered the multiple emails Lorraine had cc'd to the entire school during lockdown, decrying the university's closure and resulting 'loss of community'. As such, Anna had – correctly, it turned out – surmised that the odds of Lorraine working from home when the option of coming into the office was on the table were slim in the extreme. Little that went on at the university escaped her attention, and she could normally be persuaded to part with whatever gossip she'd gleaned – provided you were willing to work for it.

If anyone was in a position to know what had been going on with Hugh, it was her.

Now, she watched as Lorraine cut a tiny piece from a giant

slice of carrot cake, skewered it with her fork and daintily transferred it to her mouth. She chewed it studiously for upwards of half a minute before eventually swallowing.

'Things were never the same after the reorganisation,' she declared. 'The work, the general atmosphere … the people to whom you're required to kow-tow.'

Anna was in no doubt, from the curl of her lip, to whom she was referring. Lorraine had never made any secret of her disdain for Fraser – ample evidence, in Anna's mind, of her sound judgement of character.

'Is that why you transferred to Registry?' she asked. 'Are you happier there, at any rate?'

Lorraine shrugged dismissively. 'It's a living. My colleagues are a pleasant enough lot, though the work ethic isn't necessarily always there – particularly with the younger generation.'

Anna made a show of nodding understandably, as if this was a problem she herself encountered on a daily basis, while Lorraine raised her cup and saucer – Earl Grey, as Anna had predicted – to her lips and sucked noisily, before setting them down again with a sigh.

'Yes, it's all change and no mistake. A lot of good people no longer with us, one way or another.'

As she spoke, she began attacking her carrot cake with the edge of her fork, slicing it into smaller and smaller pieces.

'And, of course, it's not just me who's saying this.'

'Of course not,' Anna agreed.

'Morale has been at an all-time low for a while now.'

'I don't imagine the pandemic's helped in that regard.'

Lorraine waved her fork dismissively. 'Excuses. The *pandemic*' – she said it as if she was far from convinced it really existed – 'has become a convenient catch-all to excuse every abysmal decision made by those in charge. Who needs to accept responsibility for anything when every last failing can be blamed on the *pandemic*?' She jabbed her fork at Anna. 'Well, I can tell you for a *fact* that people are *not* happy. In fact, I have it on good authority that several long-standing faculty members are planning to jump ship.'

Anna knew Lorraine wanted her to ask who these supposed faculty members were, so she could enjoy refusing to elaborate, drawing things out for as long as possible before finally caving in and revealing all. She was determined not to play that game – not least because she didn't think it was fair to the colleagues in question, who, regardless of whether the rumours were true, would be unlikely to relish learning that their career plans were the subject of office gossip.

'I was so sorry to hear about Hugh,' she said instead.

She meant it sincerely, but invoking Hugh's name was, at least in part, a strategic choice on her part – a bid to steer the conversation towards why she was really here.

'*Hugh.*' It was as if merely uttering the name spoke volumes. 'Now *there* was a good man. A man you could be proud to work for. A man who never leant on you for anything but for whom you were always happy to go the extra mile, because pleasing him was reward enough.' She shook her head, her expression murderous. 'They never afforded him the respect he deserved. The way they cast him onto the rubbish heap, all because they, in their infinite wisdom, decided they wanted a younger model. One who wears Lycra and rides an *eco*-bike.'

She gave a dismissive wave. 'Ah, what's the use? What's done is done, and it's not as if my opinion counts for anything now – if indeed it ever did. I am but a cog in the great machine.' She lifted her cup and saucer again, preparing to take another sip. 'Not that I was sorry to make the move. As a wise individual once put it, in every adversity lies an opportunity. And, given the option, I'd far rather go where I'm actually wanted, even if the circumstances weren't wholly of my own choosing.'

Anna nodded in understanding. The inference was clear: Fraser had made it known that Lorraine's services were surplus to requirements and she was, at the very least, strongly encouraged to jump before she was pushed.

As Lorraine set her cup down again, Anna decided it was time to pick up the pace.

'After the restructuring, you continued to see Hugh on more or less a daily basis – at least until the start of lockdown.'

'That's true,' said Lorraine, in the sort of tone that indicated she already knew there was a question at the end of this preamble.

'And it's safe to say you knew him better than just about anyone.'

Lorraine attempted an indifferent shrug, but it was clear she was pleased by this description.

'You'd have been well-placed to know, then, if he was experiencing any sort of difficulties.'

Lorraine looked up sharply. 'Why? Has someone said something?'

Bingo, thought Anna.

'How did he seem to be adjusting to the change in his circumstances?' she pressed, ignoring Lorraine's question. 'It can't have been easy for him, going from running a department to being, as you put it, just another cog in the machine.'

'Well, I mean,' Lorraine huffed, curiously unable to meet Anna's eye, 'I don't expect *anyone* finds it easy to adapt to a loss of status – particularly one orchestrated by unscrupulous and shameless career opportunists.'

'But we're not just talking about anyone,' said Anna, '*are* we, Lorraine? We're talking about Hugh – a much loved and missed friend and colleague … and I think you know something, don't you?'

'Well, I …' Lorraine began, still avoiding Anna's gaze. She stopped. Shook her head. 'No. I shouldn't say.'

'Lorraine.'

This time, Lorraine lifted her head with a vague 'Hmm?'

and a feigned look of surprise, as if surprised to find Anna still there.

'I know you have Hugh's best interests at heart. That you're trying to protect his memory. But I'm not asking because I've developed a sudden, uncharacteristic hunger for salacious gossip. You know me better than that – don't you?'

Lorraine gave an inconclusive half-shrug, but Anna sensed she was getting through to her.

'I'm asking because I cared about Hugh too,' she went on, staring deep into Lorraine's eyes to stop her looking away again, 'and because I think he'd got himself into some sort of trouble before … before the end. I want to get to the bottom of it if I can – if nothing else, so I can stop imagining the worst.'

This wasn't strictly true. She'd been so preoccupied with the practicalities of answering the question of what sort of trouble Hugh had got himself into that she hadn't really given any meaningful thought to what the answer might be. Perhaps it was because she found it hard to imagine Hugh – in her mind a bastion of fairness and integrity – being involved in anything suspect.

Lorraine sighed heavily. She sat, arms folded, her eyes glazing past Anna to some indeterminate point on the far wall. Anna knew she was wrestling with the conflicting forces of her loyalty to Hugh and her own implacable desire to share any smidgen of gossip to which she was party. She waited. She'd done her part in stirring the pot. Now it was up to Lorraine to either take the bait or not.

Eventually, Lorraine's posture seemed to slacken ever so slightly. She glanced around, as if making sure there were no prying ears in the vicinity, then gestured to Anna to lean in closer. Feeling slightly ridiculous, Anna did as she was bidden.

'All right,' Lorraine said in a low voice, 'I'm telling you this because I know you won't go blabbing about it to any old Tom, Dick or Harry, and because I'd rather you heard it from me than get some cock-and-bull version from someone else. It's fairly well-known that Hugh was having money issues in the last six months or so of his life.'

'What sort of money issues?'

'I don't know the specifics,' said Lorraine, sounding vaguely irritated that Anna had the audacity to ask a question she couldn't answer, 'but I heard that, during the latter part of 2019, he approached several colleagues and asked to borrow money from them. And just so we're clear, we're not just talking about the odd tenner here and there to tide him over till payday. We're talking about *substantial sums* – as in more than you can withdraw from a cashpoint in a single go.' She gave Anna a look of surprise that might not have been entirely feigned. 'He never approached *you*?'

Anna could only shake her head helplessly. This was complete news to her.

'Well,' said Lorraine grudgingly, 'perhaps he was concerned you'd think less of him.'

'Perhaps,' said Anna, unconvinced.

She wasn't sure why, but she almost felt slighted. Or perhaps it was simply regret at the fact that, whatever difficulties Hugh was facing, he seemed to have turned to multiple other people before attempting to come to her.

'And do you know if he managed to resolve these money issues, or … ?' She trailed off, not knowing how to end the question.

Once more, Lorraine grew circumspect. 'I'm not sure it's my place to say,' she demurred, prodding at a bit of cake with her fork.

'Lorraine …'

'I'm just saying,' Lorraine continued to prod violently, as if the cake had done something to personally offend her, 'people are entitled to their privacy. Would *you* be happy if your private affairs were being passed around for the consumption of all and sundry?'

Anna felt tempted to point out that, in fact, she had a

better idea of what that was like than most people, but she managed to restrain herself.

'Lorraine,' she said firmly, 'Hugh's gone. It's not going to make any difference to *him* whether or not you tell me. But if you don't, then I'm going to have to ask someone else – and, as you implied yourself, far better that I get the truth from you than a bunch of supposition and innuendo from someone who hasn't the first idea what they're talking about.'

She was stroking Lorraine's ego, playing to her well-honed reputation (in her own mind, at any rate) as a font of all knowledge with her finger on the beating pulse of the university. And she saw, from the slight, involuntary curl of Lorraine's lips, that she couldn't help but relish being placed on this pedestal.

'Well,' she said at length, and in a tone that suggested she was making a magnanimous concession, 'all right.'

Once more, she beckoned Anna closer.

'I haven't spoken about this to anyone else,' said Lorraine, her voice a tight whisper, 'so if any of it gets out, I'll know exactly who it came from.'

Anna nodded, not daring to interrupt.

'In the spring of last year, about three weeks into the first lockdown and shortly before Hugh left us, I got a phone call from His Majesty.'

Anna had no need to ask her to clarify that she was referring to Fraser.

'It was late in the afternoon, and I was just getting ready to knock off … We were all working from home by this time, of course, but I always observed regular hours – to try to maintain some semblance of normality, you understand.'

Anna nodded in understanding and tried not to look like she wished Lorraine would get to the point.

'Anyway, I pick up the phone, and without so much as a "How do you do?", he immediately launches into this spiel. "Lorraine," he says, "I need you to do something for me urgently. I need you to send out an email to all staff within the school who have access to research budgets, telling them that, going forward, all expenses claims must be submitted to, and cleared by, me. Effective immediately."' She gave a derisive snort. 'Which, I might add, is *entirely* typical of his approach to management: instigate a new policy without any warning – one that just so happens to allow him to further consolidate his power, might I add – while leaving the actual *implementation* of that policy to the first available flunky.

'Well, of course,' she continued, 'straight away, I picture the pitchfork-wielding mob beating a path to my door to shoot the messenger. I know this is going to create the most almighty bottleneck, everything going to one person – and one who doesn't exactly have a reputation for tackling his admin in the timeliest fashion, at that.

'I start to ask him what all this is in aid of, and he near enough loses the plot. Tells me it's not my job to question school policy. Above my pay grade to do anything other than keep my mouth shut and follow orders – that sort of thing.' She snorted at this obvious insult to her pride.

'Naturally, I do as I'm told and send out the email – with predictable results. But a couple of weeks later, I start to hear rumours about certain irregularities cropping up in expenses claims submitted to the finance office. Supposedly, someone there brought them to His Majesty's attention and that's why he decided to start acting like a tinpot despot – more so than usual, that is. But here's the thing. Guess whose name I heard being bandied about as the member of staff whose expenses had raised a red flag.'

'Hugh's,' said Anna, her voice barely a whisper.

Lorraine gave an emphatic nod. 'The very same. Allegedly' – the air quotes were implicit in her tone – 'the irregularities all related to submissions for expenses incurred on a research project he was doing on austerity and crime.

'Of course,' she added immediately, 'I didn't believe a word of it. *Hugh MacLeish* cooking the books? It would be laughable if it wasn't so offensive. But that's the trouble with rumours. A lie can travel halfway round the world while the truth is still lacing its boots. But folk don't care about the truth. All they care about is getting their hands on the latest juicy bit of tittle-tattle and passing it on to the first person who'll listen.'

Anna couldn't help noting the deep irony of Lorraine, of all people, having the temerity to cast aspersions on others for gossip-mongering.

'So you never managed to establish what lay behind these rumours?' she said.

'No,' said Lorraine, 'but they *refused* to be put to bed. They continued to do the rounds, even after poor Hugh passed. Eventually, I started to wonder if His Majesty might not have been the one who started the whole gossip train.'

'*Fraser?*' said Anna, unable to fully mask her incredulity. 'Why would he do that?'

Lorraine snorted. 'Surely it's obvious. Hugh was known to be having financial problems. That made him the ideal scapegoat.'

Unable to follow the tortured logic of this, Anna could only shake her head.

'As like as not,' said Lorraine, in a tone of strained patience, 'someone in Accounts slipped up – accidentally added an extra zero where there wasn't supposed to be one or what have you. But rather than acknowledge a straightforward case of carelessness, or admit that the whole fiasco occurred under his watch, our dear leader saw fit to organise a witch hunt against the very person who, just one year earlier, he'd forced out in a *coup d'état* that would have made General Pinochet himself blush.'

Throughout this speech, she'd been getting increasingly irate, her voice rising in both volume and intensity. Now, however, having reached the apotheosis of her argument – or perhaps belatedly realising she'd abandoned any semblance of self-control – she reverted to a tone that was quieter, though no less intense.

'There are two types of people in this world, Professor Scavolini. Those who see a man who's down and extend him the hand of friendship … and those who see it as an opportunity to kick him some more.'

There was no room for any doubt as to which of these two archetypes she believed Fraser Taggart embodied.

12

Anna walked Lorraine back up to the university. As they tramped up the hill, Lorraine shared various minor items of news relating to mutual colleagues – for instance, that Fiona Straker had taken early retirement at the end of 2020 and that Sophie Hennessy had recently been appointed Reader in Social and Public Policy. For Anna, it was yet another reminder of how long she'd been away, and how little contact she'd had with the people who were, at one point, her colleagues – and, in many cases, her friends. She realised that, on some level, she'd assumed the world she'd left behind would simply stand still while her own continued to turn and change. It was an oddly disconcerting feeling, as if her centre of gravity was not what she'd previously thought.

They reached the West Quadrangle and came to a halt just outside the cloisters.

'Thanks for talking to me, Lorraine,' Anna said. 'I really appreciate it.'

Lorraine was silent for a moment. When she next spoke, it was in an uncharacteristically reticent tone.

'They never did tell us how Hugh died. We were just left to imagine. They said it was a brief illness, but …'

She took a step closer to Anna, her voice lowering even as her tone intensified.

'I can read the tea leaves as well as anyone. That's what they always say when they don't want folk to know the real reason. I'm not suggesting someone has blood on his hands – not *literally*, at any rate. But I've seen firsthand what stress can do to a person, particularly those that are getting on in years. I'm just saying …'

She stopped. Glanced past Anna's shoulder. A couple of young women strode past them, talking animatedly as they headed for the stairs. Lorraine waited till they'd disappeared from view before continuing.

'I'm just saying, if it turns out someone drove him to this, I want you to see to it that they face justice. Promise me that.'

She gazed at Anna expectantly, eyes boring into her. It took all Anna's self-control not to look away.

'I promise,' she said.

Lorraine continued to hold her gaze for a moment, as if searching for some sign that she was being less than truthful. Then, seemingly satisfied, she gave a curt nod, turned and headed off into the cloisters, making for the registry office.

Anna remained where she was, on the edge of the lawn at the centre of the quadrangle, listening to the sounds of birdsong and the distant hum of traffic. The university chapel on one side, the tall turrets that flanked the cloisters on the other – it was a timely reminder that Perugia didn't necessarily have the monopoly on grand, historic architecture.

She was about to make a move when she heard a thud behind her, followed by a muttered '*Oh, et puis merde!*' She turned and saw, in the shadow of the cloisters, a young woman with short, dark hair, wearing Windsor glasses and a sleeveless floral pattern dress, stooping as she attempted to gather up the multiple textbooks that lay strewn across the stone floor. For a moment, Anna remained rooted to the spot. Then the woman glanced up in her direction, and their eyes met.

'Anna?'

Anna hesitated for a split second before breaking into a smile. She set off across the quad as Farah Hadid got to her feet, somehow managing to appear sheepish and overjoyed at the same time.

'But this is incredible!' Farah exclaimed as Anna came to a halt at arm's length from her. 'How … When … ? What are you doing here? How *are* you?'

'Good, yeah,' Anna replied, nodding a trifle too emphatically. '*Really* good. God, I didn't expect to run into *you* here. Not during summer hols.' Then a thought struck her. 'Wait – don't tell me they finally gave you a faculty position?'

Even as she said it, she realised what an absurd proposition this was. If Farah *had* finally got her foot on the lecturer scale, it would surely have come up in one of the umpteen calls or emails they'd exchanged in the last eighteen months.

Farah shook her head ruefully. 'Alas, no. I'm still waiting patiently for my turn. No, I'm only teaching some summer classes – you know, so I don't become rusty.'

'Oh,' said Anna, feeling guilty for even having raised the matter, and, in the process, no doubt rubbed salt in this long-standing wound. 'Sorry.'

Farah dismissed this with a wave. '*Bof!* It's like water off the back of a duck.'

'Here,' said Anna quickly. 'Let me give you a hand with these.'

They both dropped to their knees and began gathering up the textbooks, shoving them back into the canvas bag out of which they'd evidently fallen.

'So, when did you arrive?' asked Farah. 'And does this mean to say you're back?'

'Yesterday afternoon. Sorry I didn't give you any advance warning. It's all been a bit last-minute, and I've had a million and one different things to take care of. Anyway, how are *you*? How's Émile?'

Anna knew she was babbling, filling the space between them with as many words as possible to avoid giving Farah the opportunity to repeat the question she hadn't answered.

'We're both well, yes,' said Farah, 'though the lockdowns have hurt his business badly. It's not easy to be a personal trainer from your own bedroom.'

'I can only imagine. Luckily the likes of you and me don't have that problem.' Anna rolled her eyes. 'The joys of Zoom, huh?'

Farah pulled a face, appreciating the reference only too well. 'Listen,' she said, as they finished gathering up her books, 'I have to hurry. I have another class to give. But we should catch up properly, some time when we're not both so pressed, yes? Are you free this evening?'

'I should be, yes,' said Anna, aware that she'd hesitated just a fraction of a second at the thought of providing Farah with a further – and more prolonged – opportunity to interrogate her about her impending return to work. 'I mean,' she clarified, 'I'd really like that.'

Farah beamed with undisguised pleasure. 'Fabulous! I should be finished here by around six. Will we say Yousef's Kitchen at seven?'

'Sounds perfect.'

They both smiled, and, for a brief moment, Anna saw, with painful, far-reaching clarity, everything she'd be losing if she really did go through with her plan not to return to work at Kelvingrove. Then Farah cleared her throat and hoisted up her canvas bag, once more loaded with its precious cargo.

'Seven o'clock, then,' she said.

'Seven o'clock,' agreed Anna.

They looked at each other for a moment, both clearly feeling they should do something besides merely turn and go their separate ways. But, in the end, go their separate ways was precisely what they did, the rules of the reality they now inhabited too firmly ingrained for either of them to even contemplate transgressing them. As she reached the stairs, Anna stopped and turned to watch Farah striding across the quad, one shoulder weighed down by her bag of textbooks, thinking, for the umpteenth time, just how much better she deserved than this.

Anna made her way back down the hill towards Byres Road, deep in thought. Her encounter with Farah now receding in the rearview mirror, her mind had once more turned to Hugh, and to Lorraine's revelations. She found it as hard to believe as Lorraine evidently did that Hugh would ever have been involved in anything as corrupt as manipulating the expenses system. And yet, she found Lorraine's suggestion that Fraser had knowingly set Hugh up as a scapegoat every bit as far-fetched. Fraser might be many things, but a master schemer he was not. And, if he *was* up to no good, why task her with looking into Hugh's affairs, knowing there was a good chance it would lead to him being found out? By the same token, if it was true that Hugh had been fiddling expenses and Fraser had known about it, why the hell hadn't he said anything about it to her? He could hardly claim it had no bearing on the circumstances surrounding Hugh's death. Whatever the truth of the matter, she'd be having words with him at the nearest opportunity.

She also, she belatedly remembered, really needed to speak to him about her future at Kelvingrove, or lack thereof.

The rumour – that Hugh had been submitting falsified claims for expenses incurred on his austerity project – was specific enough that it seemed unlikely to have originated from nothing. And yet, even on its own terms, the scenario didn't make an iota of sense. For one thing, Anna's understanding was that the project in question had never got past the preliminary concepting phase. Why, then, would he be submitting expenses claims for it, either real or fabricated? For another, the expenses that a fully paid-up member of staff could actually claim were basically limited to car mileage and specialist hardware or software, neither of which she could imagine being particularly relevant to the project in question – at least inasmuch as she understood its parameters.

She began to make her way up Byres Road, her mind still churning. She wasn't heading anywhere in particular, her course determined purely by muscle memory as she turned the puzzle over and over in her head. She was so preoccupied that she didn't see the suited figure coming towards her on the pavement, phone clamped to his ear, until it was too late for either of them to correct their course. The collision was swift and inevitable, the pair of them walking slap-bang into each other with enough force to almost knock Anna – by far the smaller of the two – off her feet.

'Why don't you look where you're bloody *going*?' the man demanded as she drew herself up to her full height and glared up at him, trying to assert some control over the situation.

They both stopped and stared at each other, neither seemingly able to believe what they were seeing.

'Detective,' said Anna, aiming for cool indifference, as if this sort of thing happened to her every day.

'Anna,' said Paul Vasilico.

Of the two of them, he seemed the more surprised by far.

13

'Perugia all it's cracked up to be, then?' said Vasilico.

They were heading south down Byres Road, walking side by side at a leisurely pace, having seemingly have settled on their direction of travel by unspoken mutual agreement.

'It's wonderful,' said Anna, emphasising her point with a sharp, decisive nod. 'Truly wonderful.'

She hadn't intended it to sound quite so emphatic – but then, now that she thought about it, there was no reason to be surprised by the strength of her conviction. It *was* wonderful. Why should she feel guilty for shouting it from the rooftops?

Why she was so keen to convey to Vasilico that she had no regrets about the choice she'd made – now *that* was another matter.

'It's funny,' she went on, opting to double down. 'Until I left Glasgow, I didn't realise just how much tension I was carrying around inside me. How much I was struggling to just … you know … to *breathe*.'

'That good, eh?'

'Oh, you've no idea. I mean, I could go on about the climate, the work-life balance, the lack of aggro from my colleagues, the quality of life in general, but …'

'… but you wouldn't want to rub it in for us unlucky sods who had to stay behind.'

She caught the twinkle in his eye and couldn't help but smile in return, though she quickly forced it into a grimace.

'Precisely.'

'And Jack? How's he settling in?'

'Like he's lived there all his life.' Again with the over-the-top positivity. 'I know they say kids adjust in no time at all, but if you'd told me it'd be this easy … well, I'd probably've told you to get your head checked. He's made a bunch of friends, and he picked up the language like *that*.' She snapped her fingers. 'He's practically bilingual.'

All right, perhaps she was gilding the lily just a *bit*.

'I mean, he still mentions friends and old haunts from time to time – but I don't think he *misses* them per se. I was all set for having to field an endless stream of "I don't like it here" and "When are we going home, Mummy?" But it's as if, overnight, he just decided, *This is my life now and I'm making my peace with it.* And quite right too – I mean, what's the point of looking back on life and having regrets?'

'The wisdom of the young, eh?'

'Exactly. If you ask me, we could all stand to learn a thing or two from them.'

'Sounds like the two of you have got it made.'

Once more, Anna felt herself smiling involuntarily. 'You know,' she said, 'I think we have.'

'Which begs the obvious question.'

'Which is?'

'What are you doing *here*?'

'Come again?'

Vasilico affected an airy shrug. 'You're living it up in Perugia, happy as Larry, the pair of you … and yet here you are. You know, when I first clapped eyes on you back there, I thought at first things hadn't worked out and you'd come back to pick up the threads of your old life. But to hear you talk, it sounds like wild horses couldn't drag you back.

'So I return to my original question: how comes it that I run into you on Byres Road on a Friday afternoon, stomping around with your usual single-minded sense of purpose, barrelling headlong into random pedestrians?'

Anna was silent for a moment, considering her answer.

'I suppose I'm here to put my affairs in order.'

'That sounds rather ominous,' said Vasilico.

'Not from where I'm standing, it doesn't. Honestly, it's just a handful of boring administrative matters that got put on hold by the pandemic.'

They walked on in silence for several paces, until they arrived at a set of traffic lights. They halted at the pedestrian crossing, Vasilico reaching past Anna to press the button.

As they stood side by side, waiting for the lights to change, she realised he was looking at her.

'What?'

'Your hair. You've let it grow. I've never seen it this long before.'

She instinctively ran a hand through it, as if making sure it was still there. It had already been starting to grow out when she'd left Glasgow and now reached down almost to her waist.

'Oh, yeah, that,' she said, a tad bashfully. 'It was either let it grow or cut it myself during lockdown, and quite frankly I didn't trust myself not to make a pig's ear of it. And then, after things started to open up again, it just hardly seemed worth the effort. I mean, I go through shampoo like there's no tomorrow, but—'

'It's nice,' Vasilico said.

She started to smile, then caught herself and swiftly straightened her face.

The traffic came to a halt and the green man appeared on the screen. They crossed the road and walked on.

Anna cleared her throat, attempting to banish the feelings

of awkwardness that now seemed to be coursing through her. 'So what about you? Any major, transformative events in *your* life?'

Vasilico considered the question for a moment, then shook his head. 'None that come to mind.'

'Still with the Specialist Crime Unit, then?'

'They haven't given me my jotters yet.' He gave an amused chuckle. 'You know, it's funny – everyone talks about how lockdown put everything on hold. How, all of a sudden, they found themselves with all this free time on their hands and nothing to do except scroll Twitter and watch Netflix. It wasn't like that for us. Crime didn't go on pause just because there was a global pandemic on.'

'And of course you also had to contend with little old ladies who'd gone to sit in the park when it wasn't allowed and joggers who'd been out for more than their single allotted hour of exercise. I can see why you'd be kept busy.'

The words might have sounded harsh, but Vasilico beamed, receiving them in the spirit in which they'd been intended.

'Precisely. I'll have you know I took the responsibility tremendously seriously.'

'And what about DS Kirk? Is she still to the fore?'

'Actually, it's *DI* Kirk now. Climbing the career ladder quicker than a squirrel on crystal meth, that one.'

'Careful. She'll be your boss before you know it.'

They'd turned off Byres Road onto a residential street now and were heading in a westerly direction, flanked on either side by sandstone tenements that had been carved up and converted into flats. Again, they didn't seem to be going anywhere in particular – though, for reasons that escaped her, Anna found herself glad of the degree of privacy this more secluded route afforded them. Already, the thrum of traffic from Byres Road sounded far-off, like a distant memory.

'So come on – spill the beans.'

Vasilico's voice shook Anna from her thoughts. She turned to glance up at him searchingly.

'Hmm?'

'Why are you *really* here?' He smiled at her less than convincing attempt at a look of incomprehension. 'Come on – "a handful of boring administrative matters"? You expect me to believe you came all this way just to check your bank balance?'

'It's a *bit* more complicated than that. On which note, I don't suppose you've got the number of a builder?'

'What? No. I don't. Sorry. What I mean is, it all sounds suspiciously like a cover story to me. Or at least a pretext. I'm sure, whatever it is you need to take care of, you could have dealt with it long-distance if you really put your mind to it.' He gave her a shrewd look – one which left her feeling exposed in all sorts of ways. 'You've got yourself mixed up in something again, haven't you?'

'I have *not!*' she retorted, too quickly. Then, 'I mean, I hardly think I have to justify myself to *you*.'

'Of course not. Perish the thought. But I know you, Anna Scavolini. You and I have done this dance too many times for you to pull the wool over *my* eyes. Come on – what's really lured you back?'

For several seconds, Anna said nothing. She continued to walk in silence, not looking at Vasilico but aware of his eyes, holding her firmly in their crosshairs.

At length, she made a decision. She knew he wasn't going to give any credence to her denials – or let the matter drop until he got an answer. And besides, she might as well try to exploit every resource at her disposal – even if it was a seriously long shot.

'Oh, all right.'

As briefly as possible, she explained the mission Fraser had tasked her with carrying out and her progress so far, culminating in the revelations about Hugh's apparent money woes and alleged abuses of the school's research fund.

'The trouble is,' she explained, 'I've no way of properly getting inside his head. It's one thing to ask the people who spent time with him in the weeks and months before his death whether anything seemed off about his behaviour, but it's another thing entirely to know what was going through his mind during that time.'

Vasilico nodded soberly. 'Mm. It's a pickle all right. One I myself have had to contend with on many an occasion, believe it or not.'

'If I could – I dunno, get inside his bank account, it might at least give me some idea as to whether he really *was* having money problems.'

'You could always ask this Miriam character. You never know – she might prove more forthcoming than you think.'

Anna scoffed. 'You mean bang on her door and ask if she happens to have his login details written down somewhere? Or say, "Excuse me, but by any chance was your dad knee-deep in debt when he died and could someone've been using that to blackmail him?"'

'I wouldn't use that particular sledgehammer to crack the nut in question myself, no. But I'm sure you'll think of something. You can be quite adroit when you want to be.'

'Oh, piss off.'

Vasilico chuckled, altogether too pleased with himself. 'All I'm saying is, if you put your mind to it, I'm sure you'll find a way. You've done it before.'

They walked on, rounding a corner onto another residential street.

'Actually,' said Anna, after a pause, 'if you want to be helpful instead of just making arsey remarks, you could start by telling me what you know about the investigation into Hugh's death. I already know there *was* one, so don't try to pretend otherwise.'

'Good for you,' said Vasilico jovially. 'As it happens, I wasn't directly involved. Took a passing interest, though, on account of you and he going back a ways.'

'Well, seeing as you're such an expert, perhaps you'd be able to tell me whether they looked at his finances for a motive.'

'Why don't I just purloin the case file for you so you can read it for yourself?'

'*Could* you?' said Anna, too quickly.

Vasilico scoffed. 'What do *you* think? No, of course I can't do that. Nor am I at liberty to comment on the specifics of an individual inquiry, even to someone as tenacious as your good self.' He paused. 'What I *will* say – speaking purely hypothetically, of course – is that the time and resources allocated towards investigating a fatality are usually proportionate to the likelihood of a suspicious cause of death. If there's clear evidence the death was self-inflicted and the victim's motivation is readily apparent – say a suicide note, for example – then it's vanishingly unlikely that the senior investigating officer would deem it appropriate to comb through every last corner of their life.'

Anna nodded slowly as she digested this. She concluded this was the closest she was going to get to explicit confirmation that the police hadn't probed too far below the surface. Nonetheless, she felt she had to try for one last push.

'So the chances of me getting to see the file for myself …'

'Non-existent,' said Vasilico cheerfully.

They walked on. They'd been heading steadily west for a while now, and, as Anna took proper notice of her surroundings for the first time in a while, she realised she had only a vague sense of where they were. She knew the arteries of the West End like the veins in her own hand, but the terraced houses on either side of her were unfamiliar, and there were no street signs in sight with which to orient herself. How long had they been walking for? She'd completely lost track.

'I still can't get over it,' Vasilico said, breaking the silence she belatedly realised had settled between them.

'What?'

'You and me, meeting like this. What were the odds?'

'Don't get ahead of yourself. I hate to break it to you, but ours is only the second chance encounter I've had in the last hour.'

'Well, shit,' said Vasilico good-naturedly. 'Should I be jealous?'

'And what possible reason could you have for that?' she shot back, too quickly and too defensively.

'Oh, none, none at all,' he replied airily – which, for some reason, infuriated her beyond all reason.

'No, go on,' she said, aware of the brittle edge in her voice. 'Tell me why my having had a prior encounter with another person today would be cause for you to experience feelings of jealousy.'

She knew she was seizing on a flippant remark and making a bigger deal of it than it warranted. She also knew she could have shut down the whole 'jealousy' angle by simply stating that the person she'd run into had been Farah – but she didn't see why she should have to. On what planet was she obligated to explain herself to *him*?

For several seconds, Vasilico didn't respond. His pace had slowed, his arms were folded behind his back and his head was bent in contemplation. When he broke the silence, his tone had changed. Where previously it had been playful and whimsical, now it was sober and contemplative.

'Do you remember our conversation on the bridge on Great Western Road? The one where you told me you weren't ready for a relationship with me?'

Anna continued to walk, keeping her eyes fixed firmly in front of her, not trusting herself to look at him.

'You said you needed time. Time to figure out what you wanted. But that's not how things panned out. You took off for a new job in a different country, leaving me with no idea whether I'd even see you again.'

Anna bristled defensively. 'That wasn't something I foresaw at the time. An opportunity came along and I felt I needed to take it. And even if I *had* stayed in Glasgow, it's not like there was some sort of signed agreement between us saying there was a guaranteed future for us at the end of it. You're right – I told you I needed time. And, well … times change. *People* change.'

Vasilico came to a standstill, just outside the mouth of a cobblestoned alleyway between two rows of tenements. Anna turned to face him as he stood, jaw set, his temporal vein visibly pulsating.

'You could have said something. You could have put me in the picture. But you never picked up the phone.'

She couldn't believe what she was hearing. 'Oh my fucking *God*! Would you listen to yourself? Neither did *you*!'

'You'd moved to another country,' he retorted, his tone risibly petulant.

'You still had my number!'

'Well, I didn't know whether it would've still worked, did I?'

'You could always have *tried*!' she exclaimed, her own voice rising to match his.

He looked at her incredulously. Shook his head.

'You know,' he said, lowering his voice to a more reasonable level, 'in case you've forgotten, *you* were the one who said you needed time. Don't you think, therefore, that put you under a certain obligation to make the first move?'

'Oh, I *see*. You were being gentlemanly.'

He said nothing, just glowered at her defiantly. His silence, coupled with his obvious lack of anything vaguely like remorse, caused her resolve to harden.

'Fine,' she said, throwing up her arms and letting them fall to her sides. 'I kept you waiting by the phone for me to call and tell you I was ready for us to get it on again. You got me. I'm self-centred. I'm a bitch. I've been stringing you along for eighteen months, and now, at long last, I'm finally putting you out of your misery, telling you, beyond a shadow of a doubt, that there's no future for us. Is that what you want to hear?'

Vasilico had listened to her diatribe in its entirety without trying to interject, his expression unreadable. When she fell silent, he stood there in silence for a long minute, lips pinched, jaw tight.

'Well,' he said quietly, 'it certainly draws a line under things.'

'I'm glad you think so.'

'Good.'

'GOOD.'

'Then we're both good.'

For a few moments, they stood facing one another, each glaring daggers at the other.

And then, before Anna even realised what was happening, their lips were locking, their hands all over each other, pawing, clutching, squeezing, and they were staggering backwards into the alleyway as a single, conjoined entity. Vasilico lifted her up against the wall, almost knocking the breath from her. She felt the rough stone pressing into her back, his tongue in her mouth, her hand on the bulge inside his trousers. He hoisted her skirt up around her waist. She felt the elastic of her underwear snapping as he tore it aside. And then he was deep inside her, thrusting into her, once more smashing the air from her lungs. She cried out, but the sound was lost beneath the blood pumping in her ears and his rhythmic groans as his hips continued to slam against hers.

She wasn't sure how long it took her to come. It felt like both an eternity and no time at all. She was aware of the spontaneous contractions throughout her body; of the deep ache that she both yearned to be satiated and didn't want to end; of everything being connected, all building together towards a single, all-engulfing climax. She felt the long, low moan building up inside her. Tried to hold it in, but to no avail. She gave a shuddering cry and her whole body turned to water, melting into the wall behind her.

When the stars in front of her eyes cleared and she could see daylight again, she realised she was still whole, still in his arms with her legs coiled around his back. He was panting for breath, his head buried in her shoulder, his brow hot and damp through the fabric of her dress.

'Get off me,' she heard herself saying; then again, more forcefully, both hands pushing against his chest, 'Get *off* me.'

His grip on her loosened. Gently, he lowered her to the ground. Somehow, she managed to remain upright, leaning against the wall for support, as Vasilico fumbled to cram his semi-flaccid penis back into his fly. Her skin crackled with a million tiny bursts of electricity, and the ground felt off-kilter under her feet, as if she was standing on an incline.

'I have to go,' she heard herself mumbling.

She turned and made her way shakily towards the mouth of the alleyway. She was aware of his voice behind her, asking her where he could find her and if he could see her again, but she kept walking, step by shuffling step, one hand continuing to trail the wall in case she lost her footing, the other clutching her torn underwear in a clenched fist. She reached the street, picked a direction at random and started walking, her pace steadily increasing as her sense of balance returned, until she was striding at a brisk clip, her breath coming out in short, heavy puffs with each step.

As the fog lifted from her mind, shock swiftly set in at what she'd just done. She'd just had frantic, unplanned sex in an alleyway. She wasn't the sort of person who had sex in alleyways – frantic and unplanned or otherwise. What on earth had possessed her? What was she *thinking?* Actually, she wasn't going to answer that. Thinking couldn't possibly have come into it – because, if it had, she'd never have done something so utterly reckless. Had anyone passed the alley while they were doing it? Had they been *seen*? She thought about the saliva they'd just exchanged – among other bodily fluids. Had Vasilico tested for COVID recently? Did *she* need to test? How long would it take for her to begin showing as positive? Could she bring herself to break all the rules and travel when she couldn't be sure she wasn't infected? Would she end up trapped here for another week, or even longer?

It was only when she finally emerged from the warren of vaguely familiar residential streets and found herself near the bottom of Hyndland Road that her conscious mind finally acknowledged what the unconscious part had probably registered more or less as soon as she'd laid eyes on him – and of which it had *definitely* been aware when she'd felt it pressing against her skin as he held her.

The ring on his third finger.

14

Anna sat in the outdoor seating area of the little deli on the corner of Park Road and Gibson Street, at a table for two enclosed inside a clear plastic tent – one of around half a dozen similar contraptions lining the pavement – and toyed with the laminated drinks menu as she waited. Her heart was still pounding, though, at this point, she concluded it had less to do with her ill-advised frenzy-fuck and more to do with how quickly she'd had to leg it here from the hotel, after making a pit stop to freshen up and replace her underwear. Going commando for the rest of the day was not an option she'd been willing to countenance.

Her eyes strayed to her phone, lying face up on the table, showing a Facebook profile. Paul Vasilico's, to be precise. It was the first time she'd ever thought to look him up on there. In fact, until she'd keyed his name into the search bar, she hadn't known whether he even had an account. She normally gave social media, in all its various manifestations, a wide berth, and regarded those who made a habit of snooping on the status updates of their friends and acquaintances as little better than the sort of people who raked through others' bins in search of a juicy scandal. But the ring on Vasilico's finger had changed everything. One way or another, she had to know what it meant. And there, sure enough, near the top of the page, were five words which left her unable to pretend, for a second longer, that it had been a mere fashion accessory:

Got Engaged to Lauren Calder
June 24, 2021

A photo further down showed Vasilico and a diminutive and extremely pretty blonde woman a good few years younger than him with their arms around one another, smiling radiantly at the camera.

She glowered at the image of the happy couple, her blood fizzing. She'd asked him if there'd been any major developments in his life, and he'd told her, with a completely straight face, that he couldn't think of any. Going out and getting bloody *engaged* wasn't exactly the sort of thing that simply slipped one's mind. It certainly made his whining about her failure to get in touch even *less* endearing than it had been at the time. He'd moved on fast – and during lockdown, no less; a period that wouldn't exactly have been conducive to pursuing a lengthy and meaningful courtship. She wondered whether he'd spared a thought for his poor fiancée while he was practically balls deep inside her in that alleyway …

She heard footsteps and quickly slammed the phone face down, then looked up to see a familiar figure approaching, dressed in her usual attire: ripped skinny jeans, white V-neck top, unseasonable black leather jacket with giant rubber spikes. Tall, tanned and looking effortlessly cool, Jen Brinkley slid into the seat opposite Anna with an easy grin.

'*Aloha, chica.* Fancy *you* coming crawling out of the woodwork.'

Anna returned the smile. 'Hey. Thanks for meeting me.'

'Ah, c'mon. The sun's shining, the birds are singing – and, out of the blue, I get a call from one of my faves saying she's back in town and do I wanna hang out and shoot the shit? What the hell else did you think I was gonna do? Say no?'

There was a brief pause in their conversation as a barista arrived to take their orders. Once she'd left, Jen gazed around at her surroundings with an air of wry amusement.

'So, some setup, huh? Guess we've all finally turned into the pod people.'

'I can't help thinking these things have got to be doing more to help the spread of infections than prevent it,' Anna admitted.

'Reckon you could have a point there. Mind you, I can see the logic behind 'em. 'S not as if we've normally got the weather for dining *al dente*. Or is it *al fresco*? Either way, impeccable timing on your part, popping up on the *one* nice day we've had this summer.

'So listen, how the hell *are* ya? I mean, I can tell just to look at you, you've been getting some much-needed Vitamin D – and not before time, I might add. Least Zoe's got her ginger disposition to account for her being so peely-wally.' She wagged a chiding finger. '*You*, missy, ain't got *no* excuse.'

There was another brief pause as the barista returned with their coffees. As she departed once again, Jen crossed one leg over the other and leaned towards Anna with an inquisitorial look.

'How's your boisterous boy, by the by? The twins are forever asking after him.' She mimicked their high-pitched voices. '"When's Jack coming back?" "When can we go and see him?" Don't think they understand the concept of other countries, let alone a worldwide travel shutdown. Mind you, looks like things might be slowly but surely getting back to normal, hmm? God, with this virus, I sometimes think the cure's worse than the disease.'

Anna – who couldn't avoid feeling a pang of guilt at the mention of Jack, 1,500 miles away and waiting for her to come back to him – sipped her coffee and opted to count her blessings that the topic of conversation had already moved on.

'So.' Jen drummed her fists on the tabletop and gave Anna a briskly businesslike look. 'What's the story, morning glory? Odds are roughly, oh, say, infinity squared to one you've summoned me here for more than just a friendly chinwag.'

Anna blinked in surprise and dismay. 'Am I *that* transparent?'

Jen smiled. 'Honey, if you were any more see-through, I'd be able to read today's specials on the board behind you without asking you to move.' She folded her arms and leant back in her chair, fixing Anna with a mock-severe look. 'So spill, Jill.'

Anna pushed her cup to one side. 'Jen,' she said, choosing her words carefully, 'how would you feel about helping me get inside someone's computer?'

Slowly, Jen leant forward, placing her elbows on the table and folding her hands, resting her chin on them as her lips slowly spread into a smile that was both incredulous and intrigued, but very much with an emphasis on the latter.

'Do tell,' she said.

15

'OK,' Jen said, 'so you're clear about what you need to do.'

Anna nodded. 'I think so.'

She held the tiny USB dongle Jen had given her in her lap, toying with it absentmindedly as they sat side by side in Jen's Prius, parked under the shadow of a leafy oak tree at the end of a row of houses.

'So run it back to me one more time.'

Anna shut her eyes, mentally going through Jen's instructions. Then, staring straight ahead and feeling for all the world like she was back in primary school, she slowly and deliberately recited them aloud.

When she'd finished, Jen nodded approvingly. 'Ten out of ten. If I had a pack of gold stars with me, I'd be sticking one on your forehead right about now.'

'It's not the remembering that's the tricky part. It's putting it all into action right under the nose of my host.'

Jen gave a dismissive snort. 'You'll be grand. Just remember, if you're not feeling the vibes or she tells you to take a running jump, you abort the mission, meet me back here and we'll come up with something else.' She patted Anna's shoulder. 'Now go break a leg.'

Anna inhaled deeply, steeling herself. Then, in a fast, impulsive movement, she got out of the car, strode to the end of the street and turned onto Hendon Drive.

'Anna!' Miriam sounded surprised but not altogether displeased to find her standing on the doorstep. 'What are *you* doing back so soon?'

Anna clocked both the smear of green under Miriam's right eye and the fresh paint flecks on the denim shirt that she was fairly certain was the only thing the younger woman was wearing.

'Have I … come at a bad time?' she said.

'Not in the slightest!' said Miriam, opening the door wider. 'Get your butt *in* here!'

'You know,' she mused, as Anna dutifully stepped over the threshold, 'I was *hoping* you'd stop by again. I so enjoyed our wee chat yesterday. What can I get you? Water again … or perhaps something a mite stronger?' she added, a touch hopefully.

'Nothing for me today, thanks,' said Anna.

As she spoke, she glanced around at her surroundings, re-familiarising herself with the general state of neglect, and the bundle of envelopes wedged behind the key bowl, still unopened.

She forced these thoughts to the back of her mind. 'So, actually, this is a little awkward.'

Miriam smiled pleasantly. 'How so?'

'Well, the truth is, I was wondering if you could do me a slight favour. Actually, quite a big one.'

Miriam raised her eyebrows comically. 'This is all starting to sound a bit ominous.'

'Hopefully not. Um …'

There really was no delicate way to put this.

'When your dad … when he passed away … did the police

take his electronic devices? Like, his phone, or ...' She hesitated. '... his home computer?'

Miriam's eyes narrowed. 'That's a very strange thing to be asking.'

'I agree,' said Anna, increasingly feeling like she was losing her grip on the situation. 'It is. But ...' Again, she hesitated. 'Well, before I left for Perugia, your dad was working on some research – research he'd been trying to persuade me to take over from him. To tell the truth, I didn't really give him a proper hearing at the time. I felt there were people more qualified to do it than me. But now ... well, lately, I've been thinking it might not be such a bad idea after all. It'd be a shame if the work he already did never got to see the light of day, and ... and I suppose a part of me would like to do something to honour his legacy.'

The words almost stuck in her throat – the knowledge that she was effectively exploiting Hugh's memory to get what she really wanted. But it was either that or admit defeat and go home.

Miriam frowned and nodded slowly, far from wholly won over by this pitch. 'I see. And what exactly is it you'd need?'

Anna winced internally, aware of how crass what she was about to say would sound. 'I don't suppose you could let me have a look on his computer – you know, to see whether it's still got any of his old notes?'

A flicker of something passed through Miriam's eyes, and, for a moment, Anna suspected she'd blown it. But, after a few seconds, Miriam's expression relaxed, and she gave an easy, almost indifferent shrug.

'Sure. It's not like you'd be digging up his grave, is it?'

The best Anna could manage was a strained smile.

Miriam thrust open the door to a small, wood-panelled home office. The curtains were drawn, and it took Anna's eyes a moment to adjust to the gloomy half-light. When they did, she saw that the walls were lined with shelves, overflowing with far more books than they were ever intended to hold. More books were piled on the floor and on virtually every other available surface – including the desk, where an aged, square LCD monitor, mouse and keyboard also sat, alongside a small, squat tower unit with a 'Windows 8 Compatible' sticker. Everything, including the screen, was coated in a layer of dust.

'The boys in blue came and took it away the day after it happened,' Miriam explained. 'They returned it a week later. I've my doubts they even switched it on.'

From her tone, it was difficult to tell whether she was expressing disapproval or something akin to vindication, as if she'd anticipated all along that the police wouldn't make much of an effort and had merely had her suspicions confirmed.

'It hasn't been on since,' she continued. 'To be honest, I don't even know if it still works.'

Fortunately, however, it did – once, between them, they'd managed to reconnect all the peripherals and figure out how to power it on; Miriam, it turned out, was every bit as tech-clueless as Anna. While it was slowly running through the start-up sequence, Anna settled into Hugh's padded office chair and wiped dust from the screen with her hand, conscious of Miriam hovering just behind her, giving off a faint whiff of paint thinner.

After a while, the familiar Windows lock screen appeared, prompting Anna to enter a pin code. She glanced over her shoulder at Miriam, seeking guidance.

'Try 2307,' said Miriam; then, by way of explanation, 'Twenty-third of July. Alfie's birthday. He used it for just about everything.'

Was it Anna's imagination or was there more than a hint of bitterness in the way she said it?

She entered the pin code, prompting a 'Welcome' message. The hard disk groaned and whirred, the desktop slowly populating with icons. A succession of notifications popped up in the corner, warning that the operating system was dangerously out of date and required urgent updating. Anna swiftly rejected them, each tap of the mouse more impatient than the last. Icons continued to appear until virtually the entire screen was covered by them.

'Gosh,' said Miriam. 'I know Daddy wasn't one for keeping things in order, but this is a bit much.'

She leant past Anna to examine the screen, one hand resting on the desk, the other on the back of the chair. In the process, her shirt, its top buttons undone, slipped down over her shoulder, exposing both the spider's web of dark armpit hair protruding from under it and the adjacent tiny, upturned breast. She either didn't notice or simply didn't care; both possibilities, to Anna's mind, seemed equally plausible.

'Sooo ...' she mused, 'where d'you figure we should start?'

'Dunno,' said Anna, not liking the sound of that 'we'. She was sincerely hoping Miriam didn't intend to hover over her shoulder throughout the entire process. 'My Documents folder?'

'Go on, then.'

Anna made a show of trying to find the corresponding icon, dragging out the process as much as possible in the hope that Miriam would lose interest and leave her to her own devices. In fairness, it didn't require much play-acting: Hugh's computer desktop really *was* as cluttered and disorganised as the real thing had been.

Miriam jabbed a finger. 'There.' She shook her head. 'Honestly, that man. It's no wonder he could never find anything when he needed it.'

Anna obediently clicked the icon, once again wishing Miriam would hurry up and go back to her painting.

The disorganisation evident on the desktop extended to the contents of the folder. All Hugh's files were simply sitting there in a single, mammoth list – a far cry from the neat collection of subfolders, organised by year and subject matter, that characterised Anna's own computer. It quickly became evident that Hugh had not been in the habit of deleting anything: there were files going back as far as 1998, as well as multiple redundant copies of what seemed to be the same material. It wasn't unusual for a document's name to begin with 'Copy of Copy of Copy of …'

'*Sacre bleu,*' sighed Miriam. 'We're going to be here till St Steven's Day.'

'Actually,' said Anna, having a sudden idea, 'I think maybe I *will* take you up on the offer of something to drink.'

'Yeah?' said Miriam disinterestedly, eyes remaining fixed on the screen.

'Yeah. It's a hot day, and—'

'I get it. This "playing detective" malarkey's thirstful work. What's your poison?'

Anna thought fast. She knew it needed to be something that would take time for Miriam to prepare. A glass of tap water wasn't going to cut it.

'Maybe some of that orange squash if you've still got any? Diluted with some sparkling water?'

Miriam straightened up. 'I'll see what I can manage.'

She turned to leave.

'And ice!' Anna called after her.

'My, my,' said Miriam good-naturedly, 'we *are* picky today, aren't we? Coming right up!'

Anna continued to scroll through the screed of documents, eyes only glancing over the file names as she listened to Miriam heading towards the door. She was aware of her footsteps stopping for several seconds, no doubt watching her from the doorway, before continuing down the hallway.

Immediately, Anna sprang into action. Jumping to her feet, she fished the USB dongle Jen had given her out of her bag. Remembering Jen's instructions – '*If at all possible, connect it to one of the ones at the back. Less noticeable that way*' – she ignored the ports on the front, instead turning the tower to a forty-five-degree angle so she could inspect the tangle of cables and sockets at the back.

'Go for one with a blue connector, if there are any. They're ten times faster than the black ones.'

She cast around, trying to identify what Jen had described to her. It was hard to make out much of anything in the gloom of the office. She considered turning on the overhead light, but that would only waste precious seconds. Just then, she noticed a small lamp on the other side of the desk. She grabbed it, switched it on – mercifully, it was plugged in – and angled it towards the computer.

'How are you getting on in there?' Miriam called through from the kitchen.

'No luck yet!' Anna shouted back, truthfully.

Continuing to angle the desk lamp's beam at the back of the computer, she fought against the feeling of information overload as she examined one port after another. There were multiple different types, most of them only minor variations on the same basic shape. She'd never understood the differences between HDMI and Thunderbolt, Firewire and Ethernet, not to mention the seemingly endless incarnations of USB, other than that you couldn't plug a device made for one port into a different kind – not without doing considerable damage. Why the hell couldn't they just make one standard connector for everything? Plus, they *all* seemed to be black.

Her heart rate rose. The seconds continued to tick by. Miriam could be back at any moment. Then, suddenly, she spotted a couple of rectangular ports, each with a small strip of blue plastic inside it. These must be what Jen had been referring to.

She tried to insert the dongle. It didn't fit. She turned it upside down and tried again. It *still* didn't fit.

In desperation, she turned it the original way up and pushed it in again, concluding that, if this didn't work, she was going to have to abandon ship altogether. Miraculously, it slotted in perfectly. She let out the breath she belatedly realised she'd been holding in.

She heard footsteps approaching from the corridor. Frantically, she switched off the lamp, turned the computer back round and resumed her seat, returning the lamp to its original location just as Miriam came breezing in, carrying a tall glass of orange juice, complete with ice and a straw.

'There we go. Sorry about the hold-up.'

'That's OK,' Anna managed to say, accepting the glass from her.

'Oh! Coaster.'

Miriam snatched the glass back and, with her free hand, began to rummage about on the desk, setting reams of paperwork astray. As Anna, half-amused, watched her, out of the corner of her eye she spotted the 'New device detected' popup in the corner of the screen. Hastily, she clicked the little X button to close it, just as Miriam let out an 'Ah!' of satisfaction and produced a faded plastic coaster, stained with the dried residue of countless mugs of tea.

'Good thinking,' said Anna, a tad breathlessly, as Miriam placed it in front of her and set the glass on top of it.

Miriam shoved some books off a nearby footstool, dragged it over to the desk and settled herself on it, legs turned inward, bare knees pressed together.

'Right, then – shall we crack on?'

For the next three-quarters of an hour, Anna continued to trawl semi-aimlessly through the contents of Hugh's computer, mindful all the while of Jen's instructions.

'Drag things out for as long as possible. If, during that time, I manage to get everything I need, I'll stage a diversion so you can retrieve the dongle. If that's not possible, you leave it in situ and we just hope it goes unnoticed.'

'That thing's making a helluva lot of noise,' Miriam observed at one point, nodding towards the computer. 'Sounds like a stuck drainpipe. Hope it's not about to go up in flames,' she added with a theatrical eyebrow-wiggle, as if she positively relished the idea.

Anna, who'd been aware of the sound of the computer's hard drive grinding away for some time, presumably as the concealed dongle did its job, felt her shoulders tensing involuntarily. 'It's probably just old and tired,' she said – then added, in a half-hearted attempt at a joke, 'A bit like me.'

Miriam slapped her arm playfully. 'You're not *old*, Anna! You've only a few years on *me*. Anyway, they say you're only as old as you feel.'

'If that's true,' said Anna ruefully, 'then I must be positively ancient.'

Time slipped by, and Anna continued to make a show of combing through Hugh's files. In fairness, she did find *some* evidence of the austerity project she'd claimed to be looking for, but there was nothing to suggest he'd made any meaningful progress on it, beyond a handful of extremely preliminary notes – certainly nothing that would have justified the expenses claims Lorraine had told her he'd been submitting.

With it becoming harder and harder to drag things out as she waited for Jen's signal, she turned to increasingly desperate attempts at small talk, further interrogating Miriam about the fallow period her work had experienced during lockdown and listening as she railed against the unique challenges people in her position had had to contend with.

'Everyone always bangs on about how they had *soooo* much free time,' she snapped; 'how they binged all seven seasons of *Buffy the Vampire Slayer* and learned how to bake banana bread and speak bloody Esperanto. *You* try doing all that if you're self-employed and getting no financial assistance whatsoever from the government.'

Anna nodded and made appropriate noises of understanding. Her enquiry hadn't merely been an idle one: ever since her conversation with Lorraine, she'd been wondering about the relationship between Hugh's apparent money woes and Miriam's own financial situation. It seemed reasonable to assume Miriam had inherited control of her father's savings along with the house and its contents, which meant she probably had an intimate knowledge of the state of his bank balance. It occurred to her that Hugh's alleged misappropriation of university funds could, at least in part, have been a desperate ploy to conceal the extent of his money problems – and, vicariously, whatever trouble he'd got himself into – from his daughter.

It would all have been so much easier if she could simply have put all this to Miriam directly. But there was no earthly way she could have brought up the matter of Hugh's finances without giving away the true purpose of her visit – to say nothing of coming across as crass in the extreme. So she continued to tiptoe around the subject, hoping that, by gently steering Miriam in the right direction, she might coax her into revealing something of her own volition. But Miriam remained infuriatingly unreceptive to Anna's gentle steers, continuing, instead, to rail against the politicians she regarded as having thrown her under the bus.

They'd been at it for nearly an hour, and Anna knew she was on the verge of running out of files to look at, when the phone began to ring in the hallway. Miriam briefly glanced over her shoulder, a spark of irritation registering in her expression, before turning her attention back to the screen.

Anna glanced up at her. 'Aren't you going to get that?'

'Oh, that? I always let it ring out.'

'It could be something important.'

Miriam shrugged, unconcerned. 'In that case, they should know better than to ring the bloody landline. What is this, the nineteenth century?'

Yes, Anna thought, *they could try sending you a letter, only for you to ignore that too.*

She fixed Miriam with a pointed look. 'I really think you should get it.'

For a moment, Miriam met her gaze with a look that bordered on insolent. Then, with a theatrical sigh and roll of her eyes, she got to her feet and strode from the room, bare feet stomping up the hallway corridor with exaggerated force.

'This is the MacLeish residence,' Anna heard her say in a high, officious voice. 'Who's calling, please?'

A pause, then:

'You're selling *what?*' A beat. 'Well, actually, now that you mention it, yes, I *could* do with having mine replaced …'

That was Anna's cue. She put her ear to the computer to make sure the hard drive was definitely no longer churning, then reached behind it, fumbling for the dongle. She successfully retrieved it and slipped it back into her bag, then spent the next couple of minutes clicking and scrolling aimlessly while Miriam's voice continued to rise and fall in the hallway, her tone growing increasingly irritable and abrupt.

'Well,' she snapped eventually, 'if that's going to be your attitude, you can eat an entire bag of dicks, and hopefully choke on them while you're at it.'

Anna heard the phone being slammed back into its cradle. A moment later, Miriam came storming back in, her features puce with rage.

'Honestly,' she said, 'I'm amazed they manage to sell any windows at all, if they're prepared to take that sort of tone with a potential customer.' She clocked that Anna was on her feet, bag resting on her shoulder. She blinked in surprise. 'You're going?'

Anna nodded. 'I reckon I've already taken up far too much of your time.'

'Oh. Found what you needed, then?'

She sounded unmistakably disappointed.

'I think so,' said Anna.

'And you're leaving straight away?'

Anna attempted a perky smile. 'No time like the present.'

She moved towards the door, but Miriam stepped in front of her, blocking the way. She gazed at Anna with an expression that was positively suspicious.

'What about the notes?'

'Notes?'

'You know – for this project? Don't you need to save them to a memory stick or something?'

Rookie mistake. For a moment, Anna couldn't think what to say. Then, she had a sudden idea.

'Oh – I emailed them to myself while you were on the phone.'

'Right.'

Miriam continued to hold her gaze for a fraction longer than was comfortable. Then, she gave a decidedly petulant shrug and stepped aside.

Anna headed towards the front door, aware of Miriam walking behind her, sullen and silent.

'Thanks for this, Miriam,' she said, turning to her host at the door. 'It was really good of you.'

'Don't mention it,' said Miriam, in a flat, borderline ill-tempered tone that matched her facial expression.

She feels used, Anna thought. And well she might. After all, wasn't that precisely what Anna had done: exploited Miriam's transparent longing for some sort of a human connection, only to cut her loose the moment she'd got what she really came for? If you thought about it, it wasn't all that far removed from a fuck-and-run – and she'd already participated in one of *those* today. The enthusiasm with which Miriam had greeted her yesterday – treating her like a long-lost bestie when, in reality, their previous encounters could be counted on one hand – certainly indicated that she didn't have a whole lot going on in her social calendar. The truth was that she was probably just desperately lonely, holed up in this massive house with no one but the occasional deliveryman for company.

Anna resolved, then and there, that she couldn't leave things like this – not with her conscience intact, and not if she wanted to have any prospect of interrogating Miriam again at a later date.

'Miriam …' she began, a little hesitantly. 'You know what you said yesterday about dinner?'

Miriam nodded sourly.

'Well, I'm afraid I've already made plans for this evening … but, if the offer still stands, maybe we could do something tomorrow?'

Miriam appeared dubious. 'Yeah? You're sure?'

'Of course. I'd love to.'

For a moment, Miriam's expression didn't change. Then, the cloud seemed to lift from her. The effect was transformational. Suddenly, she was all smiles and sunshine, her earlier bad mood instantly forgotten.

'Oh my gosh,' she gushed, gripping Anna's hand with her sharp little fingers, 'you've no idea how much you've made my day! We'll have such a great time. What do you like to eat? Any special dietary requirements? Veggie? Vegan? Halal? Kosher? They're basically the same thing, aren't they?'

'Oh, I'll eat just about anything,' said Anna. 'Except squid.'

'Damn. There goes my masterplan.'

Anna extracted her hand as gently as possible. 'Seriously, I'll take whatever's going. And listen, don't be putting yourself out on my account.'

By now, Miriam was practically bouncing up and down with delight. 'Nonsense! Let's push the boat out. Make it a night to remember. No point doing anything if you're only gonna do it by halves, right?'

'Right,' Anna agreed, her cheeks increasingly aching from the smile she was forcing.

With a considerable effort, Miriam succeeded in dialling

down her excitement enough to stand still. She regarded Anna with a look that was almost comical in its forced formality, and nodded curtly.

'Shall we say six-thirty, then?'

'Sounds ideal.'

'Right. In that case, till tomorrow.'

'Till tomorrow,' Anna confirmed – realising, as she said it, that she was effectively committing herself to still being in Glasgow come Sunday.

'Oh my *God*!' exclaimed Jen, her eyes theatrically wide, when Anna slid back into the passenger seat. 'That Miriam's something else! I made out I was selling double-glazing, thinking I could keep her on the line for about a minute tops. I just about shat myself when she actually said she *wanted* to buy some windaes.'

'She was fizzing when she got off the phone!' said Anna. 'What did you *say* to her?'

'I couldn't think of anything a window-seller would actually say, so I improv'd: told her she sounded awfy young to be answering the phone and to let me speak to a grown-up, then refused to believe her when she repeatedly insisted she was the lady of the house.'

'She probably gets that a lot,' said Anna, fighting the urge to laugh. 'No wonder she popped her cork.' She turned serious. 'You get everything?'

Jen leant behind her and patted the heavy-duty laptop lying open on the back seat, its external casing more reminiscent of a military attaché case than a normal computer.

'Every last nanobyte, ready for inspection.'

16

They pulled up outside the row of converted townhouses on Havelock Street, overlooking Dowanhill Park in the heart of the West End, and headed up the stairs to Jen's first-floor flat. As they stepped over the threshold, Anna heard the sound of small, scurrying feet, and, a second later, Ewan and Maisie came barrelling into the hallway. As Anna hung back, Jen dropped down to her knees to hug them both and plant kisses on the relatively few parts of their faces that weren't covered in glitter paint.

'*Well!*' she laughed. 'Now that's what I call a proper welcome. Been having fun tormenting Kylie?'

As if on cue, a diminutive teenage girl emerged from the living room, her hair in twin braids. She too was covered in glitter paint, including several handprints on her T-shirt.

'There she is,' Jen proclaimed, 'savaged within an inch of her life!' She flashed Kylie a moue of commiseration. 'Hope that wasn't your favourite top. Lemme know the damage and I'll comp you the cost.'

Kylie waved dismissively. 'Ach, it's no bother. Was gonna chuck it out anyway.'

As Jen released the twins and got back to her feet, she appeared to belatedly remember she had Anna in tow.

'Oh, beg pardon. Kylie, Anna. Anna, Kylie. Kylie stays next door,' she explained to Anna. 'She watches the gargoyles for me when I'm out and about. Keeps her in juice money and them out of mischief.'

Kylie gave Anna a rather bashful wave and folded her arms about herself, eyes on the floor.

Jen turned to the twins. 'Are you remembering Auntie Anna? Jack's mum?'

Immediately, the twins erupted in a babble of excited questions – 'Jack? Where's Jack? Is he coming? Are we going to see him?' – none of which Anna felt remotely equipped to answer. As she stood there, wide-eyed and tongue-tied, Jen, sensing her discomfort, stepped in on her behalf.

'Now, now,' she declared in a loud, soothing voice, 'that's quite enough of that. Jack's not here right now. Anna's come on her own …' Cue a tumult of disappointed *awww*s. 'Maybe we'll see him soon, but not right now. *So*,' she placed her hands on her hips and eyed them both firmly, 'are you going to settle down, or am I going to have to take that great big chocolate cake I bought this morning for pudding and put it in the bin?'

The transformation in the children was instantaneous. In a flash, they became completely silent and still, staring up at their mother with wide, angelic eyes, like a pair of impeccably trained dogs awaiting their next command.

Jen nodded approvingly. 'That's better. Now, Anna and Mummy have to do some work, so I want you both on your best behaviour.' She turned to Kylie, lowering her voice. 'Listen, are you needing to get off straight away or can you stay an extra hour or two and fix the goblins their tea? Double time, obviously.'

· · ·

For Kylie, the prospect of some extra 'juice money' evidently held considerable appeal, and she readily accepted this proposal, herding the twins through to the kitchen while Jen and Anna retreated to the area officially known as the Dungeon of Pain.

It was the first time Anna had ever been invited into Jen's inner sanctum – a dark and thoroughly cramped little room at the back of the flat, crowded with multiple computers and various other electronic devices whose roles Anna couldn't even begin to guess, all generating a substantial amount of heat and noise. The curtains were drawn, and the overhead lamp Jen switched on seemed woefully inadequate for its allotted role. Anna supposed, if you spent all day staring at glowing computer screens, you probably didn't have much use for natural light.

'Right,' said Jen, relaxing into a well-used office chair and flicking on a desk fan, which immediately began to rattle and turn, bringing a slight but welcome draught to the stuffy room. 'Grab a pew and let's get stuck in.'

She retrieved her laptop from her shoulder bag and popped a button on its side, causing a tray to slide out. From this, she extracted a hard drive no more than a few millimetres thick, which she hooked up to a well-worn disk reader. Anna, now perched on a chair she'd wheeled over from the opposite end of the room, watched as Jen switched on one of the several screens on the desk in front of her, then proceeded to tap away at the keyboard with the practised ease of someone who did this sort of thing all day, every day.

'What we have here,' said Jen, continuing to hammer away at the keys as lines of code scrolled past on the screen, quicker than Anna could read them, 'is a perfect one-to-one copy of your man Hugh's hard drive, including the master boot record, operating system and file structure, which means we get to peruse the whole thing at our leisure as if we were sitting right there in his office – only without the nosy adult daughter peeking over our shoulders.'

She tapped the mouse a couple of times, and a small window opened on the screen, displaying the same startup sequence Anna recognised from earlier.

'Our ultimate goal is to log into his bank accounts and check the state of his finances. If he's a *complete* luddite and does all his banking face-to-face, we're hosed. But the way things are going, banks closing left, right and centre, I'm cautiously optimistic.'

The lock screen appeared, prompting them for a passcode. Jen glanced expectantly at Anna.

'Any clues?'

'2307,' said Anna. 'Supposedly, he uses it for everything.'

Jen grinned. 'Music to every hacker's ears.'

The operating system finished loading. Immediately, Jen was off like a rocket, clicking icons and opening windows at dizzying speed, as if she already knew Hugh's computer like the back of her hand. Anna, watching, wiped her clammy neck with her hand, wondering how Jen could bear to wear her leather jacket inside this hothouse.

'Because it's his finances you're interested in,' Jen explained as she worked, 'we're gonna start by going through his browser history, looking for the names of the firms folk usually stash their money with.' She tapped away for a few seconds. 'Here we go. He was with Bank of Scotland. A nice, safe, familiar choice.' She shot a gleeful leer in Anna's direction. 'All the better for us.'

Over the next quarter of an hour or so, Anna watched as Jen continued to work, periodically giving a running commentary of what she was doing. Anna nodded and made appropriately interested noises, but she'd long since given up trying to understand what was happening, and was content to take a back seat and let Jen do her thing. She watched as Jen jumped from screen to screen, pages of text appearing and disappearing quicker than Anna could read them. She caught fleeting glimpses of the same Microsoft Outlook interface she used herself, the DuckDuckGo search engine, and various websites with dark backgrounds and garish, barely legible text which, without needing to ask, she somehow understood were of seriously dubious provenance. She considered asking Jen whether what they were doing was completely above the board, then concluded it was better if she didn't know. Better for whom, though – now that was the question. For now, she contented herself with the thought that this sort of thing was Jen's bread and butter and, as such, she was presumably sufficiently adept at covering her tracks.

In what seemed like no time at all, they were inside Hugh's Bank of Scotland account and gazing at its utilitarian white and navy-blue interface, consisting of a current account and a savings account.

'Here.' Jen pointed to the screen. 'Take a gander. He's got just under four hundred quid in savings, but his current account's as good as cleaned out.' She clicked on the latter, expanding the view to show a list of recent transactions. 'In fact, it's in arrears. Lookie here: a whole bunch of attempted direct debit payments, all in the last couple of months, all declined cos there wasn't enough in the kitty to pay 'em.'

Anna ran her eyes down the list, clocking the names of the various recipients. Scottish Power, East Dunbartonshire Council, Greenpeace ... and, not too surprisingly, the ubiquitous Wine Society.

'It's pretty obvious what's happened,' said Jen. 'After he died, the university, not unreasonably, stopped paying into his account, but all his existing direct debits remained in place, and the companies in question kept taking his money till ... well, till there wasn't any.' She jabbed a finger at the screen.

'Here. Looks like that happened around the seventeenth of June.'

Anna nodded, saying nothing. She'd more or less worked this out for herself, though Jen voicing it aloud certainly helped hammer it home. She experienced a fleeting flashback to the 'FINAL NOTICE' envelope on the console table at the MacLeish house.

'Safe to say Miriam isn't abreast of any of this,' said Jen, snapping Anna back to the present.

'Sorry?'

'Hugh died in May of 2020, right?'

'Right. The fifteenth.'

Miriam pointed to some text at the top left-hand corner of the screen. 'Last login before today was the tenth – in other words, back when he was still in the land of the living … just. What's that all about? If my old man popped his clogs and I was still living in his hoose, depending on his savings to keep the lights on, you can bet your bottom dollar I'd be doing my due diligence.'

'I'd say she's living in a state of extreme denial,' said Anna quietly.

'Well, might wanna have a word with her about it. Otherwise, odds are, before too long, she'll wake up one morning to find the bailiffs on her doorstep.'

Anna had been thinking much the same. She didn't like to think how she was going to approach that conversation without letting on to Miriam that she'd hacked into her father's bank account, but she recognised it as one that, for Miriam's sake, she really needed to have.

'What's this?' she said, suddenly noticing something. 'I don't recognise *that* name.' She pointed past Jen's shoulder towards the screen.

Frowning, Jen followed the line of her finger. '"Capercaillie Research Limited"? Me either. Sounds like they could have something to do with his work at the uni, though?'

'If it is, I've never come across them,' said Anna.

Jen continued to scroll. 'There's a bunch of transfers from this account to the Capercaillie one, all different amounts, starting in September 2019. The most recent was on 5 May last year.'

'Just ten days before Hugh's death,' murmured Anna. She turned to Jen. 'So how do we find out more about this Capercaillie Research?'

Jen shook her head. 'I'm surprised you have to ask. Where do you normally go if you want to find something out?'

Anna shrugged, mystified.

Laughing, Jen leaned over and knocked gently on Anna's forehead. 'Earth to Anna! Good old Google, of course!'

Feeling somewhat inadequate, Anna watched as, once again with lightning speed, Jen called up a new browser window and tapped the words 'Capercaillie Research Limited' into the search bar. A handful of results appeared, the first of which was a link to an entry on the Companies House website. Jen clicked the text, taking them to a stark, black-on-white page with the name of the organisation at the top and various details below.

'Registered address: 84 Hendon Drive, Westerton G61,' read Jen, following the words on the screen with her cursor. 'Incorporated on 23 August 1997. Sole director …'

But Anna didn't need to hear any more, or to see the words on the screen. 'Edward Hugh MacLeish,' she murmured.

Jen stroked her chin. 'Curiouser and curiouser. So what d'you make of it?'

'I don't know *what* to make of it,' Anna admitted, when she found her voice at last. 'I know Hugh did a fair bit of freelance consulting work over the years – advising governments, NGOs, think tanks, that sort of thing. I can only think he must have set up a limited company for his income from that – for tax purposes or whatever. He hadn't done that sort of work for years, though.'

'In which case, why make multiple transfers to the account over a period of months right before his death?'

'I've no idea,' said Anna, more tersely than she'd intended. She forced herself to adopt a more amenable tone. 'If the Capercaillie account belongs to Hugh, that means, presumably, we can get into it the same way we got into his Bank of Scotland account – right?'

Jen smiled indulgently. '*Waaaay* ahead of ya, babe.'

Once again, Anna took a backseat and watched as Jen bounced from screen to screen with dizzying speed, the clacking of her fingers on the keyboard providing a virtually non-stop soundtrack to her activities. It took her seconds to discover a number of visits to the NatWest banking website in the browser history, minutes to find several annual statements in Outlook, and roughly a quarter of an hour to gain access – again through a variety of dubious means which Anna preferred not to dwell on – to the account itself. Clicking through to the transaction history, they were presented with multiple incoming transfers, whose details matched those of Hugh's personal account, as well as several more, of varying amounts, from another. The sender for the latter was listed as 'Kelvingrove University Finance Office'.

'Jesus,' Anna murmured. 'So Lorraine was right. He *was* receiving expenses payments.'

'And using his account to pass the proceeds on to someone else, by the looks of it,' said Jen, pointing at the screen with her pinkie. 'Look.'

Anna's eyes ran down the list of transactions in the outgoing column. Again, they ran from October 2019 to early May 2020. They were sporadic, with a gap of roughly six weeks between the penultimate payment and the last, and the amounts varied wildly, from a few pounds to nearly three hundred. Each time, however, the outgoing amount matched the amount that had most recently been transferred from either Hugh's personal account or the university finance office, down to the last penny.

In every instance, the recipient was the same.

Ms E. Bright

Anna stared at the screen, trying to parse what she was seeing, the words blurring together as her eyes became increasingly unfocused. None of it made any sense: the shuffling of money from one account to the other, the apparent defrauding of the university, the multiple payments to the same individual … It was as if she'd entered some parallel universe – one in which the Hugh she thought she knew had been replaced by an unscrupulous money launderer who'd got himself involved in all manner of shady activities.

Slowly, Jen leaned forward towards the screen, elbow resting on the desk, massaging her chin thoughtfully.

'So, then, Ms E. Bright,' she mused, 'just who the hell *are* ya?'

PART III

CHEATING ON YOU

17

Yousef's Kitchen, a tiny Lebanese restaurant in Pollokshields on the city's Southside, had been in the Husseini family's hands since they first came to Scotland forty years ago. Farah was distantly related to the proprietor, though the precise details of the genealogy had always eluded Anna. According to Farah, it was the only place in Glasgow that did Lebanese cuisine properly, and, while Anna suspected she might have been a tiny bit biased on the subject, she herself lacked the culinary experience to mount a credible counterargument. Not that she would have anyway, and nor had she ever had cause to complain about the lavish spreads Yousef and his wife, Souad, always put on for them, each course tailored to their individual tastes.

Anna was the first to arrive, a few minutes before seven. Yousef – a short, pot-bellied man of seemingly endless good cheer – greeted her effusively at the door, lamenting how long it had been since he'd last had the pleasure of her patronage – to which Anna could only apologise over and over, invoking the pandemic as the ultimate cause of this most disagreeable state of affairs – as if, had there not been a moratorium on travel, she'd have been over every other week. Yousef took her jacket and showed her to a table near the back of the otherwise empty restaurant, where he furnished her with a glass of water and the menu, which he left for her to peruse at her leisure.

She'd left Jen continuing to trawl through the contents of Hugh's hard drive, with Jen promising to update her later that evening whether or not she discovered anything of note. Before heading out, Anna had tentatively asked whether she owed her anything, not knowing what sort of rates Jen normally commanded for this sort of work. The affronted look that had taken hold of Jen's face was both so instantaneous and so absolute that Anna immediately regretted raising the matter.

'We're *mates*,' she'd insisted, as if that was all that needed to be said. Then, when it became clear that further explanation was required, 'I'm doing this as a *favour*. Hardly counts as one if it comes with a big old price tag attached, does it?'

Anna saw her point, but she nonetheless felt inexorably guilty at the thought of Jen potentially sinking hours of her time and energy into this project with no recompense. She made a mental note to, at the very least, treat Jen to a slap-up meal before her return to Italy.

Farah was fashionably late, a tad frazzled and somewhat more demurely attired than when Anna last saw her, having added a wool cardigan on top of the sleeveless dress. Yousef and Souad came out from the kitchen to greet her, and she dutifully submitted to a succession of hugs and kisses which were most assuredly *not* compliant with the current COVID guidelines, before they escorted her over to the table to join Anna.

'I was saying to Souad – Farah, she's looking awfully thin these days,' Yousef declared, addressing Anna. 'Tell her she looks thin.'

'They *both* do,' said Souad firmly, sparing Anna the dilemma of having to decide whose nose she was going to have to put out of joint – Farah's or Yousef's. 'Girls these days, they're all far too skinny. No meat on their bones at all. It's such a shame.'

'We'll feed you both up,' promised Yousef, hands cupping his own formidable gut as if to advertise the intended result. 'No customer leaves Yousef's Kitchen without a full stomach.'

And, on that unwavering promise, he and Souad headed through to the back to continue with the preparations.

'Ouf!' Farah exhaled, once they were alone. 'I thought the day would never end. I hadn't time for lunch, so I apologise in advance if I eat like a pig tonight.'

'I fancy I'll be joining you at the trough,' said Anna with a smile. Late-morning elevenses at Clarissa's with Lorraine Hammond already seemed an eternity ago.

'Then we'll be happy little hogs together,' Farah declared, with an air of satisfaction. 'Now, tell me all your news.'

And so, as they tucked into the first of the night's dishes, they traded accounts of the last eighteen months. Farah might well have summed up hers as *'plus ça change …'*, for it quickly became apparent that her position at the university was as precarious, and her workload as intolerable, as ever. The industrial action at the end of 2019 had won the teaching associates a handful of minor concessions but few meaningful changes, and the slight increase in their salaries had ultimately been paid for by an across-the-board 5% reduction in their numbers, with further dismissals occurring during lockdown, when it became apparent that the move to remote learning afforded an opportunity for the powers that be to embark on a process of what was euphemistically referred to as 'rationalisation'. Farah was one of the lucky ones: several of her contemporaries were now either out of a job or else had subsequently been hired back, once restrictions eased and it turned out they were needed after all, on lower salaries than they'd previously been paid.

'It just goes to show,' she said, waving her fork airily, 'there are always people who see in each crisis an opportunity.'

'You're not kidding,' said Anna grimly. 'They don't call it disaster capitalism for nothing. Still,' she went on, forcing herself to sound cheerful, 'all in all, everyone's coping? How's the old department getting along?'

She still thought of it in those terms, even though the Department of Law and Social Sciences had long since ceased to exist as an official entity.

'They're all well, yes,' said Farah, matching Anna's tone of somewhat strained buoyancy. 'Rosanna had another baby – she's just returned from maternity leave – and you know about Dr Hennessy being made Reader.'

'And Simon? He still keeping the show on the road?'

Simon Basford, a senior lecturer in his forties with a reputation for not rocking the boat, had been appointed acting course director of the criminology programme in Anna's absence – an uninspired but, on balance, probably safe choice.

'Yes, he makes sure we stay on the straight and narrow,' said Farah. 'He asked me to tell you he continues to keep your seat warm.' She accompanied this with an encouraging smile that was clearly meant to cue Anna up to announce her imminent return.

Anna looked at Farah, at the expectation and hope in her continuing smile, and felt nothing but regret. She hated the thought of putting a blight on their evening, but she realised that to lie to Farah, even by omission, to give her false hope, would be far crueller.

She set down her fork. 'Farah ... I don't think I'm coming back.'

For a moment, Farah's smile lingered, as if she hadn't understood what Anna had said – or didn't *want* to understand it. Then reality set in, and her smile abruptly faded.

'What?' she said, in a small voice. 'Why?'

Anna sighed. 'Several reasons – most of which you can probably guess for yourself. A lot of them have to do with The Reckoning and the way things were handled back then. I mean, you have to admit – there *are* certain perks to not having to look colleagues in the eye who've seen pictures of you naked.

'But it's about more than that,' she said quickly – as if that, on its own, wasn't sufficient justification. 'It's about what the job's become – and what *I* want out of life. I've been offered a permanent position in Perugia, and I reckon I'm going to take it. It'll mean going back to working full-time, to being an administrator again ... and believe me, I have *not* missed those things ... but I'd have a ring-fenced research budget, adequate resources, genuine autonomy ... plus, there'd be certain people I'd no longer have to deal with.'

'You mean people like Fraser,' said Farah. Her tone was husky but at the same time gently understanding.

Anna let her silence do the talking.

'You built the criminology programme from virtually nothing,' Farah insisted, a ring of desperation in her voice.

'That's a *slight* exaggeration.'

'Do you really want to walk away from that? Your ... your legacy? You won't miss any of it?'

'No,' said Anna heavily. Then, 'And yes. There's a part of me that wants to just say "to hell with the lot of it" and start again with a clean slate. Of *course* there are things I'll miss. There are things I miss *now*.' She reamed them off one by one, counting on her fingers. 'I miss tablet, I miss films at the GFT on wet Saturday afternoons, I miss the colour of the leaves in Victoria Park in autumn, I miss spaghetti carbonara at La Lanterna – which, by the way, is *seriously* ironic given that I've only gone and moved to Italy ...'

She almost went on, then realised she'd got so carried away she'd skipped right past the single most obvious point in Glasgow's favour. She let her shoulders sag. Gave a soft, affectionate smile.

'I miss all these things, but most of all I miss the people I care about.'

The fond, bittersweet look that passed between them left neither of them in any doubt as to who, specifically, she was referring.

'So *stay*,' said Farah, making it sound so simple in her earnestness.

Anna sighed. 'There's a world in which Kelvingrove is the more attractive option. A world where I get to work part-time, with a full research budget and no managerial responsibilities, and no Fraser Taggart. But this isn't it. I've done all I can here. It's time for me to move on.'

Farah said nothing, her expression remaining one of deep unhappiness. Yousef, who'd clearly been hovering for some time, not wanting to intrude, chose this moment to swoop in to replace their empty plates with fresh ones.

'I want you to promise you won't say anything to anyone,' said Anna, as soon as he was gone. 'Not yet. I'm not ready for people to know.'

'Of course!' said Farah instantly. 'Absolutely. Your secret is secure.'

She'd tried to hide it, but Anna had seen the look of hope that kindled in Farah's eyes as she immediately latched onto the possibility, however faint, that the decision might not be fully set in stone. That there was still time for her to undergo a change of heart. She decided there was nothing to be gained from disabusing Farah of that notion, so instead she smiled gratefully and scooped a forkful of lentils and rice into her mouth.

Farah blew out a bright, breezy breath, as if the matter had been fully resolved to her satisfaction, then folded her hands on top of the table and pasted on an eager smile.

'Come on, then. Tell me what you've been doing since you got back.'

. . .

In the end, Anna told her absolutely everything. Everything, that is, except for her encounter with Vasilico and their ensuing alleyway fuck. There were some things you just didn't share – not even with your closest friends. She hadn't originally planned to come clean about her mission – Hugh, she felt, deserved to be able to count on her discretion. But, in the moment, she realised that, until now, she'd overlooked Farah as a potentially rich mine of information. Farah and Hugh's subject areas might have been different, but they were, as Fraser had been so fond of telling them, 'all one big family' within the School of Social and Political Sciences, and Anna had often marvelled, in the past, at Farah's almost preternatural knack for knowing everything that was going on within the university, thanks to her connections within the wider TA body.

So she told her all about Fraser's summons, the task he'd set her, and what she'd found out so far – right up to her and Jen's discovery of the Capercaillie Research account and the multiple transfers in and out of it.

'Lorraine Hammond said there were rumours he'd been making fraudulent expenses claims,' she said. 'Have *you* heard anything along those lines?'

Farah sat, brows pursed. 'There were *rumours*,' she said carefully. 'I don't know whether there was any truth behind them. But Gail Coburn from the finance office repeated them to me, and ...' She shrugged. '... she would be well-placed to know if they were accurate, yes?'

Anna agreed that she would. 'All the transfers out of the Capercaillie account were to a Ms E. Bright. Does that name mean anything to you?'

Farah thought for a long moment, during which Yousef deftly swooped in to refill their glasses.

'I wonder if that could be *Libby*,' she said eventually, frowning as if she couldn't quite believe it.

'Who?'

'You know – *Libby*.' She said the name again, as if Anna

had simply misheard. Then, realising Anna wasn't merely being obtuse, 'Sorry. Probably you *don't*. Know this, I mean. A lot of it happened after you left. There was a sociology student, Elizabeth Bright – Libby. She dropped out last summer, less than twelve months into her doctorate, despite finishing top of her class in her undergraduate degree and winning the MacArthur Prize the year before. It was quite a big scandal at the time,' she added, as if she still couldn't quite believe word of this hadn't reached Anna in Perugia. 'Certain people were left with very red faces.'

'Certain people?'

'Those who decided that she should receive a full scholarship from the school.'

Anna gave a silent 'Oh' of understanding.

'And she was Hugh's PhD student?' she said after a moment, still unable to shake the feeling that she was being somewhat slow on the uptake.

Farah shook her head. 'That's the part that's most strange. They had nothing to do with one another, as far as I know – at least, not in respect of her doctorate.'

'Who were her supervisors?'

'Stuart Colgan and Leila Hobart. You know Leila? She has her office next to the TAs' room.'

Anna shook her head. The name seemed vaguely familiar, but she wouldn't have been able to put a face to it.

'One moment.' Farah got out her phone and began tapping the screen. 'I'll call her for you.'

Before Anna could protest – say that she wasn't ready; that she needed time to prepare her line of questioning – Farah had the phone to her ear and was waiting for the call to connect.

'*Allo*, Leila?'

A pause, then she raised her voice against the pounding music Anna could hear leaking out of the earpiece.

'Leila, it's Farah. Are you free to talk?'

She glanced at Anna; mouthed what was presumably

meant as an explanation for the noise but which Anna's lip-reading skills weren't up to deciphering.

'I'm here with a colleague,' she continued, voice still raised. 'Anna Scavolini. You know Anna?'

She gave Anna an amusingly triumphal look, clearly intended to convey that Leila did indeed remember her.

'Anna wants to talk to you,' she said.

And then, before Anna had time to either object or give any thought whatsoever to what she was going to say, Farah was thrusting the phone towards her. Rather reluctantly, Anna put it to her ear.

'Hello? Leila?'

'Anna, hi. Listen, you'll have to speak up. It's absolutely mental in here, and I can't exactly ask the band to turn down the music.'

Due to the need for both of them to repeat themselves multiple times at various junctures, the entire process ended up taking far longer than it should have, but, in the end, Anna and Leila agreed to rendezvous outside the Kibble Palace in the Botanic Gardens at 10.30 the following morning to discuss things further. Anna had a sneaking suspicion Leila hadn't properly grasped what they were meeting to talk about, her explanation having coincided with a particularly intrusive guitar solo. From a certain perspective, though, that might prove advantageous. She was far from positive Leila would have agreed to this meeting if she knew Anna planned to ask her to dish the dirt on one of her ex-students. Of course, there was no guarantee she'd cooperate once she *did* know what this was all about, but Anna knew from experience how much harder it was to refuse a request face-to-face than it was over the phone.

'Got all that, I'm guessing?' she said ruefully, handing the phone back to Farah.

Farah smiled. 'Yes. Me and half of the Southside, I think.'

'I wasn't *that* loud, was I?'

Farah's only responses were an ambivalent 'mm' and the 'so-so' hand gesture.

Anna winced. 'Sorry, Yousef,' she called, leaning over the back of her chair.

Yousef shrugged amiably from the kitchen doorway.

As Anna turned back to the table, Farah raised her eyebrows encouragingly. 'Well, this seems like progress – yes?'

'I suppose it does,' said Anna, feeling somehow reluctant to entertain the possibility.

'Well, then. Tomorrow, perhaps you find the answers you're looking for.'

'Or maybe just a whole lot more questions,' said Anna darkly.

They ended up staying there chatting until long after justice had been done to the final course, only making a move when it was approaching ten o'clock and Yousef had begun putting the empty chairs on top of the vacant tables, making his point without doing anything so crude as to explicitly tell them it was closing time. Anna knew, from past experience, that they could easily have found a late-night bar and talked for several hours more, but she was already feeling the tendrils of sleep creeping up on her, aided and abetted by a full stomach. She steered things to a conclusion with the help of a few well-placed (and not entirely feigned) yawns, and Farah, it seemed, took the hint.

'You'll be going straight to bed?' said Farah, as they emerged into the last lingering dregs of daylight. It was more an observation than a question.

'Probably,' said Anna. 'My internal clock's still running an hour ahead. Plus, I'm increasingly coming to believe there's some truth in the adage that everything goes south past the age of forty.' She gave a dry chuckle. 'You've got it all to look forward to.'

Farah gave an ironic eyeroll. 'Ah, you surprise me! I turn thirty next year and I'm still subjected to weekly interrogations by my mother about when I'm going to have the house, the kids, the mortgage – you know, all the traditional markers of adulthood.'

Anna hesitated for a moment, before concluding that, if she didn't say what was on her mind, she'd only regret it later.

'Farah ...'

'Yes?'

'You know ... you really should think about applying for lecturing positions elsewhere. I know we talked about this before, and I know you said you wanted to stay in Glasgow, but ...' Her shoulders slumped helplessly. 'Well, job prospects at Kelvingrove aren't looking any more hopeful now than they did eighteen months ago, are they? And I just worry that, the longer you leave it, the harder it's going to be to ...'

'Pull myself out of the shit?'

'That's not an entirely inapt metaphor.'

For a moment, Farah didn't respond. She appeared to be studying her toes intently, as if they held the answer to this particular quandary. Finally, she lifted her head to face Anna.

'Did I tell you about the hoops Émile and I were made to jump through after Brexit to get settled status?'

Anna shook her head.

'Well, it was exhausting and it was demeaning and ... and I don't intend for all that to have been for nothing,' she concluded hotly.

Anna was about to say she understood, then realised it would have been a lie – or at least profoundly disingenuous. She'd been able to waltz straight into both a job that had been tailor-made for her and indefinite leave to remain in Italy on the strength of her EU passport. How could she hope to put herself in Farah's shoes?

'I hear what you're saying,' she said instead, 'but, you know, there *is* such a thing as the sunk cost fallacy.'

Farah thought about this for a moment, then huffed out a long sigh and faced Anna with a tired, strained smile.

'Well then, perhaps you'll put in a good word for me in Perugia.'

Anna felt a pang of sadness at those words. They both knew it was far from as simple as that; that one didn't simply walk into a job on the strength of a recommendation from a colleague who'd only just got a foot in the door herself. But she was determined not to let the grim forces of reality spoil the end of a most enjoyable evening, so, instead, she chose to return the smile and continue the charade.

'I might just do that,' she said.

18

They went their separate ways, with the promise of a further catch-up at some point next week, this time by phone, once Anna was back in Italy. In keeping with these wary, uncertain times, there was no farewell hug, but Farah did give Anna's hand an unexpectedly insistent squeeze, telling her not to rush into any rash decisions and emphasising that she was there if Anna wanted to talk anything through with her.

Anna caught a train into town and then another out to Hyndland. As she relaxed in a seat by the window, fighting the rocking carriage's attempts to lull her to sleep, her mind kept returning to Farah's employment situation. It frustrated her beyond all measure to see her protégé's career continuing to languish. It was in Farah's nature not to rock the boat; to take on all the work that was asked of her and more, driven by an unquenchable desire to be helpful. And rather than being rewarded, she was instead seen by certain individuals as a pushover; people who saw her willingness to go the extra mile as an opportunity to dump yet more work on her, all the while paying her less than she was due. And, though she told herself the people who deserved the lion's share of the blame were the ones in lofty positions who thought nothing of exploiting another person's goodwill to save a buck or two, Anna knew that, in having taken her extended sabbatical, she was partly responsible for the impossible workload with which Farah now had to contend. Farah, who'd taken on most of Anna's postgraduate students and all her teaching commitments because it had made sense to give them to someone who already knew the material inside out. That, she supposed, was the price you paid for being such a diligent understudy.

'The next stop is Partick,' the robotic voice intoned as the train continued its westward crawl. Anna felt her chin nodding to her chest. Her eyes closing.

Suddenly, she was jolted awake by the ringing of her phone. Drowsy and disoriented, she fumbled in her bag for it and checked the caller ID.

'Jen?'

'Howya, secret squirrel? Not interrupting yer beauty sleep, I hope?'

'No, not at all,' said Anna, blinking forcefully and sitting up straighter in an attempt to banish the lingering drowsiness. 'What's up?'

'Figured you were due an update on my deep dive into the contents of Hugh's drive. You OK to take this now? I can call back later if it's a bad time.'

'No, no, it's fine,' Anna insisted, getting to her feet and moving to the opposite end of the carriage, away from its sole other occupant, in a bid to give herself some more privacy. 'What have you found?'

'Not a whole lot, is God's honest truth. He led a fairly uneventful life, your man. Most of what's on there is work-related stuff, plus snaps of his holidays to Prague and Lausanne, the odd bit of Mozart he downloaded from iTunes … I've had a quick nosey through his emails; found nothing to set alarm bells ringing, 'less you regard a major spam infestation as proof of an underlying character flaw. Put it this way:

there's nothing here that points to him being involved with any international money-laundering cartels.'

'Don't sound *too* disappointed.'

'Hey, I'm just a lowly tech-head. I get my kicks where I can. Oh – while we're at it, I also found he had another savings account with Santander. Balance, as of today, is a paltry £3,017. I'm not saying it's nothing, but not exactly a comfortable little nest egg to retire on, right? End of the day, from what I can make out, old Hugh just wasn't that hot at handling his finances.'

The train pulled into Partick and came to a juddering standstill. The carriage's sole other passenger remained seated.

'That's about as far as I've got so far,' said Jen. 'I tried to get into E. Bright's bank account too, but that was a total bust. Doesn't help that I don't have a clone of *her* hard drive to comb through, but even if we *weren't* faced with that not-so-minor handicap, I fancy I'd still've been on a hiding to nothing. My usual bag of tricks – data breaches, reused passwords and the like – was as much use as a urinal in a nunnery. Whoever she is, she's a whole lot more security-conscious than old man Hugh ever was.'

The train set off once more on what, for Anna, was the final leg of the journey. In the three minutes or so that it took to reach Hyndland, she filled Jen in both on what she'd learned from Farah and the meeting she'd arranged with Leila Hobart for the following morning.

'Well, aren't *you* the busy beaver!' Jen said once she'd finished. 'The plot's thickening nicely. All of it, of course, begs the obvious question: what's an ageing professor doing paying off a young female student to the tune of several thousand quid?'

'I don't know *what* to think,' said Anna, doing her best to ignore Jen's rather pointed reference to the age and gender of the student in question, and the places in her mind to which this led. 'I'm hoping Leila might be able to shed some light, even if it's just a steer on the current whereabouts of this Libby character.'

The train came to a stop at Hyndland station. Phone still clamped to her ear, Anna got off and made for the footbridge out of the station.

'So listen,' Jen went on as she climbed the steps, 'I reckon I've given this lark about as much time as I can justify. For now, anyroad. I mean, not to sound like a filthy, avaricious capitalist, but if I leave 'em hanging any longer, my paying clients're gonna start thinking I've fallen out of love with 'em.'

'Of course. You've already gone well beyond what I could reasonably ask. Time for me to get my skates on and do some of the heavy lifting.'

'See, that's what I like about you, Anna: you know when not to take the piss. But I was gonna say, keep me posted, willya? This old riddle's well and truly got my brainbox buzzing. I'm dying to see where it all leads.'

Anna followed the footpath up to towards Great Western Road, the trees to her right sighing in the gentle breeze. As she drew within sight of the Great Western Inn, her eyes strayed to the other side of the road, and to Kelvinside, with its warren of upmarket residential streets. The Taggarts lived in that direction, she remembered. Unless he was running *seriously* late, Fraser should be back from his trip by now. She hadn't forgotten her plan to confront him about his failure to inform her about the business with Hugh's expenses claims.

She checked the time on her phone. It was a quarter to eleven, and by rights she really should have turned in some time ago. Her body clock was, after all, still calibrated to Central Eastern Time. But the brisk walk from the station had reinvigorated her to the extent that she was no longer in any danger of nodding off on her feet. More to the point, now that she had the matter firmly lodged in her mind, she knew she wasn't going to be able to switch off till she'd spoken to Fraser about the expenses ... and found out if there was anything *else* he'd neglected to tell her.

She made her decision. Bed could wait.

Continuing past the hotel, she crossed the road and headed up into Kelvinside.

19

Fraser's house was a rather impressive-looking sandstone semi on Kirklee Road, just north of the Botanic Gardens. As she headed up the short footpath to the front door, it occurred to Anna that she had no idea what time the Taggarts normally went to bed. They could be fast asleep for all she knew. Still, she was here now, and she wasn't going to lose too much sleep herself if she ended up rousing Fraser from his stupor. She rang the bell.

The door was opened by a skinny, lank-haired girl in her mid-teens, wearing tartan joggers, a Slipknot T-shirt and a borderline obscene quantity of kohl. She leaned heavily against the door, regarding Anna with a baleful expression.

'Hi. It's … Matilda, isn't it?' said Anna, hoping she'd got the girl's name right. 'Um … is your dad about?'

Looking for all the world like this was the most unreasonable imposition to be asked of anyone, ever, Matilda tilted her head over her shoulder and hollered in a loud and unexpectedly gravelly voice:

'*DAAAAD!* It's that woman you used to work with. The short one,' she added, with a rather pointed look at Anna.

After about twenty seriously awkward seconds, during

which Matilda stared indolently at Anna while Anna focused her attention on the brass plaque by the door engraved with the words 'THE TAGGARTS', Fraser appeared by his daughter's side, in his chinos and silk shirt, the top button undone.

'Ah,' he said, sounding a little perplexed. 'Anna.'

Her job done, Matilda slid back inside the house and out of view, giving a convincing impression of an unusually sardonic human slug.

Fraser regarded Anna with a somewhat bemused smile, clearly a little discombobulated by her unscheduled appearance.

'To what do I owe the occasion?'

'Can we talk?'

The bluntness of her tone seemed to focus Fraser's mind. He only hesitated for a moment before giving a short nod of acquiescence.

'I'll get my jacket.'

They set off in the direction of the Botanic Gardens, with Whisky, Fraser's overly excitable labradoodle, in tow. As the woolly mutt trotted on ahead, nose to the ground, tail swishing frantically, Anna and Fraser walked side by side at a more sedate pace.

It quickly transpired that Fraser was disappointed to realise Anna hadn't solved the entire mystery and come here to present it to him in a neatly wrapped package. Not feeling particularly disposed towards coddling him, she got straight to the point of her visit.

'I've heard from multiple sources today that Hugh had been falsifying expenses claims – and that, apparently, you were perfectly aware of this fact.' She looked at him expectantly. 'Well? Is it true?'

Fraser continued to walk on, avoiding Anna's gaze. She took his silence as all the confirmation she needed.

'You didn't think this might have *some* bearing on the very matter you tasked me with looking into?'

Fraser visibly winced, but still didn't deign to respond.

She sighed in exasperation. 'For God's sake, Fraser! Is all this just a game to you? Did you think it'd be a jolly wheeze to see how much of my own time and energy I'd have to waste finding out what you already knew?'

Fraser responded with a haughty scoff. 'Of course not!'

'Then why the hell didn't you say anything?'

'I had my reasons.'

'Well, I'm dying to hear what they are.'

'IT WAS BECAUSE OF HOW IT MADE HIM LOOK, ALL RIGHT?'

Anna stopped in her tracks and stared at him, completely wrongfooted by his sudden paroxysm. Fraser, too, seemed shocked by his own outburst. He glanced around quickly, as if making sure there was no one else in the vicinity who might have heard him. There was no response except for the light rustle of leaves in the wind and the excited snuffling of Whisky, a few metres ahead.

'I think you'd better explain, hadn't you?' said Anna quietly.

Fraser sighed and ran a hand roughly over his face. 'Come on,' he muttered, and continued along the road towards the park.

'At the start of May last year, someone from the finance office drew my attention to an anomaly pertaining to a sizeable claim submitted late the previous year for travel expenses to a conference at University College London. There *was* no conference at UCL on the day in question. The claim was in the name of a researcher going by the name of Penny Black. I did some digging. There was no Penny Black on the student register, and I could find no trace of her anywhere online – or, at any rate, no one with that name who credibly matched the profile of a sociology researcher doing work for Kelvingrove University. So I asked Finance to send me copies of this and any other claims submitted by this Penny Black.

'It turned out there were over a dozen of them, most of them travel expenses and all for varying amounts. The total value ran to over a thousand pounds.' He paused. 'Every last one of them was countersigned by Hugh.'

This time, it was Anna's turn to be reduced to uneasy silence. They crossed the Ha'penny Bridge and entered the park. Whisky disappeared into the trees, nose to ground.

'I procrastinated for ages about what to do,' Fraser continued. 'I refused to believe Hugh was on the take. For the longest time, I tried to convince myself there was a perfectly rational explanation for all of this. But if there *was* one, I couldn't for the life of me see it – though not for lack of trying, believe me.

'If we'd still been in the office it would have been easy enough to make some covert enquiries. Ask him casually in passing if he was having money problems or what have you. But we'd all been sent home, and, when Zoom and email are your only means of communication, it's not so straightforward. As it is, the last time I saw him face to face was before lockdown was called.' He sighed. 'And then, before I had the chance to put the matter to him, he took his own life.'

He fell silent. They turned north at the fork in the path just beyond the bridge, following the river upstream. The darkness, and the trees, seemed to press in on Anna from all sides, making her wish they'd remained among the houses and streetlights instead of coming into the park. Almost without realising she was doing it, she traced the contours of the panic alarm on her wrist, reminding herself of the location of the activation button.

'Shouldn't you call him?' she said – more to break the silence than anything.

'Hmm?'

'The dog.'

'Oh, he'll come back on his own. Knows he won't get his bedtime Bonio till he does.'

Anna nodded as if this all made perfect sense.

They walked on for another minute or so. Gradually, their pace slowed until, seemingly by mutual agreement, they came to a halt.

'You should have told me,' Anna said.

Fraser's shoulders slumped. He gave Anna a helpless look, his expression one of deep pain.

'I just didn't want you to think less of him.'

As excuses went, it was deeply inadequate, and the apologetic tone in which it was delivered indicated that he knew this well. Anna considered asking him what he *thought* would happen if she started looking into the circumstances of Hugh's death, but there seemed little point. They were where they were, and excoriating him after the fact would accomplish nothing besides giving her a brief feeling of moral superiority.

'Is there anything else you haven't seen fit to mention?' she asked instead. 'Anything else that might have a bearing on the case?'

She was anticipating a swift denial, but she saw, from the pained spasm that passed over Fraser's features, that there was indeed more to come.

'Fraser?'

He turned to her, arms spread wide in a gesture of surrender. 'All right. Cards on the table. I'd had my concerns about Hugh for some time – before all this came to light, I mean. Several of us had.'

'What do you mean?'

'Just this: that, in the final few months before the restructuring, back when he was still head of department, there was a broad consensus that he'd taken his eye off the ball with a vengeance. He was constantly distracted, missing appointments, failing to carry out the basic functions of the role he was being paid to do. He used to turn up to meetings smelling of alcohol, for God's sake!

'You were on sabbatical at the time,' he added a touch defensively, 'so you didn't see what the rest of us saw. But it was plain to all of us that the man was no longer giving the job his undivided attention. The entire senior management team felt it would be better for all concerned – including Hugh himself – if he was transitioned to a position with less responsibility.'

'Yes, I'm sure his wellbeing was at the forefront of your mind,' retorted Anna.

She knew it sounded petty and vindictive, but she couldn't help herself. When all was said and done, Hugh had been her friend – someone who, throughout her tenure at Kelvingrove, she'd always felt she could count on to have her back. The thought of Fraser and the university management plotting against him and usurping him while she was conveniently out of the picture was almost too much to bear.

'I know perfectly well what you think of me,' Fraser snapped. 'That's your prerogative. But know this: I highly doubt Hugh had more of a staunch defender in that place than me. You weren't there for the meetings when I stuck up for him, made excuses for him, did everything I could to save him from having to lose face.'

Anna said nothing. She had no idea whether he was telling the truth or just trying to save face himself. Like he said, she wasn't there. She still didn't trust Fraser as far as she could throw him, but there was an earnestness in his tone that made it difficult not to take his words at face value.

'If you really want to know,' Fraser went on, 'the research funding was my idea. Something to make him feel like he was doing something worthwhile while removing him from the day-to-day running of the school. No one ever expected it to amount to anything. At worst, we assumed he'd spend the next eighteen months faffing around, accomplishing nothing, at which point the money set aside for it would be recouped and dispersed to more worthwhile endeavours. That's why I was so surprised to discover he was spending it willy-nilly.' He paused, then added, rather tentatively, 'You haven't got to the bottom of what he was doing with it all, have you?'

'Not yet,' said Anna.

She decided, there and then, to keep what she'd discovered about Libby Bright and the Capercaillie Research account to herself – at least until she had a clearer picture of what had really been going on. Fraser was hardly in a position to complain. It wasn't as if he had a leg to stand on after what he'd withheld from *her*.

'And you're sure that's everything?' she asked again. 'There's nothing else you might have overlooked?'

'That's everything.'

He said it with such intensity that she found she had little choice other than to believe him.

'In that case,' she said, 'I'm going to need you to forward me copies of all the Penny Black expenses claims.'

'I'll do it the moment I get home,' said Fraser, clearly eager to make amends. 'Where is that dog?' He made a show of looking around. Whisky!' He gave a loud, trilling whistle. 'Whi-iiis-keeeeey!'

There was a sound of trotting feet in the undergrowth and Whisky emerged from the shadows, tail wagging and tongue lolling.

'What have *you* been getting up to, then?' Fraser enquired, addressing the dog as if it understood every word. 'Actually, on second thoughts, I should know better than to ask.' He bent down to reattach the lead.

'I'll leave you to it, then,' said Anna. 'You won't forget to send those forms?'

'Yes, yes, of course. Consider it done.'

'One other thing. Those dots in Hugh's diary.'

Fraser looked at her blankly. 'Which dots?'

'Never mind.' His response had told her this was not a line

worth pursuing further with him. 'Also, you don't happen to know what became of his diary from the following year, do you?'

Fraser shook his head. 'I hunted for it high and low. Not a trace of it. Perhaps he took it home with him?'

'Perhaps.'

She turned to go.

'Oh, and Anna ... ?'

She halted in her tracks. Turned to face him, trying not to look as impatient as she felt.

'You'll stick around to see this through, won't you? I know how much you hate leaving a job unfinished.'

It was such a transparent effort to manipulate her that she almost laughed in his face. But, with a considerable effort, she resisted the temptation.

'I'll be here for a couple more days,' she said instead. 'If, in that time, I get to the bottom of what Hugh was mixed up in, I assure you, you'll be hearing from me about it.'

Fraser dipped his head in acknowledgement. It was too dark now to see clearly, but she thought she caught a flicker of a triumphant smile on his lips, and a fresh wave of anger bubbled up inside her. Before it could find its way to the surface, she spun on her heel and strode off into the night, leaving Fraser and his miscreant dog to find their own way home.

20

Saturday 14 August

She slept late the following morning, coming to in a panicked lurch at ten minutes to ten. No time for either breakfast or her morning run – just a quick shower and a change into the last of the outfits she'd brought with her. Making a mental note to swing by one of the numerous clothes shops in the West End before the day was out, she hurried downstairs and set off for her 10.30 appointment with Leila Hobart. En route, she hopped on a number 6 bus heading in the same direction as her – an unexpected boon, and one that allowed her to arrive at the Kibble Palace, on the eastern edge of the Botanic Gardens, with a couple of minutes to spare.

She'd got back to the hotel the previous night to find that Fraser, true to his word, had forwarded her the expenses claims she'd requested. 'Penny Black's' handwriting bore a striking resemblance to that found in Hugh's diary. Most of the claims were for car mileage – which, it occurred to Anna, would be by far the easiest type of expense to claim fraudulently if one felt so inclined, given that there was no way of proving you'd actually driven the distance claimed ... or, for that matter, driven at all. It just didn't make any sense. The Hugh she'd known would never have done anything like this. And yet, there it all was in black and white, down to his distinctive but illegible scrawl as the authorising signatory.

Before finally turning in, she'd rung Matteo to update him on her travel plans. She could tell he wasn't best pleased to be roused at what, she'd belatedly realised, must have been well past midnight for him, and even less so when she'd told him she'd be staying in Glasgow for 'another day or two' – a rather dishonest effort on her part to imply that there was still some possibility of her joining them before the weekend was out. He didn't actually *say* he was annoyed, but she heard it in his voice clearly enough, and certainly in his rather pointed remark that Jack had asked 'When's Mummy coming?' on several occasions over the course of the day. She'd rung off, feeling a curious mixture of irritation and guilt – the latter only amplified by her belatedly remembering about her antics in the alleyway several hours earlier.

The purr of an approaching motor vehicle drew her back to the present moment. She turned from the sprawling glasshouse with its collection of rare plants to see a figure trundling along the footpath towards her in an electric wheelchair.

'Anna!' she called, raising her hand in a wave. 'It's me – Leila.'

Anna wasn't sure why, but for some reason she'd always assumed Leila Hobart would bear something of a resemblance to Farah: slender, dark-haired and fine-featured, with a vaguely 'Parisian beatnik' air to her wardrobe. Instead, the woman now cruising towards her was short and squarish, sporting a blonde bowl cut and a polka-dotted jumpsuit. She also hadn't expected her to be a wheelchair user. Not that it mattered, but, all told, the multiple discrepancies between the image Anna had held in her head and the one now facing her were so extreme that it took her a moment to reconcile them.

'Leila!' she said, hoping she'd successfully masked her surprise. 'Thanks for coming. How are you?'

'Bloody knackered!' said Leila cheerfully, bringing her chair to a standstill just shy of Anna's toes. 'I didn't get in till nearly two and I was still absolutely buzzing so of *course* sleep wasn't on the agenda. My first gig since BC.'

Anna looked at her blankly.

'You know – Before COVID.'

'Oh.'

'Funny, isn't it, how that's become the prism through which we now view everything? Like before indoor plumbing or the Berlin Wall coming down.' She gave Anna a bright, expectant look. 'So. How d'you wanna play this? We could go for a stroll, or we could find a nice park bench for you if you'd prefer to put your feet up.'

Realising she probably looked like she'd just staggered out of bed, Anna opted for the stroll in order to save face. They set off, Leila adjusting the speed of her chair to match Anna's stride as they followed the north-westerly curve of the wide main footpath.

'So, what is it you wanted to talk about?' said Leila. 'I mean, don't get me wrong – I'm always game for a blether, me, but from what I was able to make out on the phone – which wasn't much, I'll grant you – it all sounded a bit cloak and dagger.'

'I suppose it is,' said Anna. 'Maybe. It's about one of your former PhD students. Libby Bright?'

Leila's demeanour immediately grew warier. 'Ah. Yes. Well, *there's* a name to conjure with.'

Anna kept walking, watching Leila out of the corner of her eye as she waited for her to elaborate.

'Truthfully, she wasn't really *my* student as such. I was just the second supervisor – there to play devil's advocate; to be good cop or bad cop as the situation required. Right from the start, she was Stuart's little project.' She turned to Anna. 'Why d'you ask about her?'

'Oh, only because her name came up in relation to a separate matter I've been looking into,' said Anna, feigning nonchalance. 'I want to establish whether it's just a red herring or something I should be paying attention to.'

Leila said nothing, waiting for her to explain herself. It was a technique Anna used from time to time herself, especially on students who were being evasive, and it unnerved her slightly to have the tables turned on her like this.

'Farah told me she came top of her class,' she said, ignoring the question implicit in Leila's silence. 'That she was awarded full funding for a PhD, only to drop out before the end of her first year. I've got the bare bones of the story. I was hoping you might be able to fill in some of the details.'

They continued along the path, Leila giving Anna serious side-eye. Anna could tell Leila viewed this lack of candidness as more than a little unfair given what she was expecting in return.

'All right,' said Leila at length. 'Most of this is fairly common knowledge anyway, so it's not like I'm breaking anyone's confidence. Truth be told, I always thought she was a bit of an odd duck. Capital L loner; didn't seem to have any real friends among the student body. I never got much of a feel for her background or what had drawn her to study sociology. She mentioned once that she was from Dunoon originally, and I got the impression there wasn't much of a relationship with the parents.

'She wasn't really on my radar initially. I mean, looking back on it, I realise now that I must have taught her in a couple of classes at undergrad level, but we'd never exchanged so much as a word before she started the PhD – or, if we had, it was so unmemorable I'd blanked it from my mind completely.

'But Stuart thought very highly of her. She wrote her fourth-year dissertation on social interaction – which, if you'll recall, is his bread and butter. It was on the strength of it that he'd started pushing her to do a PhD – and then, when she aced her finals, that clinched it. I did read it at one point,' she clarified, not uncharitably. 'Well, skimmed it. And I'll grant you, it was a first-rate bit of work. Streets better than *most* undergraduate dissertations I've come across. But the thing is, I never got the impression she was the *wunderkind* Stuart made her out to be. She was pretty unremarkable, face to face, if that's not too blunt a way of putting it.'

'How so?' said Anna.

'Taciturn, uncommunicative, almost surly – like she resented having to perform the standard social niceties, know what I mean? Our supervision meetings tended to be a bit like pulling teeth – even *before* we went into lockdown and she started her downward spiral.' She gave a philosophical shrug. 'But the written work was always top notch – at least to begin with – and that seemed to be what Stuart cared about. And I said to myself, "You're riding shotgun on this, Hobart. This is *his* rodeo. No sense rocking the boat."' She glanced at Anna. 'Sorry – was that a mixed metaphor?'

'You said she went into a downward spiral during lockdown? What did you mean by that?'

'To be fair to her, it's hardly unheard of. Lockdown did a number on a lot of students – even the really strong, self-motivated ones. Some of them just aren't cut out for flying solo, not having the buzz of the campus and the day-to-day interaction with their peers. Though, in my experience, it's generally the outgoing ones that don't cope well with remote learning. I mean, stands to reason, right?'

Anna nodded.

'Libby, though – she always struck me as the sort of person who'd be perfectly happy shut up in her room for months on end, not having to interact with other humans.'

'But she wasn't?'

'Whatever was really going on with her, her work nosedived, and I mean *nosedived* – pretty much from the moment everything shut down. At first, she stalled us, saying she'd been poorly and that she needed more time to submit the chapter she was working on. Which we gave her, obviously,' she added hastily, as if it counted as an important point in their favour. 'It was a crazy, mixed-up time for everyone. Seemed churlish to expect her to adhere to some arbitrary deadline when we didn't even know if any of us would still be *alive* in six months' time.

'But more and more time passed, with little, if any, evidence to show she was actually working on anything. She kept promising us she almost had a draft ready; that she just needed a bit more time to finesse it. Eventually, even Stuart ran out of excuses for her. He told her, "Just send us what you have, even if it's a bit rough around the edges. That's the whole point of a first draft."'

There was a brief pause in Leila's account as Anna stepped aside to allow an elderly couple, fully masked despite the outdoor setting, to pass them in the opposite direction. They were in the northwestern portion of the park now, the children's playpark to their left, the River Kelvin obscured by the line of trees to their right. Leila waited till the couple were out of earshot before continuing.

'What she submitted, I'm sorry to say, would have been embarrassing coming from a first-year undergrad: a barely coherent string of poorly thought-out arguments and chunks of text that were obviously copy-pasted from published sources with the bare minimum of rewording. Well, after Stuart and I had a confab about it, we scheduled a Zoom call with Libby – and even *that* took some doing, she made it that hard for us to pin her down.'

She gave an incredulous laugh. 'I mean, I'm not exactly sure what she assumed we'd think she was *doing*, locked up indoors day and night just like the rest of us. But eventually we managed to get her on Zoom, and, not to put too fine a point on it, we asked her to account for herself. At first, she trotted out the same line about having been unwell, but she could tell we weren't buying it, so then she went on to spin this yarn about a personal bereavement.'

She glanced up at Anna with a grimace, as if she knew how what she was about to say would make her sound.

'I hope this doesn't seem unduly callous, but I didn't believe a word of it. I mean, I *might* have, if she hadn't already tried to sucker us with the "illness" line, only to pivot when it became clear that excuse wasn't cutting the mustard. Hell, it's not like the finite nature of our existence wasn't on all our minds at the time. But it was so insincere, so over-the-top. She sat there, choking and gasping and trying her hardest to squeeze out a tear, then glancing at her webcam as if she was checking to see whether we were buying it. And bear in mind, this was someone who, until that point, had barely emoted at all.' She shook her head. 'The whole thing was an act, and nothing anyone says will ever convince me otherwise.'

Anna said nothing, though she privately wondered which of them Leila was trying harder to convince.

'So how did you respond?' she asked, after a moment.

Leila shrugged. 'We took her at her word. What else could we do? Even if neither of us was buying it – and, to this day, I'm still not entirely sure what Stuart was thinking – we could hardly turn round to her and say, "Actually, we think you're full of horse manure. Got any other lines you want to try on us?" So we nodded and made sympathetic noises about how awful it was, and all the while she was begging to be given another week to rewrite the chapter.'

They were passing the Rose Garden now, following the path southwards along the park's western perimeter before it swung sharply around to the left, running parallel with Great Western Road in a more or less straight line back towards the gatehouse through which Anna had entered.

'In the end,' said Leila, 'we gave her *two* weeks. And, true to her word, she did send us a revised version of the chapter, but it was scarcely any better than the original. It was as if she didn't actually understand what was wrong with it and had just rearranged the words a bit, hoping it'd magically turn into something we'd accept.

'She staggered on through most of the summer, submitting a couple of further rewrites, which I honestly thought were getting worse rather than better. It was as if she'd forgotten everything she used to know – not just about the research topic but about the basics of stringing a sentence together.

'Well, the writing was well and truly on the wall by this stage. Obviously, next year's funding was contingent on her getting a positive review from her supervisors, and it was clear to all and sundry *that* wasn't going to happen. Stuart and I started holding crisis meetings, discussing various contingency plans, like trying to talk her into converting to a Masters – which, to be honest, is what I thought she should've been doing from the off. I was always sceptical about fast-tracking her to a PhD.

'But she beat us to the punch. The call started, and, before Stuart or myself could get a word in, she came straight out of the gate and told us she was dropping out. Not reconsidering her options, not looking to defer for six months, but throwing in the towel altogether. And she wouldn't be talked out of it. The subject of dropping down to an MPhil never even came up.'

The path began to curve northwards again, passing the site of the long-defunct underground railway station, its moss-covered ventilation shafts visible beyond the wrought-iron fence just off the path.

'If I'm being honest,' said Leila, 'I didn't try particularly hard to change her mind. I didn't see the point. It was obvious she'd made her decision. Stuart made more of an effort, but I think, deep down, he was more than just a tad relieved. I think he'd come to regard Libby as a millstone around his neck – this prize stallion he'd bet everything on, only for it to turn out to be a decrepit old nag.' She grimaced. 'Sorry. Not the most flattering comparison.'

'But at least, this time, it wasn't a mixed metaphor,' said Anna.

Leila considered this for a moment, then gave a shrug of acceptance, seemingly concluding that, on balance, this made the comparison acceptable.

They continued in silence for a while, following the gentle incline of the path up towards the Kibble Palace. They were almost back to where they'd started.

'Have you any idea what became of Libby?' Anna asked.

'Search me. I haven't heard from her since the day she told us she was dropping out. I assume she had to go out and find gainful employment in the real world.'

'I don't suppose you know if she ever made any mention of Hugh MacLeish, or vice versa?'

Leila frowned. 'Not that I know of. Why?'

'No reason,' said Anna quickly.

Leila gave her a curious look, as if she was itching to ask for an explanation, before seemingly deciding against it.

'And do you think it would be worth my while talking to Stuart?' Anna ventured after a moment. 'You know, asking him if there's anything else *he* remembers?'

Leila's lip curled dismissively. 'Doubt it. For one thing, he's off on his summer jollies at the moment. Pounding the Inca Trail to Machu Picchu, if memory serves. All right for some, eh? For another, I fancy he's going to be a whole lot less predisposed towards talking about this than I've been. Libby was *his* grand wheeze. *His* very public failure. Between you and me, I reckon he's still pretty mortified about the whole affair.'

They exchanged no further words till they once again came to a stop outside the Kibble Palace.

'Thanks for being so forthcoming with me,' said Anna. 'And sorry for dragging you out here on a Saturday morning.'

'That's all right,' said Leila cheerfully. 'I can't pretend I'd've said no to a couple of extra hours in bed, but that's on me for turning in at such a disreputable hour last night. I wish I had more of a sense of what this is all about ... but I'm guessing you have your reasons for being cagey.'

'I do,' said Anna, and left it at that.

'Well, in that case, I hope you got something useful out of our little chinwag.'

'We'll see. Thanks again.'

'See you 'round campus, right?'

Anna gave a non-committal grunt that she hoped Leila would take as a murmur of agreement and turned to go.

'Oh, Anna?'

Anna stopped in her tracks and turned to face Leila again.

'Just occurred to me – if you're dead set on tracking Libby down, you could do worse than to have a chat with Heather Fleetwood.'

'Who's she?'

'Oh, just another of the many Arts and Humanities graduates we foist on an oversaturated labour market every year,' said Leila cheerfully. 'She and Libby were contemporaries,' she explained, seeing Anna's uncomprehending expression. 'Started their PhDs at the same time. At the time, we'd recently introduced a semi-official "buddy" system for students undertaking research-based postgrad courses. We'd look to pair two students with the same subject area – you know, encourage them to hold writing sprints together, meet for regular catchups, generally support one another. Heather was the Cagney to Libby's Lacey. At least, that was the basic plan. I've no idea whether they ever got together again after the initial meet-and-greet we arranged for them. It's not like any of this was mandatory, or like Libby made a habit of cosying up to anyone. But, if by any chance the two of them stayed in touch ...' She shrugged, inviting Anna to follow this train of thought to its logical conclusion.

'Heather Fleetwood, you said? Any idea where I might find her?'

'You're in luck,' said Leila with a grin. 'She works weekends at Café Zen on Byres Road. You never know – she might be able to give you a steer. Just be warned: she can be a bit …'

'A bit what?'

Leila merely smiled enigmatically. 'Oh, you'll see.'

21

Café Zen was a noisy, bustling affair, the worthies of the West End having evidently decided it was *the* place to frequent on a Saturday morning. Anna, mask firmly attached to her face, found herself feeling decidedly ill-protected as she threaded her way through the throng of hipsters and yummy mummies, inching towards the counter. It was the first time she'd been in such a packed enclosed space since she'd flown into Glasgow on Thursday, and at least in the airport and aboard the plane, everyone else had been masked too. But you couldn't very well drink your skinny flat white mocha latte with your face covered, meaning the only people who were masked were the staff, all wearing thin cloth coverings bearing the Café Zen logo, which Anna suspected were more effective as a branding exercise than at halting the spread of infection.

Resisting the urge to hold her breath, she pushed through to the counter, where a young man with a ponytail and an eyebrow piercing was operating a coffee press.

'Excuse me!' she called over the general clamour. 'Do you know where I might be able to find Heather Fleetwood?'

The young man turned. 'Heather? Aye, she's about.'

He looked around, scanning past the sea of bobbing heads,

then shoved two fingers under his mask and blew a piercing whistle.

'Heather!'

At the far end of the shop, a tall woman in her early twenties with jet-black hair, dressed in a pleated miniskirt which showed off the elaborate network of tattoos running up her surprisingly muscular thighs, turned, a tray of empty glasses balanced on her shoulder.

'Someone here to see you!'

Heather made her way over, deftly weaving through the crowd, the tray remaining impressively level despite each twist and contortion. She came to a stop, towering over Anna – who, right now, felt every inch her five foot two – and eyeing her expectantly.

'How can I help?'

'Heather *Fleetwood*?' Anna clarified, in the distant off-chance there was more than one Heather working here.

'Do I know you?'

'We haven't met, no,' said Anna, aware that she was having to raise her voice over both the general clamour around her and the muffling effect of her mask. 'But I gather we've a mutual acquaintance. Leila Hobart? She said I'd find you here?'

'Did she now?' Heather looked nonplussed.

'She said you might have information about someone I'm trying to track down: Libby Bright.'

At that name, Heather's eyes narrowed. She continued to gaze down at Anna, her silence giving nothing away.

'Please. If there's anything at all you can tell me about her, I'd be extremely grateful.'

For several seconds, Heather's expression didn't change.

'At least order something,' she said eventually. 'That way it won't look like you're *completely* taking the piss.'

. . .

'We were both fast-tracked to the PhD circuit,' said Heather.

They were sitting at a small, round table not far from the counter, Heather perched on the edge of her chair with her legs at a ninety-degree angle, ready to make a speedy getaway. She seemed to have cleared things with her ponytail-wearing colleague, but the implication was very much that, should the need arise, she'd get back to work immediately, even if it meant abandoning their conversation mid-sentence.

''Course,' she went on, 'Libby was the one who bagged the fully funded scholarship. Benefits of having Stuart Colgan wrapped round your little finger.'

'And of coming top of your year,' Anna couldn't help pointing out.

A look of irritation crossed Heather's face at this, but she swallowed whatever retort she'd been on the verge of making.

'Yeah, well,' she said eventually, 'worked out for me in the long run. Turns out, bars and restaurants are crying out for staff, post-Brexit and COVID. And they're willing to pay accordingly.' She picked something, possibly imaginary, off the front of her T-shirt. 'Between this and the OnlyFans, it's not as if I'm struggling.'

Anna, who'd never been particularly adept at picking up on sarcasm, wasn't sure whether Heather was joking about the latter and felt it would be rude to ask. Instead, she sipped from the latte she'd ordered to show willing and passed no comment.

'But yeah, Libby,' said Heather. 'What is there to say about her?' She arched her back, thrusting out her chest as she stretched luxuriously. 'I had a couple of tutorials with her in third and fourth year. Plus, I saw her in lectures and from time to time around campus. Never really got the sense she was all that. She was kinda … reserved, like? Subdued. Didn't contribute much to group discussions unless she was prompted – and then, when she *did*, she never really seemed to have anything particularly interesting to say.'

She shrugged. 'And, like, that's fine. You can be a perfectly competent student and not have a single original thought in your head. Ninety-nine percent of an undergraduate degree's just showing you've done the reading, right?'

Anna thought there was a *little* more to it than that, at least as far as the course *she* taught was concerned, but she suspected Heather wasn't asking her because she expected a frank debate about the quality of the curriculum.

'And yet she must have had *something* going for her if she came top of her year,' she said instead. 'And to have convinced the panel to fund her PhD.'

Heather gave a thin smile. 'From what *I've* heard, Colgan basically railroaded them into it. Bigged her up like she was the second coming of Jesus Christ himself; said he'd never read a dissertation quite like hers; that she'd had offers from all over and that, if they didn't give her the funding, some other uni would be only too happy to snap her up.' She shook her head. 'Bollocks. That's not the Libby *I* knew. I'd've said she was sucking his cock-a-leekie if I didn't know for a fact that he's as gay as a French bassoon.'

'How well *did* you know her?' said Anna, studiously ignoring the vulgar choice of words. 'Leila said the two of you were paired up as part of some sort of student support system.'

'Oh, *that*,' Heather laughed, rolling her eyes. 'Let's just say there wasn't a whole lot of support going in *either* direction. I mean, don't get me wrong – *I* did my best to abide by the spirit of the game, but Libby refused to play ball. Said it was all a crock of shit. That she didn't need help. Eventually, I got tired of trying. You can lead a horse to water, but you can't ... well, you know how it goes.'

'So what you're saying is that you didn't spend much time with her.'

'Enough to get the measure of her,' retorted Heather hotly. 'Just because we weren't BFFs doesn't mean I was incapable of forming an opinion about her. And my opinion was: "nothing to write home about". I mean, she was a looker, don't get me wrong, and I don't doubt that opened doors for her that're closed to the rest of us. But there's only so much a blonde bob and a tight little arse can do to compensate for a serious personality deficit and a head devoid of any original thought.'

Anna said nothing, but her disapproval must have been writ large on her face, for Heather gave a weary sigh and rolled her eyes, as if she resented having to justify herself.

'I'm just saying, when it came to dishing out the funding, there were other candidates who were more deserving.'

Anna didn't have to ask if she had anyone particular in mind.

'So I'm assuming you weren't all that surprised when word got out that she'd dropped out,' she said.

Heather frowned, seemingly surprised by the question. 'Actually, I *was*. I always figured it'd be another year at least before she got found out. Take it from someone who's just coming to the end of her second year: this is the hardest part of the whole ordeal by far. First year's a doddle in comparison. You're basically just faffing about, reading up on the subject, figuring out what you actually want your thesis to be about before you commit to anything. Second year's when you've properly got to shit or get off the pot.'

Anna resisted the urge to point out to her that she *had* done a PhD herself and had some idea of what it entailed.

'I always figured,' Heather continued, 'if she was gonna crash and burn, it'd be round about now. But I guess she was even more of a phony than I thought.' She shook her head. 'Poor Stuart. I'd feel sorry for him if he wasn't such a sap.'

Anna found herself having to resist the urge to tell Heather to wind her neck in. She was firmly of the belief that no one should be above criticism, but there was only so much open denigration of one of her colleagues she could listen to. She wondered if Heather would be quite so unfiltered if she realised she was talking to a member of staff herself. But then, perhaps she *did* realise and that was all part of the fun for her.

Was a member of staff. Emphasis on the past tense.

'I take it the two of you didn't stay in touch, then, after she dropped out,' she said, already perfectly aware of what the answer would be. 'Um … what I mean is, have you any idea where I might find her?'

Heather laughed derisively. 'Are you taking the piss? I only heard she was gone a few months after she'd already dropped out, and it's not like she left a forwarding address.'

'But she *has* left, then?' said Anna, seizing on Heather's choice of words. 'As in, she's no longer in Glasgow?'

'That's the word on the street. She used to stay in a flat in Shawlands. Proper swanky, by all accounts – guest room, open-plan kitchen, the works. Makes you wonder where she got the cash to splash out like that. But supposedly she cleared out round about the time she dropped out, leaving the last month's rent unpaid. Would *you* stick around town waiting for the repo men to catch up with you?'

'I suppose not,' said Anna, reminding herself that Heather hadn't supplied any actual proof – just, at best, second-hand rumours. 'But still …'

'Word is, she owed a *bunch* of people money,' said Heather archly, casually inspecting the chipped black paint on her nails. 'It was a bit of a running joke among us students: "If you see Libby Bright coming, keep an eye on your wallet." She seemed to be forever lurching from one financial crisis to the next, asking someone to spot her enough to cover her weekly shop or the lecky meter or what have you, then weaselling her way out of paying them back.

'Even I got burned by her once. Took pity on her and lent her twenty quid when she told me she was on the verge of getting turfed out of her flat.' She sighed theatrically. 'And so began the long saga of my attempts to recoup my loss. At first, when I confronted her, she claimed she'd already paid me back.' She gave Anna a withering look. 'I mean, do I have "mug" written across my forehead? Do I *look* like my asshole's lubed up and ready to take a twelve-inch dildo?'

'I've no idea,' said Anna. 'I haven't seen your OnlyFans.'

Heather stared at her for a couple of seconds, then threw back her head and gave a rich, throaty cackle. 'You're funny, you are. I like you.'

Anna opted to treat this as a positive development.

'Well,' Heather went on, 'when that didn't fly, she immediately changed her story – said oh yes, she remembered now, and she'd give it me once she got paid next week. She was waitressing at a restaurant in Thornwood at the time, I think. Then the week after, then the week after that. At one point, after I'd asked her for, like, the dozenth time, she coughed up a couple of pound coins. Practically threw them at me, like *I* was the unreasonable one.

'I never did get the rest back. In the end, I gave up asking. But that was the last time I lent her so much as a hairpin. And, to be fair, she never chanced her arm with me again. Went and found herself other, easier marks. But my story's far from unique.' She shrugged. 'What can I say? Girl must've had expensive tastes.'

Anna thought back to the dates of the bank transfers to E. Bright from Hugh's Capercaillie account.

'Was there any period in particular when she seemed to be unusually short of cash?'

Heather pursed her lips, thinking. 'No, she seemed to be pretty much in a state of perpetual crisis. Though I reckon she went on a bit of a spending spree towards the end of … I guess it would have been spring of 2019? We were getting towards the end of the teaching period of fourth year, and I remember noticing a change in her at the time.'

'What kind of a change?'

'She started dressing … I dunno, sluttier? I mean,' she said, forestalling any objections to this characterisation, 'you're looking at the number one proud reigning queen of the hoes here, so I can get away with saying it. One hundred percent sex-positive all the way here. But she got her hair done, started wearing more makeup, dressing more provocatively – you know, short skirts and low-cut blouses, that sorta thing. And we're talking designer labels here. All stuff that would've cost more than a bob or two. I'm pretty sure she got her teeth whitened too.' She said it as if this was *the* cardinal sin. 'I'd say she got a serious cash injection from somewhere – otherwise how could a girl who was always skint to the point of having to beg off other students suddenly afford to splash out on new outfits and dental cosmetics?'

Anna gave a small shrug but said nothing. Jen Brinkley's words the previous evening, which had never been far from her thoughts, were once more at the front of her mind.

'What's an ageing professor doing paying off a young female student to the tune of several thousand quid?'

'So come on,' said Heather suddenly. 'Spill. Why's it you're so keen to track her down?' She gave an amused smile. 'She doesn't owe *you* money too, does she?'

Anna shook her head, feeling she really should have come up with a semi-plausible explanation by now. 'Nothing like that, no. I just ... need to ask her about something, that's all.'

It was clear, from Heather's nonplussed expression, that she regarded this as a highly unsatisfactory response.

'Suit yourself,' she said, when it became clear Anna wasn't going to elaborate further. 'I oughta be getting back to it anyway. They don't pay me to sit on my arse shooting the breeze.' She swung her upper body round to face the same direction as her legs, ready to leave.

'Just a minute,' blurted Anna, hearing the ring of desperation in her voice.

Heather stopped and swung back round to face her, a *this better be good* expression on her face.

'I don't suppose there's anyone else you could put me in touch with – or anyone you could ask who might have any idea what became of Libby after she dropped out? Someone who might have had a closer relationship with her than you?'

For a moment, Heather merely looked irritated, as if she couldn't believe Anna wouldn't let the matter drop. Then an amused glint appeared in her eyes.

'Are you some sort of private investigator?'

Anna decided silence was the best response to this surprisingly tricky question.

Heather smiled, eyes widening indulgently. 'You *are*, aren't you? What's really going on? Did someone she stiffed hire you to track her down?'

'I mean, not in so many words,' said Anna, concluding that dropping just enough of a hint that Heather might be on to something would be the best policy here.

Heather nodded to herself, her smile widening. 'All *right*.' Then, seemingly remembering she was supposed to be conveying an air of aloof disinterest, she shrugged. 'Fair enough, then. I'll ask around – see if anyone's heard anything on the old jungle drums. How'm I supposed to get in touch?'

They exchanged numbers, Heather keying Anna's into her phone and then – rather reluctantly, Anna thought – reciting hers so Anna could enter it into her own device.

'So you'll be in touch?' said Anna, as Heather got up to go.

'If I hear anything,' replied Heather curtly, not looking back.

And then she was off, leaving Anna to finish her now decidedly chilled latte alone.

22

Over the last few days, Anna had spent so much time in cafés of one variety or another that she was beginning to think she wouldn't care if she never experienced the smell of coffee again for as long as she lived. That said, the morning was getting on and she found herself craving solid food. Not overly keen on the idea of hanging around Café Zen, lest Heather think she was expecting her to whip out her address book and start phoning her fellow students there and then, she headed to one of the many other coffee shops on Byres Road, where she ordered what she supposed probably counted as brunch: ham and cheese focaccia and a bottle of sparkling water.

While she ate, she forced herself to tackle the matter that had – allegedly, at any rate – brought her back to Glasgow in the first place: the water damage at her old house. She was aware that more than twenty-four hours had already passed since she'd inspected the damage, and she'd still made no progress on persuading a professional to come out and take a look. The one builder whose details she had from a past job had ceased trading during lockdown, and, while Google offered up an impressive roster of potential alternatives, the reviews for them were the very definition of 'mixed bag'. With little to go on, she decided to take potluck, and started calling them at random. Of the ones she managed to get through to, most had too much work on to attend to the matter within the sort of timeframe she was looking for, but one, a Kilmarnock-based tradesman called Terry with a four out of five rating on TrustPilot, gave her some hope.

'Aye, I'll try and swing by in the next couple of days and take a peek,' he said languidly. 'No promises, but. I'm lined up to do some work on a bathroom in Springburn, and if the plaster gets delivered the morra, it's all hands on deck.'

She wished she could have got something more definitive from him. In her admittedly limited experience, builders were the most frustratingly vague people on the planet when it came to pinning them down on timescales, but she recognised she was lucky to have got even this flimsy commitment, so she thanked him and rang off, then called Colin and Justin to let them know to expect a visit at some point in the next forty-eight hours … perhaps.

With that chore taken care of, or at least advanced as far as was possible at the present time, she once more turned her attention to the Libby Bright question. It was true that she'd yet to land on any definitive proof that Libby was the 'E. Bright' to whom Hugh had made the various payments, but the coincidences were stacking up just a bit too much for her liking. Assuming Heather's account was to be trusted (and Anna saw no reason to doubt her, despite her obvious personal biases), Libby had seemingly been beset by financial worries throughout her time at Kelvingrove, though she had, on one occasion, seemingly come into a not insubstantial sum of money from unknown quarters. The timeframe Heather had described didn't line up with the payments from Hugh's Capercaillie account, but it seemed indicative of a certain pattern of behaviour.

She suspected the odds of hearing back from Heather were slim in the extreme. In any event, she didn't plan to rest on her laurels, simply hoping someone else would do all the legwork for her. And so, with her plate now cleared and a fresh bottle of water within reach, she once more turned to her phone and began to take what steps she could towards tracking Libby down herself.

She began with the phone book, searching for anyone named Elizabeth or Libby Bright within the city of Glasgow. She was somewhat surprised to get a big fat zero in terms of results. True, it wasn't the commonest name in the world, but she'd been expecting to have to sift through at least a handful of contenders. There was one in Edinburgh, but given that her title was 'Mrs', it was safe to assume 'Bright' was her married name, ruling her out of the running. Similarly, there was an Elizabeth Bright in Aberdeenshire, but she'd been registered at her current address since 2016, which allowed Anna to quickly eliminate her too.

As Anna expanded the parameters of her search, trawling the whole of Scotland and eventually widening it to include England and Wales as well, the story remained the same. Each result that looked initially promising turned out, for one reason or another, to be a no-go. She reminded herself that people of Libby's age were considerably less likely than those of her generation to even *have* a landline, meaning that this was, in all likelihood, a suboptimal way to conduct her search. She briefly considered the electoral roll, before dismissing it for the not dissimilar reason that people under the age of twenty-five were the demographic least likely to be registered to vote. Eventually, she settled on the tried and tested truism that folk in their twenties live out their lives online and tend not to be particularly circumspect about the details they share. As such, she could do a whole lot worse than to focus her attention on social media.

Zoe had once sat Anna down and explained the social media hierarchy to her. 'Facebook and Twitter's for boomers and geriatric millennials like oursels,' she'd said, in a tone of considerable authority. 'Snapchat's where the kids are at. That and TikTok.' The only problem was, Anna didn't have a Snapchat account *or* a TikTok one, and had no idea how they worked. She'd had a particularly ugly experience with Twitter a couple of years ago and had avoided it like the clap ever since, though she suspected she could probably find her way around it if she absolutely had to. Still, she'd prefer to give it a wide berth if at all possible. That left Facebook – which, if Zoe's assessment of the social media predilections of the different generations was accurate, was unlikely to herald any results. Still, there was nothing to be lost by trying, except time.

Upon opening the Facebook app, the first thing that greeted her was Vasilico's profile page, still open on the photo of him and his aggravatingly pretty fiancée. Swiftly averting her eyes, she tapped the magnifying glass icon and entered the words 'Libby Bright' into the search bar.

The app threw up around a dozen possible candidates, which she spent the next ten minutes ruling out for one reason or another. Only one seemed like it had any potential: a Libby Bright with a grand total of 17 friends and virtually no identifying information publicly available. No location was given, but the 'Vote Remain' logo which served as her profile picture suggested that she'd been living somewhere in the UK at the time of the Brexit referendum. It also suggested it was unlikely she'd updated her account since then. Only a handful of posts were publicly visible. Of these, none shed any further light on her identity or whereabouts, though a link to an academic paper on social interaction did allow Anna to experience a brief surge of optimism.

She hovered her finger over the 'Add Friend' button. She suspected she was probably on a hiding to nothing, but she figured she had nothing to lose. She went ahead and tapped the button.

Concluding that she ought to widen the parameters of her search, she switched to the web browser and entered 'Libby

Bright' into Google. The results were sorted based on her current location, showing the most relevant ones first, including a one-paragraph article in the *Kelvingrove Chronicle*, the university newspaper, about her winning the 2020 MacArthur Prize after coming top of her year. This was, to date, the only verified reference she'd found to the Libby Bright she was looking for since she'd begun her search. Many of the other results were merely the same Facebook profiles and telephone directory listings she'd already discounted, and, beyond the first couple of pages, became increasingly unhelpful, throwing up links that had only the most tenuous connections to the words she'd typed into the search field.

More out of idle curiosity than any hope of gleaning anything useful from them, she opened a handful of them. There was a Libby Brightman in Oklahoma City who'd recently celebrated her one hundredth birthday and been feted by the mayor in a ceremony that seemed to have been more about bolstering his re-election chances than celebrating his constituent's longevity. Judging by her facial expression in the picture accompanying the article, Ms Brightman knew perfectly well that she was being used as a political pawn and was treating the proceedings with the contempt they deserved. A little closer to home, there was a Lizzie Wright who worked for a wildlife sanctuary near Moffat and, along with three of her colleagues, had raised over £2,000 for operational costs by running a sponsored half-marathon. A photo posted on the sanctuary's rather outdated website showed the four of them looking sweaty but triumphant at the finish line. There was no clarity as to which of the two women in the picture – both in their twenties, both slim and dark-haired – was Lizzie Wright and which was Rhona Calder, the other woman named in the article, but it didn't much matter. Clearly, neither of them was the person Anna was looking for.

She glanced at the time at the corner of her screen. It was nearly one o'clock. Two o'clock in Central European Time.

On impulse, and because she was aware she hadn't spoken to Jack since Thursday afternoon, she switched to FaceTime and rang Matteo, only for it to serve her with an 'Unavailable' message.

She scowled at the words on the screen, frustrated and feeling vaguely uneasy. She told herself it was nothing to worry about – that Matteo might have simply forgotten to charge his phone or not been in a position to answer it. *Whatever,* she thought. She'd try again later.

Just then, her phone pinged an alert, startling her enough for her to drop it on the aluminium table with a clang. A handful of other patrons glanced briefly in her direction before returning to their coffee and conversations. Silently cursing her own clumsiness, she picked up her phone and examined the text that had appeared on the screen.

PAUL VASILICO

Busy?

She hesitated for a moment, thumbs hovering over the screen, before tapping out a response.

ANNA SCAVOLINI

Not as such.

The little thought bubble with its ellipsis appeared, indicating that Vasilico was formulating a response. It came through a moment later, accompanied by an all-too-innocent-sounding 'woop'.

PAUL VASILICO

Fancy a fuck?

23

Anna relaxed her grip on the sheets and opened her eyes in time to see the top of Vasilico's head rising from between her legs. She let out the shuddering sigh she'd been holding in and allowed her head to sink back onto the bed.

The two of them had convened in her hotel room just after two. In contrast to their frenzied rutting in the alleyway the previous day, their lovemaking this time had had a gentler, more sedate pace to it, no longer driven by a seeming need to get it over and done with as quickly as possible. She'd forgotten what a consummate lover Vasilico was: generous, attentive, tender when she needed him to be, more assertive when that was what she craved. Not that Matteo wasn't all those things, but with Vasilico it was different. *They* were different – their bodies, their approach to sex, their whole personalities. It wasn't so much that one was better than the other – more that each scratched a different itch. They were … complementary, if it was possible to think of it in those terms.

She felt him crawling up the bed and flopping down next to her. She rolled onto her side to face him. Their eyes met.

'Hello,' said Vasilico.

'Hello yourself,' she said.

He chuckled softly to himself. She gave a bemused smile.

'What?'

'Nothing. Just ...' He gestured to their surroundings. 'This. You. Me. Here. Now. Who would have thought?'

'Who indeed?'

He rolled over onto his back and, gazing up at the ceiling, let out a contented sigh. She remained on her side, watching the steady rise and fall of his chest; the beads of sweat on his bare skin. If she could freeze-frame this moment in time, this feeling, capture it and seal it away in a box, so she could return to it whenever she felt the urge, she would gladly do so. As long as they lay like this, not moving, not speaking, it was as if nothing that existed beyond this room, this moment, was real. Not Glasgow, not Perugia, not the separate lives they now led, the relationships they'd formed – none of it.

'How long did you say you were going to be in town for?'

And, with that one seemingly benign question, the barriers came down and the real world came flooding back in.

'Not long,' she said, the words catching unexpectedly in her throat. 'A couple more days at most.'

'And you're spending the rest of summer in Perugia?'

'No. Lake Trasimeno. I'll be heading out there as soon as I get back. You know – eloping to the country like a proper native.'

Vasilico gave a slight smile. 'And who's watching Jack while you're over here?'

'What?' she half-choked, unprepared for the question.

'I mean, at first I thought you might have brought him with you. But I see now that's not the case. Not unless you've got him stashed in a closet somewhere – in which case, this whole scenario just took on a decidedly awkward bent.'

Anna laughed out of obligation. 'He's not here, no. He's back in Italy. A neighbour's looking after him for me.'

'That right?'

'Yes,' she said, more defensively than she'd intended.

Vasilico scratched his chest carelessly. 'In that case, you must trust her a lot, leaving him with her while you're off on manoeuvres.'

'I do,' said Anna. She had no intention to correct his assumption.

She told herself she had nothing to be ashamed of – certainly not where *he* was concerned. She wasn't the one who'd only gone and got bloody *engaged*. And yet here they both were, naked and sweaty in a hotel bed together – the ultimate cliché. She was tempted to throw it all back in his face; tell him she knew everything there was to know about him, but that there was a hell of a lot *he* didn't know about *her*. And yet, for some reason, she couldn't bring herself to do it. Couldn't give voice to the fact that she, like him, had a life that existed beyond these four walls. Was it about power? About withholding something of herself from him? Or was she simply in denial?

They settled into silence, lying side by side, their breathing finding a shared rhythm. The noise of traffic on Great Western Road, muffled by the window-glass, sounded a million miles away.

At length, Vasilico stirred. Pushing himself upright, he swung his legs over the bed and got to his feet. She levered herself up onto her elbow and watched as he strolled over to the small desk facing the window and retrieved his trousers from the back of the chair.

'You're going?'

He turned to face her. 'I really have to make a move. Sorry.'

'Back to ... the office?'

She nearly said 'your fiancée', but managed to stop herself in time. No point spoiling the illusion for both of them.

Vasilico stepped into his trousers. 'No rest for the wicked.'

'Not even on a Saturday. It's positively criminal.'

'Criminal, you say? Sadly, we've yet to convince *them* to take the weekend off.'

'And you with your limitless powers of persuasion? I don't believe it.'

'Your faith in my abilities is, I fear, misplaced.'

He'd taken off his ring before coming here, she noticed. The thought caused a twisting sensation in her gut. She settled into silence while he finished getting dressed.

'And you?' he said, as he fastened his cufflinks. 'What are your plans for the rest of the day? Back to chasing the elusive Libby Wright, I take it?'

She'd given him a potted account earlier of her progress since they'd last seen one another, in between bouts of lovemaking.

'I suspect I've done about as much chasing as I reasonably can for now,' she said. 'I seem to have hit a brick wall. And it's Libby *Bright*.'

'Close enough,' said Vasilico cheerfully, pulling on his jacket. 'Anyway, if I know anything about you at all, you'll find a way to smash straight through that wall. Even though, as an officer of the law, I really should be strenuously advising you against taking matters into your own hands.'

'What makes you think I'd listen?'

'Absolutely nothing – which is why I'm not going to bother.'

That got a smile out of her. He turned to inspect himself in the mirror, briefly pausing to straighten a strand of his closely cropped hair before crossing over to the bed.

'I'd like to see you again before you go, if that's possible,' he said.

'Sure you'll be able to fit that into your busy schedule?'

Vasilico stroked his chin, making a show of thinking about it. 'Well, it's going to be tricky, but I'll see if I can find an empty slot in my diary.'

'Don't put yourself out on *my* account.'

'Wouldn't dream of it.' His features relaxed into a smile. 'Seriously, though, you know how to get in touch.'

'As do you.'

He smiled fondly. Then, bending down, he cupped her cheek in his hand and drew her into a kiss. It lasted for several seconds, during which she had to resist the urge to drag him back down onto the bed with her for another round. When they finally broke apart, her sense of longing for him was no less intense, but she managed to contain herself, watching as he headed to the door, gave her one last tender look, then slipped out, the soft click as he shut it like a final, definitive full stop.

She sank down onto her back and lay there, allowing her mind to soften until it was in that liminal space between wakefulness and sleep, free to go wandering where it pleased and make its own connections. She found herself wondering what life would have been like if her exposure by The Reckoning had never happened; if she and Vasilico had continued seeing each other, becoming something more than just two people who met in alleyways and hotel rooms to satiate their carnal desires. Would they still be together now? Or would the relationship have withered on the vine like so many others in her past? She'd never been with the same man for any great length of time, seeming always to become consumed by a restlessness, a desire to cut and run, a deep discomfort at the thought of 'settling down', once things started to become serious. Just over two years was her all-time record. If she and Vasilico had remained together, they'd be coming up on that anniversary right about now.

Realistically, what chance could they possibly have had? What chance did she have with *anyone*?

The ringing of her phone, lying on the floor next to the bed, startled her out of her state of semi-reverie. Rolling onto her stomach, she hauled herself to the edge of the bed and reached for it.

Matteo was FaceTiming her.

Firmly drawing a line through the idea of letting him see her in her present, post-coital state, she set the phone to audio only and accepted the call.

'Matteo?'

'Mummy!' Jack's high, excitable voice came chirping through the speaker.

'Jack? Is that you?'

'Where are you, Mummy? I can't see you.'

'Oh. Hold on.'

She hurriedly tugged the bedsheet around her torso, then switched to video mode. Jack's face filled the screen, his dark hair wet and tousled.

'How's that? Can you see me now?'

Jack nodded eagerly.

'What's happening over there? Have you been swimming?'

That would explain why she wasn't able to get through to Matteo earlier.

'Uh-huh,' said Jack, a tad breathlessly. 'We went swimming and then we went to a shop and had tara … tara …'

'Taralli?' Anna suggested.

Jack nodded again.

'That sounds lovely. And what are—'

'Mummy.'

'Yes?'

'Why are you naked?' He spoke with evident disapproval.

'Oh.'

Anna glanced down at herself, as if she too was surprised by her state of undress. The sheet hadn't slipped off, but it would have been abundantly clear to anyone with eyes that she had nothing on underneath.

She thought fast.

'Well … as it happens, I was just getting ready to have a shower when you called.'

'In the *afternoon?*'

Jack's incredulity was so absolute that Anna almost burst out laughing. A creature of unvarying habit, she'd always had her daily shower first thing in the morning. To Jack, the notion of having it at any other time of the day was probably an alien concept.

'I know,' she said with a sheepish laugh, intended to convey that she, too, recognised the absurdity of this situation. 'Silly Mummy. But I'm so discombobulated by the change in time zone, I hardly know whether I'm coming or going.

'Anyway,' she went on, changing the subject, 'it's really nice that you called. And I'm so glad you're having such a lovely time there. I can't wait to come and join you.'

She regretted saying it as soon as she saw the change in Jack's expression. Gone was the incredulous frown, replaced by a look so forlorn that it almost tore her heart in two.

'When *are* you coming, Mummy? It's been *weeks.*'

'Now, Jack,' said Anna firmly, 'you know it's only been a couple of days. And I'll be there really soon, I promise. But there are some things I have to take care of here first. Once I've got them out of the way, I'll be able to relax properly and spend all day long with you.' She gave an encouraging smile. 'That'll be nice, won't it?'

'S'pose,' mumbled Jack. He clearly felt he'd heard it all before.

At that moment, Anna heard Matteo's voice at the other end of the line, calling out to the two children in Italian, asking if one of them had his phone.

'Listen, Jack,' she said hurriedly, not relishing an encounter with Matteo in her present state, 'I'm going to have to go. But it was really nice to talk to you. I'll call again tomorrow ... and I'll see you soon, all right?'

'OK,' said Jack, clearly not convinced.

'OK. Love you. Bye.'

She stabbed the End Call button and dropped the phone as if it was radioactive, letting out the heavy breath she'd been holding in. She sat cross-legged on the bed, the sheet pooled around her waist, consumed by the feelings of guilt that – for the last couple of hours, at any rate – she'd succeeded in burying somewhere deep and unreachable inside her. It wasn't just guilt about the knowledge that Jack was over there in Italy, waiting for her, hurt and confused as to why she hadn't come – though, needless to say, that was bad enough. It was the knowledge that Matteo, too, was waiting for her, hoping to make a life with her – a life she still had no idea whether she wanted. It was hard not to feel that he was entitled to better. That, at the very least, he deserved more honesty from her than he was currently getting, even if it meant shattering whatever illusions he was currently clinging to.

She lay back again, one arm flung behind her head as she gazed up at the ceiling. What was she doing here, pretending to Matteo and Jack that she was just taking care of some simple administrative matters when, in reality, she'd once again got herself involved in something that was none of her business? What would Matteo say if she came clean to him; told him she was actually investigating the circumstances of an ex-colleague's death and trying to track down a girl who may or may not have been involved with him in some ill-defined way, and which may or may not have had something to do with his decision to end his life? He'd probably ask her if she was taking the piss – *prendendo per il culo*. And she could hardly blame him.

Libby Bright. Strange that someone with such an unusual name should be so hard to track down. It wasn't as if she was Jane Smith, of whom there must be hundreds, if not thousands, living in Scotland alone. Perhaps she'd changed it. Heather had claimed she'd left town without having paid her rent. And it sounded as if she'd been in an almost perpetual state of financial hardship. Perhaps she'd owed other people money besides her landlord. Maybe she really *had* wanted to completely sever the link to her old life and start again with a blank slate.

She'd heard once that members of the security services operating undercover often chose an alias that sounded relatively close to their real name – the logic being that you'd be less likely to slip up and fail to respond to someone addressing you by it if it had, for example, the same number of syllables or a similar overall sound.

Think. If you were Libby Bright, what would you call yourself if you wanted to throw off pursuit but still protect yourself against the occasional slip-up?

Lizzie Wright?

It couldn't be – could it?

It would be the very definition of hiding in plain sight, but it would also be just enough to throw off anyone doing a cursory Google search.

And, if you got yourself a job in a field completely unrelated to your degree, and changed the colour of your hair into the bargain …

She lurched upright, skin clammy and heart pounding with sudden nervous energy. It was the long shot to end all long shots, but *God*, it was worth a punt. She grabbed her phone again and, stumbling unsteadily to her feet, brought up Heather Fleetwood's contact details and tapped out a hasty message to her. She attached a link to the photo on the wildlife sanctuary's website and hit 'Send'. And waited.

She wasn't left in limbo for long. She was still standing by the side of the bed, stark naked, when her phone, still in her hand, began to vibrate and jingle as a call came through. She immediately accepted it and snatched it to her ear.

'Heather?'

'It *is* her! Oh my fucking *God*!'

'It's her? It's definitely Libby?' Anna lowered herself onto the end of the bed, hardly daring to let herself believe it.

'Oh, it's her all right,' said Heather, sounding both surprised and amused in equal measure. 'The one on the left in the blue vest. She's cut her hair and dyed it brown, but I'd know that smug wee face anywhere. Well, well – little Miss "I Bagged Myself a Scholarship I Didn't Deserve" shovelling pig shit in some scuzzy pound in the arse-end of nowhere. Talk about a turn-up for the books!' She cackled uproariously to herself.

'I see. Well, thanks for confirming it.'

'No sweat. This has brightened up my day no end. Wait'll I tell all my pals!'

'I'd rather you didn't,' said Anna, far from amused by this unabashed display of schadenfreude. 'It's pretty obvious she doesn't want to be found.'

'Are you going to go see her?' said Heather, ignoring Anna's remonstrating completely. 'I'd give my left butt-cheek to see the look on her face when you show up and call her by her actual name.'

'Perhaps,' said Anna, hoping Heather wasn't entertaining any thoughts of doing the same herself. 'Well, like I said, thanks for getting back to me.'

'Hey, you'll let me know how it goes, yeah?'

'We'll see,' said Anna, and ended the call.

A quick Google search revealed that the sanctuary was located just off the M74, roughly three miles from Moffat. Despite what she'd said to Heather, Anna had no qualms whatsoever about heading down there in search of Libby. In fact, she'd have set off now if it wasn't already so late in the day. According to Google Maps, the sanctuary was just over thirty miles away. None of the public transport options looked ideal, with just one bus every two hours in either direction, and nothing on the return leg after 5:30 p.m. However she went about getting there, she would obviously have to wait till tomorrow.

She was still mulling things over when she glanced at the corner of the screen and caught sight of the time.

17:07. She was due at Miriam's for dinner in just over an hour.

24

'Anna!' Miriam exclaimed as she opened the front door, wearing a 'Caution: Man in Kitchen' apron over a striped T-shirt dress. 'Is it that time already? Come in, come in. Make yourself at home. I'll be with you momentarily.'

'Is there anything I can help with?' Anna asked as she stepped into the house.

But Miriam was already scuttling back down the hallway towards the kitchen. 'Oh, nothing to worry about!' she called over her shoulder. 'Just a minor culinary upset!'

Anna lingered in the hallway, reluctant to stray too far in case the upset blossomed into a full-blown emergency. From beyond the kitchen door came the clanging of metal, followed by a shout of 'Oh, pissflaps!' from Miriam. A moment later, a smoke alarm began to emit its piercing wail.

Anna took that as her cue to step in. Hurrying down the corridor, she opened the kitchen door and was hit by a wall of steam, the source of which quickly turned out to be the oven under the hob. On the other side of the room, Miriam was on her tiptoes, frantically flapping a dishcloth in front of the trilling alarm.

Striding into the room, Anna thrust open the windows

above the sink, then turned her attention to the source of the smoke. She switched off the oven before grabbing a pair of oversized mitts and using them to open the door. Great clouds came billowing from it, accompanied by the overpowering smell of charred meat. She stepped out of the direct path of the smoke, covering her mouth with her arm as she stifled a coughing fit. Meanwhile, Miriam, who was now teetering at the top of a mini stepladder, pulled the cover off the alarm and wrenched the battery out of its socket, finally silencing it.

As the smoke gradually dissipated through the open windows, the two of them cautiously approached the oven. Miriam turned wordlessly to Anna with an expression that was somewhere between apologetic and expectant. Still wearing the oven gloves, Anna bent down and extracted the charred remains of a roast chicken, its juices sizzling in the pan.

As the smoke continued to dissipate, Miriam gazed down at the remains with a crestfallen expression.

'The instructions online made it all sound so easy,' she said.

In the end, they succeeded in salvaging a vague approximation of a meal between them. The potatoes Miriam had been planning to roast were still in their plastic bag, and, with the inside of the oven resembling that of a crematorium, they decided to forego them in favour of some microwavable potato waffles Anna found in the freezer. To these, they added raw carrots cut into strips and some low-fat Greek yoghurt which Anna fashioned into a dip. They sat on opposite sides of the oversized dining room table, picking edible bits from the desiccated chicken with their fingers while drinking Cabernet Sauvignon – purloined from the extensive supply of bottles in the hallway – from a pair of mismatched highball glasses. Miriam was largely silent, chewing slowly with her eyes downcast, her embarrassment palpable.

'Sorry,' she said, after a while. 'I'm not used to cooking for other people. I don't normally eat a sit-down meal – just wait till I get hungry, then grab whatever's to hand.'

'It's OK,' Anna assured her. 'This is nice. I'm not that big on the whole "three-course dinner" thing either.'

Miriam gave a flicker of a smile but otherwise made no response. She stuffed a carrot stick into her mouth and chewed morosely.

Anna racked her brains for something to say that would lift the mood. Her acceptance of the invitation to dinner had been partly to give herself a further opportunity to probe Miriam about her father, and, more specifically, her knowledge about the state of his finances. But now that it came down to it, she couldn't think of a single way in. Perhaps, if she hadn't spent so much of the afternoon fooling around in bed with a certain someone …

'I like your dining room,' she said weakly. 'It's very … spacious.'

Miriam glanced around at her surroundings. 'Yes,' she agreed, as if she'd never considered this before. 'Daddy used to use it to wine and dine the university elite back in the day. You never attended any of his soirées, did you? They could become quite raucous once the alcohol got flowing.'

'I didn't, no,' said Anna, reflecting, not for the first time, that perhaps she and Hugh hadn't, in fact, been as close as she'd liked to believe.

'This was mostly before your time, of course,' Miriam went on, as if reading Anna's thoughts. 'Back when I was still a youngling. After Mum got sick for the first time, they didn't hold them nearly as often. For a while, though, it seemed like there were folk here almost every weekend. Daddy always enjoyed a glass or two, and Mum could more than hold her own. I used to hear them carrying on for hours after I went to bed, making a frightful racket. My room's right above this one. It's a big house, but, you know, noise travels. They certainly livened the old place up, but I'll not pretend I was sorry once things calmed down a bit, even if I'd rather it'd been for happier reasons.'

'You've lived here all your life, then?' Anna asked. 'I mean,' she clarified as Miriam frowned at the question, her shoulders arching defensively, 'you never went away – you know, for university and whatever.'

'There just didn't seem to be much point. The art school was only a train ride away, and my parents always made it clear I was welcome to stay as long as I liked. It's not like they needed the space.'

Anna couldn't get her head round this. 'But surely there must have been times when *you* craved space of your own?'

'Not really.'

'Not *ever*?'

Miriam merely shrugged, meeting Anna's gaze without blinking.

Anna was beginning to feel a bit flustered. 'Sorry, I just …' She gave a sheepish smile. 'Well, I mean, I can't even *begin* to picture still living with my mother after all this time. Not without one of us attempting to murder the other.'

'Well,' said Miriam coolly, 'I suppose that's the difference between us, Anna. We don't all regard time spent with our parents as something to merely be endured.'

Anna felt her insides withering at this assessment.

'No,' she agreed, and lowered her eyes, chastened.

'Still,' Miriam went on, 'I'm not going to kid on I'm overjoyed to have been left holding the baby, as it were. I mean, don't get me wrong – I love this old place. But, just sometimes, I wish my folks had chosen somewhere more … manageable.'

'I understand. It's a lot for one person to handle.'

'Mm. A lot to take care of.'

'The electricity alone must cost a fortune.'

Miriam said nothing, but Anna thought she caught a brief flicker of something in the younger woman's eyes.

'Would it not make more sense to sell up and move to

somewhere that's a bit … you know, easier to manage?' she ventured. Then, as Miriam seemed to visibly bristle at the suggestion, 'I mean, it needn't be purely a money thing. It can be good to draw a line in the sand, after … after a loss. Good to make a fresh start somewhere without so much … history.'

'But you see,' said Miriam, 'that's just it.'

Anna looked at her uncomprehendingly.

'History.' She spread her arms wide. 'It's all around me. In these walls. All my memories of them are bound up with this place – the bad *and* the good. This house … it's all that's left of them. I don't want to leave that behind. It'd be like I was walking out on them. Abandoning them.'

'I'm sure they wouldn't see it that way,' said Anna gently. 'I think they'd want you to have a life of your own – one not yoked to the past.'

Miriam said nothing, but her expression told Anna she was far from convinced.

Anna shifted her position, as if that was going to make what she was about to say any easier. 'When my dad died, he left me some money to put towards buying my first house. It wasn't something I asked for, and, at the time, I felt hypocritical and grubby for even taking it. We, uh, hadn't seen a whole lot of each other towards the end.'

She cleared her throat, stalling for time. She always found it difficult to talk about things as deeply personal as this, and she was basically winging it, throwing the words together as she went along.

'The point is, he wanted to give me something I could use to get a start in life – something that would set me up for the future; let me stand on my own feet. A nest-egg, if you like. And I think you should be looking at this place in the same way. Your dad obviously trusted you to do what was best when he left it all to you, and I reckon he'd want you to do what's in your own interests – use it to get yourself some capital so you can make a life for yourself.'

Miriam gazed back at her from the other side of the table, her face emotionless. 'You think I know nothing about the way the world works – is that it?'

'No,' said Anna, flustered. 'I just—'

'I'm not as naïve as you think, Anna. As it happens, I do know a thing or two about money and how it makes the world go round. Just because I present as this daft wee girlie who whiles away the hours painting pictures instead of getting a *real* job doesn't mean I'm *completely* wet behind the ears.'

She drained her glass and pushed her empty plate away from her, then got to her feet.

'Come on. I want to show you something.'

It took a while for it to become clear what they were watching. It started as merely static on the screen, before an image appeared: blurry, out of focus, garish colours merging together.

A child's voice – a girl's. 'Daddy, is it on?'

Then a gruff, older male voice. 'Hold on ... just need to ...'

A woman's voice, remonstrating playfully. 'Sure you know what you're doing with that thing, Hugh?'

The male voice, responding with just a trace of irritation. 'Yes, yes, of course. Nothing to it. I consulted the manual carefully.'

The girl's voice again. 'He doesn't know what he's doing, Mummy!'

'No, darling, you're right. He doesn't.'

Hugh's voice. 'Yes I do. Hold on – here we go!'

The image snapped into focus, overshot, went blurry again, then came back into focus.

The setting was the same living room they were in now, though a large portion of it was taken up by a Christmas tree, its multicoloured lights almost eye-searingly bright. The whole image was garish and oversaturated, the colours bleeding outside the lines like a child's colouring book, the two figures facing the camera seeming almost hyperreal. At around ten years old, Miriam was clearly the one in charge, standing with her feet planted wide apart, hands on hips, staring into the lens impatiently. She was wearing a witch's outfit: black pointed hat, black cape, plastic wand with a pointed star on the end. Standing beside her, barely reaching up to her chest, was a boy about half her age, as sturdy and ruddy-cheeked as she was lanky and pale.

'Well?' she demanded. 'Is it filming?'

'It's *videotape*, Mim,' Hugh replied from off-screen, gently but firmly. 'Film is an entirely different medium.'

Miriam rolled her eyes and tutted in frustration. '*Daddy*,' she sighed, her highly mannered delivery – no doubt copied from something she'd seen a middle-aged woman do in an old movie or TV programme – rendered incongruous by the childish soubriquet.

'Ignore your father, Mirry,' said the woman's voice, gently chiding. "He's just being pernickety.'

'I am *not*!' Hugh objected, sounding positively wounded. 'It's important to be precise in one's language.'

'Tell him to stop, Mummy!' Miriam pouted, fists balled by her sides.

'Are we done now?' whined the little boy, tilting his head back and staring up at Miriam plaintively. 'Is it finished?'

Miriam responded by grabbing him by the back of his jumper, forestalling any potential effort on his part to effect an escape.

'All right, all right,' said Hugh jovially, the image vibrating as he attempted to stifle a laugh. 'That's enough preamble, I reckon. On with the main show. But first, allow me to introduce the cast.'

He swung the camera round a hundred and eighty degrees to face the sofa, upon which a woman in her early forties reclined, one arm flung behind her head. She had blonde hair in a perm and wore a red silk gown which accentuated her generous curves. As the camera zoomed in on her, she gave a squeal and tried to cover her face.

'Here taking her ease on the *chaise longue*,' declared Hugh, adopting a booming, stentorian voice, 'the fairest maiden in the realm – the lovely Lady Geraldine, who I must declare is looking *particularly* resplendent this evening in her Christmas present from her doting husband.'

'*HUGH!*' shrieked Geraldine, batting at the camera with the hand she wasn't currently using to cover her face. But there was a light-heartedness to it all; a sense that she was only pretending to be mortified.

Hugh swung the camera back to face the two children. 'And here, under the eaves of this mighty pine, is the most fearsome sorceress in all the land: the dastardly, the dreadful, the unrepentant source of all wickedness, the diabolical Madam Mim and her arch-nemesis, the gallant Sir Alfred the Witch Slayer!'

'I'm not Madam Mim!' retorted Miriam, indignant. 'I'm Mildred Hubble, and this is my familiar.'

She gave Alfie a sharp nudge in the ribs. He responded with a decidedly unenthusiastic 'Woooo.'

'That was the Christmas before Alfie died,' said Miriam, glancing across the sofa to Anna. 'It's the last tape I have with the four of us.' She paused. 'Did Daddy ever tell you how it happened?'

Anna stared back at Miriam, lost for words. How was one supposed to respond to a question like this?

'No,' she said eventually – and truthfully. 'And you don't have to either,' she quickly added. 'I mean … not if you don't want to.'

Even so, she couldn't deny that a part of her was more than slightly curious. For almost as long as she'd known Hugh, it had always been there on the periphery, never directly acknowledged but nonetheless an integral part of who he was. She couldn't remember who it was who'd first told her about it, and under what circumstances, but she couldn't remember a time when she *didn't* know that Hugh had lost his youngest child at the age of six.

Miriam reached for the remote and pressed the mute button, silencing the back and forth between the children and their parents. The action continued to play out on the screen, the silence, in conjunction with the ropey image quality, causing it to assume an eerie, ghostlike quality, like one of those 'found footage' tapes.

'It was on a Summer's afternoon,' said Miriam, eyes still on the TV. 'A lot like this one, actually. Daddy was in his study, working on some paper or other. Mum was … you know, I honestly can't remember. Whatever her latest fleeting hobby was at the time. Horticulture, maybe, or basket-weaving. Either way, no one paying attention to us kiddos. I was out in the front garden, laying on a picnic for my dollies. Alfie … he must have wandered off.

'There's a deep freeze in the garage. You know, one of those massive big things with a lift-up lid, long enough and deep enough for a grown man to lie down in. Somehow, Alfie must have managed to climb inside and then the lid shut on him. If he ever cried out, no one heard him.'

She paused, eyes fixed on the screen, where the children seemed to be putting an impromptu show, Miriam attempting to simultaneously perform and issue stage directions to an uncooperative Alfie, who clearly regarded the whole endeavour as unworthy of his time and effort.

Eventually, she continued.

'When they realised he was missing, they hunted high and low for him. The whole street turned out to help look. It wasn't till hours later that Daddy thought to look inside the freezer. By that time, it was too late.'

Anna was silent. Her mouth was dry, tongue thick and unwieldy. She gazed at Miriam with a mixture of disbelief, horror and pity, wishing she wasn't so useless; that she could find the right words to say. Once again, she found herself reflecting on how hard it was to comprehend so much tragedy being heaped on one family.

'And you … ?' she somehow managed.

'I never saw the body.' Miriam's voice remained flat, matter-of-fact. 'Mum made one of the neighbours take me away. But I heard Daddy's cries coming from inside the garage. I'd never heard him make that sound before. I didn't even realise grown-ups *did* that. At the time, I didn't understand precisely what had happened – the business with the deep freeze. And yet somehow I *knew*.'

A fresh silence settled on the room. Anna gazed at Miriam, trying to comprehend what it must have been like, ten or maybe eleven years old at a push, still utterly naïve as to the workings of the world, having never known death before, only to have it visited on her in the cruellest possible way. She tried to imagine all the conflicting emotions Miriam must have experienced in the aftermath: the confusion; the sense of loss; the shameful feelings of resentment towards her parents as they, consumed by their own unimaginable grief, struggled to lavish their surviving child with the same love and attention they once had. Perhaps even an inchoate form of survivor's guilt, born out of being the one inexplicably left behind when Death stopped at this house.

'Look,' said Miriam, eyes still fixed on the screen. 'Look at us.'

Anna followed Miriam's gaze. The show appeared to be over. Geraldine, presumably, now had the camera, and was recording Hugh – less grey-haired than the man Anna remembered, and marginally less rotund, but still unmistakably Hugh – crawling in circles around the living room floor, giving Alfie a piggyback, while Miriam followed behind, periodically whacking his posterior with her wand.

'We were happy,' Miriam murmured by Anna's side. 'For all their foibles, of which my parents had more than their fair share, Alfie and I always knew we were loved. You can't buy that sort of thing – not with all the riches in the world. And that's the honest truth of the matter. I don't want fortune or fame or even a roof over my head. I just want my family back.'

In that moment, she appeared so small, so childlike, so utterly helpless, that Anna found herself fighting a sudden, uncharacteristic urge to lean across and fold her into an embrace.

'So no,' said Miriam, with an air of utter finality, 'I don't think I'll be selling up and shipping out. I'd rather hole up in here with nothing but the ghosts of the past for company till the bailiffs show up to turf me out.'

'Does that mean—' began Anna, before she could help herself.

'No. I haven't touched Daddy's accounts. I mean, that's what you've been driving at with all this money talk, isn't it?'

Anna didn't know what to say. Miriam didn't sound angry, just resigned – as if this was simply something they had to get out in the open so they could check it off the list.

'I know you've seen those scary-looking letters in the hallway,' she continued, 'so let's not dance round the maypole here. I know Daddy was never much cop at keeping his finances in order; that he made one dodgy investment after another and frittered away money willy-nilly without a care for the future. So yeah, I don't need to have done an audit of his accounts to know the money's dried up. Suppose I should be mad at him, right?'

Anna didn't feel qualified to answer that question. She just shrugged weakly.

'Well, I'm not. I can't hold it against him. It's just who he was. I knew it, Mum knew it – hell, *you* probably knew it, or at least had an inkling. Expecting him to change would be like expecting … I dunno, expecting a horse to turn into a zebra or something.'

'In that case, surely all the more reason to sell up and make the most of the proceeds. I mean … I don't think your dad would want you to cling to the past.'

Anna was aware of the hint of desperation in her voice as she spoke, but she didn't care. This was no longer about trying to find out what Miriam did and didn't know about her father's finances. It had been confirmed pretty conclusively that she had no specific knowledge about the money going into and coming out of his accounts but was nonetheless under no illusions as to the general state of play. Rather, it had become about trying to save her from what could only be regarded as the road to ruin; convincing her to take control of the situation before it was too late.

'But the past is so much nicer a place to live in than the present,' said Miriam. 'Don't you think so?'

Anna, who couldn't bring herself to agree with this statement at all, declined to answer.

Miriam gave her a small, sad smile and shook her head. 'Nah. I'd rather hunker down and stand my ground. I know it's only a matter of time before I get that knock on the door …' She turned her head towards Anna, and for a brief moment, her features contorted in a twisted little grin. '… but they won't take me without a fight.'

Anna said nothing. If she was honest with herself, she found Miriam's smile vaguely disconcerting. Not for the first time, she worried that the younger woman's grip on reality wasn't all that robust.

She turned and gazed at the TV screen. Hugh was on his back now, limbs flailing as the two children crawled over him, giggling and tickling him all over. The sound still muted, Anna watched as he silently begged for mercy, his protestations unable to disguise his utter delight at the situation in which he found himself.

. . .

It was dark by the time Anna finally made a move. She would have left earlier, but she was reluctant to leave Miriam in such an obviously fragile state. Only when Miriam began to yawn did Anna gently suggest that it was time she herself was heading to her bed, to which Miriam reluctantly agreed.

'Thanks for coming,' said Miriam, as she saw Anna to the door. 'I know this evening was a bit of a disaster, and …' She gave a small, self-deprecating laugh. 'Well, I fancy you didn't sign up for a front-row seat at my own personal pity party … but I really appreciate you keeping me company, and for listening.'

She reached out and touched Anna's forearm, meeting her eyes with that familiar intense stare from which Anna found it impossible to look away.

'That's all right,' Anna said. 'And you don't have to apologise for anything. Really.'

Miriam gave a wan smile. 'You're very kind. A crummy liar, but kind.'

Not sure what to say, Anna forced a smile of her own and gently withdrew her arm. For several seconds, they simply stood facing one another at the door, neither seemingly knowing how to draw things to a close.

'You're looking into his death, aren't you?' said Miriam suddenly.

Blindsided by the accusation, Anna could only stare at her, frozen to the spot, her mouth suddenly dry.

'S-sorry?' she eventually managed to stammer.

Miriam gave a dry chuckle. 'It would hardly be your first rodeo, now, would it? A bunch of the questions you've asked me over the last few days have had a certain … probing air to them, no matter how wily you've tried to be about it. Besides, I can't think why else you've kept coming back here. Not for *my* scintillating company, that's for sure.'

'I …' Anna began helplessly, then realised she had no idea how to respond to any of this.

'I can't pretend I haven't wondered, from time to time, whether Daddy had got himself mixed up in something before the end,' Miriam went on. 'I mean, don't get me wrong – it's not as if I'm *happy* at the thought of you rooting around in our lives, going through all our dirty little secrets. But …' She shrugged limply. 'Well, better *you* rooting through my knicker drawer than some policeman, I suppose.'

'I can assure you, I haven't been anywhere near your knicker drawer,' said Anna, horrified at the very thought.

Miriam gave a high-pitched little giggle, covering her mouth. 'It was a figure of *speech*! You don't have to be quite so literal *all* of the time, Anna.'

'So people keep telling me.'

Miriam's expression turned serious. 'I want you to promise me you'll tell me anything you happen to find out – *before* anyone else hears about it.'

As the younger woman's eyes bore into her, Anna wondered, for an uncomfortable moment, whether Miriam, in fact, had some inkling as to just who it was who'd put her up to this in the first place. She forced herself to dismiss her own paranoid thoughts, reminding herself that, if Miriam had even the slightest notion of Fraser's involvement, she wouldn't have got over the threshold. At least, not in one piece.

'I promise,' she said, more to get Miriam off her back than anything. 'And I want *you* to promise you'll give some thought to selling up.'

Miriam pulled a dubious face. 'We'll see. No doubt it'd need a ton of work done before it's fit to go on the market. And you can't let just any old cowboy builder loose on a place like this. This is an Outstanding Conservation Area for a reason, you know.'

It sounded to Anna like she was getting her excuses for continuing to bury her head in the sand lined up. But she recognised that this was likely to be the closest she was going to get to an agreement under the circumstances, so she decided not to rock the boat any further.

'You take care of yourself, Miriam,' she said, with the warmest smile she could muster, then turned and let herself out.

Anna caught a train to Hyndland and walked back to the hotel. Before she turned in, she opened Facebook on her phone and checked to see whether Libby Bright had responded to her friend request. She wasn't particularly surprised to discover that the answer was in the negative. She told herself it made little difference; that, by this time tomorrow, she could well have all the answers she needed.

As she lay in bed, waiting for sleep to claim her, her phone lit up on the nightstand as a text came in. She reached across and angled the screen towards her.

PAUL VASILICO
Still awake?

She groaned, then disconnected the phone from the charger and rolled onto her back, resting the device on her stomach as she tapped out a response.

ANNA SCAVOLINI
Just about.

PAUL VASILICO
What are you wearing?

ANNA SCAVOLINI
Not much.

PAUL VASILICO
Prove it.

ANNA SCAVOLINI
Uh-uh. Once bitten, twice shy.

> PAUL VASILICO
>
> Spoilsport ☹

> ANNA SCAVOLINI
>
> You'll just have to use your imagination. Sweet dreams X

She grinned to herself, buoyed by the salacious thrill of what they were doing. Then she set her phone to silent, returned it to the nightstand and rolled over onto her side, closing her eyes as she sank into the soft pillow.

She went to sleep and dreamt about going at it with Vasilico in the alleyway. As she was on the verge of climaxing, she turned her head towards the street to see Matteo and Jack standing hand in hand, watching her. Matteo's expression was one of bland disinterest, but Jack's brows were furrowed in sullen, studied disapproval.

25

Sunday 15 August

Anna had a leisurely start the following morning. She kicked things off with a forty-five-minute run, then returned to the hotel for a shower and breakfast, before heading into the West End to spend an hour or so clothes-shopping. By now, she'd well and truly exhausted the wardrobe she'd brought with her and had been relying on mixing and matching the least offensive-smelling items, bolstered by the sort of liberal application of deodorant that inevitably leaves anyone catching a whiff suspecting that the wearer has something to hide. In contrast to the previous day, the weather was shaping up to be far more typical of a Scottish summer. There was a light breeze in the air and the sky was heavy with clouds. According to her phone, it was going to rain, though not till late evening.

Before heading out, she'd had a short and rather strained call with Matteo, which had felt uncomfortably like a chore to be endured rather than something that held any pleasure for her. There'd been no further discussion about when she'd be returning to join them, but it had remained the elephant in the room throughout the call. In contrast, Jack had seemed in high spirits when she briefly spoke to him before ringing off, his unhappiness about her absence the previous day apparently forgotten. He'd babbled excitedly to her about the activities they had lined up for the day, including a speedboat ride around the lake and a vespa tour of the local villages.

It was approaching midday when Anna made her way down to the Budget Rent a Car office at Anderston Quay, and, having completed the requisite forms and handed her credit card and driver's licence over to the clerk, left in a newish Ford Fiesta with a slightly stiff clutch but no other obvious imperfections.

The MOT on Anna's own car, currently out of commission in a storage unit in the city centre, had expired over a year ago. Having re-examined the public transport options under the fresh light of day, she'd concluded that it would be far less of a headache to simply hire a car for the day and drive to the wildlife sanctuary herself. As she followed the M8 out of Glasgow and began the roughly hour-long journey south towards Moffat, she ran over the plan for her coming encounter with Libby.

She knew she was taking something of a chance by banking that Libby would be working today. It might, perhaps, have been more prudent to have phoned beforehand to confirm she was on site. But then, if Libby really *was* on the run, the last thing she wanted to do was spook her into taking flight by tipping her off to the fact that someone was looking for her. She could, too, have left it till Monday, when there'd be more likelihood of her actually being there. But she didn't fancy letting an entire day elapse without at least having *tried* to move the needle forward. She'd been here for long enough already. She was just going to have to chance it, and, if Libby wasn't there, come back tomorrow.

And the day after, and the next day after that? How long are you going to keep them waiting, Anna?

To that, she had no answer.

. . .

Shortly before 1:30 p.m., she saw a sign indicating the turn-off for the Auchen Wildlife Rescue Centre. She followed the rough gravel track for a couple of miles until she came to an open space that housed several low, mismatched huts and a larger, single-storey unit that was clearly the main base of operations. A handful of cars were parked haphazardly in the vicinity of the buildings, most of them caked with mud and looking seriously run-down. Everything about the place screamed 'shoestring operation'.

Anna came to a stop at a respectable distance from the other vehicles, turned off the engine and sat, pondering her next move. Originally, she'd planned to march straight into the office and ask to speak to Lizzie Wright. Now that she was here, though, she wasn't convinced that was wise. She wanted to avoid creating a scene unless she absolutely had to and figured it would be better to get Libby on her own if she could. That meant she had little choice but to sit here and hope to spot her coming out of one of the buildings at some point. At least, from her current vantage point, she had a good view of the entire complex. She glanced down at her phone and the picture from the sanctuary's website, reminding herself of what Libby looked like, and settled in to wait.

For the next three quarters of an hour, she did just that, listening to Max Richter's 2004 album *The Blue Notebooks* on her phone's speaker from beginning to end before moving on to its 2006 follow-up, *Songs from Before*. During that time, she observed a handful of people heading to and fro, all moving with considerable purpose. At 1:55, a middle-aged woman emerged from one hut and strode across the grounds before disappearing into a different one on the other side of the grounds. At 2:15, an older man came out of the main building, got into a battered Land Rover and drove off. Neither of them paid Anna any heed. Either she'd parked in a sufficiently secluded location that they hadn't noticed her gleaming rental, so out of place amid this array of mud-spattered hand-me-downs, or else they had better things to do than ask the driver of said vehicle to account for herself.

It had just gone 2:30 and Anna was beginning to think she was going to have to chance her luck marching up to reception and asking for Libby when the door to the main building opened and two young women in matching olive-green fleeces emerged, engaged in earnest discussion. One was carrying a clipboard. Both had dark hair in ponytails. They set off across the grounds, continuing their conversation. Anna glanced down at the image on her phone. There was no question about it: they were the two women from the sponsored run.

She got out of the car and set off towards them, striding quickly across the gravel in the hope of intercepting them before they reached their destination. The two girls continued to talk, the sound of Anna's footsteps drowned out by the wind whipping across the open grounds.

'Lizzie?' she called. 'Lizzie Wright?'

The pair came to a halt, turning to face her. One – the one carrying the clipboard – looked decidedly warier than the other.

'Yes?' she said, shoulders squaring defensively. 'Do I know you?'

'We haven't met, no,' said Anna, choosing her words carefully and with one eye on the other girl, who appeared more than a little confused by her companion's reaction. 'But I believe the two of us have an old acquaintance in common. Hugh MacLeish.'

A flicker of something passed over the girl's face. Anna couldn't read the meaning behind it, but it was clear that the name had made some sort of impact on her. When she next spoke, there was a harsh, threatening edge to her voice, but tinged with something else as well. Something that sounded suspiciously like fear.

'What do you want?'

'Just to talk,' said Anna.

Libby – for there was no doubt whatsoever that that was who she was – glanced briefly at her companion, then turned her gaze back to Anna.

'I don't know anyone of that name,' she said, her voice catching in her throat.

This claim would have been a whole lot more convincing if it had been her first response to hearing Hugh's name rather than the belated denial it so clearly was.

'Be that as it may,' said Anna levelly, 'I'd still like to talk to you. I think you might be able to help me get to the bottom of something.'

'Is everything OK, Liz?' said the other girl – Rhona, by process of elimination – as Libby continued to meet Anna's gaze, jaw set.

'Go on without me,' said Libby through gritted teeth, her eyes not leaving Anna's. 'I'll not be long.'

'Are you sure?'

'Yes, I'm sure,' Libby almost snapped. *'Go.'*

With that, she virtually shoved the clipboard into Rhona's hands before turning to face Anna once more. With an uncertain backward glance, Rhona scurried off, disappearing into the hut at the far end of the grounds.

'Now,' said Libby, scowling at Anna with undisguised fury, 'what is it you want?'

'First things first,' said Anna, forcing herself to keep a level tone in the face of the other woman's flagrant aggression, 'your real name isn't really Lizzie Wright, is it? It's Libby Bright, and you were a sociology student at Kelvingrove University.'

'You obviously know the answer, so why bother to ask?'

Despite the harshness of her tone, her accent was soft;

recognisably Scottish but not tied to any particular region – like a carving that had had all its rough edges sanded down.

'Well, since we're on the subject of names,' said Anna, 'mine's Anna Scavolini, and until a couple of years ago, I taught criminology at KU. Hugh was ... well, I suppose he was the closest thing I had to a mentor in that place.'

'Bully for you,' said Libby. 'You still haven't told me what you want.'

'You know he's dead, I take it?'

'What if I do? And why the hell can't you just get to the point?'

'I wanted to establish a few facts first,' said Anna, continuing to sound perfectly reasonable in the face of Libby's increasingly belligerent ripostes. 'Now that we've confirmed that you *are* Libby Bright, that you *did* know Hugh MacLeish and that you *were* aware he'd died, I reckon we can make some progress. What I want to talk to you about is Hugh, and the fact that, between September 2019 and May 2020, he made multiple bank payments to you – payments totalling several thousand pounds. I hoped you might be able to explain to me why he made them and what he was getting from you in return.'

There was a wild look in Libby's eyes now. Her entire face blazed with fury, but behind the rage, Anna detected something else. The fear that had only been hinted at before was now palpable, her aggression driven as much by her brain's innate 'fight or flight' mechanism as by anger.

'Why don't *you* tell *me*,' she snarled, 'seeing as how you seem to know so fucking much already?'

'I think the two of you were having an affair, and he was buying your silence.'

Libby didn't respond. Her expression didn't change, but Anna saw, from the rapid flaring of her nostrils, that she was breathing heavily, struggling to keep a lid on the emotions broiling inside her.

'I want to make something clear,' Anna went on, feeling she really needed to say this. 'I didn't come here to make trouble for you. All I want is for you to tell me what really happened between you and Hugh, and then I'll go away and leave you alone. You'll never hear from me again. How does that sound?'

'Or,' said Libby, spitting the words from between her pinched lips like bursts of venom, 'I've got a better idea. How about I give you one minute to get back in that car of yours and go back to wherever the fuck you came from before I march into my boss's office and tell him a woman I've never met before today is harassing me and won't fucking leave me alone? How's *that* sound?'

Anna suppressed a sigh. She'd hoped it wouldn't come to this, but she'd come here fully prepared for Libby to refuse to play ball.

'I said I didn't want to make trouble for you,' she said, once again making sure her tone remained level and eminently reasonable. 'That doesn't mean I *won't*.'

Libby stared back at her, the fear in her eyes now unmistakable.

'What do you mean?' she said, in a much smaller and meeker voice than before.

'Just this. If you involve your boss, I'll have no option but to give him a full and frank explanation as to why I'm here. In the process, that will unavoidably mean telling him that your real name is Elizabeth Bright and that you're a former Kelvingrove University graduate. I'm guessing you lied about your identity on your job application? Probably falsified your employment history and references too.

'Now, I'm not saying that'll definitely be enough to get you sacked. Your boss might feel that, on balance, the work you've done here is good and that he doesn't want to lose you over a small case of identity fraud. But then again, he might not. He might be someone who values honesty above all else; who feels that trust, once broken, isn't something that's easily regained. The question is, is it a risk you're willing to take?'

Libby just stared at her, wide-eyed and speechless. Anna saw the whites of her eyes; saw the carefully maintained façade she'd created, and all the barriers she'd put up between her new life and her old one, on the verge of crashing down. A part of her hated herself for what she was doing; for the depths to which she was allowing herself to sink in pursuit of the truth. But she also knew she couldn't bring herself to walk away empty-handed – not now that she'd come so far and was so close to getting to the bottom of what had really been going on in the final stages of Hugh's life.

'Come on,' she said, adopting a kinder, gentler tone. 'You've carried this for at least the last couple of years. That's got to have taken its toll on you. I'm willing to bet there's a part of you that wants to get this whole thing off your chest. I'm not the police, and I give you my word on this: whatever you say to me, whatever you have or haven't done, none of it will find its way back to them. Not from me.'

Still, Libby didn't speak. A glassy look had come into her eyes. She appeared to be gazing off into the middle distance, no longer quite present in the immediate moment. At length, she shut her eyes. A great, heaving sigh escaping from her as she made her peace with whatever decision she'd just made.

'All right,' she said quietly. 'I'll tell you what happened. But first I need to square things with my boss.'

26

Libby emerged from the main building five minutes later and made her way over to Anna, waiting for her on the other side of the grounds.

'I told him something'd come up and I needed to take off for a bit,' she said, refusing to make eye contact. 'We fixed it so I'll stay behind till Gareth gets here to do the night shift.'

'Is there someone here all night?' asked Anna, surprised.

'There is right now. We're rearing a couple of baby barn owls and someone needs to be on site 24/7 to do hourly checks. It's a ball-ache, and I'm forever picking down out of my clothes, but you get … I dunno, a sense of purpose or something.'

As she spoke, a sense of warmth entered both her face and her voice as she briefly became lost in talking about a subject about which she was clearly passionate. Then, she seemed to belatedly remember she was still furious with Anna and pasted on her familiar scowl once more.

'Right,' she said. 'We're not doing this here. Let's take a walk.'

They set off, Anna gamely following Libby across the grounds until they came to a path leading away from the sanctuary, barely more than a faint, uneven line of dirt amid the overgrown grass. The ground gently rose and fell beneath their feet, the trees on either side of them periodically giving way to reveal undulating fields and, in the distance, mountains dotted with thickets of trees. Overhead, the sky was slate-grey, the bruised clouds threatening to burst at any moment. Anna hoped they weren't going too far; she pictured the heavens opening when they were miles from shelter.

'I want to make it clear I'm not here to judge you,' she said, feeling she needed to at least try to get things off on a more cordial note than had so far been achieved. 'I'm not interested in the rights and wrongs of anything you did. I just want to know what happened.'

'I remember you,' said Libby. 'You're that professor who had her nudie pictures seen by half the uni. You've lost weight since they were taken.'

Anna ignored the lurch in her stomach at the memory conjured by those words. She knew Libby was trying to bait her – or perhaps trying to pay her back for her own invasion of *her* privacy, showing up here and confronting her with the life she'd left behind.

'So I've got to ask,' said Libby.

'Sorry?'

'How was it you tracked me down?'

Anna found herself momentarily thrown by the question. 'The photo on the shelter's website. The sponsored run?'

'Oh,' said Libby. 'That. Knew it was a mistake posing for that. But I could hardly say no, could I? I mean, it was for *charity*.'

'I suppose not,' Anna agreed.

They walked on for a few more paces, then Libby came to a sudden, unexpected halt and turned to face Anna. Anna managed to stop herself from ploughing on into Libby only just in time.

'Shall we get on with this, then?' said Libby.

'No time like the present.'

Libby said nothing. She just stared back at Anna expectantly, arms folded.

'Well?' she said after a moment.

'Well, what?'

'Phone. Hand it over.'

It took nearly all Anna's willpower not to laugh.

'Is that really necessary?'

Libby merely extended her hand, palm up, and raised an eyebrow expectantly.

Realising she was in no position to argue – and also that she had nothing to lose, as the thought of recording their conversation would never have crossed her mind anyway – Anna fished her phone out of her bag and handed it over. Libby examined it for a moment, then switched it off and slipped it into her pocket.

'You can have it back when we're done.'

Then, without another word, she turned her face to the wind and set off along the path once more. She waited until Anna, walking fast to match the brisk stride of Libby's longer legs, had fallen into step with her once more before speaking again.

'So where would you like me to start?'

'I find the beginning's usually the best place,' said Anna.

Libby nodded philosophically, conceding the point.

'The beginning,' she murmured to herself. Then, addressing Anna, 'Well, then, let's see. I suppose it would have been just over two and a half years ago, one night in the middle of January …'

PART IV

A DOWN AND DUSKY BLONDE

27

Tuesday 15 January 2019

At the time, I was just going into the final months of my sociology undergrad, and I was working part-time at Gianetto's, this snobby wine bar on Hyndland Road, to help keep a roof over my head. You know the kind of place: the kind that puts on all sorts of airs and graces; thinks it's posher than it really is. The manageress was this proper hard-nosed woman who thought she was really something. Far as she was concerned, the serving staff were the lowest of the low, and being shat on by her was a rite of passage we all had to go through so's we didn't get too comfy and start thinking of waitressing as a long-term career choice. I lost track of the number of times I had to stop myself from telling her where to go. But I needed to pay my way somehow, and it was either that or go back to flipping burgers at McDonald's, and I never could stand the smell of chip pan fryers.

So, this night, my shift's finally over and I'm on my way out the door when this old bloke keels over right in front of me. Turns out he's having a heart attack. I was the designated first aider, so I dumped my bag on the nearest chair and dove right on in there. It was mental. His wife was sobbing and wailing, and Nicolette – that's the manageress – was just stood there saying 'Oh my God oh my God oh my God' over and over again. Anyway, about fifteen minutes later, the ambulance shows up, whisks him off to hospital, and I'm free to go.

Only trouble is, I can't find my bag. It was one of these big, fake leather shoulder bags – plenty of room in it for all the essentials. My flat at the time was out in Royston so I'd normally just go straight to work from uni, or vice versa – so of course all my coursework was in there, including a couple of essays due in next week which I'd made a decent start on writing. Naturally, I panicked – hunted high and low for it, accused everyone within earshot of lifting it. Nicolette was about as sympathetic as you can imagine. Told me I was responsible for any personal property I brought onto the premises, not her.

In the end, I'd no choice but to give up and go home – accept that someone had made off with it in the commotion. I thought that was the last I'd ever see of it.

Few days later, I arrive for work and there's this woman waiting for me – and wouldn't you know it? She's got my bag with her. Says she was walking home the other night and spotted it sticking out from under the hedgerow just up the road from the bar. She figures whoever stole it realised there was nothing valuable in it and chucked it away. I'd had my purse and my house keys in my coat pocket at the time, so that pretty much tracks. Says she had a look inside and saw my name on one of my essays and realised it must be mine.

Right at that moment, I'm just so over the moon to have it back, my brain's no good for much else besides saying 'thank you' over and over and asking her how I can pay her back. And she says to me, 'I'm not looking for any payment … but I *have* got a proposition for you. You can either accept it or not. All I ask is that you listen to what I have to say before you make a decision.'

I agree to meet her at the pub round the corner once my shift's over.

It's only after I leave and have time to think that it suddenly dawns on me: what the hell use was my name on an essay to her? How did she connect it to *me*?

By the time she arrives at the pub, I've had plenty of time to mull that question over, so as soon as she's sat down facing me, I come straight out with it and say to her, '*You* were the one who lifted my bag, weren't you?'

She insists she didn't – swears blind she just found it lying under the hedge. And who knows? Maybe that much is true. But either way, any fool can tell she's being less than a hundred percent transparent with me.

I say, 'I don't know you from Adam. So how come you see the name "Libby Bright" on a bit of paper and straight away think, "That's the girl with blonde hair who waits tables at Gianetto's"?'

And, just as I thought, she admits she's had her eye on me for a while. Says she was at the bar a few weeks back and I caught her attention.

I say, 'Am I supposed to be flattered?'

She goes on to say she went rooting through the rest of my stuff – trying to find some clue to who it belonged to. Yeah, *right*. And she came across my Social Justice coursebook and sees I've got Hugh MacLeish as one of my lecturers. And before I know what's going on, she's grilling me about him – asking me whether I reckon he's any cop as a lecturer; what I think of him as a person. I'm still too bamboozled by the direction this conversation's taken to ask what's it to her, so, like an obedient wee schoolkid, I answer all her questions. Say he's all right – bit of an old fuddy-duddy, reckon he's got his head in the clouds most of the time – but he's not a *complete* stuck-up old tosser, unlike some whose names I could mention. And then she starts asking me about his interactions with the students, 'specially the girls. Have I ever seen him say or do anything inappropriate with them? Has he ever been inappropriate with *me*?

I'll tell you the same thing I told her: at that point in time, me and Hugh MacLeish had had maybe half a dozen interactions tops, and at least half of those were me saying, 'Sorry I'm late, Professor.' He'd taught me for four years and I'd put good money on him not even knowing my name. I tell her, 'If you're looking for someone to dish the dirt on the old coot, I'm not your girl. Go bother someone else,' and get up to leave.

'Wait,' she says. 'Please, stay a moment. You haven't heard my proposition yet.'

So I sit down again. Tell her she's got five minutes to come to the point.

And she does, pretty much. Says that, years ago, someone close to her got hurt really bad by Hugh, and that he got away with it scot-free. She doesn't tell me any specifics, but given she's just been asking about inappropriate behaviour, and given what comes next, it doesn't take a genius to guess what she's driving at.

I say to her, 'Someone close to you? Or do you mean you yourself?'

She doesn't answer me, but I dunno 'bout you – I find that pretty telling.

So she gives me her pitch, and it's this: she wants to pay me to seduce Hugh. Says she'll give me two hundred quid a week for however long it takes me to get my claws into him, plus another five thou' as a bonus if I'm successful and bring her incontrovertible proof.

Yeah. The look on your face is pretty much the same one I had on mine when she said it. I'm like, 'Is this a fucking piss-take?'

And she swears to me she's dead serious. Says it's always haunted her that Hugh got away with what he did and she's willing to do whatever it takes to bring him to justice. She tells me she knows how skint I am; says she overheard me grousing to one of my colleagues the other week about how my landlord had jacked up my rent and my studies were taking a hit on account of how many extra shifts I was having to take on just to cover the essentials. And that was all the proof I needed to know she'd been camping out at Gianetto's for a while, scoping me out, biding her time. Wouldn't surprise me if she'd been following me too. For whatever reason, she'd clearly made up her mind I was the one to carry out her little scheme, and she knew enough about my money worries to know I'd be … suggestible.

So I looked her square in the eyes and said, 'Double what you're offering and *then* we can talk.'

In the end, we compromised: £300 a week and a completion bonus of £8,000. Truth was, I'd probably have settled for the original amount or less. I mean, I don't want you to think I'm the kind of person who sells herself on the cheap or anything, but *you* try putting yourself through uni, paying all the rent and bills, all with no support from your parents. Anyway, she folded pretty much straight away and I wasn't going to look a gift horse in the mouth. I figured it was easy money, and, as like as not, it wouldn't come to anything and, after a few weeks, she'd run out of patience and call the whole thing off. But if she was willing to fork out that much dosh on the off-chance I'd manage to persuade one of my professors to shag me … well, I was hardly in a position to say no, was I?

Before we go our separate ways that night, I ask her what I'm to call her. And she thinks about it for a moment – you know, brows all furrowed like she's trying to squeeze one out – and then she says, 'Call me Emily.'

28

'Emily?' repeated Anna.

Libby shrugged. 'That's what she said, and that's what I called her from that moment on. It wasn't her *real* name, of course.' She rolled her eyes, as if to even consider the possibility would be ridiculous. 'But it was no skin off my nose. I'd've called her "Your Royal Highness" if she was prepared to cut me a cheque for three hundred a week.'

'And *did* she?' asked Anna. 'Cut you a cheque, I mean.'

Libby scoffed derisively. '*Fuck* no. She paid me in cash. Fifteen crisp new twenties, fresh out the ATM. 'Least, that's how they always seemed. I never actually stood behind her and watched her withdrawing them, but they always had that "new money" smell.'

'And is there anything you can tell me about her? Age, appearance, any distinguishing features?'

For a moment, Libby seemed to bristle, as if she regarded providing these sorts of additional details as outwith the parameters of what they'd agreed. A moment later, though, she shrugged, seeming to relent.

'She was pretty unremarkable, all in all. Average height, I guess. Curly hair. Light brown, I think? No massive hairy moles on her face or anything. She dressed … like a businesswoman, I suppose? Plain skirts, blouses, that sort of thing. I always thought she looked like she'd come straight from the office. And I think she might've been English – or at any rate someone who'd spent some time there. Had those drawling vowels and couldn't pronounce her Rs.'

'What sort of age was she?'

Again, Libby had to think seriously about this.

'Dunno,' she said eventually. 'What age are *you*?'

'I'm forty.'

'Yeah. About that, then. Way older than *me*, at any rate. Actually, she was like you in a lot of ways. Sanctimonious, hoity-toity, acted like she was the only one in the room whose shit didn't stink.'

Anna ignored the obvious attempt to get a rise out of her.

'All right,' she said, 'so the two of you made your agreement. What happened then?'

29

At first, not a whole lot. She said from the start I wasn't to rush into anything. Told me, if I just went and threw myself at him right from the word go, it'd never work.

'We need to lay the groundwork,' she said. 'Get him to notice you, then slowly reel him in.'

I remember, that first week, we met up on Saturday morning and she took me clothes shopping. She picked out a bunch of different outfits; everything from sexy librarian – you know, knee stockings and pleated miniskirts – to slutty sorority sister. She said she wasn't sure what would work on him, so we'd need to try a few things.

I got my hair done too, and my nails, and my eyebrows waxed. And she bought me enough makeup to open my own branch of Charlotte Tilbury's. She even gave me lessons on how to carry myself. You know, head high, tits out, sway my hips – like I was a fucking runway model or something. And she set me up with this voice recorder thingy, so I could tape my conversations with him, as well as this camera thing to attach to my shoulder bag – you know, one of those ones that looks like it's a button but it's actually a micro lens.

I'm not going to lie – a part of me kinda got a kick out of it all. I'd never really been one for dolling myself up to the nines – always seemed like too much effort, if I'm being honest. But … I dunno, there was something about the thought that I could be this honey trap – that's what they call it, isn't it? – that was … sort of a turn-on, y'know? I suppose a part of me was kind of a bit flattered that she thought I was that much of a knockout that she could turn me into this sex-bomb with just a bit of blusher and a plunge neck top. Plus, there was the whole thrill of doing something a bit clandestine – like I was a secret agent and she was my handler.

Anyway, you've got to understand, I still thought nothing would come of it. I figured it wouldn't take long till she realised she was basically burning money and told me the deal was off. So I kept going, doing like she said and taking it slow.

'For now, we just want him to notice you,' she said to me. 'Try to catch his eye, smile at him, maybe hang back after class to ask him something about the coursework. You want to convey to him that you're more switched on than the average student. Let whatever develops play out naturally.'

We'd meet up every week for me to make what she called 'progress reports'. That first night we met, she gave me this rinky-dink old pay-as-you-go phone. That was our way of staying in touch. The night before we were due to meet, she'd text me the time and location. Usually, it'd be some pub or bar, in different places all across the city. So there was less risk of someone remembering seeing us, I guess. Not that what we were doing was *illegal* or anything, but I figured she had her reasons for wanting to keep below the radar, and I didn't feel it would do me any good to ask what they were.

Besides, she was paying me good money for all of this. When you're basically being handed a no-questions-asked tax-free allowance every week, you don't feel all that inclined to ask too many questions. I was a bit worried about the lack of progress at first; if I was making any sort of impact on Hugh at all, it wasn't obvious. But she didn't seem bothered.

'We always knew we were in this for the long haul,' she said to me when I'd told her for like the third or fourth time that there was nothing new to report. And as we moved from January into February, and I could afford to pay my rent on time and even indulge in a few luxuries for myself, I stopped worrying she was going to pull the plug and came to realise I'd landed myself this really cushy deal. End of the first week of Feb, I marched into Gianetto's five minutes before I was due to go on shift and told Nicolette I was quitting with immediate effect. You should've seen the look on the old trout's face! Left her high and dry just before the start of the busiest night of the week.

I know what you're thinking. I should have looked further ahead. You know, kept the job going so I wasn't putting all my eggs in one basket. Squirrelled away some of Emily's money so I had a bit of a nest-egg to fall back on when my circumstances changed. But I was young and daft. I'd never had disposable income before, so I went a bit doolally. I started to convince myself Emily was this crazy rich loony lady who got her rocks off doing the whole *My Fair Lady* routine on girls like me, and that the arrangement we had would just go on indefinitely. Like how, deep down, Tom doesn't actually want to catch Jerry. The chase is the whole point, know what I mean? And, if things changed, I figured I'd cross that bridge when I came to it.

I know it sounds super dumb, but that was really what I thought. Call it delusion, call it motivated reasoning, call it what you like, but I was hook, line and sinker down the rabbit hole and I never wanted it to end.

30

I think it was the second or third week of February when I had my first proper breakthrough. I'd been doing the 'slow and steady' thing like Emily'd told me – catching Hugh's eye and smiling at him on my way in and out of class; hanging back every so often to ask him about some random thing that'd come up in the lecture. And he always seemed to be tickled pink that I was wanting to know more, and to have a chance to go more in-depth with me about his pet subjects ... but it never seemed to go much beyond that. Plus, he kept getting my name wrong. Sometimes I was 'Lily'; other times it was obvious he couldn't remember it at all and would 'um' and 'er' till it got really uncomfortable for us both and then give up and move on to something else. Basically, I had the feeling I wasn't making much of an impression on him at all. If I'm being honest, I suppose I was starting to doubt my own abilities.

I figured it was time to step things up a gear.

I came up with the whole plan myself. No input whatsoever from Emily. I didn't even run it by her first, in case she told me no.

It was actually kind of brilliant, if I say so myself.

. . .

On Friday evening, there was this really intense downpour. I'd seen it on the weather forecast the night before so I knew it was coming, and I knew I'd get caught in it right when it was at its worst.

I also knew that was when Hugh normally left work.

I'd been scoping him out for a while by this stage, so I had a pretty good feel for what time he usually left at and the route he took. So, when he was driving down University Avenue towards Byres Road at a quarter to six, I just happened to be standing at the bus stop, all bedraggled and shivering in my miniskirt and denim jacket, waiting for a bus that hadn't come and was never *going* to come, on account of the bus I needed to get home not *taking* that route. And, of course, good Samaritan that he is, he sees me standing there, clutching myself, and he pulls over and winds down the window and says, 'It's ... Libby, isn't it?'

I think that might've been the first time he ever got my name right without prompting. So I gave him my sob story, all forlorn and sheepish-like, about how I'd been waiting there since four-thirty and there was no sign of my bus, and he got this uneasy look on his face, like I was putting him in an impossible situation, and for a few moments I thought he was going to say, 'That's too bad. Hope it comes soon,' and drive off. But then he seemed to, like, sort of deflate a bit, almost like he'd just resigned himself to his fate, and he said, 'Can I give you a lift somewhere?'

He ends up driving me all the way out to my flat in Royston. Silly old sod doesn't seem to've noticed it's in a totally different direction from the bus stop. Either that or he's just too polite to say anything.

We sit there for a bit, waiting for the downpour to let up so's I can make a dash for the building, trying to make small talk. It's amazing how quick you run out of things to say when you've got nothing in common and there's a forty-year age gap between you. I talk a bit about the course – how much I'm enjoying it; how *his* stuff, the social justice stuff, has really resonated with me. And he's just sitting there, nodding and saying, 'That's nice' and 'I'm so glad', like he's some clueless spotty-faced boy who's never had to speak to a girl before. Mibby I'd've had more luck if I'd asked him to tell me about his stamp collection or something.

Eventually, the rain tails off a bit and I say I'm gonna make a move. I thank him again for running me home, saying he didn't have to, and then, just as I'm about to open the door and get out, I get this impulse and think, *It's now or never.* So I lean over to kiss him on the cheek.

Right at the same moment, he turns to look at me, and our lips touch. Only for, like, a fraction of a second, and it's obvious it's an accident, but, straight away, he jumps back like I've just slapped him, his whole face turning the colour of a strawberry. And he keeps saying, 'I'm sorry, I'm so sorry', over and over again, and I'm laughing and saying it's all right, there's no harm done, but he's obviously completely mortified. I ask him if he wants to come up for a bit.

'Better not,' he says, still beet-red.

And I run my hand through my hair and give this simpering little smile – one I'd been practising in the mirror for a while – and say, 'Why? What's the worst that could happen?'

But he's absolutely insistent, saying he needs to get home – that his daughter's waiting for him. So I just play it cool and wink at him, like we're both part of this delicious conspiracy, and get out of the car, and bend down to look at him, making sure the top buttons of my shirt are undone so's he can see my cleavage, and I say, 'Thanks again for the ride, Hugh. You're one in a million.'

I'd never called him that before. Some of the lecturers, the younger ones especially, they're cool with you calling them by their first name, but with others, you just know, without even testing the waters, they're not into that. And for a moment I think he's going to say, 'That's "Professor MacLeish" to *you*.'

But he doesn't. Instead, he just steps on the pedal, absolutely *floors* it, and takes off so fast he almost runs into this car coming straight towards him.

And as I stand there, watching him drive off, I think to myself, *Well, Libby, that's you well and truly crossed the Rubicon now.*

31

'I know what you're thinking,' said Libby, briefly glancing sidelong at Anna as they continued to tramp along the path. 'Shameless little tart, throwing herself at a clueless old diddy who was just trying to do a good deed.'

'I wasn't thinking that,' said Anna.

In truth, though, she wasn't sure *what* she was thinking. The whole story seemed so incredible, so far-fetched, that morality hadn't played a big part in her thought process so far. And, to the extent that it *had*, she was a long way from being convinced that, of all the people involved, Libby was the one whose morals were the most compromised.

Libby, however, didn't seem to have heard Anna's protestation. 'Not that I expect it makes any difference to you, but for, like, at least the next week, I was so wracked with guilt I could barely concentrate on anything. I thought a bunch of times about going to Emily and saying I was calling the whole thing off; that nothing I'd tried had worked and it was obvious he was just a kindly old man who enjoyed doing right by his students. I was ready to walk away from the weekly payments; from the promise of eight grand at the end of it. That's how serious I was.'

Anna might have been more inclined to believe this had Libby not been so obviously desperate to convince her.

'All right,' she said, 'but you obviously *didn't* walk away, since clearly this isn't the end of the story. So what happened next?'

For a moment, Libby didn't respond. Instead, she produced a lighter and a pack of Marlboros from the inside pocket of her jacket. Wordlessly, she offered the pack to Anna. Anna shook her head. Libby shrugged slightly, as if to say, *Your loss.* Then, slowing to a standstill, she selected a cigarette, clenched it between her teeth and lit it, cupping her hands to guard the flame against the wind. She took a long, contemplative drag before continuing.

32

You'll know this next part yourself. At the start of the first week of March, the big restructuring the uni had been threatening for ages finally took effect. All the old departments were disbanded and reorganised into subject areas under different schools. Hugh lost his position as head of Law and Social Science, and Fraser Taggart got the Head of School gig. Word on the street was he cut some sort of grubby backroom deal with the upper management to make sure he got the plum spot.

So poor old Hugh was out to pasture and now that jumped-up little twerp was cock of the walk, strutting around in his tight trousers and fancy shirt like he owned the place. Everyone knew he'd shafted Hugh. We all felt dead sorry for him, though I don't think anyone really knew what to say to him.

And that's when I realised – that could be my way in.

Ever since the incident in his car, I'd not had any direct contact with him. I'd kept my head down in lectures, and I got the sense he was going out of his way to avoid catching my eye. I was starting to think mibby I'd pushed things too far with the kiss; that I'd scared him off for good. Emily seemed to think so too. When I told her what'd happened, she gave me this whole lecture about how she's told me from the start not to rush things. And I was like, to myself, *Bitch*, you're *the one who wanted me to seduce the old fucker. Don't take it out on me just cos* your *harebrained scheme didn't pan out.*

I went looking for him in his office. Found him just sitting there at his desk, looking like this lost little boy who'd just found out Santa isn't real.

'Libby,' he says, looking up at me. 'What are *you* doing here? This isn't my drop-in hour.'

And I tell him I know, but I just couldn't hold off any longer. I *had* to tell him how livid I was about the way he was being treated. I said he'd been nothing but good to me, that he was my favourite lecturer and the best thing about my time at uni; that I'd've probably packed the whole thing in years ago if it wasn't for him.

'They're a bunch of scum-sucking parasites,' I said to him. 'They wouldn't know loyalty if it bit them on the arse.'

And for, like, a whole minute, he just sits there, gazing up at me with this look of wonderment in his eyes. And eventually, he says, 'You know, Libby, I think that's just about the nicest thing anyone's ever said to me.'

And then, while I'm busy wondering how fucking disappointing his whole life must've been if *that's* the highlight, he hits me with:

'How would you like to have dinner with me on Friday?'

I'm so gobsmacked, I can't think of anything to say. And while I'm standing there, jaw hanging open like a professional mouth-breather, he says quickly, 'I mean, I hope it doesn't sound too forward. It's just, I had reservations at the Kirkhouse Inn with an ex-colleague who's just called to say he's going to have to pull out, and it'd be a shame to cancel. I just don't think I've ever met another student quite like you, and I'd really like to do something to thank you properly for all your kindness.'

I'm paraphrasing a bit, but that was the gist of it. Anyway, it's so much of a bolt from the blue that I've no idea how to respond. Eventually, I manage to mumble something about having to check to see if I've anything on that night, and then I hightail it out of there as fast as I can.

I texted Emily straight away and said we had to meet. She seemed a bit miffed when she got to the pub that evening – like *me* being the one to set up a meeting was this grievous breach of protocol. But as soon as I told her what it was about, she changed her tune pretty sharpish. Said I was right to call her.

To be honest, I couldn't make out whether she was over the moon about this development or properly spooked. She seemed to go back and forth a few times – like, *oh my God* versus *oh my GOD*. Then, when I said should I tell him I wasn't gonna be able to make it, she was like, 'No! Absolutely not. You *must* say yes. We might never get another opportunity like this.'

To be honest, I didn't know how to feel about it myself. I suppose there was a part of me that was a bit nervous – like, after so long playing 'slowly, slowly, catchy monkey', I wasn't ready for things to shift so suddenly, so fast. But there was an even bigger part of me that was curious about what was going to happen next. Like, I'd obviously managed to worm my way in with him. Clearly I wasn't just A.N. Other Student to him anymore.

I guess a part of me wanted to see if I could actually pull it off. You know, could I actually convince the old duffer to go all the way with me?

So I said I'd do it. I'd go there, wearing my shortest skirt and lowest-cut top, and bat my eyelashes and tell him how amazing he was. I asked Emily if she was gonna be there too – like, camped out in some strategic location so she could watch the whole thing and catch him in the act.

It was like I'd set a rocket off under her. She practically

jumped up out of her seat, and was all, like, absolutely not! Are you crazy? No chance, no way, no cigar.

By this point, I was pretty much convinced she was this ex-student of his who he'd shagged and then hung out to dry, so I wasn't too surprised she didn't wanna run the risk of him spotting her and recognising her. But I hadn't expected her to nearly blow a gasket at the mere *idea* of it. And it got me wondering – just what *had* gone down between the two of them? Like, I'd always told myself I didn't care to know the ins and outs, as long as the money kept coming in. But after that, I couldn't help inventing all sorts of sleazy scenarios in my head about what they'd got up to and how he'd done her dirty.

Guess I've always had kind of a vivid imagination.

We didn't end up fucking that night. We didn't even kiss. So, in that respect at least, it was a bit of an anticlimax. I'd been psyching myself up for fireworks all week, but it ended up just being more of the same.

He picked me up after he finished work for the day, in this out-of-the-way side street near the uni. I can't remember whether that was my idea or his. His, I think. Like, even at this stage, he knew what we were doing wasn't *completely* innocent. We drove to this pub out in the middle of nowhere, miles from the West End. I know he said he'd been planning on coming here with an old colleague, but, if the goal all along'd been to make sure we'd not be seen by anyone who knew us, he couldn't've picked a better place.

I drank a lot of wine that night, and did a whole lot of stroking of his ego. You know, going on about how much I admired and respected him and how appallingly he was being treated by the place he'd devoted practically his whole life to. He told me I was wise beyond my years; that, when he talked to me, he often had to remind himself I was a student and not one of his contemporaries. That was the word he used – 'contemporaries'. And I giggled and fanned my boobs and said, 'Oh, Hugh', over and over again.

I don't know what the staff and other punters must've thought of us. I suppose, at a pinch, they might've assumed we were father and daughter. Or maybe *grand*father and daughter. But I was basically spilling out of my top and doing everything short of stroking his leg under the table, so I don't suppose anyone was under any illusions.

Honestly, I think, out of everyone there that night, *he* was probably the only one who didn't realise what was going on.

After he'd settled up for both of us, he drove me back into town – back to the same side street he'd picked me up from. As I was getting ready to make tracks, he told me how much he'd enjoyed our evening together, and how he hoped we could do it again sometime.

'I hope so too, Hugh,' I said, and got out and headed off into the night.

33

Over the next few weeks, we saw each other a bunch more times, always going to bars and restaurants in out-of-the-way places where there was less risk of us being spotted. We did have one near miss – when a couple he knew came into the same restaurant as us and he practically had a coronary right on the spot. We snuck out the back way, ducking behind the pony wall so they wouldn't see us. I think he actually got a bit of a kick out of it – you know, the idea that we were doing something *verboten*. I dunno – mibby, for him, it was like reliving his adolescence, going behind his parents' backs, seeing some girl they didn't approve of.

And all this time, we were getting closer and closer. I started talking to him about my background – where I'd come from, what my childhood was like, that sort of thing. I might've laid it on a bit thicker than was really warranted. I made out I'd had a hard life; that I never had much of anything growing up; that my folks were harsh taskmasters who only ever saw me as a future investment – someone to take over the family business from them one day. None of it was, strictly speaking, a lie, but I made it sound a whole lot more Dickensian than it actually was.

I told him I was the first person from my family to go to uni – which was true – and that my parents had told me I was on my own if I left them high and dry – which, again, was true. I made out it'd been my life's ambition to come to Glasgow to study under him; that I'd made untold sacrifices to make the dream come true.

'Oh, Hugh, you have no idea how much I need this,' I said to him. 'This is the only thing I've ever wanted to do.'

Time wore on. I got the hell out of Royston and moved into a new flat. It was much bigger, in a way nicer area. Pricier too, obviously – but hey, I could afford it now. I was still feeding back to Emily every week, though I noticed I was starting to downplay things a bit. In the beginning, I'd given her chapter and verse, telling her everything I thought had any relevance … which, a lot of the time, wasn't a whole lot, I'll grant you. But now that things were actually happening, I was making out things were still in the doldrums. I'd already told her about dinner at the Kirkhouse Inn, so I could hardly walk that back, but I made out we'd only been out once more since then, when it was actually more like six or seven times.

I certainly didn't tell her about the pay-as-you-go phone I'd bought him so's we could keep in touch more easily. Did you know the old duffer didn't even *own* a mobile? Used his landline for everything. I didn't know people like that still *existed*. I told him it was our little secret, and he seemed to like that. Took forever for him to get to grips with how it worked, though. Some folk are just beyond saving when it comes to tech.

I dunno why I never told Emily. About the phone or … any of the other things I held back. I suppose I never really thought about it that deeply. It certainly wasn't a conscious effort to pull the wool over her eyes – at least, not then. I just figured she didn't need to know. Why complicate things more than they had to be? Besides, I was using my own initiative. Call it my little side hustle.

At the end of March, out of the blue, Emily summons me and announces that she's going off on a business trip. All totally last-minute, out of the blue, out of the country, doesn't know how long she's gonna be gone for, all that jazz. Naturally, first thought that crosses my mind is: is this it? Is she calling the whole thing off? I can't honestly see this arrangement we've got going working long-distance, even though there's no earthly reason in the world why we can't do what we've been doing over the phone. So I come straight out and ask her, 'How'm I gonna get paid if you're abroad?'

And she looks a bit uneasy for a minute, like this hadn't even occurred to her. And then, quick as a flash, before she's got time to actually run through all the possibilities and consider that it might be easiest just to knock this on the head, I say, 'Tell you what: give me enough to cover the next four weeks, and if you're gone for longer than that, we can settle up when you get back.'

A part of me was thinking there was no way our arrangement would possibly survive her trip; that putting some distance between herself and Hugh, Glasgow and me would make her see how completely batshit the whole thing was. So when she agreed to give me twelve hundred quid then and there, I figured that was as good as it was gonna get. One last massive blow-out for old times' sake, before she came to her senses and knocked this whole nonsense on the head.

I waited in the café while she did the ATM merry-go-round. Forty-five minutes later, she's back, and, as she hands me this wad of cash under the table, she looks me dead in the eye and says, in this cold-as-nails voice, 'I'll be expecting RESULTS when I get back. Don't make me regret this.'

. . .

Same week, the teaching period finished and exam leave started.

I had three exam papers plus a 10,000-word dissertation to do, each worth a quarter of my final grade. Sociology's one of those subjects where they don't have any exams in third year. Instead, they pile it all up at the end of fourth year, meaning you're basically expected to vomit up everything you've learned in the last two years in just a few hours in a dusty exam hall. I'd gotten complacent. There'd been essays and class assessments and the like, but I was out of practice when it came to doing any sort of long-form writing. I'd misjudged how long it'd take me to knock my dissertation out, and when it got to the end of the week before it was due in, it was still in an absolutely horrendous state. Whichever topic you did your dissertation on, you didn't have to sit the equivalent exam paper, so I'd chosen Stuart Colgan's class on social interaction on account of it being the one I'd always had the hardest time wrapping my head round. I figured, give myself plenty of time to get it right 'stead of pinning all my hopes on a two-hour exam paper. But now I was out of time and staring down the barrel of a big, fat 'F'.

In hindsight, I know it looks like I engineered the whole thing to my advantage. But I swear, when I went and knocked on the door of Hugh's office on Friday morning, I didn't have any kind of ulterior motive. I was just desperate, and he was the only person I could think to turn to. I was already close to tears and struggling to get my breath when he opened the door. I didn't realise it at the time, but I think I was having a panic attack.

He took one look at me, then pulled me inside, sat me down and got me to take deep breaths. And then, once I'd calmed down a bit, he asked me what was the matter.

I told him about the dissertation. I'm afraid I lashed out a bit. I said it was cos of all the time I'd been spending with him that I'd fallen so behind. I wasn't *trying* to be nasty – I suppose I just needed someone to blame, and he just happened to be there. But I could tell he really took it to heart. He looked so crestfallen, kneeling on the floor in front of me, that, for a moment, I thought we ought to've swapped places.

Then he said, 'I'm sure it's not as bad as all that. Tell you what – email it to me and I'll take a look.'

I tried to say no, that he didn't have to do that, but he was insistent. He told me not to worry about the deadline – said there were always ways of getting around these things; that folk got extensions all the time, for all sorts of reasons.

So I did what he asked and emailed him my piece-of-shit draft. While I was waiting for him to give me his verdict, I got out of Glasgow, spent a couple of nights in a hotel down in London, doing all the touristy things. And, first thing Monday morning, when it's still not even properly light, I get a call from him on his pay-as-you-go, telling me to meet him in his office.

I head in – it's, like, 7:30 or something like that – and first thing he does, before I can even get a word out, is hand me this printout. And I take one look at it and realise that, over the weekend, he's rewritten my entire dissertation from scratch – all 10,000 words of it. And I'm flicking through it, recognising fragments of my original ideas, but turned into something so much better than I'd've ever been able to pull off by myself – not in a million years.

And my first thought was, *You old fool. You lovely, stupid old fool. Why've you done this to yourself?*

I knew this was a massive no-no; that he stood to lose his position at the uni, his reputation, his entire career, if this ever came out. But he was just standing there with this expectant smile, like this old mutt desperate for a clap on the head, and I didn't have the heart to say anything except, 'Thank you.'

I said it over and over. I was overwhelmed by gratitude for this kind-hearted old man who'd given up his weekend – put his livelihood at risk, for God's sake – all for some silly wee girl who'd failed to budget her time properly.

And he says to me, 'Is it all right?'

And I say, 'Oh, Hugh, it's *more* than all right. It's amazing. It's fantastic. No one's ever done anything like this for me.'

And he gets all bashful and tries to say it's nothing, but I say, 'No, Hugh, it's not nothing. What you've done, I don't have the words to describe.'

And then, on an impulse, I throw my arms round him and pull him in for a hug. And he's laughing awkwardly and is like, 'All right, all right', like this is all completely out of proportion to what he's done. And then …

And to this day, I'm still not sure what I was thinking. I suppose it just felt right in the moment.

I kiss him on the lips.

For a second or two, he just freezes, eyes bugging out like they're on stalks. And then he just sort of goes with it, and before I know what's happening, he's giving as good as he gets, and the two of us are sucking face like it's going out of fashion, and he's falling back into his chair, and I'm in his lap, straddling him, grinding myself up and down against him while he tries to undo the buttons on my top.

Then a door slams somewhere in the building and we come to our senses. And then he's pushing the print-out into my hand and hissing at me, 'Just take it and go!'

And then I'm out the door and hurrying down the corridor, doing up my buttons as I go.

34

We saw a whole lot more of each other after that. Every chance we got, really. My finals were just round the corner and he helped a ton with my revision, going over everything I was meant to have learned over the last couple of years, getting the sort of one-to-one tutoring that's usually only available to toffee-nosed private school kids whose folks've got money to burn.

Sometimes, we'd meet in his office at the university after hours. More often, we'd go to my new flat in Shawlands. He'd arrive after it got dark and buzz for me to let him in, then leave before it got light the next morning. I'm not going to pretend I didn't get a bit of a kick out of it – sneaking him up the close like he was this boy I was hiding from my landlady. He started buying me presents – mostly necklaces and bracelets and other tat like that. I wasn't particularly taken by any of it. I thought they were quaint and a bit tacky, like the sort of stuff you'd see a much older woman wearing. But it's the thought that counts, right? And there was certainly a bit of me that was genuinely flattered by all the attention.

I finally started fucking him during that time, too. I think the first time was in the second week of April. It wasn't as repulsive as you might think. I mean, I'm not saying screwing a flabby old guy in his sixties was my perfect idea of a good time, but at least it didn't take a lot of work on my part to get him off, and he'd always fall asleep pretty much straight after. I'm not pretending I *enjoyed* it, but there was something ... soothing, I suppose, about lying next to him in the dark, listening to him snoring.

I was meant to have been getting all this on tape, of course – and I did try, a couple of times, early on. The results weren't anything to write home about. I mean, if you knew what his voice sounded like, you'd know it was him, and you'd know he was getting jiggy with someone a whole lot younger than himself, but the positioning was off, so all you could see was the end of the bed. I never did manage to get the money shot. I kept meaning to take another crack at it, but the opportunity never presented itself. *You* try setting up the perfect angle when you're busy tearing the clothes off one another on your way to bed. It's not exactly practical. After a while, I just stopped thinking about it.

In an odd sort of way, it was easier without Emily around. I reckon, if I was still meeting her for weekly debriefs, I'd've had a much harder time just losing myself in the moment and going with it. Like, I'd always have been wrestling with what I was going to tell her. If I was going to tell her *anything*. At least, this way, it felt a bit less like entrapment and more like something we both wanted.

And I think, deep down, perhaps a part of me *did* want it. Not necessarily this exact arrangement and not necessarily with *him*, but he was there and he was clearly besotted with me, and whenever I was with him, he always managed to make me feel like I somehow ... I dunno, *mattered*. And that was more than any other man had ever made me feel before. This was a man who was so completely in thrall to me, that, if I'd told him to lick my feet, he'd've dropped down to all fours right then and there.

A man who, if I wanted to, I had the power to ruin just like that.

My exams were getting closer and closer. It worked out that they were all clustered together, between the second and third weeks of May. I know some folk barely had a week between lectures ending and their first exam, so I suppose I was lucky in that sense. But it was still a struggle. I've never been what you might call a natural academic. I can't just absorb information. And when I look at a page of really dense text, the words tend to just sort of blur together. Maybe I'm an undiagnosed dyslexic – I dunno.

But anyway, one night, after me and Hugh've been burning the midnight oil for hours, and I'm so tired I can barely see straight, I chuck the textbook we've been going over across the room and tell him it's no good, I'll never get to grips with this. And he hesitates for a moment, and then he reaches for his briefcase and opens it and hands me this single sheet of paper. And it's the exam questions for his subject, Social Justice.

He tells me it's not actually cheating – not really. Anyone looking at the past papers from the last five to ten years would have a half-decent shot at predicting which questions would come up, he says. I mean, maybe that's true and maybe it isn't, but the point is I was able to go into that exam knowing exactly what I was going to be asked and what my answers would be.

See, we workshopped those too. After he'd shown me the questions, it was like there wasn't any point pretending anymore. I basically memorised it all, word for word, to the point that, when I actually set foot in the exam hall, all I had to do was regurgitate the whole thing from memory.

That was one paper. Another was Pop Culture and Media. A bit like how you could choose to avoid sitting a paper on one module by writing a dissertation on it instead, you could also choose, instead of doing a traditional exam paper with multiple short questions, to do a series of longform essays on a set of prepared topics. You still had to write them in the exam hall, but you got to see the topics in advance, so there was no real surprise once you sat down and opened the paper. Again, Hugh and I workshopped those for hours. I mean, he basically wrote them and I just read and re-read them till I had them memorised, though he always insisted it was a joint effort. Maybe it was. I dunno.

It all meant I was going into just one exam paper – Urban Pasts and Futures – sight unseen. And even then, we did as much prep for it as we possibly could. Hugh made sure we covered every eventuality, and he was able to make some pretty educated guesses as to what was likely to come up from what he knew about the bloke who was setting the questions.

At the end of April, Emily got back from her trip. To tell you the truth, I'd been half-expecting never to hear from her again. She hadn't contacted me once in all the time she'd been away. But then, Friday night, as I'm lying in bed with Hugh, listening to him doing his impression of a hoover on full power, my burner phone lights up, giving me a time and place tomorrow morning. I arrive early, but she's there already, waiting for me, leg jiggling up and down like a pogo stick. And I've hardly slid into my seat before she's giving it, 'Well? Has it happened? Did he fuck you?'

I look back on this now as one of the handful of key moments in this whole chain of events where, if I'd chosen X instead of Y, things would've turned out completely different. I could've told the truth; come clean about everything that'd happened. And she'd've said, 'Good work, Libby. Take your £8,000 bonus and may you live a long life.' But then, that's the thing. It'd all've been over. Hugh would've lost his job, I'd've lost my weekly payments and my odds of graduating in June would've got a whole lot worse.

So instead I said, 'I'm close, but it hasn't happened yet.'

Well, she was *not* pleased about that, let me tell you. Started giving me chapter and verse, demanding to know what the fuck I'd been doing the last four weeks. I said to her, 'What happened to taking it slow?' And that just seemed to make her madder than ever. I could see she was on the verge of tearing up the whole agreement right there, and in a fit of blind, brainless panic, I blurted out that he'd rewritten my dissertation for me. Her expression softened a bit, and then, before I knew it, I was telling her all about him letting me see the exam questions and helping me with my prep, and I could see her getting more and more intrigued.

'I've got him wrapped round my little finger,' I said to her. 'He's going to do it with me – I can feel it. I just need a bit more time.'

And she bought it. She still acted all high and mighty; like I'd somehow broken the terms and conditions of our arrangement. But she gave me this sort of grudging look and told me she'd give me another month to seal the deal. And I saw the look in her eyes and knew there was no way round it: from that moment on, I was on borrowed time.

In retrospect, I knew it was a mistake to have told her about the dissertation and the exam questions. At the time, I wasn't thinking. I just wanted to get her off my back and stop the whole thing from going up in a puff of smoke. But, pretty quickly afterwards, I realised I'd fucked up big time. I'd just given her a shit ton of leverage over me, and I knew how easily that could come back to bite me.

I think that was the point when I first started seriously looking for a way out.

Back when I first agreed to the whole seduction project, I'd not seen it as anything more than a chance to make myself a bit of fast and easy cash. I never imagined it'd go on for this long. And, back then, I really couldn't have given a stuff about Hugh one way or the other. I know, I know – that makes me sound like a heartless cow, and maybe I am, but I don't see any point trying to sugarcoat it. I figured either I'd get nowhere with him, or I'd manage to seduce him and hand over the goods to Emily – and then, one way or another, he'd get what he deserved. I mean, he'd be bang to rights. Every teacher knows not to sleep with their students, right?

But things'd moved on since then. I know this is gonna be hard for you to believe, but I think I'd actually come to care about him. I'm not saying I was in *love* with him or anything. But he was kind and he was gentle, and I think, at the end of the day, he was just lonely. I knew his wife had died a few years back; that he'd never remarried. We all need someone to make us feel special, right? I figured, let him have his bit of fun. Let him think he still had enough going for him for a twenty-two-year-old student to fall for him.

But there was another side to it too, and now seems as good a time as any to mention it. See, I'd always imagined uni would be a 'four years and done' deal for me. Like I said already, I wasn't a natural academic. I figured it'd be a stepping stone for me. A way of polishing my CV and upping my chances of landing a semi-decent-paying job so I wouldn't have to go slinking back to Dunoon with my tail between my legs and prove my parents right about everything. But, about a week after I handed in my dissertation, I'd run into Stuart Colgan. The grades weren't due to be published till June, along with the rest of our exam results, but he'd obviously read it already, and he started dropping all these not-so-subtle hints about how impressed he'd been. He asked me, 'Have you ever thought about applying for postgraduate study?'

I mean, it'd never even crossed my mind – both cos I never thought I was good enough and cos I knew there was no way I could justify putting off going out there and getting a proper job for any longer than I already had. But he wouldn't let it go.

He kept saying, 'Give it some thought', and all but told me he'd back me if I put in an application for funding.

Look, I'm not stupid. I know we wouldn't even have been *having* this conversation if Hugh hadn't rewritten my dissertation. And I know I'd've been on a one-way ticket to a Lower Second at best without everything else he'd done for me. But I guess a part of me had already started to drink the Kool-Aid. All Hugh's talk of it being a joint effort had taken root, to the point I was starting to believe it. Maybe I hadn't needed him to write a half-decent dissertation after all. Maybe I *was* good enough?

And, even if I wasn't, I knew I had someone I could call on to lend a hand.

35

My exams were on the ninth, fourteenth and seventeenth of May. Social Justice first, then Pop Culture and Media, then Urban Pasts and Futures at the very end. That was the one I was looking forward to the least, but, in the end, I got through it, no problemo. This is probably gonna sound kind of perverse, but I think the fact that I actually had to work for it – that I wasn't able to go in there and just hock up a screed of words I'd already learned – made it all the more satisfying. At any rate, it cemented the idea in my head that I wasn't just this fraud who was only keeping my head above water cos I'd spread my legs for one of my professors. I let myself think, *You know what? Maybe I actually* do *have a knack for this.*

A month had now passed since I'd managed to stall Emily, and she was back to demanding results, riding me even harder than before. She said she didn't care any longer if the two of us hadn't actually screwed.

'Whatever you've got, it'll have to do,' she said. 'This has gone on long enough.'

Of course, I hadn't actually *got* any evidence, outside of those two videos of us doing it that would probably never be enough to stand up in a court of law, plus a handful of sound recordings I made early on that I'd never listened to but which I was pretty sure wouldn't amount to much of anything. And I could sense, this time, she wasn't going to be bought off by more promises of future greatness. I'd finally run out of road.

So I think fast, and this is what I come up with.

I say, 'Supposing I *do* hand over everything I've got? What's to stop you running straight to the university authorities or whoever and completely shafting me before I've even got my degree? If you turn him in now, odds are he'll take me down with him.'

Between us, I'm not sure that's actually true. I've a feeling, whatever happened, he'd've done his best to keep me out of it. But I can tell, from the look on her face, she knows I've got a point.

So I say, 'Look – at least give me till after I've graduated. Graduation night's gonna be the big one – I can feel it. We're booked to spend a couple of nights in a guesthouse out in the sticks. Separate bedrooms, but that's how these dirty weekends always start out – right?'

It was true we'd discussed the idea of going away together once I'd graduated a couple of times, though we'd never made any concrete plans. But she didn't need to know that. Right now, it was all about buying myself just a few more weeks on the gravy train till I knew whether or not I had any future in academia. *Then* I could decide how I was going to play this.

And it worked. I could tell she was pissed, but there was no way she was going to pass up the chance of getting a full-blown Technicolor feature film of me and him doing it in a B&B. She gave this sigh and said, 'All right. But this is positively the last time you get to kick the can down the road – you hear me?'

36

I got a First. Of course I did.

The results came in the second week of June. I'd aced everything: top marks in all three exam papers plus my dissertation. More than anything, it felt like a vindication. I *was* cut out for this life. I *could* make a name for myself on the academic circuit. The fact I'd even got a First in the Urban Pasts and Futures paper proved to me it wasn't just down to Hugh. I *did* have a natural talent for this sort of thing after all.

I was still refreshing the results page – you know, just making doubly sure it wasn't some sort of glitch and my *real* results weren't about to drop – when I got a call from Stuart Colgan. He said how proud he was of what I'd accomplished; how he'd never doubted me for a second. And then he drops the bombshell: I've only gone and come top of my year.

Now *that*, I *wasn't* expecting. I'd thought I was gonna do well, but number one out of a class of how many students? I had to pinch myself to make sure I wasn't tripping. And I'm still trying to process this when he tells me they're gonna give me this big, hifalutin award, the MacArthur Prize, straight after the graduation ceremony. He asks me if I've given any further thought to postgraduate study, and that, if I apply to go straight into a PhD, skipping the Masters altogether, I'd likely be successful. Either way, he'd be honoured to be my supervisor.

I hum and haw a bit, saying I'll need to think about it, and he seems to accept that.

'Talk to whoever you need to talk to,' he says. 'Your friends, your family, whoever. But don't delay too long, or you might find the opportunity's passed.'

Right away, I went looking for Hugh – partly so I could tell him the good news, partly cos I wanted to know what *he* thought about the PhD.

I was a bit taken aback by the response I got when I told him my results. He seemed ... a bit miffed, really. I mean, he said all the right things – 'That's wonderful', 'You've done so well', et cetera – but I could tell this wasn't what he'd been expecting, or what he'd been hoping for. And when I told him about my conversation with Stuart, about the PhD, he looked like he was gonna have a stroke. Immediately, he started trying to talk me out of it.

'A PhD's a lot of work, you know,' he said, as if I couldn't've worked that out. And I was feeling pretty put out myself by this point, so I said, 'Well, I'll have you on hand to help me,' and he *really* didn't like that. He went all still and quiet, and said something along the lines of, 'Well, that remains to be seen.'

I don't mind telling you I was pretty fucked off with him. I said something like, 'Thanks a ton for your vote of confidence,' and stormed out.

The business with Hugh really put a dampener on the whole day. I hadn't realised I cared so much about what he thought, and it honestly really hurt not to have his full-throated backing.

But that just made my decision about the PhD a whole lot easier. I called Stuart back pretty much straight away and told him I was gonna go for it. Part of it, I think, was about spiting Hugh – about proving him wrong. But it wasn't just about him. No one'd ever thought I had it in me to do something like this – not my parents, not my teachers, and least of all me. And I was determined, come hell or high water, that I was gonna prove them *all* wrong.

I ended up patching things up with Hugh a few days later. He never could keep away from me for long, and pretty soon we were falling back into our old habits – meeting up in out-of-the-way places for food and then going back to my place for grown-up dessert. Term time was over now, so both our calendars were a whole lot emptier than before, and we ended up spending more and more time together. We firmed up our plan to go away for the weekend after my graduation. Hugh booked us a room at a B&B just outside Perth. We'd be heading straight off after the ceremony.

I was honestly pretty stoked about it. We'd never been away before together. I actually liked the thought of us checking in together like a normal couple – not even doing the whole 'separate rooms' thing like I'd told Emily. I'm not saying I was looking forward to the prospect of a weekend of so-called 'passion' holed up in a hotel room with him, but I figured there'd be upsides too.

What can I say? Sometimes, a girl likes to be made to feel special.

We never talked about my PhD in all that time. He must've known I'd said yes – I know how fast word travels in academic circles – but he never brought it up. It was like we'd reached this silent agreement not to mention it. To carry on as we were, pretending it wasn't a thing.

. . .

Graduation was on the afternoon of the last Friday in June. Honestly, I found the whole experience pretty miserable. The stupid gown, the chanting in Latin, the ridiculous pomp of it all – plus the fact it was obvious I was the only one who didn't have any family there. My parents hadn't been able to get time off to come down. 'The hotel's not going to run itself,' my dad said to me when I rang to invite them. I wasn't all that surprised, and I hadn't really wanted them to come anyway. But it would've been nice not to have been quite so alone.

At least I had Hugh there, looking like a prize pillock in his robes, sitting with the other faculty members. I kept trying to catch his eye, but he never once looked my way. He didn't seem happy. The other lecturers were all in great spirits, blethering away together, but he just sat there at the end of the row, staring into space. There was this almost *haunted* look about him, like he'd just gotten some really bad news, or knew he had something really unpleasant he had to do.

After the main ceremony, a bunch of us high-flyers were kept back for the prize-giving. I got my special embroidered certificate and a cheque for five hundred quid, and that was that. It felt like a bit of an anticlimax. And afterwards, as I was wandering through the cloisters, clutching my scroll, passing all these clusters of students and their parents and other loved ones, I remember thinking, *I don't have anything in common with any of you. There's not a single one among you that I'm going to miss.*

I took my gown back to the rental place and went looking for Hugh. I found him standing on his own at the stairs to the Argyll Hall, drinking Prosecco. I sidled up to him and looped my arm through his and whispered to him, 'How d'you fancy blowing this joint?'

And he looked at me and gave me this sort of wistful smile and said, 'I think that's a fantastic idea.'

. . .

I'd already packed an overnight bag, so we headed straight off. We were at the B&B by early evening, and once we'd checked in, we headed straight upstairs and went to bed. Out of all the times I slept with him, I still think it was the only time he didn't fall asleep straight away afterwards. I left him lying in bed to go to the bathroom and get myself cleaned up, and when I came back he'd put on his shirt and trousers and was sitting on the end of the bed, waiting for me.

In retrospect, I should've known what was coming. There was the way he was acting during the ceremony, and then how quiet he'd been on the drive north, barely saying a word. Plus, there'd been the whole business of his reaction to the PhD. His comment when I'd said I'd have him to help me with it. But I guess I was in a state of denial – lying to myself, kidding on all this was just going to go on indefinitely. That nothing was going to change.

He looks up at me and he says, 'We can't do this anymore.'

And I just blink at him and I'm like, 'What?'

He goes on to say he's been thinking about this for a long time. He tells me what we've been doing is wrong; that it should never have been allowed to go this far; how he's been taking advantage of me and it's not fair on me; how I deserve a chance at a relationship with a man my own age and anyway, I'm going to be far too busy with the PhD to have any time for *him* and we should call it quits and go our separate ways, no hard feelings, thanks for all the good times.

Of course, I'm standing there without a stitch on, just *staring* at him, not able to believe what I'm hearing. I think the worst part of it for me was the humiliation of it all – the fact that *he* was the one who had the nerve to try and end it with *me*. Like, I'd always figured, when the time came, it'd be me calling time on the arrangement. Like I was the one calling the shots, not him. And now here he was, flipping the script on its head, thinking he just got to wriggle out of this with no consequences.

And, in that moment, I saw red. I said, 'So what was this supposed to be – the last hurrah? You think you just get to call it quits when you feel like it, and I'll just smile and go along with it like a good little girl? Who the *fuck* do you think you are?'

And he just sits there, staring up at me, blinking stupidly.

I say, 'Did you think this was a *relationship* we were in? That I was with you because I thought you were irresistible? That I *enjoyed* fucking a disgusting, slovenly old man like you? That I *liked* sucking your shrivelled little cock every other night? I've got news for you, buster: all this time, I was putting up with it cos you were useful to me, and if you think you get to walk away from this as if it never happened, you're in for a rude fucking awakening.'

I tell him how it's going to be from now on: I'm going to do this PhD, and he's going to help me every step of the way. We both know I'll be needing it. And if he so much as *thinks* about backing out, I'll go straight to the university with everything. The sex, the gifts, writing my dissertation for me, showing me the exam questions, workshopping my answers – the works.

We headed back to Glasgow first thing next morning. We didn't say a word the whole way there. We'd slept at opposite ends of the bed. Or at least, *he'd* slept. After a while, anyway. I could tell from the snoring. I lay awake for hours, still absolutely fizzing mad, telling myself over and over that he was the one in the wrong; that I was the one who was hard done by; that *he'd* taken advantage of *me*. By the time the sun came up, I'd managed to convince myself. Almost.

He dropped me outside my flat. I told him, 'You'll be hearing from me,' then got out without saying another word. I headed up the stairs, still convinced that, somehow, this was all going to work out.

I'd finished things with Hugh. Now I just needed to do the same with Emily.

37

'I hadn't taken my pay-as-you-go with me to Perth,' said Libby, 'so I got back to about a hundred texts from her, demanding a get-together.'

She was perching on a low stile leading to a wide green field dotted with peacefully grazing sheep. The path had been growing less and less distinguishable from the tangled foliage for some time before petering out altogether, at which point they'd made a joint decision not to attempt to advance any further. Libby was still smoking, having worked her way through most of what had started out as an almost full pack.

'I went straight along to meet her at Dallamano's on Kilmarnock Road,' she went on. 'I was worn out, but I wanted to get this over and done with. Practically before I'd even got my arse in my seat, she was already chewing my head off, demanding to know whether we'd done the deed. And I looked her square in the eyes and said, "No. Sorry. Nothing happened at all. I feel like I've taken this as far as I can."

'Well, she didn't like that. Not one bit. She said the deal was I'd get him to go to bed with me and bring her the proof, signed, sealed and delivered. I said, "No, ma'am. The deal was

I'd *try*. And I did. Multiple times. I gave it my best shot and he didn't take the bait. And I'm done. I want out."'

She took another drag on her cigarette before continuing.

'We went back and forth for a bit. Then, finally, she seemed to accept what I was telling her. And, with this heavy sigh, she said, "Fine. In that case, hand over whatever you've got on him and we're quits."

'That's when I told her I had nothing. I spun this story about my bag having been snatched the other week, with the camera and sound recorder inside it. Anything I'd had on him was probably in the possession of whichever unsuspecting bargain hunter had snagged it at a knockdown price at the Barras. Of course, that was a lie. What actually happened is I smashed up her recording devices with a hammer and chucked the remains in a skip on my way to meet her.

'She hit the roof. She was purple with rage, doing so much spluttering I was practically drenched. I seriously thought she was gonna jump over the table and tear me a new hole. And I just kept as calm as possible and kept saying, over and over, "I'm sorry. It's just one of those things."

'And because I stuck to my story, just kept repeating the lines I'd rehearsed over and over, I think she eventually realised nothing she said was going to change the situation. That's when she started demanding I pay her back all the money she'd given me.'

She snorted out a dry, humourless laugh. 'I'd been half-expecting that. I'd always figured she was one of those Karens who'd eat an entire three-course meal, then demand the lot for free cos the coffee didn't come with any After Eights. But again, I was ready for her. I said, "Um, no – the deal was you'd pay me whether I was successful or not. It was compensation for time and effort, not a loan to be paid back."'

'And how did she respond to that?' said Anna quietly.

It was the first time she'd spoken in some time. Since Libby had begun her account, she'd observed multiple shifts in the younger woman's demeanour – some subtle, others more jarring. At first, she'd been sullen and irritable, doing everything she could to remind Anna that she was doing this under duress. Gradually, however, she'd grown increasingly boastful, appearing to positively revel in her multiple feats of deception and, it seemed, inviting Anna to admire her ingenuity and guile. Latterly, though, a different tenor had crept into her account: a petulant, self-justifying one that, given everything she'd heard, left an unbelievably sour taste in Anna's mouth.

Libby knocked ash from the end of her cigarette onto the ground and shrugged. 'She came round to my way of thinking eventually,' she said matter-of-factly. 'It's not like she had much choice. What was she gonna do – take me to a small claims court for services unrendered?'

'Sorry, but I find that a little hard to believe. She just accepted that she'd forked out …' – Anna made the mental calculation – 'over £7,000 for nothing in return and agreed to let you keep the lot and go on your merry way?'

Libby shrugged again, more belligerently this time. 'Believe what you like. That was the deal we made. She always knew it could turn out this way.'

'I'm surprised she never threatened to go to the university herself and expose you for what you did. The dissertation business alone would have been enough to get your degree invalidated and Hugh struck off.'

'Why?' Libby sneered. 'Is that what *you'd* have done?' Then she added, more charitably, 'Probably she figured, if she did, I'd only land her in it as well – tell them all she was the one who put me up to it all.'

'How? You didn't even know her real name.'

Another flash of annoyance crossed Libby's eyes. Anna got the impression she was someone who was neither used to nor appreciated being contradicted.

'Well, that's probably why she didn't shop me, then, isn't it? Cos it would've meant revealing who she really was. And there'd've been all sorts of questions about how she knew what me and Hugh had been getting up to.

'Anyway,' she went on, once more with that now familiar air of self-righteous indignation, 'I'm not sure why you're asking *me* to explain her actions. It's not like I could peer inside her mind and see what was making it tick. There's nothing about her behaviour that made a lick of sense. Honestly, this was just about the *least* incomprehensible part of the whole sorry saga.'

Anna considered pressing the matter, then decided against it. Of everything Libby had told her, this was still the part she had the hardest time believing, but she accepted Libby clearly had a different perspective on the matter and was unlikely to be swayed anytime soon. She had little choice but to take her explanation at face value.

'So what happened next?' she said eventually. 'I'm assuming that wasn't the end of the story.'

Libby inspected the depleted end of her cigarette and grimaced. 'Oh no, not by a long shot.'

38

I spent a good chunk of what was left of summer figuring out my research topic and questions. Hugh helped me firm those up. I mean, I already had a general idea that I wanted to do something on how technology had changed the dynamics of social interaction, so it wasn't like it was a *complete* blank slate.

Needless to say, we weren't sleeping together anymore. Our meet-ups were strictly business now. We tried to be as civil to each other as possible, but that's not the easiest thing when one of you's holding a gun to the other's head. Metaphorically speaking, obviously. Any fool could've told you he was dead unhappy about the whole situation, but I kept telling myself he couldn't have it both ways. He'd been only too happy to write my exam papers for me while I was still spreading my legs for him every other night.

Stuart arranged for me to get some funding that was going spare. Apparently, it'd been earmarked to go to another student who'd had to drop out cos of some change to his family situation. It wasn't a lot – way less than I'd been getting from Emily, and nowhere near enough to live on. I started to wonder if there was any way I could've strung things along with her for a bit longer … but, realistically, I don't think that was ever on the cards. Honestly, I'm amazed she indulged me for as long as she *did*.

Her money had pretty much run out by now, and I'd blown a chunk of it in August on a holiday for one to Majorca – you know, doing that whole student rite of passage thing. I wish I hadn't bothered. I'd timed it all wrong, and my week there coincided with the English summer holidays. I ended up at a resort with a bunch of school leavers on their jollies – and I dunno about you, but I'd rather give myself a DIY labiaplasty than be kept up all night by a bunch of randy eighteen-year-olds from Bromley all making whoopee till the sun came up. I guess I'd been spoiled by Hugh's company. At least he had the good grace to pass out once he'd shot his load.

So, basically, I went into the autumn semester skint and with outgoings that were way in excess of what was coming in. I thought about trying to get another part-time job, but my only recent employer was Gianetto's, and I couldn't exactly see Nicolette writing me a glowing reference – not after how I'd told her where to stick it. Plus, I don't mind admitting I'd gotten used to the sort of life I'd been enjoying for the past seven months. The thought of going back to some degrading minimum wage service job was enough to make me want to slit my throat.

The first time Hugh gave me money, I swear, it wasn't cos I asked him for it. We'd been meeting up, about once a week or thereabouts, to work on my literature review chapter. I'd never written anything on this sort of scale before, so I didn't have the first clue what I was doing, and he was lending me a hand. I'd been moaning to him about my money woes, saying I didn't know how they expected anyone to be a full-time student on these poverty wages, and he said, 'What if I were to write you a cheque?'

At the time, I'd been thinking about applying for one of

those living costs loans. It wouldn't have made a *massive* difference, and obviously I'd've had to pay it back once I graduated, and I really wasn't keen on the idea of getting saddled with any more debt than I already had. And now, here was Hugh, offering to hand me a cheque, no questions asked. It was as if Emily never left.

So I accepted his money, and then, a couple of weeks later, when I said I still had a cashflow problem, he wrote me another. And it just sort of became this regular thing. I even helped him get set up with online banking so he could transfer money to me directly. I'd originally wanted him to use PayPal or Monzo or something for the extra anonymity, but it was hard enough walking him through logging into his Bank of Scotland account, and I figured, better not complicate things any more than we had to in case he had second thoughts about the whole thing.

It wasn't like with Emily, where I'd get the same amount from her at the same time every week. He was obviously having to rob Peter to pay Paul, giving me what he could, when he could. But he was a bloke in his sixties with a well-paying job and a cushy pension, while I was this poor, starving student, living the cliché. I couldn't feel *too* bad about asking him to share some of the proceeds.

He did try to wriggle out of it once or twice – told me there were teaching opportunities I could look into if money was a problem. But it was never a serious prospect. I told him once, if I couldn't afford to keep doing the PhD, I might have to tell someone about how I'd got my first-class honours degree, and he seemed to take the hint.

So Autumn rolled on, and I kept working on my literature review with Hugh, and having fortnightly catch-up meetings with Stuart and Leila, my other supervisor. They seemed pleased with my progress – the written stuff at least. Those face-to-face tutorials were always a bit nerve-wracking. Like, I'd never know when one of them was going to ask me some question I didn't have an answer to. Leila always seemed 'specially keen on ambushing me about some obscure point in the latest draft I'd submitted. But I always seemed to get through it OK. What with all the subterfuge over the last few months, I'd gotten pretty good at thinking on my feet.

Me and Hugh continued to work on my lit review together. By Christmas, we'd knocked it into pretty good shape. Stuart and Leila seemed to think so, anyway. As we went into the new year, we started working on the methodology chapter.

It was all going fine. We heard all the rumours about this super-deadly, super-infectious virus that was spreading around the world, but I didn't pay them much heed. To be honest, I don't think anyone really did. Not even once it'd spread to Europe and was basically right on our doorstep. Then, towards the end of March, Bozo the Clown went on national telly and told us we were all going into lockdown, and that was that. I didn't think it'd affect work on my thesis. Not in any meaningful sense, anyway. I figured me and Hugh would find ways to work together on it remotely, same way everyone else had to adapt.

Only trouble was, Hugh decided to go to ground.

It was maddening. One moment, we were getting on … well not exactly like a house on fire, but we were at least bumping along civilly. The next, I couldn't get him on his phone for love nor money. I thought about calling the office, asking one of the secretaries if they could get hold of him for me, but I figured that was just asking for trouble. Far as anyone knew, the two of us had nothing whatsoever to do with each other. Why put the spotlight on us now?

So instead, I holed up in my flat and stewed for over a month, making fuck all progress on my chapter. It's not like I didn't try. It's just the whole thing was still such a work-in-progress when Hugh did his disappearing act, and he had such a disorganised way of working, I couldn't for the life of me figure out what was basically complete and what was still just random jottings and ideas.

And all the while, I was trying to deal with the gaping hole in my finances. I applied for an overdraft. I took out a bunch of loans. But really, I was just plugging the holes in a ship that was already going down. I figured it was only a matter of time before the whole thing capsized.

Eventually, I reached the end of my tether. I needed help with my chapter, and I needed cash, and I needed both fast. I looked Hugh up in the phone book, and, one afternoon, about six weeks into lockdown, I went looking for him at his house.

He must've seen me coming cos I was only halfway up the driveway before he came trotting out, trying to head me off. He said his daughter was in the house; that she mustn't see me. I asked him why he hadn't been answering his phone. At first, he spun this story about having lost it, but he was a useless liar and I told him as much. Eventually, he came clean.

'I can't do this anymore,' he said. 'It's wrong and it's immoral, and it's only a matter of time before we get caught. We can't see each other anymore. It has to stop.'

At the time, it felt like it came out of nowhere, but, just like with his ultimatum at the B&B in Perth, I should've seen it coming a mile away. His moods'd been getting more and more … erratic, I guess, for a while in the run-up to lockdown. Sometimes he'd seem almost chipper, like he was genuinely enjoying having this project for us to work on together. But other times, he'd seem dead lethargic, like none of it mattered; like he was this condemned man just going through the motions. At the time, I'd put it down to the way the uni was treating him. You know, taking away his responsibilities and throwing him on the scrap heap.

And it's not like I wasn't telling him all the time how much of a difference he was making to me. 'You're helping me so much, Hugh,' I used to say. 'I don't know where I'd be if it wasn't for you.' I thought he'd like that, knowing he was still doing something that mattered.

But now I could see that all my kind words had counted for nothing. After everything we'd been through together, he still wanted to throw in the towel. And what's worse, he thought he could just slink away without even having the decency to tell me to my face.

I tried begging. I tried pleading, and when that didn't work, I tried cursing him out. I called him a selfish old git who was pissing on my dreams. I said he *knew* how much this meant to me. How it was all I'd ever wanted to do and I didn't know what I'd do with myself if I couldn't have this. I even tried throwing myself at him, saying I'd let him fuck me every day for the rest of his life if he'd just help me for a little bit longer.

And when none of that seemed to work, I turned to threats. I said, if he was determined to sink me, to deny me the life I deserved, then I was going to make sure I took him down with me. I said to him, 'Perhaps I ought to meet this daughter of yours. Let her know what me and daddy dearest have been getting up to.'

That made him go as white as a sheet. He started puffing and panting, clutching his arm. I honestly thought he might be about to have a heart attack. I backed off a bit. Tried a more reasonable tack. I said this'd been a stressful time for everyone, and I understood he'd just wanted some space to clear his head a bit. I said I'd give him another week to think about his options. Said I'd be waiting for his call. That I knew he'd come to the right decision … eventually.

When I got back to the flat, I found Hugh had sent some money to my bank account. It wasn't much, and it wouldn't make so much as a dent in the debts I'd racked up, but in a way it kinda touched me. It was more of a token gesture than anything, but I guessed he'd taken pity on me, and I let myself believe it was a sign of good things to come.

So I hunkered down and bided my time. I gave him a week, just like I'd promised. A whole week without trying to get in touch with him once. He didn't call me and he didn't send me any more money, but I forced myself to be patient. And, even when the week came and went without anything from him, I still continued to wait. I told myself a week didn't have to mean a week in the absolute *literal* sense. Perhaps he'd lost track of time. God knows, during lockdown, the days all blended together, and Hugh'd had a tendency to forget what day it was even during normal times. I kept kidding on to myself, but deep down I knew I wasn't going to hear from him.

Truth be told, I'm not sure I could ever really have done the whole 'kamikaze' thing and landed us both in it. I suspect, when push came to shove, I'd probably've let him cut and run and tried to muddle through on my own as best I could. It's one thing to make grandiose threats about taking us both down in a blaze of glory. It's another entirely to follow through. I think *that's* why I waited for so long. At the end of the day, I guess I'm just not as ruthless as I liked to tell myself I was.

I was still trying to write that bloody methodology chapter when I saw on the university intranet that Hugh had died.

39

'At first,' said Libby, 'I thought it had to be a mistake. Someone'd got the wrong end of the stick. It wasn't Hugh – it was someone else who'd got mistaken for him. Or he wasn't really dead, just sick with COVID or whatever. I thought, what sort of piece of shit would make up something like that, then post it for everyone to read? My mind went through all sorts of contortions, considering every possibility except the only one that made a lick of actual sense.'

She lifted her head and faced Anna, eyes glistening with unshed tears. 'When it finally hit me, I went to pieces. I cried for hours, and I didn't get out of bed at all the following day. And I knew, deep down, I'd caused this. The post on the intranet said he'd died of an illness, but I knew he'd done it to himself. And I knew it was because of me. Because of what I'd made him do. Because I'd backed him into a corner and given him no way out. If I hadn't gone to his house that day and given him my ultimatum, he'd still be alive today. I'm absolutely certain of that.'

After that, she fell silent for several seconds, her head bowed low, lost in silent contemplation. Eventually, she drew in a long, shuddering breath and continued, her voice hollow and lifeless.

'I didn't go to the funeral. I couldn't bring myself to. I couldn't face the thought that I might have to look his family in the eye. But someone started a shrine for him at the university gates. Flowers and cards and teddies and the like. I took along a bouquet for him, early in the morning, when there was no one around to see.

'I kept going through the motions with the PhD, but it was a losing battle, and, to be honest, I hadn't the heart for it anymore. Not without Hugh. It had been our little joint effort, and it seemed … I dunno, somehow it didn't seem right to carry on without him. I knew Stuart and Leila were gearing up to tell me I wasn't cutting the mustard, and I knew I'd never get the next year's worth of funding. So I beat them to the punch. I told them I was dropping out, and that was that.'

She inspected the remains of her cigarette – little more than the filter and a centimetre of ash. For a moment, she seemed to contemplate taking a drag. Then, changing her mind, she ground it out on the stile and tossed it on the ground.

'By that point, I was behind on my rent and had a mountain of debt racked up. I needed to find work, and sharpish. I figured the best thing I could do was clear out of Glasgow altogether. It's not like there was anything to keep me there, and everywhere I went I was surrounded by reminders of everything that'd happened.

'Eventually, I found my way down here. I saw the sanctuary was looking for staff. No previous experience required, just a strong work ethic and a passion for animals. I didn't mention my degree. By then, I'd come to think of it as … you know, dirty. Something I'd obtained at a decent man's expense. Instead, I told them I'd worked waitressing and fast-food jobs till now and was looking for a change. It wasn't strictly a lie. I was able to blag my way in without references. They were desperate. They'd lost a couple of part-timers to Brexit and COVID, and I was willing to work all the hours I could get. Anything to keep my mind busy.

'I didn't set out to use a fake name. But my boss misheard me when he was taking down my details – thought I'd said Elizabeth *Wright*, not Bright – and I decided just to stick with it. Made it more of a clean break. From there, it was easier to be Lizzie than Libby. Who even *calls* themselves Libby anyway? It sounds so wanky. They agreed to pay me cash in hand till I got set up with a bank account in my "new" name.'

She got to her feet, knee joints clicking as she straightened her legs. She paced a little, arching her back and stretching her arms out behind her, fingers threaded together as she gazed up at the ever-darkening sky.

'I got myself a bedsit in Moffat – not much more than a bed, a sink and a toilet, but it was better than nothing. And it's not like I was planning on bringing anyone home. I'm not doing too badly, all things considered. It's not the future I planned for myself, but I'm in a much better place than I was. I make an honest living, and I'm doing some good in the world. Plus, if I play my cards right, there's a promotion in the offing. Is it enough to make up for—'

She stopped abruptly, the words of this rhetorical question sticking in her throat. She was silent for a moment, her back to Anna, fist pressed to her mouth as she fought to force down the emotions bubbling up inside her.

'Perhaps,' she said eventually. 'Perhaps not. But if I thought about it in those terms, I'd probably go mad.'

She turned to face Anna. Her eyes still shimmered, but there was a spark of defiance in them.

'The point is, I'm not expecting you to feel sorry for me.'

'That's probably for the best,' said Anna quietly.

Libby's expression darkened. 'I know you think I was just using him to get what I wanted. That I didn't give a shit about him. But I cared about him. Maybe not in the way he wanted me to, or the way he cared about me, but I *did* care.'

Anna didn't respond. Truthfully, she didn't know what to say, or indeed what to think. There was little doubt that Libby's distress was genuine, but it seemed to her that was motivated primarily by self-pity rather than genuine grief or remorse.

After a moment, once it had become clear Anna wasn't going to offer her any words of comfort or reassurance, Libby gave a violent, sullen shrug, seemingly dismissing any thought of them achieving any sort of breakthrough and reaching a shared understanding.

'Whatever,' she said. 'It's about time I was getting back. You'd better come, 'less you wanna stick around to admire the scenery.'

They followed the trail back to the sanctuary in silence, Libby leading the way, Anna trudging behind her, deep in thought. She'd learned more from Libby than she'd ever expected to, and, while she still had questions – most of them pertaining to the mysterious Emily, her motives and identity – she had more than enough to chew on for the time being.

As they drew within sight of the sanctuary and its mismatched, ramshackle collection of buildings, Anna broke the silence.

'Did you ever see Emily again?'

Libby shook her head. 'No, never,' she said, her voice rough and husky after the prolonged spell of not speaking. 'I threw away the pay-as-you-go after I called time on our agreement.'

'And there's nothing else you can tell me about her? Anything at all you haven't already mentioned?'

Libby frowned and, to give her her due, seemed to genuinely be racking her brains.

'I don't think so,' she said eventually. 'She went out of her way to make sure I knew as little about her as possible. Like I said, she was about forty or thereabouts, and I figured she had some sort of white-collar job. And I suppose it's possible she lived somewhere around the West End, seeing as that was where we first ran into each other. But apart from that, I've got nothing.'

'And she really agreed to just let you walk away with nothing to show for all the money she sent your way?'

'That's what I said,' replied Libby tetchily.

Anna was on the verge of pressing the matter further, then decided there was nothing to be achieved by doing so. She had the feeling Libby was holding something back, though whether that was because she had a credible reason for believing so or simply because she *wanted* it to be the case – for Libby to be in possession of some crucial piece of information that would lead to a breakthrough as to Emily's true identity – she couldn't say.

'I'm not a bad person, you know,' said Libby suddenly. 'You can think what you like, but all I did was grab hold of a chance for a better life. Plenty of other people would've done the same thing in my shoes.'

'You think so?'

'Hey – I'm just trying to survive. That's all anyone's trying to do.'

Anna said nothing, but her scepticism must have been written on her face, for Libby snorted and rolled her eyes contemptuously.

'Oh, what? Are we just going to pretend I'm the only one who did anything wrong? What about the sixty-something university professor who slept with a girl young enough to be his granddaughter? Or the woman who took advantage of that girl's money problems to coerce her into doing it? I'm as much a victim here as anyone.'

Anna considered debating this point, but decided against it – partly because she wasn't entirely convinced she'd be on solid ground if she did, and partly because she saw nothing to be gained from antagonising Libby further.

'Fair enough,' she said instead. 'For what it's worth, I'm sorry things didn't work out the way you hoped.'

'I told you, I don't want your pity,' Libby snapped, and Anna wondered why she'd bothered trying to be civil.

'All right,' she said, maintaining an even tone with some effort. 'You've been extremely forthcoming. Thank you for that.'

Libby retrieved Anna's phone from her pocket. 'Suppose you'll be wanting this back.'

Anna took it and pocketed it herself.

Libby shrugged and raised an expectant eyebrow. 'So that's it? You'll fuck off now and leave me in peace?'

'I said I would, and I will. But will you do me a favour? If there's anything else you happen to remember – any detail you've forgotten to tell me, however insignificant – will you call me? Here's my number.'

She scribbled it down on an old receipt and held it out to Libby. Libby eyed it uncertainly for a several seconds, before relenting and accepting it with a palpable lack of enthusiasm. She stuffed it into her pocket, then arched her shoulders in a shrug and exhaled heavily.

'Well, I wish I could say it's been a blast reliving old memories, but I'll not insult either my intelligence or yours. Been sort of cathartic, though, I'll grant you *that*.'

'I'm glad,' said Anna, not completely insincerely. 'Look after yourself, Libby.'

Libby gave something that was between a snort and a chuckle. 'Been doing that since I turned eighteen.'

She turned to go.

'Just a minute,' said Anna, remembering something.

Libby stopped, turning to face Anna with obvious impatience.

Anna rummaged in her shoulder bag. 'Hugh's diary had a

bunch of dots in the margins on various dates. I was wondering if any of those meant anything to you.'

She handed Libby the diary. Once again failing to disguise her reluctance, Libby took it and allowed Anna to show her some of the dates in question.

She nodded pensively. 'I'm pretty sure those're the days we met up.' She pointed to one. 'Yeah, see. This was the night we had dinner at the Burnbrae. The night we had to hide from his friends.'

She handed the diary back to Anna.

'That's what I thought. Thanks for confirming.'

As Anna returned the diary to her bag, Libby met her gaze with a sudden, burning stare.

'I meant what I said. I'm not a bad person. Not really. Not deep down. You see that, right?'

Anna wasn't sure she did, but she recognised that there was nothing to be gained by saying as much. Not trusting herself to lie convincingly, she instead gave a soft, wordless nod, then turned and began to make her way across the grounds towards her car. A few seconds later, she heard a door shutting behind her as Libby disappeared into one of the buildings.

40

The drive back to Glasgow took Anna just under an hour and a half, which gave her ample time to ruminate on Libby's story. It was safe to say that nothing she'd heard had set her mind at ease. She'd suspected, going in, that she was going to hear things about Hugh that disappointed and upset her, but she hadn't expected to encounter such a tangled web of moral ambiguities, out of which each participant emerged profoundly compromised.

That Hugh had ridden roughshod over every conceivable standard of academic probity was beyond question. She could scarcely reconcile the friend and mentor she remembered with the picture Libby had painted. At the very least, she was forced to concede that there had been a very different side to him than the one he'd presented to her – one which, had she had even the slightest inkling of it, would have caused her to shun him like the plague. When she thought of him now, the overriding emotions she felt were disappointment and disgust.

But Libby herself was far from innocent. Hugh might ostensibly have been the one with the power within the context of the traditional student-teacher dynamic. By her own admission, though, she'd manipulated him from the start, first by preying on his diminished sense of self-worth, then his basest urges, before finally resorting to blackmail to ensure his continued cooperation. And she wasn't minded to disagree with Libby that her ultimatum to Hugh, just days before his death, had been the catalyst that had tipped him over the edge. No one had forced her to do any of those things. She'd exploited him to satiate her own desire for self-enrichment.

But then, hadn't Libby in turn been exploited herself? As she'd rightly pointed out, Emily had preyed on her financial insecurity to undertake a task that was, in the most generous possible interpretation, deeply sordid. She was all too aware that many students turned to sex work to make ends meet – a sad indictment of the lack of financial assistance available to those without the backing of the parental chequebook. Was what Libby had done really so different? True, no one had held a gun to her head, but if your definition of coercion was so restrictive that it only counted if it involved literal pain of death, then you were, at best, profoundly naïve about the realities of modern capitalism.

You try putting yourself through uni, paying all the rent and bills, all with no support from your parents. At the time, she'd made no response to this bold challenge from Libby, but she'd been sorely tempted to point out that actually, yes, she *had* done all these things herself, and had done them without resorting to extorting money from anyone. And yet, she remembered only too well the precarity; the need to scrape by from one week to the next; the feeling of constantly teetering on the very edge of survival. It didn't take much in the way of mental gymnastics to imagine herself, if she'd been in just a slightly different frame of mind, doing … well, not necessarily the exact same things Libby had done, but certainly resorting to more unscrupulous practices in a bid to make life just a little bit easier for herself. And who knows? If someone like Emily had come to her when *she'd* been a struggling undergrad and presented her with a similar offer, could she really be certain she'd have turned it down?

It would be easier, she supposed, to see Libby as a victim if she hadn't exhibited so much glee about the part she'd played in ensnaring Hugh and using him to cheat the system. If everything had worked out, and Hugh was still ghost-writing her PhD for her and paying for her upkeep, would she currently be suffering any pangs of conscience? On the surface of it, it seemed unlikely. And, of course, Libby in turn had exploited Emily, lying to her about her progress and intentions in order to squeeze every last penny out of her, then delivering nothing.

She sighed wearily and rubbed her eyes with the back of her arm, her other hand remaining on the wheel as the car thundered up the M74. It was natural, she supposed, to want to see the world in black and white; to be able to categorise everyone in it purely in terms of exploited or exploiter. The reality was a whole lot murkier, a whole lot greyer. And she was damned if she could see a way to make sense of it all.

It was early evening by the time she made it back to Glasgow. She dropped the car off at the rental place, then contemplated her next move. She briefly considered ringing Vasilico to see if he was free, then reminded herself that it was a Sunday night and that, like most people who were in his position, he'd probably be spending it with his other half. What had her life become, that this was the sort of thing she had to factor into her decision-making?

She remembered she'd promised Jen Brinkley an update once she'd found out anything of significance. It was safe to say she now had plenty to tell her.

Forty-five minutes later, when Jen opened the door to her flat, she took one look at Anna and grimaced sympathetically.

'Oh balls,' she sighed, 'I can see this is gonna be a heavy one. Don't bother making yourself at home. I'll get my skates on and we'll have a proper girls' night out and you can tell me *all* about it.'

She refused to take no for an answer, and, within the space of ten minutes, the pair of them were heading up the road towards Byres Road, Kylie having been only too pleased to make some extra spending money for herself by looking after the twins for the evening. The sight of Jen – impressively glam for a rush job in low-waisted leggings, a sequin crop top and heels long and sharp enough to take your eye out – left Anna feeling more than a little apprehensive. She hoped Jen wasn't envisaging the two of them going out on the pull together after she'd shared her news.

At Hillhead Subway Station, they boarded a train heaving with similarly dolled-up groups and couples heading in the same direction as them, and no doubt for the same purpose. They emerged at St Enoch Square a short, bumpy ride later, and Anna gamely followed Jen up to Mitchell Street, then down into the bowels of The Vault, one of those basement nightclubs that played pulsating dance music and bathed everything in bold neon hues.

Over cocktails and artisanal burgers in a booth for two, Anna told Jen everything that had happened since they'd last spoken. Jen listened carefully, giving exclamations of disbelief at all the correct intervals but otherwise refraining from making any interruptions.

'Jings, crivens!' she exclaimed, when Anna had finished. 'You couldn't make it up, could you? What a conniving little trollop!'

'It's not as clear-cut as that,' sighed Anna, aware she was probably onto a losing argument here. 'Let's not you and me do what always happens and airbrush the man out of the equation.' She shook her head. 'I looked up to Hugh. I *trusted* him. I know it sounds self-centred to say, but this feels like such a kick in the teeth.'

Jen nodded understandingly. 'I get it. And you're allowed to be selfish every once in a while, so don't go beating yourself up. Plenty of other folk'll be more than happy to do that on your behalf.'

Anna looked at Jen for a moment, then laughed softly, shaking her head.

Jen grinned in amusement. 'What?'

'How is it you're able to stay so calm and clear-headed all the time? Nothing ever seems to faze you.'

Jen shrugged and popped an olive from her martini into her mouth. 'Tae kwon do.'

'Tae kwon *who*?'

'*Do*. It's a martial arts sport. Two nights a week, I head down to the Scotstoun Leisure Centre and spend ninety minutes kicking people in the face. Lets me channel all my pent-up aggression into a specific time and location, leaving me in a pure, constant state of Zen the rest of the week. That and getting laid on a semi-regular basis.'

Anna shifted uneasily in her seat. 'I gather some people find that to be therapeutic. Unfortunately, in my case, it seems only to make matters worse.'

Jen raised an eyebrow. 'What's this? Trouble in bed?'

'In a manner of speaking.'

'Yeah? Well, if you're looking for something to spice up the old love life, I've always found handcuffs and a pair of edible panties work wonders.'

'What?' Anna spluttered into her glass. 'No, no, no! No spicing up required here, thank you very much! Quite the opposite, as it happens.'

Jen raised an eyebrow and rested her elbows on the table, fingers laced together under her chin. 'Well, colour me curious! Would it be impertinent of me to ask for some contextualising detail?'

. . .

Somewhat reluctantly, Anna told Jen about both her hook-ups with Vasilico and her 'arrangement' with Matteo back in Perugia. In the process, she found herself sharing more about her personal life and her own thoughts on it than she'd ever imagined possible outside of a professional therapy setting. Jen listened, her expression attentive and non-judgemental, nodding softly as Anna articulated the quandary that, until now, had remained strictly an internal one.

'The thing with Matteo,' she said – 'if I'm being completely honest, it started out as an arrangement of convenience. Except, over time, it evolved into something more, without me realising it was happening or even consciously agreeing to it. At any rate, *he's* made it clear he wants it to be something more.'

'And what do *you* want?' said Jen.

Anna laughed grimly. 'Well, that's the nub of the issue, isn't it? If I had an easy answer to that, odds are I wouldn't be in this mess.'

She leant back in her seat, resting the back of her head against the upholstered backrest behind her. 'Before we made the move to Italy, Jack had been having …' She searched for the word. '… behavioural issues. When I confronted him, he told me he was acting out because he thought it was the only way of getting me to pay him attention. And the thing is, he wasn't wrong to feel that way. Not completely, at any rate. I *did* take my eye off the ball with him. I was wrapped up in work and … well, you know.'

Jen nodded understandingly. It had been thanks to Anna's experience of being targeted by The Reckoning that they'd first got to know one another.

'The point is, I felt, if I did *anything* to make him think he wasn't the absolute centre of my world … that he had to share me with anyone else …'

She let her shoulders sag. Managed a faint smile. 'He's much better now. But, over time, I think that morphed into a convenient excuse to avoid letting things get more serious. And I like Matteo. I do,' she insisted, wondering who she was trying hardest to convince. 'He's kind and sensitive and he makes me laugh.'

'That's not nothing,' acknowledged Jen.

'Right. But is it enough?'

Jen gave a strained, sympathetic smile but said nothing. She seemed to recognise that now was not the time for advice – that Anna had more she needed to get out of her system.

'I know I'm stringing him along,' Anna went on. 'That every day that passes is another day of letting him think he has a chance of a future with me. And maybe I *could* settle down and be a family with him and Francesca and Jack, and be happy. But there's something missing. Some …' Again, she tried to find the right word. '… some spark I keep telling myself I'd need to feel in order to countenance making a life with someone.'

'And you feel that spark with Vasilico?'

'I feel *something*. I don't know if it's just rampant lust or something more profound. All I know is, I felt it the second I laid eyes on him on Byres Road the other day. We both did.'

She reached for her martini and drowned a generous mouthful.

'A couple of years back, after The Reckoning and what they did to me, it was near-impossible for me to even *contemplate* a relationship with him.'

'And now … ?'

'Now, it's not an option. He's spoken for.'

Jen watched her silently, waiting for her to continue.

'I said I needed time,' she explained, 'and he gave me time. And then I left the country, and somewhere, in the intervening period, he got tired of waiting and moved on.'

Jen blew a strand of hair away from her face. 'Fuck me, but you lead a complicated life, Scavolini.'

'I suppose, at the end of the day, it's immaterial,' said Anna, not disagreeing. 'I won't be in Glasgow for much longer. My life's in Perugia now – and in that respect, Matteo is, if nothing else …'

'Handy?' suggested Jen.

'The more straightforward option,' said Anna, aware this didn't exactly constitute a denial. 'But it feels like … I dunno, like settling for the runner-up prize. And I hate that I think of him in those terms – believe me, I do. But not as much as I hate knowing I'm carrying on behind his back while he's over there, waiting for me.'

She raised her glass in self-deprecating mockery of a toast and gave a rueful grimace. 'I suppose it all makes me a terrible person.'

Jen gave Anna a long, hard look, leaning towards her with her arms folded on the table. 'Anna,' she said firmly, 'with the proviso that you're my dear friend and am therefore hopelessly biased – no, it absolutely doesn't.'

Anna met her gaze, far from convinced but too tired to say so.

'I'm going to give you a piece of advice my mum gave me when I was sixteen. One day, she sat me down and said, "Jenelle, I want you to listen because I'm only going to say this the once. No man is worth sacrificing your own happiness for. Whatever you do, promise me you'll always put yourself first, and never, *ever* settle for second-best."'

'But—' Anna began.

'But nothing. It's *your* life. You're allowed to be selfish, and you're allowed to make people wait while you figure out what you want.

'Take *moi*, for instance,' she went on. 'I tried to do the whole monogamous, heterosexual, 2.4 children thing for at least a year before I realised I'd never love any man as much as

I love my crotch goblins and my wee sister. I made my peace with the notion that I was never going to have the husband and the joint bank account and the Volvo; that, whenever I needed to scratch the itch, I could go out and get what I wanted and then come back home again without it having to turn into a whole thing.'

She shrugged. 'Maybe that's not for you. Maybe your idea of a perfect life looks completely different from mine. And that's totally fine. But whatever it looks like, just remember, it's for you to decide, no one else. And, for the love of almighty God, don't settle for a relationship just to keep the peace, or I promise you, it'll end in tears for everyone concerned. Including Jack.'

She drained her glass, leant back with her arms folded and shrugged, as if inviting Anna to argue with her.

Anna simply sat there and gazed at her for almost a full minute before speaking.

'Your name's *Jenelle*?'

'What of it?'

'Nothing. I just ... I dunno, I always assumed Jen was short for Jennifer.'

Jen laughed. 'My parents: not exactly the conventional sort. But that's nothing. Just wait till you learn what Sal's short for.'

'What *is* it short for?' asked Anna, suddenly curious.

Jen tutted and wagged her finger. 'Nah nah nah, that's for her to reveal, not me.'

They smiled at one another companionably. Anna realised much of the earlier tension she'd been experiencing had evaporated.

At length, Jen straightened up again, fixing Anna with an expectant look. 'So have you decided what you're going to do now?'

'Hang on a tick. You just told me it was all right to make people wait.'

Jen dismissed this with a wave. 'Oh no, we're done with all

that. I meant about the Hugh business. Where do you go from here?'

Anna blew out a heavy breath. 'Honestly, I'm not sure. A part of me feels I should be making an effort to track down this Emily, but the trouble is I've got nothing to go on, other than an approximate age and a general description. I don't even know her real name.'

Jen nodded soberly. 'It's a pickle and a half, all right.'

'And then, there's this other part of me that feels like I've accomplished what I set out to do. I've got a pretty comprehensive picture of what was going on with Hugh in the last months of his life, and a fair idea of what caused him to end it. I even know who was blackmailing him, if that's the proper word for it. Maybe it's time for me to report my findings to Fraser, draw a line under the whole thing, and go home to Perugia.'

Jen thought about this long and hard, brows etched in concentration. Then, having come to a decision, she drummed her knuckles dramatically on the tabletop.

'All right, here's what I think. I think you've had a hell of a day and've got a ton of stuff to chew on. Don't launch into any snap decisions tonight. Head back to your hotel and get yourself some shut-eye. You probably need it. Don't worry,' she added with a grin, 'I won't make you show me your moves on the dance floor.'

Anna gave a grateful smile.

41

It was dark when they emerged from The Vault, and beginning to smirr with rain. The long-threatened downpour couldn't be far off.

Jen spread her arms and turned her face up towards the sky. 'THE SCOTTISH SUMMER HAS ARRIVED!' she declared in a loud voice, then turned to Anna with a grin. 'Want me to call a cab?'

'What are our odds of actually *getting* one?'

'Eh, about ninety-nine squillion to one, but it's worth a shot. You wanna?'

Anna shook her head. 'No, it's fine. I'll walk up to Central Station and take the train. I could do with some air.'

Jen looked at her doubtfully. 'You sure?'

'Sure. It's only rain. Besides,' she added, with a sly smile, 'I figured you'd be wanting to stick around in town for a bit longer. I'm guessing you didn't get all dressed up for nothing.'

'Ah, now that *is* true,' said Jen philosophically. 'Kylie's good for another couple of hours, and it's been at least a fortnight since I last had my end away.'

Anna grinned. 'I'll bid you a good night, then, and may your orgasms be long and plentiful.'

Jen cackled appreciatively. She patted Anna on the shoulder, then pulled her leather jacket up over her head and, using it as a makeshift umbrella, headed off up the rain-spattered pavement in a brisk trot.

Anna headed in the opposite direction, making for the station. She realised, as she walked, that she felt considerably less burdened by the business with Hugh and Libby than she had when she'd shown up at Jen's door just a few hours earlier. Even though, on some level, she recognised that this was simply because Jen had helped her take her mind off it rather than because they'd actually resolved anything, she still felt a whole lot more clear-headed about it all. Whatever decisions she had to make would still be waiting for her in the morning, and she was OK with that. She'd missed this sort of thing: shooting the shit with a girlfriend on a night out, airing her worries and putting the world to rights. Perugia might have a lot going for it, but she was yet to form the sort of deep, intense relationships there that she had here in Glasgow with people like Jen, Farah and Zoe.

She was heading up Union Street when her phone began to ring. Ducking under the cover of a shop awning, she examined the screen. The number was one she didn't recognise, and the phone offered no suggestion as to the caller's identity.

She took the call.

'Hello?'

'Hello?' said a voice she didn't recognise. It was young, female and rather haughty. 'Who is this?'

'You're the one who called me,' Anna pointed out, 'so I think you'd better go first, don't you?'

'This is Detective Constable Vicky Phipps of Police Scotland,' said the voice, with more than a whiff of self-importance. 'To whom am I speaking?'

'Anna Scavolini,' said Anna promptly, then immediately cringed at her own knee-jerk act of deference to authority. 'Can I ask what this is about?'

'We're in the process of trying to establish that,' said Phipps, in that same brisk, supercilious tone. 'Did you happen to pay a visit to the Auchen Wildlife Rescue Centre earlier today?'

'Yes,' said Anna, wondering how on earth this woman could possibly know that.

'And, while you were there, did you speak to a Ms Elizabeth Wright?'

'Yes,' said Anna again, feeling a sudden, inexplicable pang of unease. 'Why? What's happened? Is she all right?'

There was a long pause, during which Anna made peace with what, somehow, she knew deep in her gut was coming next.

'Ms Sabbatini,' said Phipps eventually, and with an intonation noteworthy for its lack of anything approaching a genuinely apologetic tone, 'I'm sorry to have to tell you that Elizabeth Wright is dead.'

PART V

LOOK WHAT YOU'VE DONE

42

Cambridge Street Police Station. One of several similarly unlovely brick buildings spread throughout the city, often located in what might uncharitably be described as the most incendiary trouble spots. In Anna's case, it was the nearest one within walking distance and the one to which she'd volunteered to make her way when Detective Constable Phipps had informed her they wished to speak to her urgently as a potential witness to the final movements of Elizabeth Wright. Upon her arrival, she'd been kept waiting for over ninety minutes while the investigating officers made their way there from Moffat. Now it was well past midnight and she was seated in an airless, over-lit basement interview room at a badly stained Formica table, on the opposite side of which sat two officers in plain clothes.

Of the two, and despite being the more junior, Vicky Phipps had done almost all the talking so far. A small, moon-faced woman in her early twenties with large, round glasses and hair stretched back into a tight ponytail, she was wearing her facemask in the chin-strap configuration, her nose and upper lip plainly visible above the fabric. She barked all her questions in an arch, knowing sort of tone, as if she'd already decided Anna had had something to do with the death, even if she wasn't sure precisely what role she'd played. The other, who'd briefly given his name as DS Conway, was the strong, silent type. A large, florid-cheeked man in his forties, he sat, arms folded, gazing off towards the corner of the ceiling but undoubtedly listening to every word that was being said. He, at least, was properly masked.

Libby's body had been discovered a little under an hour before Phipps had made the call to Anna, hanging from a coat hook in the female changing room at the wildlife centre, her belt looped round her neck. Her colleague, Gareth Baynes, had arrived at 9 p.m. to relieve her but had found no sign of her. A chivalrous sort, he would never have dreamed of entering the women's changing area, and it wasn't until almost an hour had passed without sight or sound of her and he'd already looked everywhere else she could feasibly be that he finally decided to brave the forbidden domain of the opposite sex. Upon their arrival, the police had found Anna's number on a scrap of paper in her pocket.

'*Professor* Scavolini,' intoned Phipps, in a manner that all but implied *if that's REALLY your name.* She'd been placing undue stress on 'Professor' ever since Anna had corrected her on 'Ms'. 'Let's see if I've got this straight. You visited the Auchen Wildlife Centre near Moffat at approximately 1400 hours to speak to the deceased, whose name – contrary to what her colleagues believed and what is recorded on the payroll – is in fact *not* Elizabeth Wright but Elizabeth *Bright*. Prior to this meeting, you'd had no previous contact with the deceased. Is that correct?'

'Correct,' said Anna, her voice flat and emotionless. She felt numb and hollowed out, but still had enough of her wits about her to know she had to tread carefully.

Phipps feigned bemusement. She wouldn't win any awards

for acting, that was for sure. 'Forgive me, but that seems *quite* strange. You hired a car and drove sixty miles to see someone you didn't know?'

'We had a friend in common. Hugh MacLeish. He was my colleague. He died last year.'

'*Interesting,*' mused Phipps, where *I'm sorry to hear that* would have been more appropriate. 'And is Ms Wright – excuse me, *Bright* – the only mutual acquaintance of your ex-colleague to whom you've paid a visit?'

'I've spoken to several people about Hugh. I was very fond of him, and I was abroad when he died. I've been asking as many people as possible about their memories of him.'

'Indeed,' said Phipps, in a tone that suggested she didn't believe a word of this.

She made a considerable show of turning to another page in the set of printed notes in front of her, lifting the top sheet with a theatrical flourish and placing it off to one side.

'Ah, yes,' she said, after examining the page in front of her for several seconds. 'A number of Ms Bright's colleagues – *former* colleagues, I should say – attest to the fact that the two of you were observed speaking together outside the centre and that you subsequently left together for a period of *several* hours.'

She lifted her head sharply, her pupils comically large behind the lenses of her glasses. 'Tell me, what could you possibly have found to talk about for such a length of time?'

'First of all, it wasn't *several* hours. It was two. Possibly two and a half at a push. Secondly, Hugh worked at Kelvingrove University for over forty years. We had a lot to talk about.'

'Yes, but unless my arithmetic is seriously impaired, neither you nor the victim knew him for forty years. So I'll ask you again, *Professor* Scavolini: what did the two of you talk about?'

During the ninety-minute wait for the detectives to arrive, Anna had had ample time to plan her strategy. She'd resolved to tell them as much as she needed to and as little as she could get away with. One of the things she'd known she couldn't avoid was Libby's true identity – both because there was no other way to explain her visit to the wildlife centre and because she felt that, no matter how estranged they were, her parents deserved to know about their daughter's fate. On the other hand, she had no intention of furnishing the police with any of Libby's revelations about Hugh. Partly it was because she'd given Libby her word that she wouldn't involve them – and that still counted for something in her mind, even in death.

But there was another reason too. She knew that, if she gave the police even a flavour of what she and Libby had really talked about, one way or another, as surely as the sun rose, word would get out, and that would destroy Miriam. She hadn't forgotten her promise to tell Miriam what she found out, but there was a marked difference between telling her about it on her own terms, where she could control just how much sordid detail she actually imparted, and her reading that her father had had a sexual relationship with one of his students on the front page of some scuzzy tabloid.

'We talked about Hugh's life and the legacy he left behind,' she said evenly. 'Like I said, I was extremely fond of him. We both were. It shouldn't, therefore, be so hard for you to imagine that we had a lot to talk *about*.'

Phipps gave a smarmy, insincere smile and inspected her notes again.

'It's unfortunate, isn't it?' she said, without looking up.

'What is?'

'A mutual friend of yours died. By all accounts, a tragic loss. Now, a few hours after meeting to discuss said friend, a *second* individual is also deceased, under conditions which point strongly towards the death being self-inflicted.' She lifted her head to meet Anna's gaze and gave her an insolent, almost gleeful little smirk. 'Quite a thing to have on your conscience, I expect.'

The other officer, DS Conway, shifted in his seat and made a low, rumbling noise, which might have been intended as a rebuke but might equally well just have been him stifling a belch. Phipps continued to stare at Anna, clearly expecting a response.

Somewhere deep inside Anna, something finally snapped. She sat up a little straighter, folding her arms and matching Phipps' insolent gaze with one of her own, and counted to five inside her head before speaking.

'Am I under arrest?'

'You are not,' said Phipps, eyes once more downcast to her notes.

'Then I'd like to remind you that I'm under no obligation to sit here and listen to your innuendos, your insolence, and the callousness you mistakenly believe makes you sound clever. A woman I spoke to just hours ago is dead. Hard as it may be for you to believe, I'm currently in a state of shock. Now, if you want me to answer any more questions, you can put them to me in a manner that accords me the same basic respect I'd extend to you if our positions were reversed. And, while you're at it, you can learn to wear your mask like a fucking grown-up.'

As Anna spoke, Phipps slowly lifted her head. She now stared straight at Anna, a look of disbelief in her eyes, seemingly rendered mute by her outrage.

If she intended to say anything in response, she never got the chance. Conway loudly cleared his throat and eased himself onto his feet.

'Right, I reckon we've earned a comfort break. Let's reconvene in ten minutes.'

When they got underway again shortly afterwards, Phipps's manner remained terse, though the words themselves were comparatively more civil – so much so that Anna strongly suspected she'd been subjected to an all-inclusive bollocking during the intermission. She moved things along briskly, stating that the circumstances of Libby's death appeared fairly cut and dried.

'We'll wait for the pathologist's report, of course,' she said, 'but, as I mentioned previously, it seems reasonable to conclude that the deceased took her own life. Her colleagues have attested to the fact that she'd appeared withdrawn and unhappy for some time. There's also the small matter of this.'

From beneath her notes, she produced a plastic evidence bag containing a single sheet of dog-eared paper, which she handed to Anna. Anna took it and read the smattering of words written in a round, achingly childlike script.

> I'm sorry you had to find me like this. I really am.
>
> I thought I could find a way forward, but I realise now that I've been deluding myself. I've let everyone down with my lies, and I can't bring myself to go on any longer. The world is a better place without me in it.
>
> I'm so sorry.
> L.

'It was found next to the body,' said Phipps, unnecessarily, her voice cutting through Anna's thoughts.

'No,' said Anna uselessly. 'This can't be right.'

'It's her handwriting. We compared it against the personal development plan her employers had on file.'

'But she … she said she'd made peace with her lot in life,' said Anna, still unable to believe it.

'Maybe she had,' said Conway gently. 'Maybe this was what she meant by "making peace".'

'But she was in line for a promotion,' said Anna, her voice little more than a low mumble now.

Conway gave a kindly, sympathetic smile. 'Perhaps she was just putting on a brave face.'

'But …' Anna began, for the third time.

But she couldn't think of anything more to say.

They wrapped things up fairly quickly after that. Anna was informed she was free to go. Conway walked her out. Phipps had stormed off without a word or a backward glance, no doubt to brood over her feelings of persecution.

'We probably won't need to talk to you again,' said Conway as they reached the foyer. 'You mentioned you'll shortly be heading back to Italy?'

'Yes.'

'Well, if we *do* need to speak to you about anything else, I'm sure we can arrange to do it remotely.' He dipped his head in farewell. 'Safe travels.'

With that, he turned and headed back into the station, disappearing through the double doors leading to the part of the building that was out of bounds to the public.

Anna stepped out into a downpour of biblical proportions. She wasn't sure when the seriously heavy rain had started, but the fact the entire car park was awash suggested it had been underway for some time. Sheltering under the awning above the entrance, she took stock of her situation. She knew her odds of procuring a taxi were slim to non-existent, and the thought of the long trek back to the hotel in the rain was enough to make her want to curl into a ball and weep.

With a heavy heart, she got out her phone.

. . .

She was still sheltering under the awning twenty minutes later when Jen's Prius pulled into the car park. As it came to a halt, Anna could see that the twins were in the backseat, asleep under a blanket, heads resting against one another. Jen wound down the window and gazed up at Anna with an empathetic smile.

'Hop in,' she said.

43

Monday 16 August

Anna came to a few brutally short hours later to the sounds of Jen getting the twins washed and dressed. She'd conked out on the sofa more or less as soon as they'd got to Jen's flat and had slept through what little remained of the night. Now, as Jen scurried around after her progeny, entreating them in an insistent whisper not to wake their Auntie Anna, Anna shut her eyes again and, with a groan, let her head fall back onto the cushion she'd been using as a pillow.

She waited till Jen had herded the kids out the door and she'd heard the car pulling away outside before slowly easing herself into a seated position and rubbing the sleep from her stinging eyes. When she checked her phone, the screen exploded in an array of missed call alerts and voicemails from Matteo, peppered among the plethora of other notifications for emails, news alerts and all the other things she didn't currently have the headspace to deal with. She swiped left on all of them, consigning them to the ether. She'd call him later. Right now, she didn't think she could face him – or Jack.

There was a note on the kitchen counter from Jen: *Taking*

the goblins to their grandparents for the day. Back soon. Help yourself to leftover Coco Pops and Ribena. Kisses, Jx.

Foregoing the offer of sugary breakfast treats, Anna instead pulled on the trousers and plimsolls she'd been semi-conscious of peeling off shortly before oblivion took her a few hours earlier, and set off towards the Great Western Inn. Before allowing herself to process the events of the previous twelve hours, she planned to avail herself of a long, hot shower and change of clothes. At some point overnight, the rain had stopped, and the still-wet pavement glistened with the sun's pale reflection. Everywhere she looked, wide, lagoon-like puddles told the story of a lengthy, sustained downpour.

Roughly half an hour later, at around 9:45, she drew within sight of the hotel. As she approached the front entrance, she spotted a tall figure in a suit standing outside the door with his back to her. As she made her way towards him, he swung around to face her.

Paul Vasilico looked like he'd left home in a hurry that morning. He was unshaven, and his normally immaculate suit was rumpled and creased. For several seconds, they just stood there, a metre apart, staring wordlessly at each other.

'Paul,' she said eventually.

'A colleague called me first thing this morning,' he said, somewhat breathlessly. 'They said you'd been pulled in for questioning about an unexplained death. I came straight here, but you weren't in your room. I was just about to call you when—'

He was still speaking when she hurled herself at him, throwing her arms around him and sinking into his chest. He stopped talking midstream and silently folded his arms around her, enveloping her in his solid, reassuring embrace.

They retreated to her hotel room and spent the next several hours together in bed. Sometimes, they made love – a gentle, unhurried sort of love that seemed to blend seamlessly with the rest of the time, where she lay in his arms, alternating between dozing and holding snatches of murmured conversation. She knew that, for as long as they lay together like this, everything else was made slightly more bearable.

Bit by bit, she found herself telling him everything that had happened the previous day: her conversation with Libby at the wildlife centre; her questioning at the hands of the police; her conviction that Vicky Phipps had been right in her insinuation and Libby *would* still be alive now if she hadn't gone there and compelled her to relive her own role in a man's death. She found herself replaying every word she'd said to Libby, wishing she'd been kinder, less self-righteous, less determined to emphasise her own superior moral credentials.

And Vasilico gently stroked her tear-stained cheek and assured her that it wasn't her fault; that, if Libby's guilt was strong enough to drive her to take her own life, it would have caught up with her eventually – today, tomorrow, months or even years from now – but it would have happened with or without Anna's involvement. Anna didn't believe it, and she was convinced he didn't either; that he was just lying to make her feel better. But the very fact that he cared enough to lie to her brought her some measure of comfort.

When she next came to, she was alone in the bed, the warmth and firmness of Vasilico's body immediately conspicuous by its absence. Rolling onto her side, she found him standing in his boxers at the far end of the room, furtively rummaging through his trouser pockets.

'Lost something?' she said.

He glanced up at her. 'My phone.'

Anna propped herself up on her elbow. 'Did you definitely have it when you left this morning?'

'I thought I had … but then, I went out the door in such a

rush, I suppose it's possible I forgot to grab it.' He turned his pockets inside out, then shook his head, the matter seemingly settled. 'I must've left it in the charger. Dammit,' he muttered under his breath.

'Is it a problem?'

'It's not the end of the world, no – just a pain in the arse. I'll swing by the flat for it later.'

Anna pushed herself up into a sitting position, hugging her knees to her chest. 'You're heading off, then?'

Vasilico winced apologetically. 'Have to. I'm meant to be on duty, and I've already been AWOL for over four hours. Better show my face before someone tries to get hold of me on the phone I abandoned in my fit of chivalrous ardour.'

Anna raised an eyebrow. 'Is *that* what they're calling it these days?'

'Ah, don't act like you weren't delighted to see me.'

She responded by tossing a pillow at him. He dodged it effortlessly, before grabbing his clothes and disappearing with them into the bathroom before she could lob anything else in his direction.

It was twenty to two when Vasilico emerged a few minutes later, fully dressed and showing no outward sign of having just spent the morning in bed with an illicit lover. Lying on her side without moving, Anna watched out of the corner of her eye as he paused to retrieve his ring from his pocket and set it back on his third finger.

'You don't have to hide that from me, you know.'

He looked sharply in her direction, his features momentarily catching in a painful wince. Swiftly covering his unease, he attempted an easy smile.

'I didn't realise you were awake. In future, I'll poke you with a sharp stick to make sure.'

'After all this time, I feel the least we owe each other is to be honest.'

'There's nothing honest about what we're doing,' said Vasilico quietly, and it seemed to Anna that, for the first time since their encounter in the alleyway on Friday, she'd briefly glimpsed the man behind the mask, and that he was as conflicted about this as her.

Turning away from her, he crossed over to the dresser and, facing the mirror, began to fuss with his hair.

Anna eased herself upright, wrapping the sheet around her torso. 'Maybe not, but we both know what this is and what's going on, so we might as well call a spade a spade.'

Vasilico turned to face her again, his expression pained. 'I just don't want anyone to get hurt.'

She didn't force him to specify who he meant by 'anyone'.

'Look,' he went on, 'we both know that, sooner or later, you'll be back in Perugia and it'll all be moot. Until then, let's just enjoy this for what it is, OK?'

For several long, uncomfortable seconds, she didn't answer. Instead, she held his gaze for as long as she could, daring him to look away. Then, with a degree of resignation, she lowered her own eyes and gave a soft nod of acceptance.

'OK.'

He responded with a small smile of gratitude. He was silent for a moment, then asked, 'Whenabouts are you leaving anyway?'

'Sooner rather than later.'

'Will I see you again?'

Anna sighed heavily. 'Well now, that's the million-dollar question, isn't it? I imagine that's going to depend heavily on *both* our schedules.'

'I'll make time if you do.'

She met his eye. He gave a weak smile. She managed to return it.

'In that case,' she said softly, 'I'll make time.'

His smile deepened. Making his way over, he perched on the end of the bed and, cupping the back of her head, drew her in for a tender kiss. He withdrew his lips but remained leaning over her, gazing softly into her eyes.

'Do you ever wonder ...' he began, then stopped.

'What?'

He smiled slightly and shook his head. 'Nothing.'

He kissed her again – a brief, chaste peck on the lips – then got to his feet and headed out, gently closing the door behind him.

44

She continued to lie in bed for a while longer, luxuriating in the warm, drowsy afterglow. She felt a good deal calmer now. The grief and the guilt were still present, but they were less raw now; less immediate. She still didn't believe Vasilico's assertion that her actions had played no part in Libby's death, but, for the first time since she'd received the news, she found she was able to think properly both about the distance she'd already travelled in pursuit of the truth and the crossroads she now faced. And, as she gazed at that fork in the road, at the two radically different paths that lay before her, she realised what she'd known deep down, even as she'd equivocated to Jen in the basement of The Vault the previous night.

She wasn't finished yet.

And now, as she lay there, her mind making free association as it drifted unconstrained from one idea to another, she found herself returning to the various unanswered questions that continued to perplex her about the case. The identity of the enigmatic 'Emily', and her motivations for employing Libby to entrap Hugh, surely constituted the final piece of the puzzle, and she was determined not to simply leave it hanging like a loose nail. She knew from past experience that, if she did, she'd just continue to fixate on it until it drove her mad.

At length, she reluctantly concluded that continuing to lie in bed, allowing herself to indulge herself in this indolence, wasn't accomplishing anything meaningful. It was quarter past two in the afternoon, and every fresh minute that ticked by was a minute wasted. She needed to be up and about, on the move, doing *something*, even if she didn't know precisely what.

She threw back the covers, got out of bed and headed to the bathroom, where she took a shower, vigorously scrubbing her entire body with a rough washcloth in an attempt to rub away both the last vestiges of lethargy and the lingering taint of transgression that seemed to hang over her. At least, she supposed, she and Vasilico had now acknowledged the elephant in the room, albeit in a roundabout sort of way. It didn't make what they were doing any less wrong, but at least they were no longer pretending.

She forced herself to put their affair – *because that's what this is, Anna, and it's time you got to grips with that fact* – to one side and concentrate on the matter at hand. She was minded to agree with Libby's theory that Emily was a former student of Hugh's who'd had some sort of liaison with him, probably along similar lines to the one she and Libby had engineered. If that was true, and Emily had been around forty years old when Libby met her, she would probably have been a student roughly twenty years ago – in other words, at the turn of the millennium.

As she stood under the showerhead, allowing the piping hot water to pummel her, she racked her brains, trying to think if there was anyone she knew who would have worked with Hugh during that period. No one immediately sprang to mind. Law and Social Sciences had always been something of a 'young' department, most of the people on staff when she joined in 2011 having been there for less than a decade themselves. Hugh, in many respects, had been the last of the dinosaurs – a relic of a bygone era who'd first entered the university's grounds as a student in the early 1970s, rising through the ranks to eventually take his place as the head of the department in which he'd spent his entire adult life up to that point. Libby hadn't been wrong: the way they'd treated him was abominable.

It wasn't until she was towelling herself dry on the end of the bed that a thought entered her head. Well, more accurately, a face. Thin, wizened, flecked in various spots with white stubble that he always seemed to miss while shaving. And a voice: thin and reedy, but nonetheless possessing a baritone depth, hinting at the power it must have commanded in his younger years. Hugh's predecessor as head of department, who'd been seeing out the twilight phase of his career on a part-time contract when Anna had arrived there, and had retired just six months later.

What was his *name*?

She got out her phone and opened the Internet Archive, inputting the address of the university website and selecting a snapshot of the site as it had existed in 2010. She navigated to the Department of Law and Social Sciences and selected the Staff List page, scrolling through the various names, some of them barely remembered, others unfamiliar, until one stood out.

Archibald Macpherson.

Of course – *Archie*. Good old Archie, with his habit of cleaning his glasses on his tie and his insistence on rolling his Rs like Édith Piaf in full-on *'Non, je ne regrette rien'* mode. He'd seemed ancient to her at the time, but that might just have been the folly of her own relative youth talking. Realistically, he'd probably only been in his mid-to-late sixties. What had become of him? Assuming he was still alive, of course.

She briefly considered all the usual items in her people-hunting arsenal – the phone book, social media, the voters' roll – before it occurred to her that there was *one* person who was virtually guaranteed to know where to find Archie. The only other person who'd definitely been there at the same time as him and Hugh.

'Archie!' said Lorraine Hammond, practically smacking her lips with enthusiasm, as if the very act of saying the name brought her boundless delight. 'Now *there's* a man to look up to. A black, *black* day when he hung up his mortarboard, so it was. They don't make them like him nowadays, that's for certain.'

'Indeed they don't,' agreed Anna, holding the phone slightly away from her ear. 'Lorraine, do you happen to know if he's still in the land of the living?'

'I'm happy to report that he is indeed – eighty-eight years of age and still going strong. I get a Christmas card from him every year. And I always make sure to send him one of my own,' she added, clearly keen that Anna should know this.

'In that case, you'll be able to tell me his address.'

'Why?' There was an unmistakable note of suspicion in Lorraine's voice.

'So I can add him to my Christmas card list too?'

Anna's response more than half-sounded like a question in its own right.

'I see,' said Lorraine, with obvious reluctance. 'Well, I don't suppose there's any harm. You *are* ex-colleagues, after all. One moment while I consult my Rolodex.'

Anna waited as patiently as she could, reflecting that of *course* Lorraine was just the sort of person who would have a real Rolodex on her desk.

'Here we are,' said Lorraine eventually. '59 Alder Gardens, Bellahouston. A *very* desirable area,' she remarked, with evident approval. 'You know, I wouldn't mind—'

'Actually, Lorraine,' said Anna quickly, 'I'm going to have to go. Thanks for all your help.'

She hung up while Lorraine was still spluttering out a response.

She got dressed as quickly as possible and hurried downstairs to the ground floor. As she headed through the lobby, she called Jen.

'The disappearing woman!' exclaimed Jen, before Anna could get a word out. 'I was *wondering* what'd become of you.'

'Sorry about that,' said Anna with a wince. 'I needed a change of clothes and a general spruce-up and I wasn't sure when you'd be back and—'

'Hey, no sweat. Ya gotta go, ya gotta go. Trust you're all spick and span now.'

'Very much so,' said Anna.

She emerged from the hotel and set off towards Hyndland Station.

'Listen, Jen, I hate to ask you for another favour after everything you've already done, but—'

'Name it. Less time spent apologising, more time for the rendering of services.'

Suppressing the urge to shower Jen with profuse declarations of gratitude, Anna instead explained, as concisely as possible, her current thoughts regarding Emily.

'If Libby's theory was correct, she'd have been a sociology student at Kelvingrove at some point between the late 90s and early 2000s. Mid-2000s at an absolute push. I seriously doubt Emily's her real name, but it might be something close to it. Something beginning with an E, maybe. I realise it's a long shot, but—'

'Hey, I'm a dab hand at finding needles in haystacks. You just leave it to Beaver.'

Anna thanked her and rang off, quickening her pace towards the station, where she boarded a train to the city centre. As the doors slid shut behind her and the train shuddered into life, she steeled herself for what, with all her might, she hoped would be the final heave.

45

She arrived at Central Station at around quarter past three and headed to the upper level, where she caught a train on the Cathcart line to Maxwell Park, the closest station to Archie Macpherson's home in Bellahouston. Shortly before 3:45, she turned onto Alder Gardens, a quiet, wooded residential street populated by spacious detached houses, several of which bore more than a passing resemblance to the one in Kelvinside where she'd grown up. She made her way up the driveway of number 59 and rang the doorbell.

As she stood waiting on the doorstep, she belatedly remembered that the person she'd come here to see was nearly ninety years old, and, as such, had more reasons than most to fear the virus they'd all spent the last eighteen months trying to avoid. She hurriedly fished her mask out of her bag and was in the process of fixing it in place when the door opened.

The figure standing in the vestibule wore a disposable face covering and leant on a Zimmer frame for support. Stooped and with creased, papery skin that made Anna think of a walnut, Archie Macpherson looked every one of his eighty-eight years, with the possible exception of his eyes, which were still clear and bright, peering at her from behind a pair of half-moon spectacles.

'Can I help you?' he said.

'Professor Macpherson, hello. I don't expect you'll remember me, but I'm a former colleague from Kelvingrove University. My name's Anna Scavolini.'

He frowned. 'Scavolini? I'm not sure I …' Then, recognition seemed to dawn. 'No, but of course. You were the girl who … you were Susan's daughter,' he said, seeming very sure of himself.

'No, I'm afraid not,' said Anna.

'Really?' He appeared momentarily thrown. 'I swear, you have her eyes. But then,' he said, sounding disappointed, 'all I see of people these days are their eyes. Besides, I'm sorry to say my mind is not what it was.'

Not sure what to say to this, Anna offered what she hoped was a sympathetic smile. For a few awkward seconds, they simply stood there, facing each other on opposite sides of the doorway.

'I'm sorry,' said Archie, breaking the silence, 'was there something I can help you with?'

'Possibly,' said Anna. 'It may be a long shot, but … well, I don't suppose I might come in for just a few minutes? Or,' she added, seeing Archie's look of uncertainty, 'we could talk in the garden. It's a lovely day. Seems a shame to waste it.'

The least she could do, she felt, was to spare him the ignominy of having to explicitly refuse her entry.

Archie's expression brightened instantly. 'Of course. What a nice idea.' He pointed towards the side of the house. 'Round to your right, through the gate. I'll join you in just a moment.'

Following his directions, Anna made her way round to an expansive, well-tended garden. A veranda with a table and a couple of folding chairs backed onto the rear of the house. She made her way over to it and waited patiently for Archie, taking in the lush green of the lawn, drops of rainwater still glistening on the individual blades of grass.

She turned at the sound of the back door opening behind her. Archie shuffled out, still masked, and made his way over to her. She watched him struggling to manoeuvre himself from his Zimmer to one of the chairs, but resisted the natural inclination to step forward to help him. This, she sensed, was a man who believed devoutly in the two-metre rule.

Once he was settled in his chair, Anna followed suit. She kept her mask on too, recognising that she was on his territory and that the rules were his to set.

'So,' he said, eyes crinkling in a smile, 'we worked together, did we?'

'Only very briefly,' she reassured him, keen that they didn't dwell on his obviously hazy memory, about which she sensed he was self-conscious. 'You were on your way out the door when I was on my way in, so to speak.'

Archie's brows knitted together, puzzled by the euphemism. Then, seeming to get it, he gave a laugh of recognition. 'Ah, yes. Ha. Very good.' He leaned back in his chair, folding his liver-spotted hands on his chest. 'Well, it's ever so nice of you to visit, even if I'm not entirely clear as to why you *are* here. I don't get a lot of visitors these days,' he said, before Anna could explain herself. 'All these rules! One can't help feeling rather cut off.' He gave a sigh of resignation. 'But we've all got to do our bit.'

Anna couldn't help but be reminded of the way people she'd seen in documentaries used to talk about the Blitz – which, now that it occurred to her, Archie would be old enough to have experienced firsthand. She had a sudden mental image of one of those novelty mugs bearing that hackneyed phrase – *Keep Calm and Carry On.*

'Do you have *anyone* to come and visit you?' she asked, feeling a pang of concern for the elderly man. 'Any family?'

'I see my granddaughter at least once a week,' said Archie.

He chuckled. 'She brings me my shopping, and we set the world to rights from opposite sides of the living room window. She's forever trying to persuade me to let her come in, but I keep telling her: rules are rules.'

'Well, I'm glad you're keeping yourself safe,' said Anna, deciding not to point out to him that those rules had been relaxed some time ago. In her experience, attitudes towards safety measures had only hardened with the passage of time, and adherents to both sides of the ideological divide tended to take it as a personal affront if you tried to suggest they change their behaviour. Besides, if it gave him peace of mind …

'So,' said Archie, leaning forward with a sudden, hitherto unseen shrewdness, 'why *are* you here? I hope you won't think me ungrateful, but I'm sure you must have more pressing individuals to call on than someone with whom, by your own admission, you only briefly crossed paths.'

'I, well …'

She wasn't sure where to begin. She decided, in the name of expediency, to take the direct approach.

'Do you remember Hugh MacLeish?'

'*Remember* him?' Archie's eyes lit up in recognition. 'Of *course* I remember Hugh.' He shook his head wistfully. 'Young Hugh … People referred to him as my great discovery, but in truth, he was very much his own man. He ran the department after I stepped down, you know. Who's in charge there now?'

'A man called Fraser Taggart,' said Anna, choosing to leave it at that.

Archie frowned. 'Taggart? I don't think I know him … but then, my memory isn't what it was.'

'Trust me, you're better off that way.'

Archie frowned in confusion, and Anna instantly regretted her words.

'Were you aware Hugh had died recently?' she asked, moving swiftly on.

Archie nodded gravely. 'I read about it in the paper. A

shame no one thought to inform me directly – but then, I suppose their minds were on more pressing matters.' He sighed and shook his head. 'Yes, a very sad state of affairs all round. When I first took him on all those years ago as a young PhD candidate, I never for a moment imagined *I'd* by the one to outlive *him*. It's a black evil, this virus,' he added grimly.

'It is,' Anna agreed, opting not to correct him on what she imagined was the common assumption that Hugh's death was COVID-related. 'So, Hugh was your PhD student?'

'And subsequently my researcher, before he took up a permanent appointment as a lecturer. Of course, the road to a faculty position was far less tortuous in those days. I hear war stories from colleagues in the trenches about folk still stuck on teaching contracts into their forties.'

'Yes, I imagine it was a different world all round.'

'It was a less fraught one, that's for certain,' said Archie, with some zeal. 'There was a great deal less micromanagement. A whole lot less box-ticking. Folk were trusted to know how to do their jobs and to get on with them.'

'Yes,' said Anna dutifully. 'Changed days, for sure.'

It wasn't that she disagreed with him; it was just that there were only so many times you could hear the same refrain before it started to sound clichéd. And, for all her issues with the way things were being run at Kelvingrove in the months prior to her departure, she wasn't going to pretend *some* degree of managerial oversight wasn't needed. In her experience, those quickest to complain about the rules often turned out to be the very people most deserving of a short leash.

'Forgive me for asking all these questions,' she said, keen to bring the conversation around to the purpose of her visit, 'but …' She affected a slightly sheepish air. 'Well, it's just that I only got to know Hugh in the last decade or so of his life. I'm not sure the picture I have of him is … complete. Can you tell me anything of what he was like as a young man?' She paused. 'As a newly qualified lecturer?'

Archie frowned at the oddly specific nature of this question, then seemed to accept it. He sighed and leaned back in his chair, gazing up at the canopy above them as he delved into the recesses of his memory.

'The thing about Hugh,' he said, after considering the matter carefully, 'is that he was always exceptionally eager to please. He went out of his way to be helpful. He'd do all sorts of little favours for people, always without asking and even if it wasn't within his remit. And he never looked for anything in return. In his eyes, making someone else's life that bit easier was reward enough. And there were no airs and graces with him. He had one of the sharpest minds I've ever encountered, but he was always extremely self-effacing. Never acted like he was better than anyone else. He used to chum around with the university porters, cadging cigarettes from them and whatnot.'

'What about his dealings with his students? How was he with *them*?'

Archie considered the question. 'He was always very ... accessible, I suppose would be the word. There wasn't much sense of there being an "us and them" when it came to the students. He kept it all decidedly informal.'

'It's funny,' said Anna. 'That's not how I remember him at all.'

She hadn't meant to articulate her thoughts out loud, but she was so surprised by the picture Archie had painted that she couldn't help herself. As far as her own perception of Hugh was concerned, she was more inclined to agree with Libby's assessment: that he was something of an old fuddy-duddy who was always 'Professor MacLeish', never 'Hugh'. To her, he'd always seemed one step removed in his dealings with students – not unfriendly or cold, but taking care to maintain a courteous professional distance.

'I mean,' she added quickly, aware that Archie was looking at her sharply, 'don't get me wrong. People could always go to him with a problem, but I always saw him as someone who was clear in his mind that he was the teacher and they were the students. I suppose it's possible he changed as he got older,' she added, a touch sheepishly. It was, she conceded, unlikely that he'd been an old fuddy-duddy *all* his life.

'I fancy most of us *do*,' said Archie – to Anna's mind not unreasonably. 'Though, as a young man, I recall he was quite popular among the student body – with the girls especially.'

'Oh yes?' Anna tried not to sound *too* much like her ears had just pricked up.

'Yes,' said Hugh, his voice carrying an unmistakable note of amusement. 'He was part of what I've come to think of as the new guard. When I was starting out, the idea of a lecturer socialising with his students would have been scandalous – particularly those of the opposite sex. But that was Hugh in a nutshell – he wasn't bothered about upsetting the established order.'

Anna was desperate to interrogate this line of enquiry further but knew she needed to tread carefully, in case she said the wrong thing, prompting Archie to shut down.

'It's a minefield, though,' she said, trying to make her observation sound as casual as possible. 'Especially nowadays. You want to be approachable, but *some* degree of professional distance is essential.'

Archie laughed ruefully. 'Yes, changed days indeed. People now are far more mindful of – what is it they call it? Safe-keeping?'

'Safeguarding.'

'Ah, yes,' said Archie contentedly, 'that's it.'

'I suppose it must have been the equivalent of the Wild West back then. You hear such stories: the air in the staff room thick with cigarette smoke, alcohol being consumed openly during work hours, folk disappearing for three-hour lunches …' She paused, then added tentatively, 'Lecturers getting mixed up in relationships with students …'

She couldn't see Archie's mouth, but she sensed, from the

buckling of the fabric of his mask, that he was giving a rueful grimace.

'Haha, yes, that was certainly known to happen on occasions.'

'Hugh didn't ever ...' She feigned an embarrassed laugh. 'I can't believe I'm saying this ... *He* never got involved with any of his students, did he?'

She immediately saw, from the look in Archie's eyes, that he didn't consider this an absurd proposition at all. Rather than the expected shock – or, indeed, indignation – that she would suggest such a thing, his expression of unease showed that she'd hit uncomfortably close to the truth.

She leant towards him, fixing him with an intense look. 'Professor Macpherson,' she said, 'did something happen between Hugh and a student?'

By now, Archie was seriously flustered. He toyed with a loose bit of thread on his trouser-leg, unable to meet Anna's eye.

'I told you, my memory's not what it was. Besides, what's to be gained by indulging in gossip and scandalmongering? They're dreadful things, rumours. Follow you around for years, refusing to die, whether or not there's any truth to them.'

'Archie.'

The sharpness of Anna's voice caused him to jerk his head up abruptly. He stared back at her, the baggy skin under one eye twitching slightly as he struggled to meet her gaze.

'This isn't about me setting out to ride roughshod over Hugh's memory,' she said, doing her best to walk the tightrope between reassuring and firm. 'I'm not trying to dig up dirt or make something out of nothing. But I've heard something that's given me cause for concern, and I think you're better placed than anyone else to help me establish whether or not there's any truth to it.' She gave him what she hoped passed for a conciliatory look. 'Come on: if you truly believe he hasn't done anything wrong, there's no harm in telling me what you know.'

For a long time, Archie said nothing. Then, resignation seemed to set in, and he let out a weary sigh, as if the effort of continuing to pretend had simply become too much.

'Hugh was always … I suppose it would be fair to call him a "ladies' man" – or, at least, he had something of a reputation for being one. He cut rather a dashing figure in his day. Women were drawn to him like … well, not unlike a rock musician, though I expect you'll find that a difficult comparison to swallow. Accordingly, I'm afraid there were occasions where he was … indiscreet.'

'Just so we're clear, we *are* talking about *students* here – not other faculty members.'

Archie said nothing.

'Women – *girls* – over whom he was in a position of power.'

It was as if she had to say it out loud to allow herself to accept that it was real.

'He was a young man himself at the time,' said Archie, his tone one of exasperation, as if Anna was deliberately missing the point. 'And he wasn't without his trials and tribulations. He'd lost his son at an unconscionably young age. Under the circumstances, certain allowances were inevitably made.'

After Alfie's death, Anna thought. *So not THAT young.*

'It's not as if he was simply *pursuing* these girls,' Archie snapped, clearly guessing some of what Anna was thinking. 'There was mutual attraction there. *They* went after *him* too.' He shook his head irritably. 'It was a different time. You lot these days don't know the half of it. You want to group everyone into black and white – oppressors and oppressed. They were all consenting adults.'

'As a former sociologist, I'd have thought you'd understand a thing or two about power dynamics.'

Archie didn't like this one bit. 'I won't be patronised by

you,' he scowled. 'I fancy I've forgotten more about power dynamics than you've learned in your whole short life.'

Anna said nothing.

'I'm not saying his behaviour was unproblematic. I'm just saying, it's not as cut and dried as you make out.'

'And I don't suppose you happen to remember the names of any of the students he was ... indiscreet with.'

'Of course I can't remember their names!' Archie snapped. 'It was decades ago, and it's not as if I was keeping track of all his affairs. Anyway,' he went on, now aiming for a marginally more placatory tone, 'I can't fathom why you insist on dredging all this up now. The man's not around to defend himself. What's to be gained from a witch hunt?'

'The man may be dead,' Anna pointed out, 'but the women he slept with are, presumably, still alive. You don't think it's possible that some of them might have a different recollection of events than you?'

'They were *adults*!' Archie spluttered in exasperation. 'They knew what they were doing. And they were all willing participants. Not one of them ever complained, apart from—'

He stopped abruptly, the look of stricken horror in his eyes making it clear he realised he'd said too much.

'So there *was* a complaint made?' said Anna, pouncing on this momentary indiscretion at once. 'When was this? What came of it?'

She was thinking, if there was an official grievance on file, that it might just be possible to get her hands on it and, in so doing, be in a position to track down the complainant.

'I misspoke,' said Archie, backtracking furiously. 'I'm old. My memory isn't what it used to be. I don't know what I'm saying.'

'I think those excuses are starting to wear a bit thin, don't you?'

Archie groaned in frustration. 'It was a piece of nonsense! It was obvious to anyone with half a brain that there was nothing to it. Nothing that would have stood up to even a *modicum* of scrutiny.'

'If that's the case, then you have nothing to lose by telling me.'

Archie didn't respond. He merely glowered at her from behind his face covering, arms folded protectively about himself.

Well, two can play that game, thought Anna. She set her jaw, folded her own arms and faced him down.

Archie gazed back at her with the look of a defeated man. 'If I tell you, will you promise to leave me in peace?'

'Provided you give me a full and frank account. No omissions or attempts to sugarcoat things.'

Archie shook his head and scoffed softly to himself. 'Fine,' he muttered, the word barely audible behind his mask.

He fixed Anna with his gaze once more. 'There was an occasion when a colleague from a separate discipline – now deceased, I'm sad to say – brought something to my attention. A third-year student to whom he served as advisor of studies had come to him, claiming she was pregnant and that the father was one of her sociology lecturers. She hadn't explicitly stated his identity, but it was obvious, from reading between the lines, that the lecturer in question was Hugh.'

'And, presumably, it fit with his general pattern of behaviour.'

The sharp look Archie gave her indicated that he didn't appreciate this interruption.

'The colleague in question indicated to me that he suspected the girl was … "fishing", I believe, was the word he used. She wasn't doing particularly well in her studies, and it seemed not implausible that this accusation was a rather ham-fisted attempt on her part to claim special dispensation. Apparently, she'd even made noises about going to the press with her story.

'My colleague and I went and spoke to the girl together. We

asked her if she was *sure* this was the route she wanted to go down. We laid out to her what it would mean for her if she went ahead and made a formal complaint. The inquiry could drag on for months. She'd be asked to account for herself in front of an investigatory committee; to provide proof to back up her claims. It had the potential to get *very* awkward for all concerned.

'The fact she backed down more or less instantly seemed a pretty strong indication that she was making the whole thing up – the pregnancy bit, anyway. Still, we played along. Gave her the number of a family planning clinic and sent her on her way. But the Head of Faculty and I had a long talk with Hugh. We impressed on him that, if he *had* been incautious with this girl, then it was incumbent on him to do his bit to take care of the matter.

'I heard nothing further about the girl. If memory serves, she ended up dropping out a couple of months later – at which point, she naturally ceased to be the university's problem. I didn't raise the matter with Hugh again. Whether he *did* talk to the girl, come to sort of settlement with her ...' He shrugged vaguely, leaving the rest unsaid. 'I saw that as his business, not mine. Either way, we managed to head off a potential scandal for the university, and, at the time, that seemed far more important than indulging a girl who'd failed to take responsibility for her own actions.'

Listening to this, it had taken all Anna's willpower to keep her expression neutral; to not interject, on multiple occasions, with just what she thought of Archie and his colleagues' handling of the situation. She couldn't work out whether Archie genuinely believed the student had been lying or if that was just the comforting lie he told himself. Either way, she passed no comment on what she'd heard. She recognised that this wasn't the time for it – not while she still needed his cooperation.

'When was this?' she asked.

Archie shook his head. 'I couldn't give you an exact date.'

'An inexact one, then. Could it have been, say, around the time of the millennium?'

Archie appeared to give this genuine consideration. 'Yes, I suppose that's plausible. Certainly, it was while I was still head of department, but I think, by that stage, Hugh's star was in the ascendancy, and it was fairly clear he was the heir apparent. That was partly why everyone concerned was so keen to head off a major scandal.'

Well, at least you had your priorities straight, thought Anna.

'And this student,' she said, 'by any chance do you remember her name?'

Archie pursed his brow, again seemingly making a genuine effort to recollect. But at length, he gave a sigh of exasperation and shook his head.

'It's no use,' he said. 'I'm afraid it's gone.'

'Could it …' Anna decided to take a gamble. 'Could it have been Emily?'

For a moment, it seemed to her that something resembling recognition passed through Archie's eyes. But then, as swiftly as it had come, it was gone.

'Maybe,' he said unhappily. 'I don't know. Certainly, I could believe it began with an "E" … or possibly an "A". I never had much of a head for names to begin with, and my memory's …'

'… not what it was,' Anna finished. 'It's fine. I understand.'

She continued to probe Archie for another quarter of an hour, hoping to unlock some previously buried memory that would lead to further details about the student. But Archie, despite his seemingly sincere efforts to oblige her, was unable to come up with anything, and only grew more and more frustrated by his own perceived inadequacy. Eventually, Anna, sensing that she'd got as much out of him as she was going to, drew things to a close, thanking him for his cooperation – though the words very nearly stuck in her throat.

Archie walked her to the gate, leaning heavily on his Zimmer.

'Well,' he said, as she turned to face him, 'I won't suggest it's been a pleasure, but I wish you well with your enquiries, such as they are. Please convey my best wishes to Susan.'

'I will,' she said – not having the heart, in spite of everything, to correct him again.

46

Anna strode back up the road towards the station, her mind churning. It went without saying that she was sickened and appalled – not just at what Hugh had been getting up to but at the role of Archie and his colleagues in hushing it up. She didn't know Archie as well as she'd known Hugh, obviously, but she'd nonetheless genuinely thought better of him. And to hear him talk, it sounded as if Hugh's 'indiscretions' had been common knowledge among his colleagues.

It wasn't even as if these events were that long ago. The purported pregnancy incident had potentially taken place within the last two decades – when Hugh was already well into his forties and she was just a few years away from joining the department herself. All this talk of it having been a different time held no water whatsoever. At least, if it had happened before she was born, she might have been able to pretend it really *did* take place in the dim and distant past.

Whatever remnant of sympathy she'd felt for Hugh after hearing Libby's story had, she realised, all but evaporated. Exposure and being drummed out of the profession was the very *least* he'd deserved for what he'd done.

. . .

As she waited on the platform for a train to take her back into town, she called Jen and gave her a brief précis of what she'd found out. Jen was reassuringly appalled – something Anna belatedly realised she welcomed, since it confirmed she herself wasn't merely overreacting. Still, outrage and indignation weren't going to help them make progress.

'I want you to concentrate on female sociology students who dropped out during their third year,' she said. 'Same time-frame as before.'

'On it,' said Jen, keys clacking in the background. 'I'm ploughing through the old uni records as we speak.'

'How did you ...' Anna began, then stopped herself. She didn't need to know. Didn't *want* to know.

'Hell-*o*,' said Jen, 'what's this now?'

Anna was on the alert at once. 'What is it? What have you found?'

'Hang on – let me make sure it's not a false alarm.'

More key-clacking.

'No, I actually think I might have something. Listen to this: Emma Rippon, date of birth 05.05.1979. Hails from Borehamwood, Hertfordshire. Enrolled in an MA in sociology and English literature 15.09.1997. Voluntarily withdrew from study 17.03.2000. Reason for withdrawal ... "none specified".'

'Emma Rippon,' Anna repeated to herself, her voice barely a murmur.

'So whaddaya think? Could she be our Emily?'

She *could* be,' Anna admitted. Hardly definitive, though, is it?' She realised how uncharitable she must sound. 'Tell you what, though,' she conceded, 'I'm not going to turn up my nose at any potential lead, however tenuous.'

She glanced along the track. A train was crawling towards the platform on the northbound line.

'Listen, Jen, that's my train. I'm heading back to yours now. Can you work some more of your magic and find out what became of Emma Rippon after she dropped out? Maybe see if you can unearth any contact details?'

'How else did you think I planned on spending my one child-free day of the week? On second thoughts, don't answer that. I'll get cracking straight away. Toodles.'

The train was halfway to Central Station when Anna's phone pinged a text alert. She retrieved it from her bag and looked at the screen.

PAUL VASILICO

Hey

She texted back a response:

ANNA SCAVOLINI

Found your phone, then?

He responded with a thumbs up emoji, followed by:

PAUL VASILICO

Can we meet?

Semi-urgent

ANNA SCAVOLINI

????

PAUL VASILICO

We don't have to, but I've got something important to tell u

ANNA SCAVOLINI

Tell me now.

PAUL VASILICO

It'll sound better in person

She considered her options. She'd told Jen she was on her way to her place, and she didn't want to keep her waiting – not after everything Jen had already done, and continued to do, for her.

Her phone pinged again.

PAUL VASILICO

Just a quickie

Promise 😉

She suppressed a sigh. Was Vasilico *really* proposing another hookup, so soon after the last one? She found it hard to believe he had any lead left in his pencil after the morning they'd had.

She made a decision. Tapped out a message.

ANNA SCAVOLINI

I'm on the train into town. ETA 5 minutes. Meet somewhere there?

The little ellipsis appeared, indicating that Vasilico was composing a response.

PAUL VASILICO

George Square at 5:15?

Scott Monument?

ANNA SCAVOLINI

Perfect. See you there.

Still mystified, she disembarked at Central Station and headed for George Square. She wondered if it was possible Vasilico had had some sort of brainwave regarding her investigation, in which case it might well turn out to be fortuitous that he'd intercepted her on her way to Jen's. But it didn't seem likely. The sudden, horrifying thought struck her that he was going to tell her he'd broken up with his fiancée so they could be together. What was it he'd said? *I've got something important to tell you. It'll sound better in person.* Christ, she hoped not.

The square wasn't exactly heaving when she arrived, but there was a healthier crowd here than she'd seen anywhere in the city since her return on Thursday. After the previous day's downpour, today was shaping up to be almost as balmy as Friday, and the denizens of Glasgow seemed determined to make the most of this rare instance of lightning striking twice.

She arrived at the Walter Scott statue, proud and erect atop his tall column, and looked around. There was no sign of Vasilico. She checked the time. Twelve minutes past five. She headed over to one of the benches surrounding the monument and took a seat.

As she sat there, watching the various people – two young men having a heated exchange in front of the Cenotaph; a group of tourists in shorts and flip-flops hauling travel cases across the wide expanse of the square; a trio of teenage girls sunbathing on the grass in their bras – her phone began to ring. Half-expecting it to be Vasilico, calling to announce that he was running late, she checked the screen, only to see that the display gave the caller's name as Terry Finan.

'Terry, hi,' she said, taking the call. 'Thanks for getting back to me.'

'Anna. Aye, no bother. So I've been along and had a look at yer house, and … Well, listen, there's no delicate way tae put this, but that wee problem ye described? Turns out it's a wee bit worse than we thought.'

Anna felt her heart sinking.

'Go on,' she managed to say.

'So I'm no sure how *au fait* ye are with the local history, but there's a lot of old mine-working under the West End, and subsidence is a pretty recurrent issue. But, eh, I'll be level with ye, Anna – I don't think I've ever seen a case this bad.'

Fuck, she thought.

'Seriously?'

'Aye. The leak's just the symptom, no the underlying cause. And this probably isn't what ye're wanting tae hear, but realistically, if this doesnae get taken care of pronto, ye've got mibby another ten, fifteen years before the whole front of the house collapses.'

Anna said nothing. She just sat there, phone pressed to her ear, stunned into silence.

'Ye still there?'

'Yes,' she managed, 'I'm still here.'

'I was gonnae say, ye're more than welcome to seek out a second opinion. But I don't think ye'll find anyone who'll paint ye a rosier picture than the one I just have. And if it isnae fifteen years, it'll be twenty, twenty-five tops. Point is, it's gonnae happen sooner rather than later. Now,' he said, his tone perceptibly more businesslike, 'I can give ye a quote if ye're ready?'

'Let's hear it, then,' said Anna, with weary resignation.

The fee he quoted to her was so extortionate, she came dangerously close to asking him if he was taking the piss.

'Now, as I say,' he continued, his intonation irritatingly cheerful given the bombshell he'd just dropped in her lap, 'ye're welcome tae shop around, but I promise ye this: ye'll no find a better quote in the whole of Glasgow – not if I know anything about my trade. So what's the plan? Will I schedule ye in?'

Anna shut her eyes and counted to five in her head.

'I'll need to think about it,' she said, and rang off while Terry was still extolling the virtues of his over thirty years in the business.

She leant forward in her seat, clutching a handful of hair on either side of her head, and resisted the temptation to scream at the top of her lungs. She half-suspected Terry was diddling her, but she had neither the expertise nor the headspace to try to prove it. She wondered if she'd be better off cutting her losses and simply flogging the house to whoever would take it off her hands, with the structural issues factored into the asking price. It would be an undeniable relief to simply throw in the towel and let it be someone else's problem.

'Anna Scavolini?'

A woman's voice, coming from just a few feet away, cut through the mental fog.

'Yes?' she said, lifting her head and turning in the direction of the voice.

Even as she did so, a ferocious blow to the side of her face knocked her clean off the bench. She landed on the concrete and found herself gazing up at a small, ample-breasted woman in a smock dress, her blonde hair in an elaborate French twist. She was in her early thirties and glaring down at Anna with such seemingly unmotivated loathing that, for a moment, all Anna could do was stare up at her in wide-eyed stupefaction.

'Do I know you?'

It was all she could think of to say.

'No,' said the woman, 'but I feel like I've gotten to know you *quite* well through the texts you've exchanged with my fiancé.'

Even as she spoke, Anna realised why she seemed so inexplicably familiar, and yet so maddeningly hard to place.

The photo on Vasilico's Facebook page.

Oh, fuck.

Oh, FUCK.

Using the bench for support, Anna managed to scramble back onto her feet.

'Oh yes,' said Lauren, a note of unmistakable satisfaction in her voice, 'I've been wondering where he kept disappearing off to – telling me he was with his work colleagues and his work colleagues he was with me. It's nice to finally put a face to a name. I've got to say, you're not really what I expected.'

Anna racked her brains, frantically trying to come up with something to say. Every option seemed woefully inadequate.

I didn't realise?

But of course she had.

We never intended to hurt you.

Pull the other one.

I'm sorry.

Don't even *think* about it.

She realised Lauren was still speaking.

'Bet the two of you had a right good laugh about me, didn't you? About how you were pulling the wool over my eyes. Carrying on behind my back.' She adopted a high-pitched, singsong voice. '"Silly cow Lauren, she doesn't suspect a thing."' Her voice returned to its normal register. 'Well, I *knew* he was up to something.'

Finding her voice at last, Anna began to speak. 'I swear, we weren't—'

'DON'T.' Lauren held up a manicured finger, silencing her. 'I don't want to hear a single word out of your mouth. You don't get to speak.'

Anna glanced from side to side. She was aware that, all throughout the square, people were watching them. A number had brought themselves closer to the action, some managing to do it more subtly than others, like circusgoers hoping for a ringside seat.

Lauren continued to rant, pacing back and forth. It seemed to Anna that she was no longer speaking directly to her, but rather to herself or to some other imagined audience, the words pouring out of her in a furious stream of consciousness.

'It's not right, you know – taking advantage of people's trust. You give them the freedom to come and go as they please without having to justify their every movement.' She laughed grimly and wagged a chiding finger. 'This is what comes of it, you know – of assuming the best in people. Of treating them the way you'd want *them* to treat *you*. Of being a gullible fool. Well, who's the fool *now*?'

She came to a halt, hands pressed into the small of her back, breathing heavily through her nostrils.

Anna tried again. 'Lauren—'

'I'M HAVING HIS BABY!'

Anna was immediately stricken silent. She stared at Lauren, her tongue cleaving to the inside of her mouth.

Lauren gave a grim smile of satisfaction. 'Didn't tell you *that*, did he? Well, that's what you've come charging into, stomping all over in your size-whatevers, thinking you can take from me what's mine. We're CATHOLIC!' she yelled, as if that changed everything – which, now that Anna thought about it, perhaps it did. Certainly, the rushed engagement suddenly made a whole lot more sense.

'CATHOLIC,' Lauren repeated, underscoring her point with an almost triumphant nod. 'And I swear to you, if you so much as *think* about trying to mess up this chance at happiness for us, I will FUCK YOU UP.'

She fell silent and stood facing Anna, shoulders rising and falling as she sucked in air. Somewhere in the crowd, a solitary male voice shouted an approving 'YEAH!' and applauded enthusiastically. No one else spoke.

Eyes still on Anna, Lauren shook her head contemptuously. 'Stay the fuck away from him,' she muttered, then turned on her heel and stormed off, her dress billowing in the gentle breeze as she cut a swathe through the throng of onlookers.

Leaning against the bench to steady herself, Anna realised she was now the sole focus of attention. Dozens of pairs of eyes stared at her, eagerly waiting to see what she'd do next.

She did the only thing she could do under the circumstances.

She turned tail and ran.

47

She fled south across the square, crossing the road amid an angry blaring of horns, and set off down Queen Street. She made it as far as Royal Exchange Square before finally coming to a halt. There, under the statue of the Duke of Wellington, decked out with his customary traffic cone, she stood, catching her breath.

Feelings of horror, shame and embarrassment coursed through her mind. At least on some level, she'd always known there was a chance that she and Vasilico would be found out; that some sort of retribution would eventually take place. But she'd never imagined being confronted in this manner, and so publicly. She wondered if Lauren had deliberately engineered it that way to ensure maximum humiliation for her.

She'd always abhorred the idea of being 'the other woman', and yet, nevertheless, had allowed herself to slip into precisely that role. And she couldn't claim it had happened by accident or without her knowledge. She'd gone into this with both eyes wide open, fully aware of what she was doing, wilfully deluding herself into believing it somehow didn't count if they didn't acknowledge it for what it was.

That Vasilico was spoken for was something she'd always

factored into what they were doing – ever since that first, frantic coupling in the alleyway, when she'd felt the imprint of his ring on her flesh. But not for one instant had she ever considered that a *child* might be part of the equation. And, by the sounds of it, Vasilico knew Lauren was pregnant. The fact he'd allowed things to carry on under those circumstances was, in her estimation, as close to unforgivable as it was possible to get.

She massaged her still stinging cheek, trying to ignore the burning sensation in her elbow, which she now realised she must have grazed when she fell. Then, with a trembling hand, she dug out her phone and swiped through to the Contacts screen. She deleted the entry for Vasilico, then went to the Messages app and did the same with their conversation history. Finally, she blocked his number, solemnly vowing that, from this moment on, she would have nothing further to do with him, for as long as they both lived.

'What am I *doing* here?'

She asked the rhetorical question out loud, not caring who heard her. This was ridiculous. Here she was, chasing after a woman whose real name she couldn't even be sure she knew – and for what? On the off-chance that she'd been the mysterious individual who'd paid Libby Bright to seduce Hugh – Libby, who was now dead because she, Anna Scavolini, busybody *par excellence*, couldn't just let things be.

Regardless, she'd done what Fraser Taggart had asked of her. She now knew, or had come as close to knowing definitively as it was possible to be, what had been going on in Hugh's life during his final months, and what had driven him to his untimely death. She'd done what she set out to do – and yet she was *still here*. Why?

There was nothing left for her in Glasgow. She certainly wasn't wanted – that much was clear. She'd remained here far longer than she'd ever planned to, coming up with excuse after excuse to postpone her leaving. Well, no more. It was time for her to make good on her promise – long since stretched to the point of absurdity – that this would be a flying visit, and return to Italy to try to salvage whatever it was she and Matteo had, while she still had a chance.

Turning to her phone again, she called up the Skyscanner app. The last flight of the day to Perugia had already left Stansted, but there was one direct from Glasgow to Rome at 11:45 p.m. which would at least get her into the right country by early tomorrow morning. She could figure out how to get to Lago Trasimeno from there. Right now, anything was better than remaining in Glasgow for a second longer than was absolutely necessary.

Ten minutes later, her flights were booked, COVID questionnaire completed and proof of vaccination status uploaded successfully. Amazing what you could achieve when time was of the essence. She was just completing the online check-in when her phone rang.

'Jen,' she said, taking the call.

She knew she sounded tired and irritable, but she really didn't have the headspace to talk to anyone right now, nor the energy to pretend otherwise.

'Where in the name of blue blazes *are* ya?' demanded Jen. 'Don't tell me you're still stuck on that bloody train. What's the excuse *this* time? Signal failure as per?'

Then, before Anna could get a word out, 'Listen, no matter. I figured you were overdue a status report, so here's what I've managed to dig up so far, mostly from social media and the like. Looks like Emma Rippon *was* up the duff. She gave birth to a boychild a few months after she dropped out. Then, a few months later, began a relationship with a South African bloke who was over here on a work visa at the time. Just over a year later, when his visa ran out, she and the kiddo upped sticks and moved back with him to Jo'burg. That's where the trail runs cold, but I fancy, if I keep plugging away, I'll be able to—'

'Jen,' said Anna wearily, '*stop*. You …' She searched for the correct thing to say. 'You need to drop this. *I* need to drop this.'

'What? But you said—'

'I know what I said,' said Anna, with as much patience as she could muster. 'I just …' She sighed. 'I'm tired, and I'm done.'

Dead silence at the other end of the line.

'You were right. I've done what I said I'd do. You can stand down. I'm leaving tonight. I'm going home.'

'You really just want to let this go?' Jen sounded confused and more than a little hurt. 'But we're so close – I can feel it. Surely, if there's even a chance this Emma came back to Glasgow for revenge, you'd want to—'

'I'm sorry I dragged you into this. And I'm sorry you've wasted so much time on it. But I need to go. Now. Please don't ask me to explain why. Just accept that I have my reasons.'

Another long, uncomfortable silence.

'Of course I accept it,' Jen said at last. 'And you don't have to explain anything to me. You say you're leaving tonight?'

'That's right. My flight's already booked.'

'In that case, obviously I'll drive you to the airport.'

'Jen, you don't have to—'

'Have to, schmav to. I'll do it cos that's what pals do. 'Time's yer flight?'

'Eleven forty-five.'

'Get yer bum over to mine for nine. That'll leave us plenty of time. We can swing by the hotel and grab your stuff on the way.'

'Jen,' said Anna, weary gratitude oozing from every pore, 'I don't know what to say.'

'Then don't say anything. Just make sure you're here by nine.'

'I should be there a lot sooner than that. I just need to take care of something first.'

She rang off, feeling a good deal calmer now that she had a

definite plan of action. The thing she still had to take care of was telling Fraser what she'd found out. She could, she supposed, have called him once she was back in Italy, but that somehow felt too cowardly, too much like running away, and what she was doing felt far too much like that already without compounding the matter further. No, she'd go and talk to him, lay out everything she'd found out, including Jen's Emma Rippon discovery, and he could decide where to take it from there.

She set off in a southerly direction towards Central Station. Queen Street was closer, but that would mean going back up through George Square, and she wasn't prepared to risk the possibility that some of the people who'd witnessed her encounter with Lauren might still be there to recognise her.

She hadn't walked more than a few paces, however, when she came to an abrupt halt, Miriam's words to her on Saturday night coming back to her like a soft murmur in her ear.

I want you to promise me you'll tell me anything you happen to find out – before *anyone else hears about it.*

She stood there on the pavement, torn between a desire to remain true to her word and an equally powerful urge to avoid another encounter with Miriam, whose over-the-top intensity was the last thing she needed right now.

But a promise was a promise, and, right now, she felt like she could do with upholding at least *one*, if only to slightly rebalance the scales of a karmic justice she didn't believe in but nevertheless felt dutybound to honour.

She looked at her phone. It was ten past six. That gave her nearly three hours before she was due at Jen's. She had time to talk to both Fraser *and* Miriam. Miriam first, because her house was the furthest away, then back to the West End for Fraser and, finally, her ride to the airport.

Her decision made, she set off for the station once again.

48

Upon arriving at Central Station, Anna belatedly realised she hadn't eaten a thing since yesterday evening and was now seriously famished. She grabbed a meal deal from the M&S in the main concourse on her way down to the lower level, where she boarded a westbound train just as it was about to leave. She arrived at Westerton twenty minutes later and, as 7 p.m. approached, tramped up the gravel driveway and rang the bell at the MacLeishes' front door.

The woman who answered the door was, on first glance, not the Miriam Anna thought she knew. Gone were the casual, adolescent clothing and unruly mop of hair. This Miriam had her hair pinned back and wore an expensive-looking trouser suit, her sharp, pointed heels adding a good six inches to her height. She also had on a smattering of makeup. It was subtly applied, but it made her features appear sharper and more defined. She looked … like an adult, Anna supposed, for the first time since she'd met her. The only other time she'd seen her in formal wear had been at Geraldine's funeral, and the grown-up clothes on that occasion had seemed only to accentuate her childlike air. This time, all the pieces seemed to fit together far more seamlessly, creating the impression that this was every bit as natural a state for Miriam as the denim shirts and T-shirt dresses that had been her attire of choice during Anna's previous visits to the house. She looked like a smart, confident businesswoman fully in control of her life.

'Anna,' she said, clearly a little taken aback. 'What are *you* doing here?' And then, before Anna could get a word out herself, 'I mean, it's lovely to see you, of course. Always a pleasure, never a chore! Will you be wanting to come in?'

'Thanks,' said Anna, still slightly breathless from the brisk walk up from the station.

'I wasn't expecting you today,' said Miriam, shutting the door behind her. 'Actually, you're lucky to have caught me. I'm just this minute in the door myself. Haven't even had time to get changed.'

'Sorry?'

'I just got back from a meeting with a client. Wants to commission me to do portraits of him and his entire extended family. Very stiff upper lip – you know, tweed jackets, country estate, private school accent, the whole nine yards. I had to make a good first impression, hence …' She gestured to her suit. '… you know, the fancy dress.'

'Uh-huh,' said Anna faintly.

None of this seemed quite real. The juxtaposition of Miriam's trifling concerns with the bombshell Anna knew she was about to detonate under her was so extreme that it was as if the two of them were living in parallel realities.

She forced herself to get it together. 'Miriam,' she said, gently but firmly, 'can we sit down somewhere? I've got something to tell you.'

A flicker of something akin to fear crossed Miriam's eyes. 'Can't you tell me here?' she said, her voice suddenly high and shrill, like a child's.

'I really think it would be better if we sat down,' said Anna, praying that Miriam wasn't going to make this any harder than it needed to be.

For several seconds, Miriam just stared back at Anna, her eyes wide and unblinking.

'It's about Daddy, isn't it?' she virtually whispered.

Anna couldn't bring herself to say it, so she gave a slight, soft nod instead.

Miriam seemed to physically deflate. Her shoulders slumped, her posture slackened, and she suddenly seemed a whole lot smaller than she had just a few seconds ago.

'Is it … bad?'

'It's … not great,' said Anna diplomatically. '*Please* can we sit down?'

Miriam looked like she'd rather be anywhere but here. For the briefest of moments, Anna thought she was going to refuse to hear what she had to say. To order her out of the house. To slam and lock the door behind her and retreat into the comforting embrace of utter denial. But then Miriam gave a small, sad nod and gestured to the living room.

'You know the way by now,' she said.

'I can't believe it,' said Miriam, once Anna had finished. 'I just can't.'

She'd sat in silence as Anna told her story, giving as close to a complete breakdown of her investigation as she dared. She'd slightly edited it in places, making no mention of Fraser's involvement, or of her and Jen's hacking of Hugh's computer and his bank accounts. But she'd made no attempt to sanitise Hugh's actions, driven by a conviction that Miriam was entitled to make up her own mind about her father's behaviour and that she, Anna, had no right to redact it according to her own personal whims and insecurities. Whether or not that was the correct decision, she couldn't say, but at least Miriam was neither in floods of tears nor cursing her out. That was something, she supposed.

'It can't be real,' said Miriam, shaking her head. 'I mean,

I'm not going to pretend I never suspected him of playing away from home. All those late nights and unexplained absences ... but a *student?*' She spluttered the word in disbelief. 'It's unconscionable, is what it is. You don't *do* that – not to someone you're in a position of responsibility over.'

Slowly, Anna reached across the sofa and squeezed Miriam's shoulder. It was a futile, powerless gesture, but she felt the need to do *something*.

'Is there ... is there any chance this ... this Libby could have been lying?' asked Miriam, turning to Anna with a look of wild desperation in her eyes. 'Making it up for attention and whatnot?'

Anna shook her head. 'She had nothing to gain and everything to lose by making up a story like that. I don't think we'd be doing ourselves any favours by entertaining those sorts of delusions.'

Miriam gave a watery smile. 'Pity. I like them better than cold, hard reality.' She paused. 'And now you're saying she's dead too? That she took her own life?'

Anna nodded. 'The police seem pretty sure. There was a note ...'

'Just like with Daddy,' murmured Miriam. 'I suppose ...' she began, then stopped, seemingly unsure whether to articulate what was on her mind. Anna sat quietly, watching her, waiting for her to continue.

'I suppose,' she began again, 'I ought to feel sympathy towards her or something. Getting dragged into all of that ...'

'You don't have to feel *anything* if you don't want to,' said Anna gently. 'A situation like this – there's no instruction manual. No list of acceptable emotions. And if what you feel towards her is anger ... that's OK too.'

Miriam nodded slowly, gazing at the floor. She seemed to be mulling over Anna's words – that, or still trying to process what she'd heard. At length, she stirred and turned to look at Anna again.

'And this woman who put her up to all of it ... this Emily ... you don't have any leads as to who she could be?'

Anna shook her head. 'I don't know anything for sure. She *might* be a former student of your dad's called Emma Rippon, but it's a seriously long shot. And, in any event, she left the country years ago. She could have returned in the intervening period to ... you know, to exact revenge. But if she did, chances are she left again after it all came to nothing.'

Miriam nodded again, her expression distant and thoughtful. 'What will you do now?'

'Me?' Anna was surprised by the question. 'I'm heading back to Italy later tonight.'

'Your work here is done, then.'

The words sounded vaguely like an accusation, or at least an admonishment, but Anna didn't detect any rancour in Miriam's tone.

'Something like that,' she said. 'I just need to collect my stuff from the hotel, and then I'll be on my way.' *And pay your sworn enemy, Fraser Taggart, a visit so I can tell him most of what I've just told you.*

'You'll be leaving straight away, then?'

'Unless you'd rather I stayed.' She sincerely hoped Miriam wasn't going to take her up on the offer.

Miriam gave a wan smile. 'It's kind of you to ask, but no, it's fine. Actually, I kind of want to be alone, I think. I'll ... I dunno, maybe I'll open a bottle of something and take off all my clothes and put on some really loud 80s electronica and angry-dance myself into oblivion.' She paused, then smiled again. 'But I'll be fine. Honest. I'm not going to do anything stupid. Reckon this story's got more than its fair share of suicides already.'

Anna managed the smallest flicker of a smile. She wasn't sure how reassured she was by Miriam's words. The very fact she'd mentioned suicide implied that the thought had at least crossed her mind. But Anna chose to take her at her word. She had no other option. It was either that or remain here against Miriam's express wishes – and miss her flight.

'If you're sure,' she said.

'I'm sure.' A thought suddenly occurred to Miriam. 'How're you getting back?'

'To the hotel? Same way I got here: the train.'

Miriam looked positively aghast. 'Oh, no, no, no, that won't do at all. Trains are unreliable as buggery. They're always late and full of unsavoury types and are absolute disease magnets. Don't take the smelly *train*.'

'Well,' Anna began helplessly, 'I'm not sure what other—'

'Why don't I drive you?'

'You?'

Anna was surprised Miriam could drive, far less had access to a car. There was, she supposed, no reason why she shouldn't. It just didn't fit with the image she'd formed of her as being locked in a state of perpetual childhood. But then, the Miriam facing her on the sofa looked far less like a child than the one she'd picked over the burnt carcass of a chicken with just a couple of nights earlier.

'Of course me!' said Miriam, grinning at Anna as if she was being ridiculous. 'Who else? It's the very least I can do after everything you've done for me.'

She refused to take no for an answer, and, in short order, they were heading out into the hallway together, Anna feeling vaguely like she'd just been pummelled into submission. Her carefully laid plans had been thrown into disarray, the order of her itinerary hastily rearranged to factor in a stop at the hotel *before* her visit to Fraser. She told herself it made no real difference, other than necessitating the need to cart her luggage up to Kirklee Road and then down to Jen's flat on Havelock Street. She'd be saving time in the long run, thanks to Miriam's lift. But it still left her feeling discombobulated and ill at ease in some vague, indefinable way.

'You don't mind if I go and slip into something less presentable?' said Miriam, as they reached the door. 'Here.' She thrust a set of car keys into Anna's hand. 'It's in the garage. You go and make yourself comfortable, and I'll be with you in two ticks.'

Anna headed out the front door, then followed the gravel path round to the garage off to the side of the house, inside which a new-looking Ford Focus sat waiting. As she stepped out of the sun and into the semi-darkness of the cool, stone-walled building, it occurred to Anna that this was where both Hugh and Alfie had died. Instinctively, she looked for the infamous deep freeze, but there was no sign of it. She probably shouldn't be too surprised. It would have been far *more* surprising if Hugh and Geraldine had kept it after what had happened.

She settled in the passenger seat, shoulder bag in her lap. All things considered, Miriam had taken the news far better than she'd feared. There was, she supposed, still a chance that Miriam was merely experiencing a delayed reaction and that, sooner or later, it would all hit her like a ton of bricks. In that respect, perhaps the offer of a lift was a delaying tactic on her part: a ruse to postpone having to face up to it all. But there was nothing Anna could do about that, other than to hope that, if and when the breakdown finally happened, it wouldn't be too messy.

The minutes continued to tick by, and still Miriam failed to materialise. Anna checked her phone. 19:55. She hoped there really *was* still time to fit in a debrief with Fraser before she was due at Jen's at nine. She was just going to have to make sure her report was the very essence of brevity and that she didn't give Fraser any opportunity to drag things out.

She checked the time again. Only another two minutes had passed, but it felt like far longer. What was keeping Miriam?

She sighed. Might as well at least do something productive while she waited.

She started by tackling the backlog of notifications she'd ignored since the previous night. There were the missed calls and voicemail messages from Matteo that she'd already clocked and ignored, but, buried among them, was another voicemail from a number she didn't recognise. It had come in at 19:44 the previous evening, while she and Jen had been down in the basement of The Vault, where the signal had been non-existent. A cold caller? More than likely. Still, she'd better make sure. You never knew – it could be something important. *And pigs might grow wings.*

She tapped the message and listened to the automated preamble from the plummy-voiced announcer before, finally, the message began.

'It's me.' Pause. *'Um, Libby. So, uh ... so listen, there is something else. Something I didn't tell you earlier. I didn't mention it because I thought ...'* She trailed off. *'Truthfully, I dunno what I thought, 'cept that mibby I could have my cake and eat it – you know, give you what you were after without really giving you what you were after? Guess I was kidding myself I could still tell you all the other stuff and somehow it wouldn't count so long as I kept this part to myself. And mibby this is a bad idea, but I figure you deserve to know. It might make a difference to what you do with the info I already gave you. Gonna call me back when you get this? Best do it quick, 'fore I change my mind.'*

The message ended, the plummy voice providing her with a series of options, including to listen to the message again, delete it or return the call.

Slowly, Anna lowered the phone from her ear, the words of this veritable message from beyond the grave churning over and over in her head. What had Libby been trying to tell her? What did she mean by 'it wouldn't count'? And why the hell hadn't she checked for messages earlier?

She was still pondering these questions when the door next

to her abruptly opened, jolting her back to the present. Miriam dropped into the driver's seat, breathless and a trifle manic.

'All right?' she said, grinning expectantly at Anna.

She looked more like herself now, in a lightweight tweed blazer, an oversized T-shirt and baggy denim jeans. She'd washed off the makeup too, her face red and slightly shiny from scrubbing. Anna wondered if she'd been crying and if that accounted for the delay – though, if she had, there was no telltale sign of redness in her eyes.

'All right,' she replied, hastily stuffing her phone back into her bag as if it was contraband.

Miriam buckled her seatbelt. 'Best get to it, then.' She held out her hand. 'Keys?'

They set off, cruising east along Maxwell Avenue towards Switchback Road, the long, straight stretch of road connecting Canniesburn Toll to Anniesland. It was just after 8 p.m. and eerily quiet, the rush hour – such as it was these days – having long since passed. The street was all but deserted, apart from the occasional figure glimpsed in the front garden of one of the houses on either side of them. Even the purr of the car's engine was barely audible. Neither Miriam nor Anna spoke. It was as if they'd exhausted all there was to say back at the house.

Anna was still preoccupied by Libby's message. She hadn't wanted to trouble Miriam with this further twist in a story she'd already presented to her as having a clear beginning, middle and end … but that didn't stop her ruminating on the implications herself. If Libby had wanted to tell her something, why kill herself less than an hour later? It just didn't make sense. For reasons she couldn't fully explain, a cold sense of dread and foreboding slowly began to creep over her, beginning in the pit of her stomach and working its way up to the back of her throat.

They turned up Ilay Avenue and came to a halt at the traffic lights at the junction onto Switchback Road. The still-bright sun, hung low in the sky behind them, elongating the shadow cast by the car in front of them. The lights remained red. The occasional car zoomed past in either direction in front of them, but, otherwise, the intersection resembled a ghost-town.

'Not many people out tonight,' observed Anna, for no reason other than to fill the silence between them.

'No,' said Miriam.

Anna waited for her to say something more, but nothing was forthcoming. Perhaps she was one of those people who didn't like talking while she was behind the wheel.

As the lights remained stubbornly stuck on red, despite the complete absence of traffic on the road in front of them, Anna looked around, trying to find something to distract her from the increasingly suffocating silence. Her gaze fell on Miriam's arm, where a white, downy feather was embedded in the fabric of her sleeve.

'Oh,' said Anna, pointing, 'you've got …'

Miriam barely glanced up from the wheel. 'Hmm?'

'Here.'

Anna reached across and plucked the feather from her jacket, then noticed another a little further down, close to the elbow. She was about to pick it off too when she noticed several more tiny, fluffy feathers stuck to Miriam's seat.

'What's been going on here?' she said, half-laughing. 'Have you been having a pillow-fight or something?'

Miriam's expression remained impassive.

Anna opened her mouth to speak again. But even as she did so, she remembered something Libby had said to her the day before at the wildlife sanctuary.

'We're rearing a couple of baby barn owls and someone needs to be on site 24/7 to do hourly checks. It's a ball-ache, and I'm forever picking

down out of my clothes, but you get ... I dunno, a sense of purpose or something.'

They both heard Anna's sharp, involuntary intake of breath. Their eyes met. The look that passed between them told Anna that each knew exactly what the other had just worked out.

Out of the corner of her left eye, Anna was aware of the lights changing from red to amber. In the same instant, she sensed movement to her right. Then she felt Miriam's hand grabbing her by the scruff of her neck and shoving downwards with all her might, smashing her forehead into the dashboard.

Anna briefly saw stars.

Then, only darkness.

PART VI

WHAT YOU DO WITH WHAT YOU'VE GOT

49

Jen took a large bite out of her shawarma wrap and dropped it back into the polystyrene container by her keyboard. She chewed morosely, eyes on the glowing multi-monitor array in front of her. To say that this was a bitter end to her investigation was putting it mildly.

After she'd got off the phone with Anna, she'd found herself singularly unable to let the matter of the current whereabouts of Emma Rippon lie. Whatever Anna had said about being done, there was, she'd concluded, no reason for her not to continue the search herself. It was her own time, after all, and she'd already devoted too much of it to simply throw in the towel with so many questions unanswered. So, she'd kept digging.

As it turned out, what had thrown her was that Emma Rippon had got married in South Africa, but not to the man with whom she'd moved there to make a new life for herself and her young son. Their relationship appeared to have soured within a couple of years, and she and her son had relocated again, this time from Johannesburg to Durban. There, she'd met a local property developer, Jacob Okeke, and, a few years later, married him. Thus, Emma Rippon had become Emma

Okeke, and it was in that name that her death certificate was issued when she was killed in a hit-and-run in July 2015, at the much too young age of 36.

Which, apart from being an appalling tragedy, both for Emma herself and for her husband and her now teenage son, meant only one thing: Emma Rippon couldn't possibly have been Emily.

Jen reached for her shawarma, only to set it back down again, uneaten. She'd lost her appetite. Not unreasonable, given the circumstances.

She glanced at the clock display in the corner of her main screen. It had just gone 20:15. What on earth was keeping Anna? How long could it possibly take for her to get from the city centre to the West End? She'd promised to be here by nine, so she had time yet …

Still, though, where could she have got to?

50

Fragments.
Brief snatches, images and sensations, punctuating long, extended bouts of oblivion.

Driving. The car's vibrations deep in her bones. The tops of tall buildings passing above her.

Turning, slowing. Crawling past a great mass of scaffolding erected at the front of a multistorey terraced house built from rough sandstone blocks.

Still now. The car's engine silent. Somewhere, a door slamming.

Arms curling under her armpits from behind, hugging her torso, crushing her boobs against her ribcage.

The feeling of being dragged backwards, heels scraping on concrete.

Hauled up a steep flight of steps, one at a time. The dull, distant ache as the sharp edges rake her back.

Landing, facedown, on some hard, smooth, cool surface.
Drifting into unconsciousness again.

51

Anna came round suddenly and violently as a splash of water hit her square in the face. She raised her head, blinking and spluttering and wondering where the hell she was.

'Ha!' said Miriam. 'I can't believe that *worked*!'

Anna opened and closed her eyes forcefully, trying simultaneously to banish the miasma of fog that seemed to hang over her and to take stock of her situation. She was sitting on a hard, straight-backed wooden chair, her ankles tightly bound to the front legs. Her arms were pinned behind her, hands tied at the wrists. When she tried to move them, she found she couldn't raise them more than a few centimetres before coming up against heavy resistance. At first, she couldn't work out what was wrong with them. Then, as she tried again and felt the rope digging into her wrists, she realised it must be attached to something further down – perhaps a crossbar below the seat. Whatever the mechanism, it was clear she wasn't going anywhere.

And there, in front of her, stood Miriam, clutching a half-empty plastic water bottle and looking altogether too pleased with this state of affairs. She had a nervous restlessness about her, as if she'd been waiting for Anna to come round of her own accord for ages and couldn't wait to get started.

Started with what? *That* was the question.

'You knocked me out.'

It was the only thing Anna could think of to say.

'Yes,' said Miriam, cheerfully.

'You smashed my head into the dashboard.'

'I did,' Miriam agreed, with perhaps the faintest hint of regret. 'It seemed the right thing to do under the circumstances.'

Anna fought down a rolling wave of nausea. Her forehead was throbbing, like a slow, heavy heartbeat.

'I think I have a concussion,' she said.

Miriam gave a dismissive wave. 'Oh, I'm sure it'll pass in a moment. You're a tough old bird, you. Been through worse scrapes. You know, it's funny, I was just thinking the other day that—'

She was cut off mid-flow by Anna projectile vomiting in her direction. She sidestepped just in time as Anna's partially digested M&S meal deal hit the hardwood floor where she'd been standing a mere fraction of a second earlier. As Anna's stomach roiled and she fought to swallow down a fresh wave of nausea, Miriam's features crumpled into genuine concern.

'Oh, you poor thing. Here.'

Moving towards Anna, she gently wiped the corners of her mouth with a tissue, then raised the water bottle to her lips, tipping it back for her. Anna drank obediently, mainly because she didn't have much choice in the matter. Once she'd finished, Miriam withdrew the empty bottle from her lips and crushed it in her fist.

'There, all better now. You need to give me advance warning if you're thinking of doing that again. Good thing this floor's a doddle to clean.'

As she spoke, Anna finally managed to focus her eyes for long enough to take in her surroundings. They were in a square, high-ceilinged room which, on a first impression, seemed almost cavernously large, though that might just have been because, apart from a metal bedframe and the chair to which Anna was tied, it was completely unfurnished. The heavy curtains were drawn shut, and a single, naked bulb hung from the ceiling, casting long shadows across the walls, which still bore remnants of hastily stripped paper.

She spotted her shoulder bag, presumably still containing her phone, lying in the far corner, and wondered if there was any way she could get to it. If there was, she couldn't see it. She was trussed up tighter than a Christmas turkey, and probably just as doomed.

'Where are we?' she asked, her voice sounding strange and distant in her own ears.

'In one of my properties,' said Miriam matter-of-factly.

'Your properties?'

'That's right. What, you didn't think I made enough to live on just from my *paintings*?' She gave a high-pitched giggle, tickled pink by the very idea. 'There's no money in art, not unless you're prepared to be a complete corporate sellout – in which case, it hardly counts as art anymore, does it? No, Mum always pushed me to be self-sufficient, especially after she got sick. "Your father's never been sensible with money," she said, "so it's no use looking to him to bail you out." And she was right. A year or so after she died, a friend of his persuaded him to invest a bunch of money in some hare-brained business venture that was going to revolutionise the world of hydrogen production or something. And, like a chump, Daddy went along with it hook, line and sinker. Just about wiped out his savings, leaving him living virtually paycheque to paycheque.

'That was the kick up the backside I needed to realise I couldn't rely on him to pick up the pieces for me if everything went south. So I got smart, made the right sort of investments, bought up rundown properties on the cheap to do up and make myself a pretty penny. There's good money to be made in this racket if you know what you're doing.' She affected a drawling American accent. 'Livin' the capitalist dream, baby.'

'And you ... you *own* this place?'

Anna was still struggling to process all this, the fog that seemed to engulf her brain stubbornly refusing to lift.

'Plus the flats on either side. The previous tenants cleared out during lockdown, and I haven't been able to replace them yet. And, as you can see, this one's something of a work in progress. So it's not like we're going to be disturbed.'

'But ... but I thought you were broke. The "final notice" letters. The bailiffs ...'

'Hey, *I* never said I was broke. If you assumed that, that's on you. OK, so I haven't exactly gotten on top of Daddy's finances, and that old house is a repossession waiting to happen, but it's not as if I'm *destitute*. I do all right for myself, all things considered – though there are less stressful ways to earn a living. Still, could be worse. To paraphrase the great Klaus Kinski, letting flats is better than cleaning toilets.'

Anna was beginning to think she'd woken up in some sort of parallel universe. As she stared up at Miriam, standing before her with a huge, demented grin stretched over her features, something finally clicked into place.

'You're Emily, aren't you?'

Miriam mimed taking an arrow in the heart, head flung back, hands pressed to her chest. She grinned and shrugged a trifle sheepishly. 'Ya got me!'

'But *why*?'

'Suppose I've always just liked the name. There's something ... I dunno, sophisticated about it. Something a bit fey. Plus, I wrote my dissertation on Emily Mary Osborn, who was only, you know, one of *the* most significant female painters of the nineteenth century and a leading light of the Pre-Raphaelite movement. I thought it was quite apt, no?'

Anna said nothing. The impetus behind her *why?* had been

rather more all-encompassing than just a desire to learn the origins of a pseudonym.

'Just me, then? Oh well.' Miriam shrugged, clearly trying to hide how miffed she was behind a show of nonchalance.

'And Libby didn't kill herself, did she? You murdered her and dressed it up as suicide.'

'Of *course* she didn't kill herself.' Miriam rolled her eyes impatiently. 'Though I take it as a compliment that both you and Moffat's finest bought the little scene I staged for you. The suicide note was a nice touch, I thought.'

Anna stared at her, wide-eyed and open-mouthed, unable to believe the indifference with which she'd made this admission.

'*Why*, though?' she said again. Her tone was less forceful this time, more plaintive. More resigned to the knowledge that whether she got an answer to her question would be down to Miriam's own mercurial whims.

'Why?' Miriam looked like she couldn't believe what she was hearing. 'Because she broke the rules, that's why! Took a great big shit all over the terms of our agreement and then dragged her arse-cheeks over the proceeds for good measure. She wasn't meant to talk to anyone about what we'd done – least of all a bossy busybody who fancies herself as a private eye and can't mind her own business for love nor money.

'You see, Anna,' she said, as Anna stared up at her, dumfounded, 'I was onto you right from the start. Right from our first conversation, when you showed up out of the blue at the house, I had my suspicions. That business with the computer only went and confirmed it. "Carrying on his research", my hairy arsehole! It was as clear as a bloody big neon sign you were trying to piece together what happened to him.

'I thought at first there was a limit to how much harm you could do. Figured I'd covered my tracks thoroughly enough that there was no risk of you finding out anything that led back to me.' She shook her head. 'I should've known better. Once you get your teeth into something, you don't bloody let go, do you?'

She began to pace back and forth, striding briskly, arms ramrod straight and sticking out behind her, fists balled. Anna noticed she'd taken off her shoes and was wearing just a pair of invisible socks, startlingly white against the dark finish of the floor. The left one had a hole in it.

'After the computer business,' she went on, continuing to pace, 'I followed you everywhere – always several paces behind, of course. I couldn't risk you spotting me, even though I was in disguise the whole time. Nothing too elaborate – just a hat, some tinted glasses and a good old facemask. Mad, isn't it, how no one blinks twice anymore when they see someone with their entire face covered up, even out in the fresh air? They just assume you're immunosuppressed or a hypochondriac or something.'

She laughed and shook her head, as if reminiscing about a fond experience. 'Such a merry dance you led me! All over the city, talking to all those fellow busybodies. Leila and Heather and your pal Jen – and that hunky toy-boy of yours!' She tutted playfully. 'Naughty Anna, helping yourself to a hot slice of action on the side! I must've spent hours parked outside that hotel on Great Western Road while you and he were in there getting up to all sorts of hanky-panky. It's no wonder the chicken dinner ended up getting burned, the rush I was in to get home and get things ready before you arrived.'

Anna listened to this diatribe with growing disbelief. Miriam was quite obviously mad, the faint streak of mania that she'd always suspected lurked just below the surface now given unapologetic free rein. There was clearly no point in trying to reason with her. The best she could do was play for time, using any and all means at her disposal.

'But your dad,' she said, leaning into the desperation she

felt and letting it seep into her voice. 'The whole business with Libby … Why would you set him up like that?'

'Because I had to *know*!'

Miriam stopped in her tracks and whirled around to face her, a ring of exasperation in her voice, as if she couldn't believe Anna had failed to grasp this.

'I had to know whether he really was guilty of all the things they said he'd done.'

'Who's "they"?'

Miriam laughed and shook her head in disbelief. 'Seriously? You're going to make me do the whole "villainous victory monologue" thing? Don't you think that's all a bit old hat?'

Not knowing how to respond, Anna just stared up at her in helpless silence.

Miriam laughed softly and shook head. 'Oh, why not? The old ways are the best, I suppose. Besides, after all this time, I suppose there's a part of me that's dying to tell *someone* how it all went down.'

She clapped her hands together, the matter evidently settled to her satisfaction. 'But first,' she declared, 'I'm going to need a drink. Care to join me?'

52

'Let's see,' said Miriam. 'It must be … what, getting on for three years now? Three years since I got that letter claiming Daddy had been getting up to no good with his female students.'

She stood in the centre of the room, facing Anna, clutching the half-bottle of whisky she'd produced from one of the other rooms in the flat. She'd already offered Anna first dibs (Anna had declined) before proceeding to unscrew the lid and knock back a generous measure. She'd also taken the time to mop up the vomit and scour the floorboards with stain remover. She was clearly houseproud – quite a contrast to the state into which she'd allowed the family home to fall.

'It came with the regular mail,' she went on, gesticulating with the bottle, 'in a plain brown envelope. Typed, not handwritten. Purported to be from "a concerned member of the public", though it was obvious, from the way they knew the inner workings of the department, that they were a colleague of his. Said he'd been carrying on for years, *including* while Mum was on chemo.

'At first, I couldn't believe it. How *could* I? Daddy was …' She shrugged helplessly. '… *Daddy*. I thought it was someone's sick idea of a joke. Maybe someone who got passed over for a promotion and figured they'd get their revenge by blackening a good man's name. But, after a while, doubt started to creep in. What if they were telling the truth? Why write to me, then never follow it up, if they were after revenge or hush money or whatever? I had to know.'

She paused to take a swig of whisky, knocking it back like it was orange juice. 'I couldn't *confront* him, obviously. If I just walked straight up to him and said, "Daddy, is it true you've been rogering your students?", things would've never been the same between us again, whether he confirmed or denied it. And if he *did* deny it, how would I know if he was telling the truth? If he'd already been lying to us for years, for *decades* – why stop now? I had to come up with a way to find out for sure.' She flashed an unnervingly eager grin at Anna. 'Go on – ask me what I came up with.'

Anna considered whether indulging her was likely to do her more favours than maintaining a stony silence. In the end, she concluded she had little to lose either way – and she really *did* want to know.

'What did you come up with?' she asked obediently.

'*Glad* you asked. Actually, in the end, it was like all the best ideas. It came along the very moment I wasn't looking for one.'

Turning, she strode over to the bedframe, as if intending to sit down on it. As she reached it, she seemed to abruptly change her mind and, performing a sharp one-eighty, headed back over to Anna, bottle still in hand.

'A few months later, I was in Gianetto's on Hyndland Road one evening. I was supposed to be meeting this bloke, but he'd stood me up.' She pulled a face. 'Tinder. Anyway, while I was sitting there, working my way through a whole bottle of Malbec and wishing suppurating sores on the genitals of the entire male species, all of a sudden, I spotted one of the waitresses.

'Hopefully it's not too much of a spoiler to say it was Libby

– though, of course, I didn't know her name at the time. I'm still not sure if it was purely her looks that caught my eye or something else as well, but there was something about her that just grabbed hold of me and refused to let go.

'I spent the whole evening watching her bouncing from table to table, always with a smile on her face, laughing at all these middle-aged blokes' dad jokes and barely batting an eyelid when one of them quote-unquote "accidentally" brushed up against her arse – which, FYI, was *after* he'd told her how much she looked like his daughter. And I thought to myself, *Now there's a girl who knows how to put on an act.*'

She paused for another swig. Anna watched her warily. She wasn't convinced a drunk Miriam was necessarily any less dangerous than a sober one – but at least she was talking, and every minute she spent talking was a minute where she hadn't bashed Anna on the head or poisoned her or whatever it was she intended to do.

Hanged. She hanged Libby with her own belt.

Not that Anna held out much hope of an eleventh-hour miracle rescue. It wasn't as if anyone knew where she was. *She* didn't even know where she was. She hadn't told Jen she was heading to the house in Westerton, so it wasn't as if there was any hope of Jen going there to look for her and then somehow following her trail to wherever they were now.

There was no getting around it: she was seriously fucked.

'Afterwards,' Miriam went on, 'I found I couldn't get her out of my head. There was just something about her. Something ...' She searched for the word. 'Something vulnerable, and yet also stoic. You could imagine men going nuts over her, wanting to take care of her. Wanting to *save* her. Particularly men of a certain age.'

She gave Anna a conspiratorial little eyeroll, as if to say, *WE know the type.*

'After that, I kept going back to the bar, week after week – as often as I dared, really. I didn't want to draw *too* much attention to myself. She was on most nights, so I soon realised it didn't matter which days I went there.

'It sounds silly, I know,' she said, a touch ruefully, 'but I felt like I really got to know her. I watched her turning on the charm like she was flicking a switch, flirting with dirty old men for tips, making it look so effortless. And one night, I heard her mouthing off to one of her co-workers about how cash-strapped she was; how she was sure she was going to fail her degree thanks to all the shifts she was having to put in. And I thought, *Bingo*.'

She made to raise the bottle to her lips again, then stopped, eyes falling on Anna as if she'd just remembered she was there. Again, she held out the bottle to her. Again, Anna shook her head. Miriam shrugged, then knocked back another mouthful herself.

'I think,' she said, 'in retrospect, the plan had been taking shape for a while – just sort of percolating away in my subconscious without my knowing it. She told you about the business with her bag getting nicked, I take it?'

'She did,' said Anna.

'That, honestly, was a complete spur-of-the-moment thing. I just saw my chance and did it. I don't think I was really *thinking* of anything, beyond this vague sense that I might use it to get some leverage over her. I'd already come up with the idea that I was going to try to get her to seduce Daddy. But I swear – and look, I know you're not going to believe this, but it's God's honest truth – I swear, I had no idea she was one of his students till I looked inside her bag. It was, like … I dunno, like it was *fated* or something.'

She tipped back her head and gave a delighted little giggle, as if, even now, she couldn't quite believe the serendipity of it all. Then, she made a show of regaining her composure, holding up her hand as if to forestall any criticism from Anna and adopting an expression of studied solemnity.

'When I met her a couple of days later – to give her back

her bag and make my little proposition – I went in disguise, of course. I bought a wig, makeup, a whole 'nother wardrobe. And I came up with a backstory and everything, even though I was the only one who'd ever know it. I figured I was … I dunno, this hoity-toity business professional who worked in finance or something. I even adopted a whole different accent. Copied it off some politician I'd seen on the telly. You know the kind – the ones that get elocution lessons cos they think they'll never get taken seriously by the big beasts down south unless they speak this ungodly mashup of Kelvinside and southern English.'

A gleeful glint flashed in her eyes. 'It was *fun*! You've seen the home videos. You know I've always loved playing dress-up. It was like the shows me and Alfie used to put on, only a whole lot more serious. I loved putting on Emily's clothes and the wig and turning into her for a couple of hours a week. Honestly, it was my favourite part of the whole farrago.

'I thought Libby might take some persuading, but I figured she'd not be able to resist what I was offering her for long – not if she was as skint as she made out. And yeah, there was a bit of haggling, ironing out the fine details and whatnot, but in the end I got her for pretty much exactly what I wanted. I even lowballed her to begin with cos I knew she'd try and get me to go higher. Let her think she was the one getting one over on *me*.' She laughed again, clearly delighted with her deception.

'And where was it all coming from?' Anna couldn't help but ask. 'All this cash you agreed to pay her.'

A flash of irritation crossed Miriam's face. 'I told you, I've always been smart with my money. I had a nice, steady stream of income coming in from my various investments. Plus, you seem to have forgotten I was living at home this whole time. Gotta be *some* perks to shacking up with the 'rentals, right? So yeah, suffice it to say, I wasn't hard up.'

So that was why she'd been so content to essentially flush money down the toilet, Anna thought – month after month, with nothing to show for it. When it came down to it, on some level this really *had* just been about a bored little rich girl playing at spies.

Miriam gave Anna an expectant look, as if making sure she was quite finished asking questions. Not daring to risk a further interruption at this stage, Anna kept her expression as neutral as possible and met her gaze.

'Anyway,' said Miriam at last, 'where were we? Oh yes – I always figured there were two possibilities. Either Daddy wouldn't take the bait, in which case I'd feel a whole lot more confident in writing off the letter as just some pathetic little shitweasel trying to stir the pot. Or he *would*, and then … well, that would be a whole different kettle of fish, wouldn't it?

'Of course, I was burning through money like no tomorrow, but I told myself it'd be worth it to get the answers I was looking for. And Libby took to the role like she'd been born to play it – with a little help from yours truly, obviously. I was the one who picked out the right clothes for her, taught her how to carry herself and whatnot. She might've been playing the part, but I've got at *least* equal dibs on character rights.

'I thought at first about tailing her – y'know, keeping tabs on her to see how she was getting on. As you can attest yourself, I'm quite adept at following people and not being spotted. But I decided it was too big a risk. Last thing I wanted was for Daddy to see me. I always figured, no matter how good my disguise was, he'd still've recognised me – even if I was wearing a bloody burka. Your wee boy'd know *you* no matter what, right?'

Anna, bristling at this mention of Jack and not trusting herself to respond verbally, instead gave the closest approximation possible, within the confines of her restraints, of a shrug.

'Exactly,' said Miriam, pleased that Anna agreed. 'I couldn't risk it. So I kept her on a fairly long leash, and contented myself with our regular catch-ups. And at first they *were* regular – as regular as clockwork. I've always liked that phrase – "as regular as clockwork". I wonder where it came from. Don't s'pose you've any idea?'

'I can't say I've ever given it much thought,' said Anna.

Miriam continued to ponder the question for a moment, the bottle pressed under her chin, before dismissing it with an unconcerned shrug.

'Anyway, at first, everything seemed to be going to plan. "Slow and steady wins the race" and all that. Then, in March, Daddy was stabbed in the back by that fermented sack of shit Fraser Taggart, which turned out to be a blessing in disguise from the point of view of the mission, cos it ended up being Libby's way in. Him all sad and dejected; her stroking his knee, telling him what a fine figure of a man he truly was – honestly, I couldn't've planned it better myself.

'I noticed Daddy spending more and more time out of the house, of course. All the late nights. The meals out. How could I not? I only bloody *lived* with him. And that all tallied with what Libby was telling me, though I knew she was trying to play it down. The number of times Daddy was late coming home, either she was spending a whole lot more time with him than she was making out or she wasn't the only girl he was seeing ... and I wasn't sure which option I'd've preferred.'

She took another glug of whisky. The bottle was getting seriously depleted now, and she was starting to slur her words a bit, her movements becoming increasingly floppy. This might, Anna supposed, be a positive. If whatever Miriam ultimately intended to do to her involved untying her first, and it came down to a physical fight, Miriam's state of intoxication could put her at a disadvantage.

'But, of course,' said Miriam, 'as fate would have it, young Libby had ideas of her own. Even as I was handing over great wads of cash every week so she could live the life of Riley, she was busy making plans to stiff me. I ought to have smelt a rat even then, though for the longest time I told myself it was nothing – just my own natural tendency towards mistrust.' She grimaced. 'Should've listened to my gut.

'But no. Instead, I kept on indulging her, accepting all her excuses and her big promises of a grand exposé if I'd just wait a few weeks longer.' Her expression soured. 'Until the day after her graduation, when she admitted she had nothing and said she wanted out.

'Of course, I never bought all that crap about her bag getting snatched with all the evidence in it. I figured either she'd been lying to me the whole time – that all that about her having Daddy eating out of the palm of her hand, writing her essays for her and helping her cheat on her exams, was something she made up so I'd keep paying her – or else that she was deluded enough to've actually *fallen* for the old sap; convinced herself they were going to make a proper go of it.' She turned to Anna with a sharp look. '*You* spoke to her. Which was it?'

'Neither. She *was* sleeping with him but realised exposing him would bring her dreams of a future in academia crashing down.'

For several long, uneasy moments, Miriam didn't respond. She just stared at Anna, a blank, almost vacant expression on her face. Anna was on the verge of asking her if she was all right when she stirred and shook her head, a strange smile slowly spreading across her lips.

'Well I never – the devious little *cow*.' She sounded more impressed than angry. 'If I'd known that was her game, I'd've put up more of a fight when she said she wanted to bail.'

'But you didn't,' Anna put in. 'You let her walk away with everything, leaving you with nothing. Why?'

Miriam didn't respond immediately. She drew her shoulders in and hugged her arms about herself, refusing to meet Anna's eye.

'She … was unexpectedly persuasive,' she said at last.

Anna stared at her in disbelief. A part of her wanted to ask, *Is that IT?*

Seeming to sense what she was thinking, Miriam stared back at Anna obstinately, chin jutting out in defiance.

'What?'

'"Persuasive"?' Anna repeated, unable to hide her incredulity.

No matter how precarious her own situation, she couldn't help but be baffled and perplexed by Miriam's refusal to elaborate. It had, she suddenly realised, been exactly the same when Libby had told *her* side of this part of the story. And, just as it had been with Libby, this was by far the least convincing aspect of Miriam's account. They were both holding something back – but what, and *why*?

Miriam shrugged belligerently. 'She kept insisting she'd fulfilled her end of the bargain. And even if she hadn't, it's not like I could prove it. What was I going to do? Shop her and Daddy for the exam business out of spite? Then Daddy'd be out of a job and I *still* wouldn't have the proof I wanted. It was in no one's interests.'

'But hadn't you already decided you were going to shop him to the university if Libby had brought you proof he'd had sex with her? He'd have been out of a job for sure after *that*.'

'Actually, I *hadn't*,' said Miriam tersely.

'Hadn't what?'

'Decided I was going to shop him. I hadn't got as far as figuring out what I'd do if it turned out it was all true. I mean it,' she insisted, responding to some criticism Anna hadn't actually made. 'I thought about exposing him, but who the hell knows whether I'd've been able to follow through if push came to shove? I just needed to *know*. I figured, once I had proof, I could make up my mind about whether I was going to do anything with it. You do understand that, don't you?' She looked at Anna entreatingly, anxiously seeking reassurance. 'This was never about fucking Daddy over. It was about finding out THE TRUTH.'

And now he's dead, thought Anna. She felt like asking Miriam if she considered that a price worth paying – but, of course, that would have been suicide. Instead, she tried again to surreptitiously raise her arms, but there was so little slack in the rope securing them below the seat that they barely moved at all.

And now Miriam was pacing again, going in circles around the room, the nervous energy inside her making it impossible to stand still. She continued to clutch the now considerably depleted whisky bottle, the golden liquid sloshing around inside it with each step.

'But she'd already admitted he'd written her dissertation for her and helped her cheat on her exams,' said Anna. 'Plus, he was wining and dining her on a regular basis. What they were doing essentially amounted to a full-blown affair between a lecturer and a student, whether it went as far as actual intercourse or not.'

Miriam ignored her. She continued to pace, the circles getting increasingly smaller and more frenzied.

Anna knew perfectly well that none of these questions helped her own plight one iota. Nonetheless, she felt somehow compelled to get to the bottom of why Miriam seemed to have put such stock in one transgression over all the others.

She tried again. 'Why was sex this great big tipping point that would put his behaviour beyond the pale when you were prepared to give everything else a pass?'

'BECAUSE THAT'S WHAT THE LETTER SAID!' yelled Miriam, coming to a sudden standstill and whirling around to face her, sloshing whisky all over the floor. 'That was the original accusation. It didn't say he was tongue-wrestling them or showing them exam papers – it said he was FUCKING them, and I HAD TO KNOW.'

Anna was so taken aback by this sudden eruption that all she could do was stare back at her, speechless.

Miriam glared at Anna, swaying slightly as she tried to remain still. 'I'm not saying it's OK,' she went on, quieter now, her tone more plaintive. 'I'm not saying taking your students out to dinner or buying them presents or helping them cheat is acceptable behaviour, but it's a world away from putting your dick inside them. I was hardly going to end his entire career over a few nights out and perhaps the odd peck on the lips. Haven't you ever kissed someone and it not meant anything? I know *I* have.'

As she spoke, her voice cracked with a sudden, raw vulnerability, and, in that moment, Anna understood. Miriam, who'd adored and idolised her father beyond rational thought, had been doing everything she could to give him the benefit of the doubt. She'd been so unwilling to think less of him that she'd set an almost impossibly high burden of proof for him – one that, unbeknownst to her until this evening, he'd still managed to clear.

'If you must know,' said Miriam, her tone abruptly shifting to one of haughty defiance, 'I did actually wonder once or twice if he'd ever tried it on with *you*.'

'With *me*?' Anna spluttered.

'Well, can you blame me? The two of you were always so close. Thick as thieves, to coin a phrase.' Her expression changed into a benevolent, slightly patronising smile. 'But, of course, deep down I knew you never would. You'd never do anything so underhand. So ... sordid.' She paused. 'You never did, did you?'

'No,' said Anna quietly, 'we didn't.'

'Well, then,' said Miriam stiffly, 'that's all right, then.'

Her voice still carried a note of lingering brittleness, though whether because she wasn't fully convinced by Anna's denial or because she was still annoyed by her earlier question, Anna couldn't tell.

'All right,' she said gently. 'But that wasn't the end of the story, was it?' Reassurance, she concluded, was the best policy under the circumstances.

'No,' said Miriam quietly, 'you're right. It wasn't.'

53

'Soon after, I started to notice a change in Daddy. He was around a whole lot more – no more late nights and last-minute meals out. Instead, he hung around the house like … I dunno, this lovelorn puppy. Whatever really happened between him and Libby, it was clear it was well and truly over.'

She'd stopped pacing now and had settled on the edge of the bedframe, perched on the siderail with her arms hanging between her knees, the whisky bottle dangling loosely between her fingers. There was a different energy about her now: less frenetic, more subdued, as if her outburst had drained nearly all her stamina and she was conserving what little remained by moving as little as possible.

'If you're going to ask me if I felt guilty, of course I fucking did. I'd done this to him. I'd put temptation in his way, let him get besotted by a bit of skirt, knowing full well what it might do to him. Whatever it was they'd had together, it clearly meant something to him.'

She raised her head to meet Anna's eyes. 'I didn't give a stuff about the accusations anymore. I just wanted him to be happy again. I tried everything I could think of to cheer him up – cracking jokes, spending time with him – but he didn't seem to want it. Just kept muttering about how busy he was and shutting himself up in his office.

'He limped through the rest of the year and the start of 2020. Then, the pandemic hit and, suddenly, we were in lockdown. He was teaching over Zoom, or trying to. Daddy was never much cop at tech. And I was painting, or at least that was the idea. You don't appreciate just how reliant you are on the outside world to keep the creative well full till you're cooped up all day apart from your hour of government-sanctioned individual exercise. Daddy didn't seem to be getting on much better. Whenever we ran into each other, he always seemed sort of hollowed out – like all the life had been drained from him and he was just this walking sack of bones and organs, shuffling around like a zombie, still performing all his routines even though he'd forgotten the actual point of any of it. Still, I figured we were getting by.'

She shut her eyes and inhaled a long, slow, deliberate breath. Anna waited on tenterhooks, even though she had an inkling of what was to come.

'Then, one day, I came home to find him dead.'

A stillness settled on the room. The very air seemed to have been sucked out of it. No sound came from the street outside. Anna's own breathing was slow and shallow. It was as if her very respiratory system recognised that to make any extraneous noise would be inappropriate at this juncture.

Miriam drew in another long, shuddering breath, then continued.

'It was late afternoon. I'd gone out for my daily walk. I had this route mapped out that got me to Dawsholm Park and back within the hour. See, I was a good girl. Always played by the rules. Unlike *some* folk I could mention.

'There was no sign of Daddy when I got in. At first, I figured he'd gone out for his own constitutional. He'd been out already that day, but he was always getting mixed up, not remembering he'd been out just a few hours earlier, or forgetting to go out at all. Going out twice in one day, not leaving the house at all the next – I figured his books more or less balanced.

'Anyway, I didn't worry too much at first. But then, as more and more time passed, I started to get skittish. I worried he'd had some sort of accident. I'd never managed to persuade him to get a mobile phone, so for all I knew he could've been lying in a ditch somewhere with a broken leg and no way to summon help.

'I don't know what precisely it was made me check in the garage. Call it a sixth sense if you believe in that sort of thing, or some distant memory of Alfie being found in there years earlier, but when I opened the door, the place was absolutely *reeking* of exhaust fumes, and I knew straight away what he'd done.'

She paused to lift the whisky bottle to her lips. Then, seemingly thinking better of it, she set it down on the floor, untouched.

'There was no note or anything. Just him sitting behind the wheel with his head tilted back and his eyes wide open, staring up at the ceiling like he'd been waiting to meet his maker.

'I went to bits. What the hell else was I going to do? Dropped to my knees and bawled myself hoarse for a good quarter of an hour. It's a wonder none of the neighbours heard – but then, maybe it's not so surprising. Everyone locked up in their own houses behind the double-glazing, thinking the world couldn't hurt them as long as they shut it out.

'Then, pretty quickly, I pulled myself together. I knew he'd done it because of her. Grief over losing her or guilt over what he and her had done or some combination of the two – I don't know. All I knew was, if I couldn't provide the police with a plausible motive for him killing himself, they'd be all over his life like a bad rash, combing through everything, trying to work out what'd driven him to it. And then, chances are, someone'd remember seeing him and Libby together at some point or other – and from there, it'd be a hop, skip and a jump to the whole thing coming out. And I didn't want that for him. Didn't want that to be how people remembered him. Or for it all to lead back to me somehow.

'So I didn't waste any time. I ran to his office and scrubbed his computer of anything that looked halfway incriminating, then I sat down and wrote a suicide note. It was easy enough to fake his handwriting. I used to do it all the time back in school – "Mim's got a gammy knee so she can't do cross country" and the like. I laid the blame squarely at the doors of the university, saying he felt worthless and didn't see any point going on. All of which was true, incidentally. He might not've said it out loud, but you ask anyone you like what that demotion did to his self-esteem, and they'll all tell you the same thing.' Another deep breath. 'Then I got on the blower and contacted the emergency services.

'The police questioned me, of course. I didn't have to do much acting, or tell them too many direct lies. They bought that I'd found him and called 999 straight away. I was basically incoherent with tears, and it's not like I had to fake *those*. He was my *everything*.'

She uttered it as a sharp, angry retort, as if Anna has suggested otherwise.

'When Fraser Taggart showed up at the funeral – and, incidentally, the fucking *nerve* of the guy, after everything he did – it was easy enough to lay into him, pinning all the blame on him. Again, not much acting required. And I figured it would help the story of a poor old man driven to his grave by an uncaring administration to take root – y'know, going full ham on him in front of a captive audience. And it seemed to work ... for a while, anyway.'

She shot a baleful look in Anna's direction. As ridiculous as she knew it was, Anna couldn't help feeling a twinge of guilt.

'You never had any further contact with Libby?' she asked, as much to change the subject as anything.

Miriam shook her head. 'Not since the end of June 2019.'

'You didn't …' Anna searched for the most diplomatic way to word this. 'You didn't blame her?'

Miriam was silent for a moment.

'Funnily enough, I didn't.'

It was as if she'd only now considered this for the first time.

'Of course, she played her part in all of it, but at the end of the day, I was the chief instigator. It was *my* idea. *My* modus operandi. I was the surgeon and she was … I dunno, the scalpel, if you want to look at it that way.'

Anna suspected Miriam wouldn't have felt quite so charitable towards Libby had she known about Libby's threat to expose Hugh just a week before his death. Still, she felt disinclined to point this out now.

'Truth be told,' Miriam continued, with an airy wave of dismissal, 'I really hadn't thought about her all that much since it happened. Not till I followed you to Moffat the other day and saw you talking to her. That's when I knew she had to die.'

'Why? What changed your mind?'

'Have you been listening to a word I've said?' Miriam snapped, launching herself back onto her feet. 'I already told you: BECAUSE. SHE. BROKE. THE. RULES.' She drew out each word, in the process managing to give 'rules' two syllables: 'ROOL-ZUH'.

'But so what?' said Anna, trying – and failing – to maintain a calming, placatory tone. 'She didn't tell me anything that could've identified you. Don't think I didn't press her. She had no idea who you were.'

'Well, of course I realise that *now*. Hindsight's a bloody wonderful thing, don't you think? But I had no idea what the two of you spent all that time gassing about. How could I? I could hardly risk following you down a one-way country lane. I had no way of knowing she hadn't told you the one thing that would've put "Emily's" identity beyond all possible doubt.'

'What *thing*?'

And, just like before, you could practically hear the shutters coming down. Miriam's face assumed a look of studied expressionlessness, and she stared off towards the far wall, as if she and Anna were distant acquaintances who'd suddenly found themselves trapped in a doctor's waiting room together with nothing to say to one another.

'Miriam?'

'Never mind. It's not important.'

'Well, I mean' – Anna even managed a slight, incredulous laugh – 'it clearly *is*, otherwise you wouldn't keep avoiding the subject.'

'I'm not avoiding anything,' Miriam huffed. She affected a shrug, but rather than appearing nonchalant, it came across as a nervous spasm.

Anna tried another tack. 'It's just us here, Miriam,' she said gently. 'You and me. No one else listening.' She gave an encouraging smile. 'Come on – don't you think it's time you got this off your chest?'

Miriam's expression faltered slightly. The flesh at the corner of one eye twitched as she struggled to hold Anna's gaze. Anna stared back at her, refusing to be the one to look away first.

'She really *didn't* tell you about my confession, then?' Miriam said, a faint expression of wonder in her voice.

'No,' said Anna. 'But I'd like to hear it.'

For several seconds, Miriam remained stock still, biting her bottom lip as she considered her next move. At length, she gave an almost imperceptible shrug.

'Well, I suppose you might as well know. It's not like you'll be telling anyone else.'

54

'It was my one slip. The one time I let my guard down with her. It was … not the greatest of days. The anniversary of Alfie's death. We'd been due to meet for a status report, only she'd got held up at the bank or the post office or some such – I forget which it was.'

She gave a dismissive wave. 'Doesn't matter. Anyway, I sat there in the bar waiting for her, and I figured: might as well order myself a cheeky glass of Shiraz while I'm waiting. Well, that one glass became two, and then three, and by the time she finally got there, breezing in like she hadn't just kept me waiting for the better part of the afternoon, I was already three sheets to the wind.' She gave a small, self-indulgent chuckle. 'Kinda like how I am now, as it happens. Funny, isn't it, how life has that … what do they call it?' She drew a big, curving line in the air with her entire arm. 'Circularity.'

She really is plastered, thought Anna. That she was still vertical was probably a small miracle – or the opposite of one, depending on whether or not you were currently tied to a chair.

'It ended up being a somewhat more … unstructured meeting than we were used to. More booze was imbibed, by both of us. She had a general moan to me about her various problems – the money situation, her arsehole parents – and I … I responded in kind. Nothing specific, not at that stage. That didn't happen till we ended up back at a flat I owned in the Merchant City.'

Anna stared at her in surprise.

Miriam gave an exaggerated grimace which, in her current state, made her briefly look like she'd suffered a right-sided facial paralysis. 'I know. Rookie mistake, right? I was *pissed* with a capital "P". I'm not even sure how it happened. We ended up in a taxi, and somehow, it ended up taking us there. Guess I must've given the driver the address. Good thing it was between tenants at the time.

'Anyway, we make our way up the stairs, her helping me stay upright, and we open another bottle she's brought with her, and before I know it, it's dark outside and I'm getting all weepy and telling her about Alfie. About how he climbed into the deep freeze; how, by the time Daddy found him, he'd already been dead for hours. And she's sitting on the settee beside me, stroking my hand and saying it isn't my fault. So reassuring, so soothing. One of those "you can tell me *anything*" voices. And I keep saying, "You don't understand. It's down to me. It's *all* down to me." And she says, "How d'you work that one out?" And I tell her.'

She sunk back down onto the bedframe, her socked heels squeaking as they slid away from her across the hardwood floor. Her eyes had a glassy, faraway look. When she spoke again, it was in a low murmur, as if she was reciting some sort of incantation.

'Our parents were never truly neglectful, but they *were* self-absorbed. Often too wrapped up in their own affairs to pay much attention to us – Daddy either at work or else squirrelled away in his office at all hours, Mum with her crocheting or her horticulture or whatever was the latest hobby of the week for her.

'Well, one day, I made up my mind I was going to teach them a lesson. I took Alfie's hand and led him down to the garage, and I knelt down in front of him and I said, "Now listen, Alfie, we're going to play a game."

'And he said, "What kind of a game?"

'And I said, "The *best* kind: hide and seek. Here's how it's going to work. You're going to hide, and then Mummy and Daddy are going to come and look for you.

'"Now, listen, Alfie."' She raised a stern index finger. '"This is really important. You've got to be *dead quiet*, you hear? You can't make a sound till they find you, otherwise the whole thing will be ruined. Do you understand? Will you be a good boy?"

'And he nodded and said, "I'll be a good boy."

'And I said, "I knew I could count on you, Alfie. Now, you're in luck, cos I've found the *best* hiding place for you."'

As she'd been speaking, her voice had grown increasingly childish, her intonation more singsong. It was as if she'd forgotten when and where she was and, in her mind, was back there in the garage, talking to Alfie, persuading him, with honeyed words, to—

Oh, God.

'It was nearly two hours before Mum came looking for him. And of course I couldn't *say* anything – not without getting into serious trouble. So I kept my mouth shut while the two of them went charging about, getting themselves into more and more of a flap, and all the while I kept silently willing them, *Go and look in the garage* – like, trying to implant the idea in their minds.'

She sighed. 'But it didn't work. Of course it didn't. And it wasn't till hours later that Daddy finally thought to look there. Maybe, if they'd gone straight there when they first noticed he was missing, maybe there would still've been a chance. *Maybe.* But they didn't, and he's dead, and I poured it all out to Libby that night.

'I didn't name any names. I don't think she ever guessed

whose daughter I was. If she did, she kept her cards *seriously* close to her chest. But either way, I must've fallen asleep or blacked out or something, cos I came to hours later and she was gone.

'She made no mention of it next time we met, or the time after, or the time after that. It's like we'd made this silent pact that we'd never speak of it.' She affected a deep American drawl. 'What happens in Vegas stays in Vegas, right?'

She continued in her normal voice. 'I cleared out for a bit. Fucked off to an artists' residency in Switzerland for a month to put some distance between us. I dunno, I guess I was hoping she'd somehow forget I'd ever told her or *I'd* forget or something. Either way, it never came up between us – not till the day she told me she was walking away and I said, "You've got to be taking the fucking piss", or other, less eloquent words to that effect. I threatened to expose her to the university; to write them an anonymous letter about her and Daddy, which at the very *least* would've been enough to make things seriously uncomfortable for the pair of them.

'And she said, "And if you do that, I'll tell the cops you were the one who caused your brother's death."'

Anna forced down a mouthful of viscous saliva as the last piece of the puzzle slotted into place with a final, hideous click.

'She'd taped the whole thing – or, at least, so she claimed. Told me she'd set her phone to record as soon as we got into the flat. An insurance policy, she called it. Made multiple backups too, just in case I was thinking of snatching her phone from her then and there.

'I tried to brazen it out. I was shitting my pants, of course, but I managed to stare her down and said, "What good will that do you? You don't even know my real name."

'And she said, "Maybe not, but I reckon it wouldn't take much for the cops to find it out. I doubt there's *that* many wee boys in the country who froze to death in a garage freezer. Plus,

I figure it'd take me next to no effort at all to find out who owns flat 2/4 at 28 Garabedian Street."

"'But I'm not *going* to,' she added. "Not if you do the sensible thing here. I swear on my life, I don't *want* to know who you are. I just want to be left alone and to live my life – same as you. It's in both our interests for us to walk away and never see each other again.'"

Miriam shrugged in Anna's direction, her mouth forming a little moue of uncertainty. 'She might've been bluffing. I'd no way of knowing. Either way, I didn't have much choice. I agreed to her demands – and, in a way, I was glad to. There was something almost ... serendipitous about the way things'd turned out. I'd rather she had something on me than I had nothing at all on her. Mutually assured destruction – that's what they call it, isn't it? When both sides possess a weapon capable of annihilating the other, so neither one'll ever risk using it.'

'That's one way of looking at it, I suppose,' said Anna quietly.

It was the first time she'd spoken since Miriam had made her confession. Since then, she'd been battling a horrible, twisting nausea in her stomach – a feeling that had only intensified with each fresh, matter-of-fact revelation. That Miriam was a cold-blooded killer was something she'd made her peace with some time ago. That she'd murdered Libby and as good as driven her own father to suicide were indisputable facts, straight from her own mouth. But the situation with Alfie was something else. She wasn't sure if it was because he'd been a child – because they'd *both* been children – or because of the self-serving way in which she'd recast the incident as an indictment of their parents, but either way, it left her shaken to her core. There was nothing redeemable about this woman. Nothing at all.

Miriam, for her part, seemed to have recovered much of her previous bombast now that they'd dealt with the matter of

Alfie's death. She was on her feet again and once more clutching the whisky bottle, though she hadn't yet put it to her lips again.

'I told her, before we went our separate ways, "Fuck me and I'll fuck you ten times as hard." Can't say she wasn't warned fair and square. Like I said before, I'd no idea how much she'd told you, but I figured there was a good chance she'd spilled everything and it was only a matter of time before there was a knock on the door and I was carted off in handcuffs. So I had to make sure I got her while I still had a chance, didn't I?

'I waited till all the other staff had left, then followed her into the staff room. Strangled her with my own tights, then dragged her through to the locker room and strung her up for her work buddies to find. Wrote a suicide note for her, too. Again, it wasn't much of a stretch copying her handwriting. She'd been carrying around a clipboard with her hourly observations on those barn owls – all super-detailed. If she was as conscientious back when she was a student, maybe she wouldn't've needed Daddy's help with her exams,' she added, with what verged on a smirk.

'Before you ask, I was wearing gloves. Always helps to come prepared for any eventuality. And, of course, my face mask. The ubiquitous face mask! So many uses, not all of them benign. Point being, no threat of any droplets of saliva having transferred from my mouth to her person in the heat of the struggle. Not that I fancy the authorities'll bother digging too deeply. After all, a "my life's a shit-show" note from a university drop-out with a low-paying job and no friends is pretty cut and dried, right?'

Anna said nothing. She hadn't the words. She just gazed back at Miriam in numb silence. After everything she'd heard, she felt almost inured to it all. She thought, perhaps, she could guess as least some of Libby's rationale in not telling her about the confession. She'd probably concluded that, as long as she held back the key detail that would have allowed her to definitively identify Emily, she could safely give her everything else she wanted, thereby staving off the threat to unmask her to her employers, secure in the knowledge that Emily would never know she'd broken her confidence. And she would probably have been right, if Anna hadn't led 'Emily' right to her door ...

As if she'd guessed her thoughts, Miriam's expression softened. 'I hope you don't feel too bad about it, Anna. None of this is on you. I mean, all right, so I wouldn't have found her without you. Plus, you *were* the one who convinced her to spill her guts – so granted, there *is* that. But you weren't the one who killed her. I'm happy to own that. I'm a big believer in personal responsibility.'

'Like you accepted responsibility for Alfie?' said Anna.

Miriam's face darkened instantly. 'That was different. I was a *child*. Below the age of criminal responsibility. If either of our parents had been any cop at, oh, you know, *parenting*, he'd be alive today. Besides,' she went on, moving towards Anna, knuckles white around the neck of the bottle, 'I never *wanted* him to die. If you think that, then you really *are* a whole lot stupider than I gave you credit for. I'd have done *anything* for him.'

'Anything, except save him.'

Miriam stared at Anna in disbelief for a moment, then snorted and shook her head contemptuously. 'Oh, fuck *you*, Anna, with your high and mighty attitude and your superiority complex. I was eleven years old. Did you never do anything wrong when you were eleven?'

'I certainly didn't kill anyone,' said Anna, her voice a low growl.

She knew she was treading on seriously thin ice here, but she couldn't hold back any longer. Besides, she could tell things were coming to a head, and the knowledge that, in all likelihood, she had little time left had aroused her fighting spirit. If she was going to go down, she might as well go down swinging.

'Well,' said Miriam, almost primly, 'perhaps that's because you're an only child who had so little regard for your own parents you couldn't even stand to live in the same country as them. It was a bit much, I suppose, to expect you to know anything about the bond that exists among families who love each other – I mean really, *truly* love each other from the bottom of their hearts. And sometimes, when you love something so unconditionally, so completely that it feels like your literal *soul* is on fire, you'd rather see it destroyed than let anyone else share even a morsel of it.'

Anna stared up at Miriam. She was standing so close Anna could practically count the hairs in her nostrils.

'You're mad,' she said quietly. 'Completely mad.'

Miriam grinned a wide rictus of a smile. 'That's love for ya, baby.'

She was silent for a moment, her eyes distant, as if thinking back to some earlier, happier time – a time before it all went wrong. Then, her expression abruptly shifted to one that was stony and businesslike, her eyes devoid of any hint of warmth.

'And now, I think that's about enough yakking. It was very clever of you, Anna, keeping me talking all this time – but if you thought that was going to save you, you're in for a rude awakening. I think it's about time we got on with what we both know has to happen, don't you?'

With that, she tossed the whisky bottle aside. It connected with the far wall and shattered into umpteen pieces. From her pocket, she produced a pair of tights – the same pair, Anna guessed, that she'd used on Libby just twenty-four hours earlier.

Panic took hold of her – a burning, unquenchable desire to live that overrode every other concern. A desire to live, and to see Jack again, even if it was for just one last time. All the myriad things she'd never told him hurtled through her head in the split second it took for her to draw a breath. As Miriam wound the tights round her hands, she found herself beginning to babble.

'Please, I don't want to die. I have a little boy. Jack. He's not even six. He's waiting for me to come home. He misses his Mum. He—'

'Oh, yap, yap, yap,' Miriam sighed.

As she stretched the fabric taut, Anna abandoned any further thought of pleading or bargaining and switched instead to the time-honoured tactic of mindless screaming.

'HELP! HELP! PLEASE! SOMEONE HELP ME!'

But that was as far as she got. In the second in which she paused to refill her lungs, Miriam yanked off her left sock and stuffed it into Anna's mouth, silencing her.

'I told you before,' she said, 'there's no point. The other units are all empty. All you're doing is wasting your breath and giving me a headache. Besides, I can't help thinking, if you care about that little boy of yours as much as you claim to, why is it he's in a foreign country waiting for you while you're over *here* getting mixed up in everyone's affairs but your own?' She shrugged. 'Just a thought.'

Breathing through her nose, Anna gazed up at her helplessly, her eyes smarting with frantic tears.

As casually as if she was going to open a window, Miriam moved behind her, getting herself into position.

'Walls are four feet thick, anyway,' she observed offhandedly. 'Even if the other flats *were* occupied, I highly doubt—'

That was when they both heard the knock on the door.

55

Anna felt Miriam freeze behind her, the tights stretched mere centimetres above her head. For several seconds, she didn't move. Then, the knock was repeated – louder, somehow more insistent. Anna craned her neck to look behind her. Miriam gave her an accusatory glower, as if, somehow, she was the one who'd caused this. Anna's only response was a helpless widening of her eyes.

For a moment, Miriam didn't move. She stood there, biting her lip, appearing to be weighing up her options. Then she made her decision. Anna saw the stretched tights passing in front of her eyes as Miriam brought them down. She managed a tiny, guttural squeal of terror at the back of her throat.

But Miriam wasn't planning to strangle her. Not yet, at any rate. Instead, she wrapped them round Anna's mouth three times before tying the two opposite ends behind her ears. Anna's eyes darted around frantically as she sucked air through her nose, trying desperately to fill her lungs while simultaneously avoiding choking on the rolled-up sock, now forced to the back of her throat by the gag. Then, grabbing the back of the chair, Miriam dragged it and Anna across the room till it was flush with the wall and Anna's hands were being squeezed painfully between it and the back of the seat.

As a third knock sounded at the door, Miriam stepped in front of Anna and jabbed a finger under her nose.

'Not a sound, or it'll be the worst for you.'

Then she inhaled a deep breath, smoothed down the creases in her T-shirt and strode out of the room, her one bare foot squeaking on the floorboards. Anna listened as her footsteps receded down the corridor, followed by her asking in a high, haughty voice, 'Yes? Who is it?'

Anna couldn't make out the answer, muffled as it was by the front door. But it was evidently to Miriam's liking, for the next sound she heard was that of a deadbolt being drawn back, followed by the door being opened.

'Well?' Miriam barked. 'What do you want?'

And then, to Anna's eternal euphoria and disbelief, the voice that answered her was that of Jen Brinkley.

'It's Miriam, isn't it? Anna's told me all about you. Had no idea you had a swinger's pad out here!'

Her tone was obliviously cheerful, as if this really was nothing more than an unexpected chance meeting between two people who happened to have a friend in common. Anna had no idea how she'd come to be here, but she mentally thanked Providence, The Fates, The Powers That Be with a fervour utterly unbecoming of an atheist.

She forced herself to remember that she was a long way from being out of the woods yet; that, far from her salvation being guaranteed, Jen herself was just one unanticipated blow to the head away from being trussed up like a turkey herself.

Willing her pounding heart to quiet, she listened to the continued sounds of conversation from the hallway.

'What of it?' said Miriam, blocking Jen's entry by leaning

against the doorframe. 'You still haven't told me what you want.'

'I want Anna, actually,' said Jen, with continuing, seemingly boundless good cheer. 'She was meant to meet me at my place, but she didn't show up. Don't suppose you've seen her?'

'Not since Saturday. She told me she was going back to Italy soon. I assumed that's what she'd done.'

'Hmm,' Jen mused. 'That's very odd.'

'Why's that?'

'Well, because her phone's GPS data puts her at this very address within the last hour.' She held up her own phone by way of illustration.

'I've been out,' said Miriam abruptly. 'I was with a client all afternoon. Maybe she *was* here and we just missed one another. I only got in ten minutes ago.'

Jen glanced at the floor. 'That'll be why you haven't had time to put on your other sock, I take it.'

'Precisely.'

They continued to face one another. Jen gave a disarming smile, as if passing some wry comment on the situation in which they'd found themselves. Miriam didn't return it.

Anna strained to listen as the voices continued. She hadn't succeeded in picking up every word, but she'd heard enough to get the gist. Jen was saying something about Anna being on the verge of missing her flight, which wasn't like her at all.

'Maybe she's already at the airport,' Miriam said, no longer even *trying* to hide the fact that she wanted Jen gone.

'Seems unlikely,' said Jen. 'We'd already agreed I was going to drive her there.'

'Perhaps she forgot?'

Anna tried once again to wriggle free. But it was no use: the cords digging into her wrists and ankles were just too tight. And shouting was impossible – that much she'd already confirmed. It was obvious Miriam had put the chair against the wall to prevent her throwing her weight back and tipping it over. She tried leaning sideways, but it that, too, was no use. The chair was solid and sturdy, and she was bound far too tightly to be able to shift her weight sufficiently to one side in order to overturn it.

Now Jen was speaking again. 'You know, I think I can hear the bounds of credibility fracturing as we speak.'

'Well, wherever she is,' said Miriam, audibly annoyed now, 'she's not *here*. Look, I haven't the time for this …'

Time. Anna suddenly remembered: her watch. Or rather, the panic alarm that looked like a watch, secured round her left wrist, ready to be activated at the press of a button. Easier said than done, under the circumstances … but it gave her an idea. There was no hope of reaching it with the fingers of her other hand; her wrists were bound too tightly for her to move them independently. But, if she could raise them up just a little bit, she might be able to snag the button on the underside of the backrest …

She tried to raise her arms. Again, the rope securing them to the crossbar prevented them from moving more than a few centimetres. She tried again, and swore she managed to get them just a fraction higher.

She halted, fighting for breath. Listened to the continuing voices coming from down the hall.

'Look,' said Miriam, with an air of finality, 'I wish you all the luck in the world hunting her down. Now, if you'll excuse me …'

In desperation, Anna gave her arms one last, frantic tug, exerting all her energy into driving them upwards. The button made contact with the backrest. For what felt like an age but was, in reality, probably less than a second, nothing happened. Then, a blinding vortex swallowed her up as one hundred and twenty-five decibels of noise exploded inside her eardrums.

. . .

As the alarm began to peal, scarcely any less deafening out there in the hallway, Jen jerked her head up sharply. For a moment, she and Miriam's eyes met, neither of them budging. Then, in a sudden, unexpected movement, Jen darted sideways to her left. Miriam moved to block her path, but it turned out to be merely a feint, for Jen immediately changed tack, diving right and around Miriam, through the door and into the flat.

Anna, sitting with her chin to her chest, teeth clenched together and eyes squeezed shut as she tried to block out the ear-rending siren, was dimly aware of a hand on her shoulder. She forced herself to open her eyes and found herself staring up at Jen, leaning over her, staring down at her in disbelief.

She saw Jen's lips move.

Holy FUCK!

She tried to respond, her half-choked groan drowned out by the still-pealing alarm. Jen shook her head, indicating that she shouldn't try to talk, then pointed a finger at her own ear, miming a wince. Anna jiggled her shoulders and nodded behind her, and Jen seemed to get it. Reaching behind Anna, she fumbled to undo the cord around her wrists. In the process, she inadvertently pressed the alarm button for a second time, bringing the sound to an abrupt stop.

As the deafening cacophony in Anna's ears was replaced by a residual, high-pitched ringing, Jen finally succeeded in loosening the rope around her wrists. As Anna felt the circulation returning to her hands, Jen removed the pair of tights and prised the saliva-drenched sock out of her mouth.

'You're OK,' she said. 'Just breathe.'

As Anna madly gulped down air, unable either to respond or to process the questions now flooding through her mind, she spied, out of the corner of her eye, the figure of Miriam standing in the doorway, haloed by the light from the hall corridor, a fireplace poker clenched in both hands. She advanced into the room, the poker raised above her head, ready to bring it down onto the back of the unsuspecting Jen.

'JEN, WATCH OUT!'

At the last second, Jen swung around, raising her arm to block the blow, even as Miriam brought the poker down. As Jen staggered backwards, thrown off balance by the impact of the weapon, Miriam swung again, but Jen managed to dodge it, and the poker hit the floor instead, the hook wedging between two floorboards. As Miriam struggled to free it, Jen kicked her legs from under her. Miriam hit the ground, landing heavily on her shoulder.

Still winded, Anna struggled to free her legs while watching as, like a wild animal, Miriam scrambled to her feet and barrelled into Jen, attacking her with her fists and teeth and nails, doing whatever she possibly could to land a blow. Too weak from her recent lack of oxygen to intervene, Anna could only look on in dazed stupefaction as the two women grappled together just a few feet away from her on the floor.

They broke apart, shuffling backwards and facing one another, both breathing heavily, hair askew. Jen raised her fists in a boxer's stance. Miriam wiped saliva from her chin with the back of her hand, nostrils flaring with each ragged breath. Her eyes darted from Jen to Anna, then back again. She seemed to be considering her next move.

Without taking her eyes off Miriam, Jen reached down, clasped her hand round the handle of the poker and gave a sharp tug. It came away easily. Slowly, Jen brought herself up to her full height, holding the poker at her side like a drawn sword.

Miriam looked at it, then at her. The corner of her lip quivered.

Then, from somewhere deep inside her, she emitted a low, guttural wail. It might have signified anger, desperation, terror – or, perhaps most likely, all three. But either way, without further ado, she turned and ran. She fled from the room and set off down the hall corridor, a banshee-like wail echoing in her wake.

Jen seemed on the verge of setting off after her. But, as Anna, who'd succeeded in freeing her legs and had somehow managed to haul herself to her feet, let out a soft moan and felt her knees beginning to buckle, Jen abandoned the idea of pursuit and hurried over to her, tossing the poker aside. Putting her arm around Anna, she caught her before she fell and allowed her to lean against her, absorbing her weight.

'Are you OK?'

Anna tilted her head to look up into Jen's eyes. 'Peachy,' she managed to groan, through gritted teeth.

Jen gave a low, grim cackle.

At that moment, they heard the front door slamming. They both hurried to the window, Jen continuing to support Anna. Jen ripped back the curtains in time for them to see Miriam tearing out into the narrow street below, one foot socked, the other bare. She hesitated for a moment, turning her head in either direction, before sprinting over to her Ford Focus, parked at the kerb just a few metres away. Its lights pulsed once as the doors unlocked. She wrenched open the driver's door and hurled herself in. The engine revved and she took off at a breakneck pace, roaring up the wrong side of the road.

The headlights of a huge SUV lit up the Focus, approaching in the opposite direction. The driver sounded the horn. Miriam corrected course, swerving to the other side of the road. Too late, she realised she'd just put herself in the path of the very scaffolding Anna had briefly glimpsed as she slipped in and out of consciousness on the way to the flat. The taillights shone as she slammed on the brakes, but to no avail. The car rammed headlong into the scaffolding. One of the long metal poles, shaken loose by the impact, shot out and crashed through the windscreen on the driver's side like a ballistic missile, finally coming to a halt as it made impact with something more solid than glass. The sustained, uninterrupted blast of its horn rent the otherwise still night air.

'Oh, *fuck*,' Jen breathed.

As she and Anna continued to watch, figure after figure descended on the previously empty street – summoned, presumably, by either the noise of the crash or the continuing sound of the horn. The first people on the scene were a pair of young men in T-shirts and shorts, both of whom quickened their pace at the sight of the car. One bent down, peering through the driver's window. He was too far away for Anna and Jen to make out his expression, but the shake of his head said it all.

Anna turned towards Jen, but even as she opened her mouth to speak, Jen beat her to it.

'I can't be involved in this,' she said shakily. 'My babies …'

And, in an instant, Anna got it. She nodded, forestalling any need for Jen to explain.

'We need to clear up first,' she said.

Altogether, it took them less than three minutes. As Jen frantically wiped down every surface either of them could conceivably have touched, Anna retrieved the sock and tights Miriam had used to gag her, as well as the crushed water bottle, and shoved them into her shoulder bag. Then, together, they slipped out of the flat, Jen bearing much of Anna's weight on her arm.

As they emerged from the building, the crowd around Miriam's car continued to swell. None of the various onlookers paid them any heed as they turned their backs on the grisly spectacle and crept off in the opposite direction.

56

They kept walking, Anna mentally and physically incapable of doing anything other than putting one foot in front of the other as Jen guided her, steering her round corners while maintaining a consistent, brisk pace. She soon began to recognise the geography. They were in Anniesland, not far from Great Western Road and less than half a mile from the traffic lights where Miriam had knocked her out. The realisation that they'd covered so little distance was strangely disorienting.

Jen's Prius was parked in a quiet side street. She unlocked it and helped Anna into the passenger seat. Neither of them spoke till they were both safely inside with the doors closed.

Anna was the first to break the silence.

'How are you even *here*?'

'GPS,' said Jen bluntly. 'I hacked your phone. Highly illegal, and yet another transgression to add to the already sizeable charge sheet against me, but I got worried when you didn't show. And every time I tried to ring you, all I got was an "unavailable" message.

'I got there, saw all the windows were in darkness 'cept for a light showing through a crack in one of the curtains. Searched the property register, saw the title deeds were in Miriam's name. I figured something suss was going down, so I hotfooted it up the stair, banged on the door and … well, you know the rest.'

A moment of silence passed as Anna digested this. Then, Jen spoke again.

'Emma Rippon can't be our Emily, by the way. She's dead.'

'I know. Miriam was Emily.'

Saying it like that, it sounded so matter-of-fact. But then, she'd had time to get used to the idea. Jen's expression of open-mouthed incredulity was a lot closer to her own original reaction.

'She *what*? But how? Why?'

Too wearied for a lengthy explanation, Anna merely shrugged.

'Then Libby's death …'

'Also her doing.'

'Jesus *Christ*.'

Jen covered her face with both hands, a muffled hiss of air escaping from behind them as she exhaled heavily. After a moment, she lowered them and turned to Anna with a stricken expression.

'I meant what I said back there. I can't get involved in this.' She shook her head. 'Fuck's sake, I *am* involved. But you know what I mean. The number of laws I've broken – hacking into bank accounts, university registries, government databases of every possible stripe …' She stared at Anna imploringly. 'If they connect any of this to me, I'll be an old woman by the time they let me out.'

'I understand,' said Anna.

All this was her fault – she knew that perfectly well. Every law Jen had broken had been for her benefit. And Anna could hardly plead ignorance. Had she not sat there in the Dungeon of Pain, watching Jen merrily clicking keys as she broke into Hugh's bank accounts? She'd known what they were doing was illegal, and yet had been content to sit back and watch, deluding herself into believing it was all somehow fine and dandy because she didn't understand the precise ins and outs of what she was watching.

'And you can't be involved either,' said Jen, interrupting Anna's thoughts. 'Mind you've got a wee boy waiting for you back in Italy. If they place you at the scene, you think they're gonna let you just waltz onto a plane and skip the country? You'll be tied up here answering their questions for weeks, months, maybe longer.'

'I know that,' said Anna.

It sounded more defensive than she'd intended. Truthfully, she hadn't considered, until now, the implications of a potential police investigation on her own freedom of movement.

'It's probably better if we don't have any further contact,' said Jen, unable to meet Anna's eye. She hesitated. 'At least, not for a while, anyway.'

'That's OK. I figured you were probably sick of the sight of me by now anyway.'

Jen managed a strained laugh. Anna grinned weakly. As jokes went, it was a pretty feeble one, but it was the best she was capable of right now. And it seemed to lift the mood.

'Missed your flight,' said Jen. ''Least, you would have by the time we got to the airport.'

'God, yeah. Don't suppose they have a policy of issuing refunds in cases of abduction and near-death.'

'First time for everything, I suppose.' A pause. 'Shall I run you to A&E? Quite a bump you've got there on that noggin.'

Anna considered it. 'Best not. It'll only lead to questions, and I'm not sure I've got a sufficient lack of self-respect to claim I walked into a door. Plus, you know what hospitals are like. Bloody disease meccas. I walk in there, odds are I'm walking out with COVID.'

'And we can't have that.'

'No,' said Anna, thinking of Jack, waiting for her in Italy, 'we most certainly can't.' She was silent for a moment, then glanced across at the driver's seat. 'Thanks, Jen.'

Jen dismissed this with an unconcerned wave. 'Oh, pish posh. Ride or die, am I right?'

'I mean it. Thanks for everything.'

Jen met Anna's gaze and smiled, before reaching across and giving her hand a brief but firm squeeze.

'So,' she said, after they'd sat in companionable silence for a moment, 'if you're not going to the hospital and you're not getting on a plane … what *are* you going to do now?'

Anna considered this. 'Well,' she said at length, 'there is *one* person I still need to talk to.'

57

It was approaching 11 p.m. when Anna made her way up the driveway to the Taggarts' house on Kirklee Road and rang the doorbell. After a moment, it was opened by a rather spaced-out-looking Matilda. She hung on the door and gazed balefully at Anna from behind hooded lids.

'Hello again, Matilda,' Anna began. 'Is your dad—'

'Out,' said Matilda flatly. 'Him *and* Mum. Some charity thing at the City Chambers.' She rolled her eyes, suggesting she took a dim view of such things.

'I see. Any idea what time they'll be back?'

Matilda raised her hands to ear level in an exaggerated parody of a shrug. 'Who knows? What even *is* time?' She snorted and chuckled softly to herself. Anna wondered if she was feeling all right.

'Could I maybe come in and wait?' she ventured, taking a hopeful step towards the doorway.

Matilda contemplated this request for longer than would be considered polite. 'I guess,' she said at last, her tone making it clear just how much of an imposition she felt this was.

Anna gave a grateful nod and stepped inside.

'Are you OK?' Matilda asked her as she shut the door

behind them, her tone not exactly awash with concern. 'You look like you've headbutted a flat iron.'

Anna declined to answer that, but, as she followed Matilda through the hallway, she found herself touching her forehead self-consciously, checking for signs of damage.

As they stepped into the living room, Anna was hit by a pungent blast of the same overpowering, musky smell she belatedly realised she'd caught a whiff of at the front door. Music was playing on the speaker system – something angry and frenetic she didn't recognise, though mercifully at a low volume. A plastic bong – the source of the smell, she quickly realised – sat on the coffee table.

Completely unperturbed, Matilda flopped down on the nearby sofa, reached for the bong and took a long hit, before leaning back into the cushions, shutting her eyes and nodding in time to the music, as if Anna wasn't even there. Anna, knowing better than to wait for an invitation to sit, chose an armchair at a ninety-degree angle from the sofa.

For almost a full minute, they sat, saying nothing to each other, like two people inhabiting different realities – which, given Matilda's presently altered state, probably wasn't an entirely inappropriate comparison.

'How's school going, Matilda?' Anna asked, once the silence had become seriously uncomfortable.

Slowly, Matilda raised her head, opened her eyes and looked at her incredulously, as if to say, *WHY exactly are you talking to me?*

Anna tried again. 'What are you studying for your Highers?'

'You don't have to pretend.'

'Pretend what?'

'Like you're actually interested. I know you're just saying it for something to say.'

Well, all right, thought Anna, *but you don't have to point it out. You could just play along.*

''Sides,' Matilda went on, folding her arms behind her head, 'it's not like any of it actually *matters*. Have you *seen* the state of the world? Whole thing's pretty well fucked.'

Anna could hardly claim that, in her darkest moments, she hadn't entertained similar thoughts. Still, she concluded it would do Matilda no good to hear that, so she opted instead for a more optimistic tack.

'Well, I agree it has its *problems*,' she said, 'but if we all just give up, doesn't it essentially become a self-fulfilling prophecy?'

Matilda stared at her for a long moment. 'Wow,' she said eventually, 'that's seriously deep.'

Anna wasn't sure whether she was being sarcastic or if, through the lens of the pot she'd been imbibing with such gusto, her words had constituted a genuinely profound observation.

'Anyway,' she said, choosing not to dwell on the matter, 'your parents must want you to do well so you'll have plenty of options when it comes to universities.'

Matilda groaned and rolled her eyes. 'Oh *God*, they're on my case the *whole* time. Never give me a moment's peace. It's always, "Matilda, have you done your homework?" or, "Matilda, why've you got your nose in your phone when you could be revising instead?" Yeah, they want me to do well.' She launched herself upright with a suddenness that startled Anna. 'But answer me this: do I look like I want to end up like them? Do they strike *you* as a solid advertisement for studying hard and landing a so-called "good" job? Mum's a permanent bundle of neuroses, and Dad – he's not been the same since the promotion.'

'Oh?' said Anna, feeling a little dazed.

'Nuh-uh. Stressed out his nut the whole time – high heid yins breathing down his neck, demanding RESULTS. And none of his underlings understand the pressure he's under. They think he's always chasing them to deliver cos he *enjoys* it. But they don't have the first clue. He works his *arse* off to keep the lights on in that place, and does he get any thanks? He gets ZIP. I keep telling him, "You're wasting your time, Dad. No one's ever gonna thank you for it." But he just shakes his head and says, "Matilda, you don't understand. It's not about being thanked or being popular. It's about RESPONSIBILITY."'

Anna could practically hear the capital letters.

'Yep.' Matilda leaned back, once more folding her arms behind her head. 'Everyone wants a piece of him. He gives and he gives, and still they aren't satisfied.' She snorted. 'Ingrates.'

Anna didn't respond, but she found herself feeling strangely moved. Despite her façade of jaded cynicism, Matilda clearly had her father's back – and that, Anna realised, made her like her more, even though she didn't much like the person she was defending.

'I hadn't realised how stressed he was,' she admitted.

Matilda gave an emphatic nod. 'Oh yeah, it's bad. 'Specially after that old guy died.'

'Hugh?' Anna was surprised at the mention of him.

'Think so, yeah. Dad was off his game for *ages* after he popped his clogs. I swear, it aged him five years in the space of a week. Kept going on about how he should have done more, how he'd let him down – even though I can't for the life of me work out what more he was s'posed to've done. I mean, if it's your time to go, well … then it's your time to go, right?'

'I suppose,' said Anna uncertainly.

'You know he came to see Dad not long before it happened?'

Something seemed to shift inside Anna. She was aware of herself sitting up ever so slightly straighter.

'I didn't know that, no,' she said. 'When was this?'

Matilda shrugged airily. 'I remember it was a Friday afternoon. Dad had decided he was packing us all off to his and Mum's cottage up at Blair Atholl for the weekend. Total breach of lockdown rules. That chief medical woman'd only just lost her job for doing the same. But then, that's Dad to a T. Big stickler for the rules – just not when it concerns *him*.

'Anyway, we'd finished loading up the car and Dad was in a hurry to get off, only Mum couldn't find her laptop charger and was going spare about how, if she couldn't charge it, she couldn't see her emails and then how would she know if there'd been some emergency at work? Everything's a drama with Mum. She'd just found it and her and Dad were about to get in the car when the old man came walking up the driveway and made a complete beeline for Dad.

'I was in the back with my headphones on so I didn't hear what either of them was saying, but I could see whatshisname, Hugh, was being really intense – y'know, getting right up in Dad's face, not letting him get into the car. There was a bit of back and forth between them, then Dad put his foot down – went like *this*.' She made an emphatic gesture with her hands. 'Again, I didn't hear what he said, but the old guy looked CRUSHED.'

Matilda frowned suddenly, as if, for the first time, considering how this must look. She contemplated the ramifications for a few seconds, then carried on, speaking quickly – suddenly, it seemed, eager to bring the account to a close.

'And then Dad got in the car and drove off, leaving him standing there in our driveway looking like …' She trailed off.

'Like what?' said Anna.

Matilda winced. 'Like a broken man, I s'pose.'

As quietly as possible, Anna let out the breath she'd been holding in. 'And when was this?' she said quietly.

Matilda shrugged. 'A Friday.'

'You said. *Which* Friday?'

'A Friday in May,' said Matilda, rather irritably. 'I can't remember the date. I just remember it was May cos I'd've been sitting my Nat 5s right about then if they hadn't cancelled them all cos of COVID.'

'Could it have been the fifteenth?' asked Anna.

'Could've been. Dunno.' A pause. Then, in a slightly more apprehensive tone, 'Why? Does it matter?'

Anna didn't respond. She was too deep in thought.

At that moment, the room was lit up through the open curtains by the headlights of a car crawling up the driveway, accompanied by the crunch of gravel under wheels. Immediately, Matilda sat upright.

'Shit – they're home!'

Jumping to her feet, she grabbed the bong and sped out of the room with it. Anna heard her feet pounding up the stairs. Moments later, she was back with a can of Febreze, which she proceeded to spray liberally around the room, replacing the smell of weed with the even more pungent smell of synthetic citrus.

'Not a word,' she said to Anna.

Anna, her mind still elsewhere, merely nodded distantly.

As the front door slammed shut, Matilda stuffed the Febreze behind a cushion on the sofa, plonked herself down and assumed an air of purity and innocence as the door opened to reveal Catriona, wearing a pearl necklace and an expensive-looking gown, both of which positively screamed 'well-to-do woman attending charity function'.

'Anna!' she said, surprised and, Anna thought, slightly perturbed to see her there. '*This* is unexpected.'

Fraser appeared behind her in the doorway, his tie loosened.

'Oh,' he said.

'Hey, Mum, hey, Dad,' said Matilda, the picture of innocence. 'I was just keeping Anna company till you got home.'

'Right,' said Fraser, sounding as if he didn't entirely believe it. 'Well, that was decent of you.'

Neither he nor Catriona appeared to have noticed the smell that clung to the air, or the fact that their daughter's pupils were twice the size they should have been. Or perhaps they just didn't *want* to notice.

Anna got to her feet. 'We need to talk.'

'Um ... can it wait? It's late, and Catriona and I are both—'

'Look,' said Anna, aware of the icy tone in her voice but long past caring, 'we can do this here in front of the family or we can do it in private. Either way, we're doing it now.'

'Fraser, what's this about?' said Catriona, eyeing her husband apprehensively.

Fraser glanced briefly at Anna, then turned to Catriona and laid a hand on her forearm. 'It's all right,' he said gently. 'You head on upstairs. I'll be up in a bit.' He turned to Matilda. 'And you, young lady, time you were in bed as well.'

Matilda pulled a face, but Anna sensed she was secretly glad of an excuse to abandon the scene of the crime. Either way, she departed without complaint, only briefly pausing to shoot Anna a fresh glare from the door, once more swearing her to secrecy.

Fraser waited till both his wife and daughter had gone upstairs before turning to Anna with a look that bordered on weary resignation.

'Right, then, shall we do this?'

58

Fraser ushered Anna into a small, stylishly furnished study at the back of the house. Unlike Matilda, he hadn't commented on the bruise on her forehead. Either he hadn't noticed, or he had and was simply too polite to say anything. Based on past experience, she concluded that the former was more in character.

'You know,' he said, 'I was actually on the verge of calling you myself to see if you had any updates. You've been very quiet the last couple of days. I wasn't sure you were even still in the country.'

'I've been busy,' said Anna shortly. She looked around for somewhere to sit.

Fraser gestured to a low wingback chair. 'Please.'

Anna took a seat, her shoulder bag resting on her lap, while Fraser slid into the executive chair at his desk, swivelling around to face her. He gave her a small, expectant smile.

'You've, ah, found out something, I take it?'

'You could say that.'

'I take it I should brace myself for bad news.'

'I wouldn't advise against it.'

. . .

She told him her story: her conservations with Lorraine Hammond, Leila Hobart, Heather Fleetwood and Archie Macpherson; the suspicious transactions into and out of Hugh's bank accounts; tracking down Libby Bright at the animal sanctuary and the account she'd extracted from her. Fraser listened in silence, one elbow resting on the surface of his desk, periodically wincing or massaging his jaw. His expression was one of mounting horror as Anna detailed each of Hugh's infractions, from rewriting Libby's dissertation to their subsequent affair to assisting her in cheating on her finals.

'And where is this Libby now?' he said quietly, once Anna finally fell silent, his voice like verglas.

'She's dead too,' said Anna. She hesitated, then added, 'Seemingly by her own hand. There was a note next to the body.'

Fraser allowed this to sit for a moment. 'Well,' he said at last, 'in a way, I suppose that makes things slightly less messy.'

'That's one way of looking at it.'

'And this Emily – you really have no idea who or where she is?'

Anna hesitated. 'There's reason,' she said carefully, 'to suspect she might have been a former student of Hugh's who got pregnant by him at some point in the late 90s or early 2000s ... though, if it *was* her, that trail has well and truly run cold.'

She knew, as she spoke, that this was the story she'd stick to till her dying day.

Silence descended on the room. The air felt close and oppressive.

Fraser shook his head. 'What a mess. What an almighty, God-awful mess.'

Suddenly, he slapped his thighs – an attempt, perhaps, to pull himself together, or to wrest back some semblance of control.

'Well, Anna,' he said briskly, 'when you set out to do a job, you certainly don't do it by half-measures. I tasked you with looking into Hugh's affairs, and you've certainly gone above and beyond the call of duty … though a part of me now wishes to God I hadn't initiated this whole debacle in the first place.' He sighed heavily. 'But we always knew this might lead to us discovering things about our friend that we'd wish we hadn't. No one can accuse us of going into this endeavour without both eyes open.'

Anna couldn't help noticing that he'd essentially parroted back the warning she'd given him at the outset as if it was an original thought of his own.

'You didn't have any inkling, did you?' she said. 'I mean, about his behaviour with students.'

Fraser looked genuinely hurt by the question. 'Anna, I give you my word, hand on heart, I hadn't the slightest idea.'

She believed him. His sincerity came across as genuine, and, in any event, it seemed in keeping with his general cluelessness about the lives of his staff. He had perfect plausible deniability.

The two of them sat in silence. Fraser's face was ashen. Anna let the moment linger for just a few seconds more, before speaking again.

'Remind me – when was the last time you saw Hugh face to face before he died?'

She kept her tone deliberately casual, though it required some effort.

'Not since before lockdown.'

Anna felt more deflated by this response than she'd been expecting to. A part of her, she realised, had been hoping he'd take this one last opportunity to come clean.

This was going to make what came next that much harder.

'That's funny,' she said. 'I heard he came to see you one Friday afternoon in May.'

Fraser chuckled incredulously. It sounded forced. 'What are you talking about?'

'So you're denying it? You're saying he *didn't* come to see you when you were about to leave for the weekend and the two of you *didn't* have a heated exchange on the driveway?'

Fraser's expression darkened. 'Matilda,' he muttered. 'She's said something, hasn't she? You don't want to go listening to what that girl says. Half the time, she's just trying to stir up—'

'It never happened, then? You can look me in the eye and guarantee that the conversation never took place?'

To give him credit, Fraser did *try* to meet Anna's gaze – for all of two seconds. Then, abruptly, he broke eye contact with her and threw up his arms in exasperation.

'Oh, what does it matter? Either way, the man's dead. What *possible* difference can it make whether we did or did not have a conversation beforehand? All right – so he did come to see me one Friday in May. What of it?'

'And which Friday was this?' Anna's voice remained deceptively calm.

Fraser practically scoffed. 'I can't possibly remember—'

'Was it the fifteenth?'

Fraser attempted a shrug that came off looking more like a violent convulsion than an expression of ambivalence.

'It really ought to be pretty easy for you to tell me whether it was or it wasn't, seeing as that was the day he killed himself.'

Complete silence.

'It was, wasn't it? He came to confess to you and you told him to get lost and his response was to take his own life.'

By now, Fraser's face had turned from grey to a deep crimson. 'All right,' he snapped, 'so it was the fifteenth! How was I to know he was going to go straight home and gas himself?'

For a moment, Anna was so taken aback by his tone, and the crudeness of his words, that she just stared back at him in silence.

'He "gassed himself", as you put it,' she said eventually, 'within hours of you and him having your set-to. Did it never occur to you that the two events might be connected?'

'If I thought that, don't you think I'd have seen fit to mention it?'

'I don't know, Fraser. *Would* you?'

Fraser had no answer to that. He picked agitatedly at a bit of loose fabric on the arm of his chair, still refusing to make eye contact with her. His entire face was flushed, a patina of sweat glistening on his brow.

'Take me through *exactly* what you said to him,' said Anna.

Fraser glanced up, briefly meeting Anna's eyes before quickly looking away again. He continued to pick at the arm of his chair. Then, eventually, he let out a heavy sigh – of defeat, maybe, or perhaps of relief at finally being able to let go of this.

'All right,' he said, 'yes. It was the afternoon of the fifteenth. I'd wanted to get out of the city for a while. I'd been going stir crazy cooped up inside the house for weeks on end with nothing but a single daily hour of fresh air to alleviate the boredom. We all had. And I thought, what difference does it make? We aren't going to have contact with any other people. It poses no risk to the health of the nation.'

Anna pinched the bridge of her nose. 'Fraser, I don't care about the sodding lockdown violations. Just tell me what happened.'

Fraser gave a small, chastened nod. 'We were just about to set off when, out of nowhere, he came striding up the driveway, demanding to speak to me. I'd recently found out about the business with the expenses claims, and, as such, wasn't exactly predisposed towards welcoming him with open arms. So, when he started prattling on at me with his vague claims about "mistakes" and secrets that had the power to ruin him, I'm afraid I gave him rather short shrift. I told him I knew all about the fraudulent claims he'd been submitting, and that if he thought I was going to help him cover them up, he had another thing coming.

'"I don't want your sob stories," I told him, "or your

excuses. I certainly don't need to hear about your gambling debts or whatever it is you've got yourself into. It's your mess and you're going to have to find your own way out of it. We'll deal with this on Monday morning through the proper channels. And now, if you'll excuse me, I've a weekend to get on with."

'I got into the car and drove off, leaving him standing there, wearing that vacant, gormless expression he always seemed to have on his face. And that was that.'

'And then he went home and killed himself,' said Anna quietly.

Fraser snorted. 'You're seeing cause and effect where there isn't any.'

It was an attempt at bravado on his part, an attempt to sound assertive, but, instead, they simply sounded like the words of a man who knew he'd been caught.

Anna shook her head, still struggling to come to terms with what she'd heard. 'I thought he killed himself because of the threat from Libby. But that was over a week earlier and he still soldiered on till his conversation with you.'

She raised her head and looked at him, and it seemed to her that, for the first time ever, she was seeing him for who he really was.

'And you lied to me, because you *knew* that was how it would look.'

Miriam had been on the right track all along, she realised. She wrote the suicide note pinning the blame on Fraser purely as a diversionary tactic, when all along she was far closer to the truth than she could ever possibly have guessed. And Fraser, in turn, had exploited Anna's guilt over her own failure to listen to Hugh at the farewell party to convince her to investigate the death, all the while covering for his own culpability. *Find your own way out of it,* he'd had told Hugh.

And that was just what Hugh had done.

'Yes, all right,' Fraser snapped, his temper well and truly up now. 'I knew, if I told you, you'd leap to conclusions with your usual holier-than-thou approach towards everything. But I never held a gun to his head. He made his own choice, and that choice was taking the coward's way out rather than facing up to his responsibilities. The man was skimming money from his employers, sleeping with his students, helping them falsify their exam results ... and *I'm* the bad guy for trying to hold him to account?' he spluttered incredulously.

Anna hadn't been conscious of getting to her feet, but she realised, at some point, she must have done so. 'You *usurped* him,' she shouted, no longer making any effort to moderate her tone. 'You made him feel like he was worthless; like the decades he'd given to that place counted for nothing. And, when he needed you most, you told him he was on his own and that you were going to hang him out to dry. And still, you have the nerve to sit there and tell me, with a straight face, that you feel *no* responsibility for what happened.' She shook her head in disgust. 'It's *you* who deserves to be held to account.'

She stood there, blood pounding in her ears, skin prickling with perspiration, feeling no emotion other than a fierce, burning desire for revenge. Despite all Hugh's many transgressions, she found it impossible to put aside her enduring fondness for the man, far less the thought of him dying alone after having been so callously spurned in his hour of need.

Fraser snorted. 'And how, pray tell, do you intend to do that? If my part comes out, so will everything else. Everything your precious Hugh got up to. His whole epitaph, such as it is, will go up in smoke overnight – I can promise you that.'

'If that's what it takes, then, as far as I'm concerned, it's a price worth paying.'

But even as she spoke, a sliver of doubt crept into her mind. Was she really ready to see Hugh's legacy trashed so comprehensively? She knew, in principle, it was no less than he deserved. And yet ...

'And the scholarship?'

Fraser's tone had changed now. Where previously there was bluster and self-righteousness, there was now only a cold, calculating calm.

'The scholarship?' Anna found herself echoing.

'You think Dame Jackie Gordon will be perfectly happy to continue funding a scholarship in the name of a serial abuser of students? All those disadvantaged little urchins can kiss goodbye to their postgraduate careers in the Social Sciences. To say nothing of the reputational damage to the university itself ... Or do you care so little about that that you're willing to burn the entire establishment to the ground just to even the score with me? Because you, with your perfect sense of right and wrong, feel that the truth must be exposed at all costs, no matter the damage you leave in your wake?'

He was on his feet now too, moving towards her slowly and purposefully, his voice growing quieter as the words themselves became ever more coldly calculating. He seemed to sense he had the advantage, a vicious glint in his eye as he came to a halt facing Anna, close enough to reach out and touch her.

'You're good friends with Farah Hadid, aren't you?' he mused, as if he'd never noticed until now. 'Her career really hasn't ended up where it ought to have by this stage, has it? One might even say it's stagnating. Be a shame if she were to see out the rest of her days as a lowly, underpaid TA ... or, worse still, on the unemployment line.'

Anna looked up at him sharply.

'The academic world's an exceptionally small one, you know,' Fraser continued, in the same philosophical tone. 'It wouldn't take much to make her radioactive. A word in the right ear, a failure to make the grade at the next staffing cull, which we all know is coming ... I can make sure she finds it impossible to get a job *anywhere* ...'

His expression hardened as he stood in front of Anna, gazing down at her from his considerable height advantage.

'... and I *will*, if that's what it takes.'

Her legs suddenly weak, Anna sank back into the chair, utterly shaken as she digested the implications of Fraser's words.

'Look.' Fraser sounded almost conciliatory now. 'We all have to play the cards we're dealt. They're not the ones you'd have chosen, granted, but there's still a way out of this. I heard through the grapevine you've been offered a permanent job in Perugia – one with very favourable conditions. My advice is: take it. Go back to your life there and forget all about this. It's for the best.'

Anna said nothing. She continued to sit there for upwards of a full minute, feeling her entire world crumbling around her. Then, wordlessly, she got shakily to her feet, and, without meeting Fraser's eye or saying a word to him, turned and walked out.

59

Anna wandered the West End aimlessly, letting her feet carry her wherever they saw fit. She stalked the leafy residential streets, the deserted back lanes and the busy main roads, constantly on the move as she wrestled with the choice that now lay in front of her. She'd have loved nothing more than to hang Fraser out to dry and recognised that, right now, she was angry enough to do it and to hell with the consequences. But then she thought of the scholarship, and of the university – the place she'd been only too happy to see the back of but which, loath though she might be to admit it, still meant something to her.

And then there was Farah.

In all the time she'd known Fraser, she'd thought him slippery and self-serving, willing to throw anyone and everyone under the proverbial bus if it was to his advantage – but never so nakedly Machiavellian. The new side of himself that he'd shown her tonight appalled and frightened her in equal measure. He'd known that the path to silencing her had not lain in threatening her directly but rather the institutions, the principles and the people she cared about. In that respect, he'd known her better than she'd ever given him credit for. And *she* knew, in her heart of hearts, that it hadn't been bluster. There was little doubt in her mind that he fully intended to follow through on his threats, if she gave him a reason to.

What price justice, Anna?

She became aware of the sound of voices nearby. She looked around and realised that, without being aware of it, she'd travelled in an easterly direction and was now within the bounds of the university campus, a mere stone's throw from her old workplace, the Hutcheson Building. Up ahead, people were streaming out of the student union, some unfastening their face coverings as they walked. All seemed to be in high spirits.

As she turned her back on them and continued on her way, a voice halted her in her tracks.

'Professor Scavolini? Anna?'

She turned as one of the students – a young woman with shoulder-length blonde hair – broke away from her friends and hurried towards her. She beamed at Anna, cheeks flushed, a few strands of hair sticking to her sweaty forehead.

'It's Grace,' she said, when Anna didn't respond. 'Grace Dunphy. Remember?'

Of course – Grace. She'd been one of Anna's undergraduate students at the time The Reckoning had been going on their spree. They'd subjected her to a violent sexual assault, causing her to miscarry. The last time Anna had seen Grace, she'd tried to persuade her, without success, to reconsider her decision to drop out.

'Grace,' she said, nodding a little too vigorously as her brain struggled to play catch-up. 'Of course, yes. How've you been?'

Grace nodded enthusiastically. 'I'm good, good. Listen, I didn't know you were back in town. How was Italy?'

'It's … you know.' She hoped that would suffice as a response. 'Have you, uh, been to a gig?'

'Yeah, this new band from Coatbridge. The shit-hot new

thing, so I'm told. I dunno, seemed to have more enthusiasm than talent – but hey, I had a blast and got all sweaty, so that's gotta count as a win, am I right?'

'I guess so,' Anna agreed.

Grace stuck her hands into the pockets of her dungarees and gave Anna an expectant grin.

'Well?'

Having neither the energy nor the headspace to engage in guessing games, Anna could only grimace apologetically.

'Sorry, Grace. I haven't a clue what you're driving at.'

'Well, I'm here, aren't I?' said Grace, as if it was obvious. Then, seeing that Anna still wasn't getting it, 'I re-enrolled last year. Finished my undergrad degree. I'm starting my Masters in a few weeks. So you see,' she concluded, still grinning, 'all your badgering totally paid off. I came back, because of you.'

Anna was aware that, at some dim and distant point in the past, this news would have filled her with joy. Now, though, she found it impossible to muster any enthusiasm for Grace having returned to this poisonous place.

'That's wonderful, Grace,' she managed to say, aware that her voice was devoid of any hint of joy. 'I'm so pleased you had a change of heart. Now, if you'll excuse me ...'

'Of course, of course. So good seeing you again, Professor.'

Anna nodded tightly, then turned and headed off.

'Guess I'll see you at the start of term?' Grace called after her.

Anna, already several metres away and walking as fast as she could, pretended not to hear.

She continued uphill, still letting her feet set the direction of travel. She drew within sight of the main building and headed into the grounds via the open gate. There, she found a bench overlooking the small garden in front of the visitor centre and sat down.

She reached across to her shoulder bag, lying next to her on the bench, and took out her phone. Unlocking it, she opened the voice memo app and played the most recent recording, starting it at a random point in the middle of the roughly eleven-minute timeline. Fraser's voice cut, mid-sentence, into the still night air.

'... care so little about that that you're willing to burn the entire establishment to the ground just to even the score with me? Because you, with your perfect sense of right and wrong, feel that the truth must be exposed at all costs, no matter the damage you leave in your wake?'

She hit Stop. Silence returned. She lowered her phone, clutching it between her knees, and let out the breath she'd been holding in. It was Libby, of all people, who'd provided her with the inspiration – or, perhaps more accurately, Miriam's angry account of Libby's revelation that she'd recorded her drunken confession about Alfie's death.

Mutually assured destruction, Miriam had called it. Well, here, certainly, was everything Anna needed to destroy Fraser. And she even had an inkling of the way in which she might go about doing it – one that, if she played her cards right, would safeguard Farah's job, Hugh's legacy *and* the broader reputation of the university. But it would involve engaging in a degree of brinkmanship that was beyond anything she'd previously been prepared to countenance. Behaviour that would, in her mind, force her to occupy the same moral abyss as Fraser himself, or close enough. And she had no idea whether that was something she could live with.

Time passed. She didn't move. Midnight came and went. Her phone informed her that it was Tuesday 17 August – the start of the sixth day since she'd returned to Glasgow. Still she didn't move.

As she gazed straight ahead, her vision unfocused, flowers whose names she didn't know blurring into a fuzzy haze of hues, she was dimly aware of footsteps approaching, and then of someone plonking themselves down next to her.

'And of aw the park benches in aw the towns in aw the world … ach, *you* know how that line goes.'

'ZOE!' cried Anna, turning in surprise.

And indeed, there she was, large as life, sitting on the bench next to Anna, grinning like a ninny. She spread her arms invitingly. Anna hesitated for the tiniest morsel of a moment before throwing all her pandemic-enforced caution to the wind and throwing her arms around her pal, rocking the pair of them back and forth and laughing with a delirious mixture of disbelief and joy.

'Oh my *God*,' she exclaimed, when they finally released each other, 'what are you *doing* here?'

Zoe shrugged unconcernedly. 'Decided tae drive up Monday night 'stead o' first thing Tuesday mornin'. Sal's got a shift at Costa at three and – eh, truth be told, we were both just a wee bit homesick. Wales is totally overrated, by the way. I mean, don't get me wrong, it's gorgeous 'n' all, but there's only so much hills 'n' valleys a girl can take. Gimme a good old-fashioned city break any day.'

'No, I mean how are you here – *here* here, sitting on this bench with me?'

'Well now, I must confess, it did involve a wee pinch o' the black arts …'

Anna stared at her questioningly.

'Got tae near midnight and I couldnae sleep for love nor money. Still too wired efter driving all day, I'm guessing. Figured I'd get out o' the flat, stretch my legs a bit. Then, just on the off chance, I looked ye up on Find My Friends, saw ye were still in the neighbourhood, and figured, why don't I come 'n' surprise ye? So …' She grinned and spread her arms like a magician at the end of some grand performance. 'Surprise!'

Anna shook her head. 'Seems the whole world's using my phone to track my every movement tonight,' she said, more out of mirth than displeasure.

'Eh? Also, anyone tell ye, ye've got a right beezer of a bump on yer forehead? What happened?'

'Long story. Listen, Zo, I'm really sorry about how cunty I was on the phone the other day.'

Zoe batted her apology away with a wave. 'Ach, forget it. I shouldnae've put ye on the spot like that. If ye wanted a quick in 'n' out wi minimal fuss, that's naeb'dy's business 'cept yours.'

Not for the first time, Anna found herself reflecting on the fact that she really didn't deserve Zoe.

'So, what's the sitch, bitch?' Zoe eyed her eagerly. 'I wanna know *everything*.'

Anna looked at Zoe helplessly. 'I'm not sure where to begin.'

Something in her face or tone of voice must have given her away, for Zoe's expression instantly grew serious.

'That bad, is it?'

'You have no idea.'

Zoe gave a strained smile and rolled her eyes as if Anna was being *really* dense. 'Well, obvz *not* unless ye *tell* me.'

'It'll take a while.'

'Aye? Well, seeing as how we're both of us sitting on a park bench in the middle o' the night, I'm guessing neither of us's got anyplace better tae be.'

Anna considered this.

'Good point.'

So she told Zoe the whole story – the *real* whole story, with the full details of Miriam's involvement, not the censored version she'd given to Fraser. She concluded with the conversation in Fraser's study, his threats to destroy Farah's career and the plan that had since started to take shape in her mind.

'I think I know what I need to do,' she sighed, 'but I'm afraid of what it says about me.'

For a long time, Zoe said nothing. She sat there, arms

spread across the back of the bench, regarding Anna thoughtfully. At length, she stirred.

'I ever tell ye what *really* happened with Dominic Ryland?'

Anna shook her head. That whole period of Zoe's life had remained shrouded in doubt and uncertainty for ... God, it must be getting on for the better part of a decade now.

'I gave him to Jim Cottrell.'

Her tone was matter-of-fact, unsentimental – that of someone who'd thought long and hard about this and had long since ceased to question her choice of actions.

'I mean, I told Cottrell he'd been double-crossing him – grassing him up tae the polis 'n' whatnot. And I knew I was signing his death warrant, or as good as. But I knew it was what I had tae do. It was a price worth paying tae get Ryland off my back – tae make sure what happened tae Carol could never happen tae anyone else I cared about. I'm no proud of it. I don't kid myself I done a good or a moral thing – but, in the balance o' payments, it was the *right* thing. Lesser o' two evils, if ye wanna think of it like that.

'Point is,' she said, cutting Anna off as she opened her mouth to object, 'I put a bloke in a wheelchair. A sick fuckin' rapist bloke who put out a hit on me that nearly cost Carol her life – but still, he was another human being, and he cannae walk or piss or shit now cos o' me. And, wi all due respect, what *you're* talking about daein' is pure chickenfeed in comparison. I've made my peace wi what I done ...'

She reached across and gripped Anna's forearm, squeezing it firmly.

'And you will too.'

She gave an encouraging smile.

'Go. Play they basturts at their own game.'

60

The official residence of the Principal of Kelvingrove University was a Victorian townhouse on Park Circus, the elegant, crescent-shaped street at the top of Woodlands Hill, overlooking Kelvingrove Park. Jim Buchanan was known as something of a night owl, but nonetheless, Anna experienced a degree of trepidation at the thought of ringing his doorbell at close to 2 a.m. on a weekday morning. When, a good couple of minutes later, a light appeared in the hallway and he appeared in his silk dressing gown, she knew there was a strong chance she'd roused him from his bed.

'Anna!' he said, seeming not in the least bit perturbed by the late hour. '*This* is an unexpected delight. You'll forgive the informal attire, I hope. If I'd known you'd be calling, I'd have changed into something more suitable.'

Anna didn't know how to respond.

He gestured inwards. 'Won't you come in?'

With something of a sense of relief, she accepted his invitation.

'You know,' he said, as she followed him into the hallway with its black and white tiled flooring, 'I've just heard the most shocking news. Apparently, Hugh MacLeish's daughter died in a car accident earlier tonight.'

Not trusting herself, Anna kept her mouth shut and continued to follow him in silence.

Jim shook his head. 'Awful, awful business. That poor family – one tragedy after another.'

They made their way through to the ornately furnished living room. Anna watched as he moved about briskly, switching on lights and rearranging the cushions on the sofa. He was a small man, with close-cropped hair, balding in the centre, and given to quick, deft movements and gestures. Anna didn't know him all that well, but, in all their limited dealings, he'd nonetheless always treated her as if they were old friends. On balance, she thought she liked him – certainly in comparison to *some* members of the senior management group she could name.

'Can I get you anything? Tea? Coffee? If you'll permit me to make the observation, you look like you've been in the wars.'

Anna shook her head. She realised she hadn't actually spoken a word since he'd opened the door to her.

Jim gestured to the settee. 'Please.'

She did as she was bidden, while he settled in a high-backed chair facing her, folded one leg over the other and smiled at her inquisitively.

'Now, what can I do for you? I can only assume, for you to have called at this indecorous hour, that it must be a matter of some import.'

For the third time that night, Anna told her story. She reverted to the edited version she gave to Fraser, omitting her discovery of 'Emily's' true identity and her subsequent ordeal at the hands of Miriam. To this, she added the conversation in Fraser's study and his efforts to blackmail her. Towards the end, she got out her phone and played the recording in its entirety. Jim listened, brow furrowed, a look of grave concern etched into his keen features.

Afterwards, he remained silent for a long time, leaning back in his chair with his fingers steepled together, deep in thought.

'Well,' he said eventually, 'how do you think we should play this?'

Before coming here, Anna had promised herself one thing and one thing only, and that was that she wasn't going to be coy about her agenda. If she was going to compromise her principles so completely, she was at least going to be upfront and honest about it.

'It seems to me,' she said carefully, 'that I have everything I need to make serious hay if I choose to do so. There's plenty in this story for the press to spend months, if not years, chewing over – from the shameful actions of a former Professor of Sociology and the colleagues who conspired to cover them up to the efforts exerted by the current Head of Social and Political Sciences to blackmail me into silence.'

Jim made no response. He continued to sit in silence, seeming neither aggrieved nor even particularly surprised by this declaration.

'I have it in my power to destroy the legacies and careers of several people,' Anna went on, 'and to make Kelvingrove University a byword for sleaze and corruption. My silence is dependent on four conditions.'

Again, Jim said nothing. He merely made a small gesture with one hand, inviting her to go ahead.

'One: Fraser Taggart is to be made to resign his position at the university with immediate effect.

'Two: an undertaking to conduct a thorough review of the university's safeguarding measures, particularly those governing staff/student relationships.

'Three: the scholarship for disadvantaged social sciences students funded by Jackie Gordon is to go ahead, but not in

Hugh MacLeish's name. Given everything that's come to light, it would be inappropriate.'

'*Entirely* inappropriate,' said Jim quietly. He paused. 'And, er, the fourth condition?'

'Four: Dr Farah Hadid is to be appointed to a permanent faculty position and backpaid for the last eighteen months of unacknowledged work as my locum.'

She allowed a moment for the dust to settle, and for Jim to digest her list of demands, before continuing.

'Now, I know you don't have the power to order any of these things directly, but you *can* exert sufficient influence to see to it that they come about.' Again, she paused briefly. 'And one last thing. I'll be needing an answer tonight. Otherwise, I'll go straight from here to the offices of the *Tribune* and wait for them to open their doors first thing in the morning.'

Jim leant back in his chair again, letting out a heavy sigh. For a full minute, he neither moved nor spoke. Anna was aware of the rhythmic tick of the pendulum clock on the mantelpiece; of the occasional, distant hum of a motor vehicle somewhere beyond the house's tall, double-glazed windows.

At length, Jim stirred.

'If I were to go along with this proposition,' he said carefully, as if selecting and considering each word individually, 'what assurances would either of us have that the other wouldn't renege on the agreement? To put it more bluntly, that either you or I wouldn't, at some indeterminate point in the future, decide to, in the common parlance, "go public".'

Anna met his gaze, unblinking. 'Mutually assured destruction. If word of this ever got out, we'd both be as damned as each other.'

Jim considered this. Finally, he nodded soberly.

'Your terms are ... acceptable.'

Anna got to her feet. Jim did likewise. For a brief, absurd moment, it felt as if they were about to shake on it.

Jim gave a brisk, businesslike nod. 'Well, it would seem I

have some calls to make. Some will inevitably have to wait till a more civilised hour. One, however, I can make straight away.'

Anna didn't need to ask which one this was.

'One question. The small matter of the scholarship. I fully agree that to name it after the late Professor MacLeish would be … unseemly. Do you, perhaps, have a more suitable suggestion?'

Anna thought about this for a moment.

'Call it the Mark Westmore Award. It's been twelve years since he was murdered on the very grounds of the university. In all that time, the contribution he made to this place has never been adequately recognised.'

Jim considered this, then gave a small nod of approval. 'Very good.'

Anna, too, nodded, then turned to leave.

'Oh, ah, just one more thing.'

Anna stopped in her tracks and turned to face him again.

Jim took a couple of steps towards her, arms folded behind his back, wincing slightly in anticipation of raising what he evidently regarded as an indelicate matter.

'It seems plain that the School of Social and Political Sciences will shortly be looking for a new head. Not unrelatedly, I'm aware you're currently approaching the end of an eighteen-month sabbatical. This is all strictly unofficial, of course, but should such a vacancy materialise, would you be thinking of returning to the fold to throw your hat into the ring?'

Anna was so taken aback by the question that, for a moment, it was all she could do not to stare at Jim like a gaping fish.

'I doubt it'll have escaped many people's notice that you've been less than thrilled by the direction of travel here for some time,' said Jim. 'Think of this, then, as an opportunity to chart a fresh course.' He smiled at her encouragingly. 'What do you say?'

EPILOGUE

Tuesday 17 August

Anna forced down the lid of her wheelie case and, by leaning all her weight on it, succeeded in keeping it shut for long enough to tug the zip closed. Hands on hips, she took stock of the hotel room, making sure she hadn't forgotten anything.

Her new flight departed Glasgow Airport at 11:15 a.m. This time, the layover was in Schiphol, with the second flight scheduled to touch down in Perugia at 18:30 local time. With any luck, she'd reach Lago Trasimeno while it was still light. She'd be glad to be back in Italy, and to see Jack again; it was almost a week since she'd last held him in her arms.

A knock on the door jarred her out of her thoughts. She wondered if reception had sent a porter up to give her a hand downstairs with her luggage. It wasn't something she'd requested, though she had mentioned to the man at the desk that she'd be checking out at nine sharp. She headed over to the door and opened it.

Fraser Taggart stared back at her with the hollow, half-dead look of someone who hadn't slept a wink. His eyes were red-rimmed, his jowls sandpapery, his shirt – which she fancied was the same one he'd had on last night – crumpled and partially untucked. The look in his eyes was one of pure hatred.

'Fraser,' she said, rather uselessly.

'I suppose you're over the moon,' he said, his voice a bitter snarl. 'After all, you've got what you wanted, haven't you?'

'What I wanted?'

She was beyond caring enough to indulge him.

'I've been given my jotters,' Fraser continued. 'Leant on. Encouraged to see that my face doesn't fit. Don't pretend you didn't know. You and Jim Buchanan cooked this up between you – sweeping away all that stands in your way.'

'Fraser,' began Anna, then changed her mind. Why say anything? She knew it wouldn't make a difference. Better to let him waste his own energy than expend her own on a fight she knew neither of them could win.

'You've never liked or respected me,' Fraser went on, in a tone dripping with both contempt and self-pity. 'You've never managed to hide it, so don't try to pretend now. I never stood a chance with you, no matter how hard I tried. In your eyes, I was never worthy of my position. How could I be? How could I measure up to your exacting standards? No one, besides yourself, ever *could*.'

He paced back and forth a couple of times. Then, hands on hips, he threw back his head and barked out a short, contemptuous laugh.

'Well, I hope you'll be very happy in your new position. And once you've remade the university in your own image – once you've driven out everyone whose views don't accord precisely with your own – perhaps, as you gaze down from your lofty perch atop the spoils of conquest, you'll finally find time for some self-reflection and see that you're nothing but a dictatorial megalomaniac who can't bear to hear an opinion that doesn't accord perfectly with your own!'

Without meaning to, Anna felt herself raising a single,

incredulous eyebrow. She couldn't help it: she'd never known him to be this florid in his speech before, which only served to make him sound all the more ridiculous.

'Well?' he demanded. 'Have you got anything to say at all?'

'Fraser,' said Anna, as blandly as possible, 'are you going to leave, or am I going to have to call security?'

Fraser's expression hardened. 'Don't worry, I'm going. But mark you me.' He jabbed a finger towards her. 'You'll get your comeuppance one day, and it won't be by my hand. I wouldn't dream of it. Not when you have friends in such esteemed places, as you've so ably demonstrated.' He shook his head. 'Oh no – your downfall will be by your own hand. People like you are always brought down by your own hubris.'

And then, having seemingly run out of things to say, he turned and stalked off, any dramatic exit he might have hoped to achieve blunted by the fact of his having to walk the entire length of the corridor before finally reaching the stairs and disappearing from view.

Anna waited till she was sure he was definitely gone and not about to come haring back up the stairs to hit her with an additional dose of overlooked vitriol, then wearily shut the door and returned to her packing.

She lugged her case down the stairs, handed in her key at reception, then continued out to the drop-off area, where the taxi she'd booked was waiting. She heaved her case into the boot, then slid into the passenger seat.

'Glasgow Airport,' she told the driver.

As the taxi pulled out of the hotel grounds and turned onto Great Western Road, she sank back into the upholstery and finally allowed herself to fully relax, her mind drifting back to a few hours earlier, when Jim Buchanan had put his proposition to her.

. . .

'I doubt it'll have escaped many people's notice that you've been less than thrilled by the direction of travel here for some time. Think of this, then, as an opportunity to chart a fresh course.' He smiled at her encouragingly. 'What do you say?'

Anna thought long and hard before giving her answer.

'Three days a week. A ring-fenced research budget. No managerial or administrative responsibility. Those are the terms under which I'll come back. I don't want Head of School. I've *never* wanted that sort of power. I just want to do my research and deliver my lectures and support my students to the best of my ability. You know – the things this job was *supposed* to be about.'

Jim was silent for a long moment, his keen eyes studying Anna while giving away nothing of his inner thoughts. Then, their corners crinkled into a smile.

'You know,' he said, 'if you'd said *two* days, I'd still have accepted.'

And now, as the taxi continued down Great Western Road, she thought ahead to the long and difficult conversation with Matteo that awaited her in Italy, followed by a separate – and probably no less challenging – one with Jack. There would be other hurdles to overcome, too, like how she was going to resolve the issue of Jack's schooling, to say nothing of the situation with the house. But, after everything she'd been through in the last twenty-four hours, she wasn't going to worry about those just yet.

The decision hadn't been an easy one, but she knew it had been the right one. In much the same way as at an earlier point in her life, around a decade ago, when she'd faced a similar choice, she'd come to the realisation that, for better or worse, and for reasons she couldn't fully articulate, her future lay here.

It wasn't because it was the easy option – far from it. And it *certainly* wasn't because of Paul Vasilico, whom she hoped never to see again. Partly, she supposed, it was about the criminology programme she'd built and her desire to play her part in taking it to even greater heights, and the connections she'd forged at the university; the friendships she'd made both within and outwith it. If she permitted herself to be sentimental about it, partly too, it might be that, while we were all a smörgåsbord of different identities and attachments, the part of her that felt Scottish was marginally stronger than the part that felt Italian – or, at least, had won this particular round of their ongoing power-play, however permanently or temporarily that might transpire to be.

But strip away all the sentimentality, all the abstract ideals about identity and belonging – at the end of the day, it was about *her* future, *her* wants and needs. No one else's.

It was time to come home.

The taxi turned south onto Crow Road, gathering speed as it hurtled towards the Clyde Tunnel, and her mind returned once more to the deal she'd struck in Jim Buchanan's living room; to, as Zoe had put it, the game she'd played. She'd got what she wanted, in a way, and far fewer people had been hurt than would have been the case had she stubbornly clung to her ideals. Whether, ultimately, it had been the right thing to do was a question she couldn't yet answer. Perhaps she never *would* be able to. But that was a matter between herself and her conscience, and so, she knew, it would remain, for as long as she continued to draw breath.

After all, she thought, what are we, in the end, but the sum of the secrets we keep?

ACKNOWLEDGEMENTS

I debated long and hard whether to acknowledge the COVID-19 pandemic in this book, for the simple reason that it's a period I doubt many are keen to revisit.

Ultimately, though, I concluded that, by pretending the events we all lived through five years ago hadn't happened, I'd be undermining the credibility of the world I've spent the last six novels creating. So, for better or for worse, what Zoe would no doubt refer to as 'the Panny D' ended up being a major part of this instalment.

I want to begin, as always, by thanking Suze Clarke-Morris, my editor for the past four books now, who always succeeds in walking the fine line between affording me a long leash and gently steering me in the right direction where necessary. Also, Neil Snowdon, for indulging me during several plot brainstorming video calls over the last twelve months, and Tim Barber, for his sterling cover design.

Thanks, too, to Eugenio Ercolani and Esteban Medaglia for their help with the Italian dialogue (there's only so far entry-level Duolingo will take you), and to my cadre of beta readers: Anne Simpson, Caroline Whitson, Catherine Mackenzie, Daniel Sardella, Luiz Asp and Sarah Kelley.

Warmest congratulations to 'Dame' Jackie Gordon for winning the competition to have a character named after you. I hope you enjoyed your namesake's role in the story.

Finally, my most abject apologies to anyone called Libby. I don't really think your name sounds wanky.

Printed in Great Britain
by Amazon